scott wellinger

the author of **CRASH** *and Venom*

Sinn

a warren dennihan prequel

Sínn

A Warren Dennihan Prequel

by scott wellinger

ISBN: 978-0-9899421-5-7

For the City of Boston.

You are so much a part of me and therefore my writing. The ability to share you with the world is my humble gift back.

PROLOGUE

TRAFFIC WAS A NIGHTMARE ON STORROW DRIVE.
The Big Dig project had ensured that the entire city of Boston was a metropolis parking lot. It had been for years before and would continue to be for the foreseeable future. The colossal construction project had begun in 1991, after two decades of planning, to alleviate the very traffic it was causing. The undertaking was supposed to be finished in 1998, but six years after the due-date there was still no end in sight.

The two lanes headed west on Storrow were just as congested as the eastbound lanes. While those that were aimed west, away from the Interstate 93 ramp towards Harvard and MIT had the Charles River and the Esplanade to view on their right, those headed toward it had only the tall buildings of BackBay to study. The luxurious apartment buildings with back terraces overlooking the Charles were admired and fantasized over by everyone including the eastbound traffic, further taunted by the signage stating '*If you lived here you would already be home*'.

Along the Charles River was the jogging path, the Hatch Shell at the Esplanade where the outdoor movie and concert season had recently begun, and the crew teams rowing their way past the onlookers stuck in traffic. The early May weather was in the mid-to-upper sixties, though lightly raining as it had all spring. The joggers were plentiful in the sun-showers as their faith in the activity was rekindled by the annual Marathon that had taken place just a few weeks prior. The Boston Pops had just played the opening weekend for the Hatch Shell, and the U2 cover band *The Joshua Tree* was supposed to play the upcoming Saturday night. The eight-oared sweep racing shells were moving in the water past the four-wheeled deadlock like they were standing still. Because they were.

The pedestrian bridges that passed over the four lanes of halted traffic had graffiti reminding all who were trapped below of the Bambino Curse. While the city did long to reverse the curse,

6

they wanted to reverse the traffic situation more. Little did anyone know that one of those two wishes would be granted later that year.

When traffic is halted to such an extent, virtually any motor vehicle violation is ignored by the Massachusetts State Police which patrol Storrow Drive. It was an unwritten rule for all of the arteries, not just Storrow. Pullovers in heavy traffic are hazardous to all parties involved. One can't speed, nor weave in and out of traffic when snails are moving past you. Derelict vehicles that overheat or cease to run are met with hand gestures and shouting, versus AAA or a tow truck because help simply can't get there. In truth, most troopers just sit on the side of the road or avoid the congestion all together during peak times. Nothing will make the already unbearable gridlock worse save for the flashing lights of a cruiser pulling over some poor slob.

The Probationary Trooper William LaDue did not receive the unwritten memo or message regarding discretion during traffic jams. He sat in his 2002 Ford *Crown Vic* patrol unit bored out of his mind. His cruiser parked off of the curb under one of the graffitied footbridges, staring ahead at the park and the General George Patton statue that stood in it. There are only so many jog-bras and swinging ponytails one can stare at to pass the time. The occasional flick of the wipers to clear the rivulets off of the windshield in order to see said jog-bras. He couldn't leave, there was no place to go. The young go-getter had only been out of the academy for slightly more than ten months, had just gotten out on his own in-fact. He sat there alone wanting more than to babysit traffic. He decided to punch in the tag numbers of the vehicles that were not passing him. One such license plate caught his fancy.

The red, white and blue MA commercial plate had a DEC 04 expiration date. That was not the problem, the end of December was about eight months yet to come. What set off bells and whistles was the fact that the tag was registered for a dark, 1999, tourmaline metallic *Econoline E350*, yet it was attached to a brand new, white, 2004 Chevy *Express Cargo* van. Against conventional wisdom, Trooper LaDue decided to ring him up.

William turned on his lights and gave a long yelp from the siren on his cruiser to alert the squatters. Nobody moved, nobody could move. All hoped the new development didn't include them.

The cruiser continued up on the lawn, pulling next to the white van being sought in the right lane. There were two passengers, definitively, one in each of the bucket seats in the front. There were possibly more in the back, though there were no side windows in the utility vehicle to discern for certain. LaDue was alone in his cruiser, which meant he needed to call a backup cruiser. The situation was already a problem and getting worse.

The Trooper pointed to the passenger, then pointed to the lawn in front of his patrol vehicle. He then reversed his Crown Vic, allowing the van to jump the curb ahead of him. Only it didn't. The van didn't move. William engaged his loudspeaker.

"Pull up onto the curb and turn off your vehicle."

The hesitation was notable, but the request was eventually adhered to. The van slowly rode up the curb and onto the newly green park lawn from the combination of wet spring rain and sporadic sun. The gap the van created in the traffic was absorbed by vehicles who were all too eager to move the few short feet forward. The pullover was garnering attention from the pedestrians on the overpasses as well as the runners along the path. Something to occupy those who were stuck in traffic. But not too much. Just another day in the city.

Dispatch was giving the young trooper grief about the backup he was requesting, reminding him of the hour and traffic. As if he was unaware. LaDue was informed that a two-man cruiser was on route but to hang tight. In the meantime, he called out the tag number over the radio to dispatch in an effort to learn more information than what he could obtain from the screen in his vehicle.

"Dispatch, this is Romeo-two again. I've got a Mass tag November-7-8 4-5-Echo. Reads here as belonging to a dark blue 99

Ford, but I got it on a brand new white Chevy. What have you got?"

"Romeo-two, that tag is coming back stolen, along with the vehicle. Take caution, hold off. Backup is on route. Over."

"Roger-that."

Probationary Trooper LaDue was officially excited. Not only did he now have something to do for the remainder of his shift, a large portion of it at least, he now had a situation that was likely to be more involved than a mere traffic citation. He was told to wait for backup but he couldn't. Excitement got the better of him.

He exited his patrol vehicle and walked up the driver side of the van. He did so cautiously, looking into the large side mirror to get a visual on the driver while unsnapping the flap over his service weapon. LaDue was sure to stay tight to the van, making it that much more difficult for the driver to fire a shot of his own at a six o'clock angle versus a seven or eight. The Trooper would have told him to roll down his window, but it was already down. He called out to the driver from just behind his driver-side door.

"Reach both hands out of your window, and open your door from the outside. Slowly. Then step out of the vehicle."

"What is this about Officer? I couldn't have been speeding, we were at a stand-still," said the driver. He stuck out his hands but did not as yet pull on the black handle to his door.

"Just step out of your vehicle and we will get to that. How many passengers are in there with you?"

"One. And me." He pulled the outer handle and the door began to open slowly as instructed. "Don't you have to have a reason to pull me over?"

"And I do. Just tell your passenger to stay calm, you do as your instructed, and we will all get through this as calmly as possible."

The driver was about the same age as Trooper Ladue. Maybe not quite as old, which is to say that they were both barely old enough to rent a car. They weren't still using acne cream but they were still about half a decade from thirty. Once out of the van, the driver was pushed against it; his right cheek pressed into the white, metal side.

The trooper then quickly dodged to his left, looked into the van and came back out of view of the passenger. LaDue was right-handed so using his weapon would not be a possibility without exposing his torso, opening himself up for taking a bullet. He again called into the vehicle while putting handcuffs on the driver.

"Inside .... I need you to put your hands forward so I can see them and slowly climb over to the driver side toward me. Do just like your friend here did and this will go nice and smooth."

"Eat a dick!" The passenger then called out to his friend, "Hey Danny. I think this pig is alone. No backup."

The cuffed driver called back, "Little late for that now. We're smoked. Backup just pulled up." Another two-toned blue cruiser pulled up behind Ladue's. This one contained two State Troopers.

"Fuck!" The shout came from inside the van.

"Listen to your friend here and just come out nice and easy."

"Why'd you pull us over?" The passenger was still not over onto the driver's side, and LaDue was in the process of getting the driver to move to the back of van and sat down on the lawn by the road. He was not yet there when he heard it.

LaDue heard the passenger door to the van open and the word "GUN!" shouted. One of his backups had tried to apprehended the other occupant. Before the passenger could be pulled from the vehicle, he fired at the backup trooper. The return fire hit the passenger. Twice. The passenger fell out of the vehicle, his weapon kicked away, relieving him of it and sending him face-down onto the lawn in the process. Then, "Clear." An ambulance needed to called. The passenger was alive but bleeding badly. The process happened in the time it took for LaDue to get to the back of the van.

Once the situation was completely under police control and a short debriefing had occurred, LaDue then moved the driver next to his accomplice and were both told that they were pulled over because the tags did not match the vehicle. The passenger while bleeding and in pain had already been read his Miranda rights as he was picking up a weapons charge along with an attempt on an Officer. For now. That gave them probable cause to search each of them and their vehicle. The troopers started with the suspect's pockets, asking if they stuck their hands in their pockets were they going to get stuck with anything? Knife? Syringe? The driver was the only one who responded, answering 'no', so both of their pockets were emptied. The writhing passenger had no ID. He was pulled further away and was trying to be stabilized by one of the backup troopers. The Driver had a license that identified him as Daniel McKennie.

"What are we gonna find in the van, Daniel?" The protocol was that LaDue would handle this suspect. His stop, his collar, his show. Rookie or not, this was his bust.

"Nothin'. I wanna talk to Warren Dennihan. He is one-ah-you. Statie. Goes by Deni. You know him?"

"Mr. McKennie, are you calling in a get-outta-jail-free-card already? What are you afraid of? You can talk to me. You *should* talk to me. What's in the van?"

"I ain't sayin' nothin' else unless it's to Deni. Nothin'."

"Have it your way, son." Nobody pointed out the fact that the man-child trooper had just called his like-aged suspect 'son'.

The second backup trooper stood watch over Daniel and helped LaDue. The other backup was still questioning the as-yet unidentified passenger, while he tried to get the bleeding under control. His only responses were the repeated insults to the trooper on top of him. "Cocksucka" being the theme while he spit up blood. LaDue opened the back double-doors to the van. It was filled from the back doors up to the front seats with crates.

"I'm willing to bet that whatever is in these crates is not good for you Daniel."

LaDue used the lever end of a tire-iron from the back of the van, after getting help pulling one of the large crates out of it.

When he opened it, he was both elated and astonished. The crate was filled with shredded paper as packing and modified Heckler & Koch *G3 Assault-4* rifles. The second backup was over his shoulder, just as stunned.

"Holy shit boys! It's redneck Christmas. Mother-load."

Part One

Metro Trailer Park

May 2004

1

I WAS RELATIVELY NEW TO THE TROOP H
DETECTIVE UNIT of the Massachusetts State Police Department.
It had been almost ten months, ten months exactly May 15th, when
I was promoted from patrol. I was still responsible for Boston and
Metrowest, but instead of sitting on the Mass Pike ticketing people
trying to get to and from work I was doing something important. I
conducted investigations for serious crimes against persons within
a certain area of greater Boston. Those areas were well-defined,
though sometimes in the course of an investigation there were
pissing contests with either the Springfield or Worcester units.

Within the various troops, there were ranks that everyone
sought to climb. The writing was on the wall for me, I was not
going to climb any ladder. I was a Detective Junior Grade, purely
by attrition, and that is how I would retire. The politics were
obscene, the bullsh more than I could stomach. To be honest, rules
aren't really my thing to begin with. Odd, I know, but sometimes

what stands between me and the objective is a rule. I like to look at the big picture, the pencil pushers like to scrutinize over whether that picture is on Polaroid or Kodak paper.

So you could say that while I liked my work, I absolutely hated my job. You could say that because it was absolutely true.

I hated my boss, I hated my partner, and I hated the back-stabbing assholes that wanted my job. One would think that in law enforcement the job should be about justice. Justice for the people who were wronged, for the people of the City of Boston. But if you think that, you would be absolutely wrong.

What it was actually about, was politics. Who owed whom what favor, who knew which of their colleagues was dirty and what that damage could do if anyone were to find out. Those little tidbits of information won you chips in a big game that I wanted no part of.

So it was customary for cops to consult with other cops on cases. Information traded in exchange for get-out-of-jail-free cards. A collar wasn't a collar until someone from the DA's office was involved. Then other deals were made. Somehow the prisons and county lock-ups were full, but don't ask me how.

What wasn't customary was for me to be called in on one of these deals, which is exactly what happened on Tuesday May11th, 2004. I remember the exact day because the Tribe was at Fenway, and Pedro was scheduled on the mound. I had tickets, but of course I didn't get to go because of this nonsense that I am about to tell you.

It was 6:15 PM and I was at The House, ready to check out for the day and get over to Fenway for the seven-oh-five start-time. That's when the kid called my name, Warren Dennihan. Only everyone calls me Deni, so I could tell right off the jump that I probably didn't know who was calling me.

"Dennihan!" The Trooper calling me looked like he was fifteen years old.

"That's Detective Dennihan, who are you?"

"William LaDue. Trooper LaDue. I got a situation from a routine stop that went sideways, guys callin' for you."

"Oooooooh, you're Billy. The new kid. Billy the Kid, I heard about you. Real go-getter that went to Brown."

Normally I would never have heard of a new trooper, even in my own building which this kid was not. But LaDue was the talk of the Staties. He was from Rhode Island, really smart, and had gone to Brown University. You don't get too many smart guys who want to be a glorified meter-maid for the Commonwealth of Massachusetts State Police. So people talked. The rumor was that he was one of those do-gooder action junkies that thought this was a noble career and he would make a difference. I gave him a year, two at the most before he figured it out. Meanwhile his mom was probably real proud to pay top-dollar for an Ivy League education for a job that pays $35k a year if he is lucky enough to get overtime. But the Massachusetts State Police is the largest police force in New England, so if he had to be a cop at least he was in the Ivy League of shit jobs.

The kid tried to fit in because he was different. Most of the guys in the department were either ex-military or ex-crooks. Either way, none of us had gone to Brown so our options were far more limited than his. This kid could be anything he wanted to be, yet he took the job away from guys and girls who needed the opportunity. Nobody liked him because he was supposedly a silver-spooner, so he tried all the harder. He even put on the fake Boston accent, which was invented to be a strong as mine. He dropped his R's, making them sound like ah's, like 'ah' instead of 'are'. He added them when they didn't exist, like 'sar' instead of 'saw'. My accent, unfortunately, is real.

"Uh, yeah. That's me. Anyway, I got one Daniel McKennie that is in a real fix and all he wants is you. After we Miranda'd him, he didn't say he wanted a lawyer or nothin'. Fuckin' punk just wants you, guy."

"Enough with the accent before you hurt yourself. Did you say McKennie? As in little Danny Mick?"

"I didn't say 'Danny Mick', but yes. He is down in room six waiting to speak with you." Thankfully LaDue dropped the accent, but now he sounded like a preppy douche.

16

I knew Danny Mick from the neighborhood. I grew up and still lived in Southie. For those that don't know Boston, Southie is South Boston. It is a rough and tumble Irish neighborhood, full of projects and three-deckers, where you are a criminal or you don't have hair on your nuts yet. I dated his older sister, Roxy for a while. By date, I mean we wrestled naked in bed quite a bit back in the day. She was a hot-mess back then and rumor had it that she still was.

"Do you know why he wants to talk to me? What'd he do?"

"Van full of assault rifles. His partner pulled a piece on us. He died on the way to Mass General. My backup called it in so Detective Hobbs is already in the loop. His case now, so you'll have to get with him." The trooper's accent was back. I could see why he rubbed people the wrong way. He definitely pissed me off.

"Hobbs is already down there?"

"Yeah. He told me to find you, but I was gonna anyway cuz the kid's been askin' for you," LaDue said.

"You wouldn't know shit if it was in yer hand would ya? I thought you were supposed to be smart? Hobbs is already my partner. So my case now."

"Whatever. I told him I would find you, and I did. Good luck. Who lets me know where to show up for the trial? You?"

"Just get outta here, Billy."

"William."

The kid had the balls to stare me down. Standing your ground is something I admire. To a point.

"Hey Billy? Kick rocks will ya?"

When I had finally gotten rid of the eager beaver, I made my way to Interview Room Six. Outside the room on the bench was my partner, Detective Sergeant Rick Hobbs, the partner that outranked me that I couldn't stand.

Rick Hobbs was the kind of guy that after being with him for twenty minutes, you would actually be so irritated that choking a baby was deemed a plausible outlet for your anger, though obviously not appropriate. Only I had to spend way more than twenty minutes with the bag o'douche, I had to spend a minimum of five days a week with him attached to my hip. He was the know-it-all, holier-than-thou type that never made a mistake. Arrogance is fine, except that he screwed up all of the time and blamed everyone else for his fuck-ups. He was so self-absorbed that he probably liked the smell of his own shit. Other than that he was okay.

"There he is. Where ya been, Deni?"

"I was gonna file my fives before goin' to the game. Pedro is pitchin' tonight."

"Why bother? The Sox do great every year until the All-star break, then they suck their way out of the division. Yankees will be in the World Series again this year, mark my words. Sox will be lucky to get the Wild Card."

"Yeah well, it's a marathon not a race and it woulda been really nice to catch the game. Whatta we got?"

"Spiv by the name of Daniel McKennie. Only twenty-four and he's got a sheet as long as my fuckin' arm. Got caught with his dick in a pig. Ten cases of assault rifles in a brand new stolen van with stolen plates from yet another stolen van. Address puts him in Southie, probably in a triple-decker. You know that neighborhood, it's a metro trailer park. They infest the area like cockroaches. Anyways, he says he knows you and I assume he wants a walk. I don't see it happen'n partner."

18

"We've been workin' together, what? Ten months right? How is it you don't know I come from Southie? What am I now? Trailer trash?"

"I remember you live there. I make it that's how you know this mutt."

"I used to date his sister, that's how I know him. And just watch your mouth. If things woulda gone different aways back, maybe I woulda been with him. Maybe drivin' the van."

"Whatever. He could be your kid for all I give a shit. But there's no way he walks on this, no matter who you're bangin'."

"I'm not gonna get into it with ya, Rick. Just gimme some time with tha kid, huh? No microphone, no video, just me and him. We good?"

"Knock yourself out. He's snagged, confession or not."

I went into room six and the kid was sitting in his chair, stoic and handcuffed. I removed my sport-jacket and placed it on top of the microphone in the center of the table and took my seat across from him. I knew what Rick agreed to and I also knew what he was capable of. Not a big trust factor between us.

"Got yourself all jammed up here Danny."

"Are we alone or are they watchin' on tha other side a tha mirror?" His accent was a bad as mine. Maybe worse. You tend to run into that in Southie. Get two of us together with an outsider as a bystander and they will tell you that we are speaking a different language, because what comes out of our mouths doesn't sound like english. I probably didn't have to cover up the microphone in retrospect.

"Yeah, just us. But I'm not sure what I can do for ya, kid. You're pretty fucked."

"What am I gonna do, Deni? Slopes is gonna shit a cow, man."

"Aaaah, Danny. Slopes? What did he get you into? Guns?"

He nodded his head. "G3s."

In the thirty-seconds I had spoken to Danny, I had already sized up what was going on. Everybody from Southie has a nickname. When you live twelve to twenty people in one three-family three-decker, you get a neighborhood with a ton of people with the same name. It's called a three-decker, or triple-decker as the non-locals called it, for the complicated reason that there is an entire community of houses with three ascending decks. The houses are practically attached to each other, side by side, the style exactly the same. A basement with three floors built up on top, each floor a different apartment, all having decks both front and back.

The Irish-Catholic community in Southie isn't devout by any means, but they follow the 'no form of birth control' rule. Nicknames were the only way to tell us all apart. Even if you were the one and only, like Warren Dennihan, you still got a nickname. Sean Teague was the given name to Slopes.

In Southie, there are probably fifty Sean Teagues. Slopes got his name because he is one of the rare cases where the disease Bell's Palsy became permanent. Either it wasn't diagnosed quickly enough or an antibiotic wasn't given soon enough, or he didn't take it. In any case the side of his face drooped like it was sliding off his face. He was very sensitive about it, but that didn't stop the nickname. Slopes was a boss for the Irish mob.

Back in the 70s, former IRA 'Volunteer' Patrick Nee came to the US and became a leader with the Mullen Gang. They then went to war against the Killeen Brothers gang over Boston turf. James J. Bulger was the boss of the KB crew back then, he got a nickname too - Whitey. When it was all said and done, the Mullens and Killeens joined the Howie Winter gang, because their war depleted the two gangs to a point where they couldn't survive. When Howie Winter went to jail in '79 for rigging horse races over at Suffolk Downs, Bulger took over the whole shah-bang. The Winter Hill Gang became the biggest confederation of organized crime in the east after the Irish Gang War. In '94 Whitey Bulger went into hiding because he turned FBI informant, but his crew was still doing business without him. They were still bookmaking and loansharking, which were some of the least horrible things they did.

The Winter Hill Gang had made the papers recently because they held a bunch of no-show jobs on the Big Dig. They had formed a dummy corporation called the C. Dáil Corp., which James Kerasiotes of the Mass Turnpike Authority awarded a contract without a bid. They got paid for literally nothing. No wonder the Big Dig project was long over the deadline and over budget.

Danny telling me that he had a cargo van full of Heckler & Koch *G3A4s* meant that they were still smuggling guns for the IRA. Those guns were one of the types of the signature weapons used by the IRA in any cause they engaged in. It also meant Slopes had a come-up and was now Mr. Big in Boston. Bottom line was that those guns were going to be paid for in one way or another, which ultimately meant that Danny Mick was fucked in the permanent sense. Prison was the least of his worries. Danny didn't want me to get him out of the hoosegow, he wanted me to get him square with Slopes.

All of the information came to me in just a few sentences, and it took me almost no time at all to connect the dots. I felt for the kid a little bit. As the gentrification had begun in Southie, yuppies taking over our neighborhoods, increasingly fewer legitimate opportunities were available to make a living. I caught a break when I was kid which allowed me to extricate myself from that life without leaving the neighborhood. I was one of the few lucky ones. Danny was on a different path. With more affluent kids like young Billy buying houses, taking over the neighborhoods, and taking the decent jobs, there would be more like Danny getting classed out.

"Jesus Danny. How many G3s?"

"Two hundred."

"And your boy tried to shoot a cop? Why didn't you just take off? Try and dust the rookie who pulled you over?"

"Ya tellin' me? Gridlock on Storrow. Nowhere to run."

"I hate to add insult, but which of you two geniuses decided to move it all during peak traffic? On Storrow of all fuckin' things?"

"Big Dig redirected us. Slopes told us the pickup and drop times."

"Well then he's the idiot. No reason to move that much hardware during broad daylight in rush hour. What's really going on here?"

"No clue, man. I just did what I was told. We got fucked cuz of tha tags. Cops don't usually do pullovers in traffic. Nobody was more shocked than me to see tha fuckin' cruisa flick his lights."

"Fair enough. You were unlucky enough to get the one go-getter with a badge. But still .... "

"So what do I do? I'm a dead man. If I PC, they'll think I ratted. If I don't I'll be on the business end of stabbing. You gotta talk to him for me, Deni. He knows you."

PC meant Protective Custody while he was awaiting trial. And he was right. It would actually be easier to kill him while incarcerated than it would out on the streets.

"I'll see what I can do, but I'm not makin' any promises. If Slopes is runnin' the mob crew here which runs guns for the IRA, I might not even get the chance to talk to him. I'm a cop and everyone within 30 blocks of the neighborhood knows it. He's gonna be pretty insulated. I don't even know where he is these days."

"He never sits anywhere for more than a minute. Go see my sister. She'll get you to him. Please Deni. You gotta help me."

"No I don't. I told you I would have a chat, but it ends there. How does your sister know where he is?"

"Just you and me talkin' here? She gets her junk direct."

"You know the shit I'm gonna take if my partner or my boss hears that I'm runnin' around trying to save your ass? Where were these guns goin' anyway?"

"In the end? I got no idea. I just go from point A to point B when I'm told. Somebody else was gonna move'em later. I'm not exactly high up the food chain ya know."

"My point."

"What's your point, Deni?"

"I shoulda gone to the game, that's the point."

2

GETTING RID OF MY PARTNER, RICK HOBBS, WAS QUITE THE CHORE. He was nothing but questions once I was finished chatting with young Danny Mick. I didn't know if he had watched the conversation through the glass in the observation room or not, but he seemed to not know what was said. He was all about if Danny confessed, where the guns were going, where they had come from, and the like.

Everywhere I turned he would be there asking me another question, practically dry-humping me up one hall and down the next one. I didn't like the guy anyway, but at that point I was ready to strangle him. I was already in a bad mood for missing the Sox game. The situation was made worse by the fact that I had to see a girl I used to sleep with back in the day, in order to find a mobster who was probably going to kill the guy I had just spoken to, because he had lost two hundred assault rifles. I really didn't need my partner nagging at me as a topper.

Hobbs knew that I knew all of these hoods and racketeers. I grew up with them. Hell I still lived near them. The entire department knew that I had a relationship with these hooligans, I had been hired specifically for the intel. When I wouldn't go undercover after completing the academy, for what I thought were obvious reasons, they sent me to watch traffic on the Pike. That was the main reason I would never get any further in the department. The higher-ups had long memories and I didn't play politics, so my fate was sealed.

At the age of thirty-two, I was younger than my partner who was a decade my senior. I was in exponentially better physical condition as well but age had nothing to do with it. The old cliché about cops eating donuts was brought to life with Rick Hobbs. But not just donuts. If the foodstuff involved massive amounts of preservatives and fat, he loved it in mass quantities. It is my personal feeling that clogged arteries also clog up blood-flow to the brain. Does that mean that all fat people are stupid, of course not. What I'm saying is that if you are a guy who is not working with a ton of brain power, lack of blood to the noggin is an added hurdle that is ill-afforded. I'm no genius by any stretch, but I would bet the ranch that I would beat him in anything from arm-wrestling to a spelling bee.

"Hobbs! Enough already. I just want to finish my shit and maybe catch the back end of the game, okay?"

"I'm your goddamned senior partner and you never treat me like we're a team. What did he say? Where were the guns goin'?"

"What are you, a broken record? 'What did he say? …. What did he do? …. Where were the guns goin'? …. Why do I have a small penis?' It gets old. I told you I was going in there alone to talk to tha kid. We talked. Case closed. He wasn't lookin' for a walk, he just wanted to talk about the neighborhood. He knows he is goin' away for a long time, and we didn't need a confession. So for the last time, back …. the …. fuck …. off. Any of this gettin' through?"

"I still outrank you last I checked, but have it your way. We're gonna be boxed out anyway. With that kind of hardware, the ATF will be down here first thing."

"They have all the fun don't they? Alcohol, Tobacco *and* Firearms is like the trifecta. Booze, guns and stogies sounds like a good time to me. So you think they will show up in the morning to haul away the lot?" I played stupid. I didn't care either way, to be honest. But he was right. The ATF would want the case especially because it was a lay-up. Maybe the FBI would want in also.

"Guns and the van are already down at ballistics in Maynard, they will probably let us analyze and run them through the database, but they will take over the investigation."

The crime lab for Massachusetts was located in the western part of the state, about an hour away off of route 62 in the town of Maynard. They investigate; blood work, for DNA and toxicology; hair fibers and skin; weapons and ballistics. It was our CSI lab. In this case they would completely strip down the van for fibers or trace evidence that could lead to other suspects involved in the gun trafficking. They will also examine every weapon to determine its origin, who has used it, and if the weapon had been used in any other documented crime. Fingerprints and ballistics would take some time and since Maynard was the only lab in the state, there was a back-log.

"Well good for them. Tie it up with a bow and get it off our case load," I said. Hobbs was following me back to my desk. Our desks.

"They are gonna want to trade him in for a bigger fish, Deni."

"I'm sure."

"Sooooo …. "

"So what?"

"Who is your little friend working for? You want me to put a bow on it? Give me the ribbon."

"Do you ever sing a different tune?" I faked sign language and enunciated extremely slowly in the hopes that he would finally get the fact that I was not going to give him Slopes. "I …. don't ….

know …. who …. he …. is …. working …. for. He knows he's going away for a long time and I used to bang his sister. He wanted me to talk to her, say goodbye and that he is sorry. Do you honestly think he would tell a cop who he is working for? Surest way to get clipped is to give up his boss. He's well-trained. He'll do his time like a man and shut his cock-holster."

"You must know who he runs with. He is from your neighborhood. Winter Hill Gang? Gotta be, right?"

Exasperated, I sat on my desk dropping my fives in my to-do pile and focused on the pain in the ass partner standing before me.

"You're not my boss. You're my senior partner and I don't know how to say it any different. You keep askin', I keep tellin', but nothin' sticks to that meat between your ears. I don't know. But let's say that you are right, he is workin' for the Winters. What in the holy fuck are you gonna do about it? They been doin' business in this city for a long-ass time. They survived the gang-wars, Federal RICO Task Force …. but you? You think that you are gonna rid the city of them when you can't understand the simple concept of 'I don't know anything more than you do'. How does that play?"

"Why do you always protect them?"

"What are you talkin' about now, Hobbs?"

"You know that metro trailer park like the back of your hand. You know who is doing what five steps before they do it. You could be a goddamned hero. Just go down there and scoop up the whole crew. But instead you let them do whatever they want and you cover for them."

"Let me ask you somethin'. Is that what you think this is? Me covering for a kid in the neighborhood? Covering for 'my people'? You've got some set on you, Hobbs. There have been probably a million man-hours spent tryin' to bring these guys down, and while they get a couple of the dregs, the mob keeps truckin' along. But let me spell somethin' out for you. Where do all of those nickel and dime crooks go if the overlords go down? Disorganized chaos. You think all of those guys are gonna just go out and get a job? No fuckin' way. They go into business for themselves and crime actually gets worse. Those bodegas that are

26

currently under protection are fair game. Pawn shops sprout up all over to take place of the loan sharking. Drugs are on every corner instead of specific ones through the Winters. Or worse? New York and Rhode Island guinea crews move in and pick up the slack. There is no eliminating them, Hobbs. You just try and control it the best way you can."

"So you cover for the kid?"

"I'm done. I got nothin' more to say to you. It's not our case anymore anyway, you just said. You don't get to be a hero on this one. Just give it to the ATF or FBI or whatever and move on."

"I'm gonna request a new partner."

"I've heard that before too. Let me know how it goes."

Hobbs stormed away from me, away from our desks which unfortunately faced each other. The desk farm that was the Troop H Detective Unit was set up in one large room with desks that were like a Tetris puzzle. There were no partitions or cubicles, that was deemed as counterproductive and obstructed teamwork. All partners had desks that were facing one another, not just Hobbs and me. I was thankful that he had decided to walk away instead of having to face him while I finished the work that should have been completed hours prior.

I removed the fives that I had to finish from my to-do pile. Fives are what detectives call the DD-5 form that must be submitted on active cases. My boss, Lieutenant Manny Titanitaukis (who we call Lieu to his face and Tits behind his back), is little more than a case manager. He has to manage our share of the 2,000 homicide cases, 9,000 rape allegations, 75,000 armed robberies, 125,000 reported assaults, 130,000 auto thefts involving a carjacking, and countless other felonies that get called-in every single year. Troop H handles most of the cases since we are responsible for crimes against persons in greater Boston, but the local stations and other departments handle a good many as well. Tits needs to file his own paperwork to keep his bosses apprised of which cases are solved and which are pending. We have to submit a form, the DD-5, for each development on each case that we handle.

I was behind on my paperwork. I was originally going to just submit the fives that Tits was having a fit over and head to the game, but it was now after 9:00 PM which meant that by the time I got over to Yawkey Way the game would be over. So I decided to hunker down and finish all of my outstanding paperwork. Tickets wasted.

The realization that the date that I was supposed to bring to the game, the one that I didn't go to, hit me like a ton of bricks. I pulled out my new Motorola *V3 RAZR* flip-top cell phone and saw what I already knew. Fifteen missed calls and twenty-two unread text messages. My ass was grass.

3

I WOKE UP ON WEDNESDAY MORNING ALONE, which was not what I had been planning when I bought the very hard to come by tickets to Fenway. I had been planning my personal opening day game for the 2004 season for a couple of weeks. I had been seeing this girl, Jill, for a while and had promised her we would go. I say promised because we had been down this road before, just not with tickets to the Red Sox. She made me say over and over again that we would definitely go see Pedro throw filth at the Indians. But in fairness, maybe not in those exact words.

She had not answered any of my phone calls last night when I realized that I was more than two hours late in picking her up. I decided against calling her again that morning. For one, I get up at 5:00 AM to go work out and then to The House and, two, she was likely still really pissed and/or sleeping with someone else. I decided instead to listen to the voicemails from the night before telling me what a shit-bag I am while I made coffee. I would have read the stored texts also but I had no idea how to on the new phone. I don't even know why she sent them because she knows my feelings about them, and I definitely never send texts because I have a bitch of a time using the numbers to type in one of the three letters on each button I want for each and every word.

By the time the Dunkin' Donuts coffee was brewed, I had been thoroughly dressed down as the calls went from concern to tears to vulgarities and anger. Needless to say I deleted them. Maybe there would be a forthcoming conversation, maybe not.

I grabbed The Globe. It said that it was going to be sixty-five and sunny. Finally a nice day. I then pulled out the sports section. The Sox won, 5-3 to an always sold-out stadium and now had a 20-13 record. *Dammit.*

The gun bust didn't make the front page, above or below the fold. Didn't even make the police log buried in the small print. I thought that odd. Instead, the front cover was a follow-up about the US bodies that were hung by Iraqis off the bridge in the Sunni Triangle the previous March. They were apologizing for the controversy surrounding the graphic pictures they had used on a story printed in late April. To be honest, I hate that newspaper. It's a rag owned by the New York Times, and I hate Nuevo York. But the Herald is worse.

After the morning shower and putting on the off-the-rack suit from Filene's Basement in Downtown Crossing, I went out to the street to find what was left of my car. My two-door silver Pontiac *Grand Am* a-la 2001 was, for lack of a better term, fucked up.

I had bought the car new in silver because silver tends to hide scratches. When you live in the city, parking is a nightmare. If you are lucky enough or rich enough to park in a lot, the cars are so tight that you need a can opener to get it out. The doors get dinged super-easily and daily. Mostly, you have to park on the street which means that you get love-tapped on both bumpers pretty much daily as well.

The car that was left for me was not love-tapped or dinged. The tires were slashed, all of them, and the only remaining glass was in shards on the inside of the car. Upon closer inspection, my

Blaupunkt car stereo with no-skip CD player was gone. It was supposed to have had an anti-theft system also but that had obviously failed. I knew better when I bought the damned thing. When I was a kid, stealing car stereos was my bread and butter. There was no such thing as anti-theft. The manufacturers use the term to charge more for them.

I didn't realize Jill was *that* pissed. So I missed a few dates, welshed on a few promises. She was a hundred and fifteen pounds soaking wet, there was no way she did that on her own. Maybe my stereo was payment for the job. Maybe she was the payment.

The car was a piece of shit anyway but it meant that I wouldn't be going to spar and I would need to take the train into work. I would also have to rec out an unmarked from the motor pool which was going to be a royal pain in the ass. All in all not a great way to start my day.

After the 'HELLOMOTO' was gone from the screen after flipping open my cellphone, I called my partner to tell him what had happened and that I was going to be late. He actually sounded relieved to not have to deal with me for a couple of extra hours and I can't say that I was distraught about that part of it either. He didn't offer to come pick me up, let's put it that way.

With the extra time to kill before   I could catch the Silver line to the Red Line on the   MBTA ⓣ system, I thought it a good time to go see Roxy.   Danny   Mick's sister.   It was early and she was probably still drunk and partying, but why not? Last I knew she didn't work nor did she have any plans to.

Roxanne McKennie, or Roxy, still lived in the same three-decker that she grew up in. Only she now lived on a different floor. Like almost everyone in that neighborhood, you either moved out to a different floor of the same building, or you moved in with someone else who was on a different floor of their same building. Roxy had moved out and back in so many times that her parents weren't able to rent out the top floor in the likelihood that she would be back. This was one of those 'she was back' times.

The rickety wooden stairs that went up to the third floor to Roxy's place sounded and felt like I was going to fall through them.

31

It was a good thing she didn't weigh much if she had to negotiate these stairs every day. I was a lot younger when Roxy and I had dated, so I was going in the front door on the first floor back then. The creaking and whining of the stairs must have alerted her to my presence because she was waiting for me at the landing at the top of the third floor.

"Warren Dennihan. To what do I owe the honor of your fuckin' presence?"

It was a bad split and she was obviously still not a fan. But looking at her, I was validated in my decision to break it off because she looked terrible. She was thirty and looked like every single one of those years was hard. She was once very pretty, or at least I thought she was back then.

"Hey Roxy. You look, eh, good?" I said it more like a question, which she registered.

"Go fuck ya self." She said it in a way that only Boston women can say it. A way that strips a man of everything he is, down to his bones. Emasculating just doesn't quite say it.

"C'mon Rox. Take the high road. I gotta talk to you about Danny Mick."

I reached the top of the stairs by then but she wasn't letting me onto the landing where she was standing, which put her waist by my face. I was looking up to her pleading my case.

"Seriously, let me in so we don't have to do this in public."

"What? You afraid that somebody might see you slummin'?"

"I still live down here, Rox. I don't wanna do this the hard way, just let me in. Your brother said that you would talk to me."

"My brother don't know shit about shit. What did he do now? If you're looking to bust him, he don't live here. Try downstairs."

"He's in lock-up, so I'm not lookin' for him. He sent me to talk to you. Are you gonna let me in or what?"

"You're a cop, ya cocksucka. Go get a warrant."

"I don't need a warrant. I'm not backdoorin' ya here, Rox. I'm tryin' to help the poor prick. He's in a lotta shit, hun."

"So whatever you find in here you can't use against me?"

"Are you gonna shoot at me? Stick me with somethin'? No? Then I think we're good."

She let me inside and it was a complete dumpster-fire. To say that she wasn't much of a housekeeper would be the understatement of all understatements. I don't think the place was rentable if she did move out for good. If the lower two floors were in the same condition, the best thing to do would be to watch it burn and collect the insurance.

"I love what you've done with the place. Jesus, what is that smell? Open a window or somethin' would ya?"

"The king has spoken. You gonna pay my heat bill? Open a window he says."

"It's sixty-five degrees outside and not raining for once. It might actually be warmer outside."

"You come up here to give me decorating tips Martha Stewart, or you gonna tell me what my brother did?"

"Enough with the attitude, smart-ass. I mean it. I'm in no fuckin' mood. He got busted yesterday moving half an arsenal for Slopes. ATF is gonna be all over the kid today or tomorrow to give up the goods. If he went over or was plannin' on goin' over state lines the FBI might want to get a foot in. Wherever those guns were going, they ain't gettin' there. Slopes is gonna be none to happy as it is, so he gets word that Danny Mick spoke with cops? It's gonna get a damn-sight worse."

"So what are you gonna do for him mister hot-shit?"

"You're gonna tell me where to find Slopes so I can try and reason with the guy. Maybe keep a shiv outta your brother's belly. He does his time and keeps his trap shut, he lives to be an old man. With a little luck, someday a free old man."

"And what do you get? You doin' this outta the kindness of your heart or do I gotta suck you off or somethin'?"

"You're a real class-act, Rox. Top shelf kinda girl. Tha fuck happened to you?"

"You, ya piece of shit. You chewed me up and spit me out. You don't like what you see? Look in a mirror."

"Don't put your shit on me. We were like a million years ago. I boosted shit, which made you get all hot and bothered. We rolled around and had a few laughs but that was pretty much it. I put that crap behind me, but I never forgot where I came from. I might not have been man of the year with you, Rox, but whatever you became ain't on me. You were never an angel but this goin' the extra mile. Just tell me where to find Slopes and I'll leave you to get junked up or whatever it is you do."

Quips and snappy digs at me were over. She was a sobbing mess. It might have been what I said, but more likely I was a reminder of what could have been for her. She had a choice when I broke it off with her forever ago. That choice was to get out of the life if not the neighborhood, or get sucked down into it. At thirty years old it was not too late. But she thought so, and that realization was painful.

I felt bad, but not bad enough to console her. Not bad enough to give her a hug and lie to her, tell her everything would turn out aces. Not bad enough to even sit down in that mess. I stood in front of her like an idiot waiting for her to get a grip. It seemed to take a while.

"Rox? Where do I find Slopes?"

Her midnight makeup from the night before was running off of her face. She looked through me not at me. "Abandoned warehouse down on Wash. I don't give a shit what happens to you, but don't go down there like a storm troopa. For Danny's sake."

"Yeah sure. I know. Try to take better care of yourself, Rox."

"Don't come back here Deni. Ever."

THE CALL TO DETECTIVE HOBBS INFORMING HIM that I was going to be later than I had expected went over without much fuss. Which was a shocker because he always wanted to be attached to my hip. If he had an inkling of what I was doing, he didn't say it. I couldn't perceive even the slightest of notes that he cared one way or the other what I was doing. Maybe he was requesting a new partner, but we had been down that road a few times in ten months. I was still his partner so we know how that played out.

I hadn't initially planned on going to see Slopes that morning. I hadn't planned on seeing Roxy that morning either, but there was no time like the present. If, in fact, the ATF was going to talk to Danny Mick that day or the next, I thought it best to discuss the situation with Slopes before hand. Better to be proactive than reactive, sorta thing. The ball was rolling, so this last errand would hopefully end my to-do list with this project.

The abandoned warehouse on Washington Avenue looked like it was a squatter's paradise. The realtor sign said that it was going to be converted into lofts but it didn't say when. That sign was covered in graffiti so either the development was postponed, out of business, or it was just wishful thinking. The windows were boarded up but there was no door preventing an easy access.

I walked right in like I owned the place. But I was glad I didn't own it. Rats were having their way with the first floor. It was difficult to see with everything being boarded up, but I assumed they were rats given the sounds. The sun outside was shining bright for a change, but not enough to provide light inside the derelict building. The sound of the movement of the critters alluded to the fact that they were many and enormous.

The Big Dig was displacing all of the rats in Boston. Tunnels and bridges were being built to send traffic under or over the city to alleviate surface road traffic. Those tunnels were where the rodents lived and had been forced out among the two legged infestation. It got to a point where restaurants in the city were having to buy cats to roam their establishments at night. Exterminators could not keep up with the number of sightings and were ineffective when they did treat. This Chinese restaurant that I frequent has three enormous cats that they let roam the restaurant at night when the place is closed. They are the biggest domesticated cats that you have ever seen in your life outside of the jungle cats you see at the zoo. The owners never feed them.

Making my way in the dark as my eyes adjusted, I was halted by a man carrying a sawed-off shotgun. He didn't have to pump it for me to know that I was in trouble. I wouldn't be able to get to my holster and retrieve my weapon before being filled with holes.

"Wrong way cop."

I raised my hands in surrender. "No need to get all cranked up. I came alone."

"Maybe yes, maybe no. Either way you need to turn around and be on your merry way, for you get tuned up."

"I need to talk to Slopes. It's urgent."

"He ain't takin' calls at the moment."

"Even if I were to say that it's about the 200 G3s that are about to be turned over to the ATF?"

There was a pause. The only sounds were the rustling of the rats and the gears in the man's brain grinding, working on a thought. I could barely see him but I wanted to get a read. I didn't get one. Nor could I tell if he was the only person in front me.

"I'm listenin'," he finally said.

"I'm sure that I have your attention, but I need to talk to Slopes. He knows me."

"Everyone knows you. Like I said, he ain't takin' calls. You could be Jesus himself and he wouldn't see you right now."

"I'm going to reach into my jacket pocket for a business card, my cell number is on it. Will you give it to him? It's extremely important that I talk with him."

"Wicked slow muthafucka."

I slowly pulled out one of cards that were loosely strewn about the inside pocket of my suit jacket. They were always in there. I sent my suits to the cleaners after every third time I wore them and always forgot to take them out. I have no idea what dry cleaning is, but those cards never get damaged.

The card was extended out in front of me between my index and middle fingers. The armed security man moved through the dark building toward me and took the card. He didn't say another word, nor did I. The awkward silence was palpable and I read the situation like that was the end of the meeting, so I turned and left.

Outside of the building I flipped open my phone, dialing my partner after my eyes adjusted back to the bright sunlight.

"Hobbs, Deni here."

"I know, I can see that it's you on my caller ID. What's up? Are you coming in at all today?"

"Yeah, I'm not too far away. I'm — "

" — you're on Wash, yeah I know. I see you. I'm parked up on the corner."

I was stunned and speechless. I turned to my right and then left to discern where my ambusher was lurking.

He flashed the headlights on the unmarked 2003 Dodge *Intrepid* that he had obviously pulled from the motor pool. We normally use my *Grand Am* to get around as it is less conspicuous. The *Intrepid* was dark blue and although not a Crown Vic, it still screamed police car. I looked behind me to make sure that the thug whom had just received my business card didn't see that I had police company, or Hobbs and I would both be dead men.

I hightailed it down the block toward my partner. Seventy-five yards later I was seated in the passenger seat.

"Were you following me?"

"I thought we were partners. But I guess after your conversation with your buddy last night, you decided to take this case over on your own."

"You're kind of a one-trick-pony aren't ya Hobbs? Same thing all the time. We don't have a case to take over. I told you last night, he wasn't askin' for a walk or for any favors other than to talk with his sister. Did you follow me over to her place this morning?"

"The crack-den? Yeah I saw it. Cozy."

"How long have you been staking me out? Did you see who fucked up my car last night?"

"No. That wasn't a lie to buy time this morning?"

"Forget it. Just get us outta here before we get killed."

"And this morning's conversation with one Roxanne McKennie led you to an abandoned warehouse down here on Wash?" He pulled out from his pseudo-parallel parking job and continued up Washington Street. We were headed toward the Theatre District and Chinatown.

"That conversation produced the concern that whomever her brother was involved with might be just a tad-bit upset that the guns are now under the control of the police. That her brother might be in danger. I wanted to see if I could try and protect him."

"Jesus H. Christ Deni. Who's side are you on? This is textbook interference with an ongoing investigation. The only way to protect him is to keep him quiet. Keeping Daniel McKennie quiet keeps Sean Teague and the mob in business and is completely against what we are trying to do here. You know as well as I do that the only play here is to put your friend into protective custody in exchange for his flippin' Mr. Big."

Hobbs had just slipped up. He already knew that Danny Mick was working for Sean Teague, A.K.A. Slopes. He had just said so. What I didn't know was if he had already known that because he listened in to the conversation I had in room six, or if he knew that the abandoned warehouse on Wash was where Slopes was temporarily headquartered.

"First of all, the suspect is not my friend. Second, how long have you known that this was an Irish thing? "

"How stupid do you think I am? We're in the South End, just on the other side of the Channel from Southie. G3A4s are like the Irish calling-card. Your metro trailer park is to the mob what Pawtucket is to the Red Sox. Nothing happens in Boston involving the Irish without Sean Teague knowing or planning it. The question is what are *you* doing?"

"I'm getting out of the way while, according to you, the ATF takes over. Danny Mick getting stabbed in prison does nobody any good. He's not gonna flip on his crew, whoever it is he works for."

"Don't bullshit me Deni. You and I both know who you just saw in there. Is he 'not your friend' too?"

"As usual I don't know what you're talkin' about and I didn't see anyone in there. Pull a bitch and go see if there's anyone in there if ya don't believe me."

"I'm not turning around, we're almost outta Chinatown."

"Where are we headed?"

"Temple. We caught another case."

I tuned the car stereo into 100.7 WZLX, the classic rock station. Hobbs protested but I turned up the volume so I couldn't hear him. Queen's *Another One Bites the Dust* blared out of the tinny speakers. I hoped Freddie Mercury was wrong.

5

WITH THE THOUSANDS OF CASES THAT COME INTO TROOP H every year, Detectives have dozens of cases going simultaneously. Real life isn't like *Law & Order* where you see cops going from place to place talking with witnesses or tracking down leads on one case at a time. In the real world, Boston anyway, we have to plan our day so we aren't jumping all over the city all day.

Traffic is always bad, with the city-wide construction it's that much worse. The Big Dig will have you re-routed one way on this day, and then you are forced onto a completely different route the next. You could never plan on how long it would take you to get from place to place.   If you were going to be in one borough of Boston, you tended to stay there for the day.

If we were on one side of the city, say Dorchester, we took care of all of our cases and made all of our stops that needed to be made in Dorchester. It saved on time and it saved on gas. With the conflict in the Middle-east that was making the headlines every day, oil prices were always on the rise. Gas was getting to be a concern for everyone, especially the pencil-pushers in the Staties.

The general public gets crazy when they read in the paper or see in the news that an error by the police has led to the release of an accused criminal. I'm actually surprised it doesn't happen more. Juggling statements from several different witnesses on several different cases in the same day; investigating leads simultaneously, sometimes we mix stuff up. Or lose them all together.

It was almost the middle of May and my partner and I had already caught over three hundred cases so far that year. Some of them were closed, most were not. You have to prioritize. It sounds horrible but some things just never get investigated. Murders and rapes are top priority while others just don't ever see the top of the pile.

Take what happened to my car for example. I'm a cop and nobody cares what happened to the *Grand Am*. What do you think happens when Cindy Citizen calls in to her local precinct? That one incident involved multiple crimes. Vandalism 1 and Larceny over. Which meant that the value of the thing that was destroyed, my car, was of a value where if there was a conviction up to ten years could be sentenced. Then the civil case which may or may not be taken up by my insurance company. Then there was Larceny over, which means that the stereo/security system that was stolen was valued at *over* $500. That was yet another punishment of up to five years. Up to fifteen years is a long time and would be a righteous bust for someone. But consider yourself lucky if you get a flat-foot to even go out and take a statement. That's what insurance adjusters are for.

The case that we caught out on Temple Place was a woman who had already complained of being stalked and threatened. She had filed a restraining order and been to court to have the temporary order upheld. But that didn't make her stalker go away.

Her apartment was allegedly broken into and her personal garments had been gone through the night before. That was yet another call that this poor woman had called into the local precinct, another case to add to the thousands. She somehow managed to go to sleep after the violation. I had to give her credit for being strong. Going to sleep would have been difficult for anyone without serious medication. But she managed, medication or no.

She woke up that morning to find her stalker in her apartment staring at her through the slats of a closet door. He had apparently never left the apartment the night before and watched her all night. The police hadn't gone out to look at her apartment yet, so she left things they way she had found them as best she could. When she found the pervert in her apartment masterbating while she showered for work, there was an altercation. She managed to get in a few good licks but took many of her own. Crimes against persons, the Staties were now involved.

The victim was in pretty bad shape but she was a fighter. She was coherent enough to give a statement of what happened before heading off to the hospital. She would live another day but she was going to have permanent scars both physically and emotionally.

This case was easy enough for us to close. Hobbs and I didn't have to wait for the Maynard lab to do the blood work. The victim had drawn blood in her struggle with the attacker, both having two different blood-types. The lab could DNA match the suspect, but the victim had told us who it was and the backlog would take forever. With the previous paper on him, his address known, and the injuries we would see when we found the asshole, this was an easy one.

We didn't have any other business on that end of the city, so we headed back to my neighborhood. The guy that was causing the victim years of therapy was from Southie. You normally stick up for your own, but not this guy. It is embarrassing that the perv lived among the people I grew up with. We might be a lot of things, but we aren't skinners.

The suspect came home after we sat on his house for about an hour and a half. The victim got more than a few good swings on her aggressor. We were twenty yards off his front stoop and we could see his wounds.

The toughest part about how that went down was that I had to go all the way back to The House to process the paperwork on that prick, then come all the way back to my neighborhood because that was the end of my shift. It would have been nicer to just go home after we collared him, I was nine blocks away. He confessed in the car ride on the way in. I wish they were all that easy.

I was still thinking about the pervert and how much he bothered me when I got home to my three-decker that night. Also rattling around my brain was the fact that Danny Mick was no longer in holding. Nobody would tell me where he was either. I went down to check on him when we got back to The House after dealing with the skinner. Tell him how things were progressing. He was gone and off the books. ATF pick him up? Shipped over to South Bay awaiting arraignment? Nobody knew.

I grabbed a bottle of cheap Irish Whiskey off of the counter as I walked into my house and turned on the TV to NESN. I wanted to forget about Hobbs, Danny Mick, Roxy, and the perv.   The Indians were at Fenway again and my beloved Red Sox were not fairing as well. Kind of a shit day all-around.

But it got worse. I took off my jacket, draped it off the back of my recliner, reacquired my bottle of booze, and made my way to the kitchen for a glass when I saw that someone was already waiting for me in there.

I reached for to my armpit for my service weapon. My hand never made it to the Glock. He had me dead-to-rights. His Smith & Wesson *Model 500* hand cannon was pointed straight at my chest. The revolver didn't hold but six shots, but he wouldn't need that many. A fifty caliber projectile through my chest at that range would leave a big enough hole to stick a hand through, let alone necessitate six rounds. Even if I had my nine millimeter in my hand I was grossly out-gunned.

I could scream. My tenants above me would hear me most likely. But would they do anything? In my neighborhood screaming and gunshots were not uncommon. People only paid attention when it got really quiet.

"You're slipping Deni. Never would have been able to get the drop on you back in the day."

"Age. It's a bitch. Nice to see ya Slopes. Maybe you shoulda called first."

"You were lookin' for me?"

"Yeah but I guess you were wicked busy and couldn't talk. Danny Mick. You seen him lately?"

"I heard he got snagged."

"Doin' your work, Sean."

"What ever do you mean, Officer?"

"If we were playin' cops and bad-guys we could do games, dance for days. But I reached out today as a guy from the neighborhood. That used to mean somethin'."

Whether that six pound cannon that he had trained on me was getting too heavy or if he felt like things were maybe getting more comfortable, I don't know. But he lowered his gun, keeping it at his side in case he needed it. He stared at me with his one sharp eye while mulling over the situation.

"Care for a Whiskey?" I raised the bottle from my hand to show him it wasn't top-shelf.

"One."

"Then be a sweetheart and hand me two glasses out of the cupboard behind you." 'Sweetheart' sounded like 'sweet-hot' from a Bostonian and it's meant to sound sarcastic. I'm not sure if I said it to throw him off or piss him off, but in any event Slopes didn't bite.

44

"Fuck that. Take a pull from the bottle."

"Fair enough."

I unscrewed the top, took a pull and handed him the bottle. He took it with his left hand, his right still on his gun. I didn't really want to share a bottle with him. His Bell's Palsy made him a drooler. There was always a small pool of saliva on the right side of his mouth that sagged with the entire right side of his face. His eye and cheek sloped downward like it was about to slide off of his skull. Thus his nickname.

He took a generous pull himself on the left side of his mouth, all the while keeping his eye fixed on me. The first sip of the cheap crap that I could afford always made me wince. Not so with Slopes. I don't know what he normally drinks but the burn I felt going down was absent from his chest. Irish boys can drink, but I think that Sean Teague could bury me. He wiped his mouth with his sleeve before he continued.

"So did you come to see me because you have information for me, or did you want some from me?" He kept the bottle.

"Let's cut the bullsh. You and I both know that Danny Mick and his boy were pickin' up and delivering a shit-ton of assault rifles for you. I don't know what you were going to do with them or where they came from, all I know is that he had them. That many guns with everything but a four-leaf clover stamped to the side of 'em means that he is a big-dog now. No state case anymore. They are gonna wanna trade up. I talked to Danny Mick last night off the record. He's scared."

"He fuckin' should be."

"Not of the time. Of you."

"Like I said."

"He says he will do the time like a man, but he wants to maybe get out someday. Whoever you got on him, have them protect him in there not kill him."

"Deni I ain't sayin' that them guns was mine. But *if* they were, they had a purpose." He took another long pull of the bottle. Apparently 'one' meant one bottle, not one drink.

"I think everyone gets that. From what I can tell we had an eager rookie who was bored. You got unlucky. In your business you win some, lose some. No need for the kid to earn a shiv."

"It is what it is. Why do you care, Deni?"

"He asked me. And I knew him since back when he was still on the tit. I used to go out with his sister, Roxy."

"Shit, Deni. Everyone used to go out with Roxy. She been rode more than the nags at Suffolk Downs, man."

"Like I said, we look out for our own."

"Irregardless, big risk for you," he said.

"No shit English professor. This is unofficial. My partner knows that it's probably you who orchestrated this thing. But without Danny Mick, nothing gets back to you. The other guy died on the way to the hospital, but I'm sure you know that. The guns will be gone through at ballistics, but if there is nothing there .... Not our case anymore anyway, like I said. I am curious as to where he is though."

"Who? Danny Mick? Fuck should I know. You got him. You just talked to him."

"Had him. He was pulled out of holding sometime today. But no record and nobody knows where he is. Which is wicked fucked up. I figured you know more about where he is than me."

"And why is that? He's at your house."

"Because you have a much more vested interest in where he is than I do. I am just curious, you should be worried."

"Rumor is that ATF has him. I'll find him. You know I will."

"Yeah I'm sure. Listen, he's a sweet kid deep down. Just let him do his time. But lemme ask you a question. Just between you and me slopes, why did you have the kid go on this one? And why in broad daylight? With stolen tags? Somethin' that big — "

" — what are we friends now or somethin'? You give me a swig of your shit booze and you get to ask me things that are outta left field? Not my guns. How many times I gotta tell you?"

"Okay guy. I guess not."

"As far as your request goes? He keeps quiet, he lives. That's my guess anyways, since it ain't my thing. It's how things work in prison. You snitch, you die. Thanks for the hospitality."

46

He put the open bottle down on the counter behind him and walked past me, out of my kitchen, out of my house.

The visit from Slopes was a bad way to end my day. If that was how it ended. But it wasn't. I was pondering if Bell's Palsy was contagious and if whatever lived in Sean's spit was killed off by alcohol and whether I needed to go to the liquor store, when I heard the locks on my front door rattling.

I was in no mood for company. My car was totaled, my partner was the same douche-bag he was every day, I risked sanctions by sticking my neck out for the kid brother of the girl I used to bang when I was a hood-rat, I had to deal with a poor woman who had begged for help and didn't get any until she was almost killed by the asshole who was tormenting her from my neighborhood, and I had received an unwelcome visit at gunpoint from none other than Sean Teague himself. I was kinda done for the day.

At some drunken point in our brief relationship I had made the mistake of giving Jill a spare key to my place. You had to unlock both deadbolts and the lock in the door knob to get inside, a process that she was having difficulty with.

When she finally did gain entrance, I was standing there with the second to the last glass remaining in the bottle of Whiskey in hand. She had been drinking. I had been drinking. One of us was swaying.

"Come right in. Please."

"I've come to tell you how much I hate you Deni."

"Take a number. Hey, couldn't you have called to tell me that?"

"I wanted to see your face when I told you that you're a piece of shit."

"Ah. How do I look? The same?"

"Why can't you be a good guy, Deni? You always make promises, and you always break'em. I'm a good girl. A catch. Why do I put up with your shit?"

"Good question. Come have a drink and we can talk about it for days."

"I shouldn't drink anymore. Besides I am very mad at you. I don't drink with people I'm mad at."

"I'm pretty pissed at you to, but a drink seems appropriate. Why did you have to trash my car?"

"What are you talking about?"

"Are you going to deny having someone kill my car? You seen it? Go look at it."

"You're drunk," she said as she held herself up with the help from the wall in my parlor.

"No shit, so are you."

"I'm giving you back your keys. I need to date someone more like me."

"Ha. Rich from Connecticut? Good luck finding one of those in this neighborhood."

"Educated with a real job, asshole."

"Yeah that makes sense. A business guy? Somebody with money is more your speed?"

"Fuckin-A. But I'm not shallow. I don't need rich, Deni. I just need the guy to be decent."

"That's nice. Keep in touch."

She left and soon after I blacked out.

THERE AREN'T ANY FEDERAL HOLDING FACILITIES OR PRISONS in Massachusetts. How Governor Mitt Romney or any other before him had managed to keep the Federal Bureau of Prisons out of the state was anyone's guess. Instead, what the US Marshals, FBI, and ATF were forced to do with any of their federal persons of interest, was to incrementally pay through the teeth.

The state of Massachusetts, like any other state, have criminals who's acts elevate them to a federal level. If you could call those acts elevated. Most states have at least one federally funded property for super-max, max, medium or minimum-security work camps to house their felons. But those from the commonwealth state need to either be shipped to another state or federal dollars are spent to house them in county facilities.

The closest federal lock-up to Boston was in Berlin, New Hampshire. Unfortunately that facility was only medium security, with only two rows of chain-link fence topped with razor wire.

49

Most men who were either waiting for such elevated trials or had already been convicted necessitated much more aggressive restraints and protocols. So the state charged the government, and therefore every taxpayer in the country, to house them in with the Massachusetts locals.

The Middlesex County jail in Cambridge sits atop the no longer used Superior Courthouse. It is one of the only high-rise maximum security prisons in the country. The courthouse is no longer used because the building was constructed when lead paint and Asbestos were used. The jail above was used with the same materials but when you get your hand caught in the cookie-jar, a little Mesothelioma is deemed part of the punishment. The jail was supposed to be abandoned as well for the same public health reasons, but with overcrowding there was no place to relocate those that call the jail their temporary home.

The high-rise was originally designed to house 160 inmates, though the building that was certified too great a health risk to hold that many routinely holds between 340-400. The cells therein that once held one inmate, possibly two, now had three and sometimes four.

This facility is where they had moved Daniel McKennie to be detained pre-trial. The ATF and the federal prosecutor wanted to move him away from his possible cohorts and put him into protective federal custody. There were a few very real problems with this design. There was no federal facility for him in the general vicinity, which meant he would need to be moved up to Berlin, NH or out to the Super-Max state facility in Walpole. Also the suspect refused to cooperate in giving up his crew. The federal prosecutor assigned to the case couldn't justify the added expense of protective custody in Walpole, nor move him north to Berlin when the person he wanted to protect wouldn't flip and wouldn't ask to be PC'd. So the prosecutor stuck him close by in Middlesex County.

Danny Mick was housed in gen-pop at Cambridge, where he shared a cell with two other inmates. This was not his first time he had been incarcerated, though it was the first time at Cambridge. Danny Mick had been in a juvenile detention center, police lock-

50

ups, even other county facilities in his young past. Consequently he had run into many of the inmates he was currently housed with from the commission of his past misdeeds or during the punishment he received from doing them.

He seemed to be getting on well with those he had come in contact with, both old acquaintances and new. The block was set up in such a way where he felt cautiously optimistic about his new living arrangement, even if temporary.

General Population on E was a long corridor with a polished-concrete floor and light blue, painted, metal caged doors to the cells on both right and left sides. Some metal picnic style tables were bolted to the floor up the middle of the corridor for when one side or the other was let out for rec or chow. There were very few times, at most once per week, when both sides of E block were let out of their cells at the same time for assembly.

Danny Mick had been in Cambridge for roughly three weeks, was getting fairly comfortable with his situation and surroundings, when all hell broke loose.

Memorial Day assembly on Monday, May 31, 2004, was scheduled to be the same as every Memorial Day of years past. Barbecued burger-like substance and hot dogs on stale white bread were served along with a movie projected onto a white, prison, bedding sheet. The same movie was shown every year, Oliver Stone's *Born on the Fourth of July.* Despite the violence in the movie, none had broken out in the jail since it was first shown in the early 90s. It was, therefore, green-lighted for every year henceforth. The prison population seemed to enjoy mixing company with those whom they were not normally allowed social contact, whether they actually watched the movie or not.

Until 2004.

The festivities were cut short because one of the best and brightest housed there decided to clog the all-in-one sink-toilet. The building was old, the plumbing just as vintage. The miscreant stuffed the toilet and continued to flush repeatedly, flooding just his cell at first then backing up the entire line on E. Others began to join in on the fun, stuffing and continually flushing their cells as well. Though the jail is a twenty-four-seven facility, the jail didn't

51

have a maintenance presence on the holiday weekend. The flooding escalated past the point of no return. The building was already more than double past the intended capacity and therefore there was no place to move the inmates. The water flowing out of the toilets and exploding out of the sinks disallowed use of the cells and bunks for sleep. There was also no longer anyplace for evacuating bladders or bowels.

Emotions and tensions ran high while the COs that had the least tenure and couldn't get out of working Memorial Day tried to figure out what to do. Mini fights broke out, which brought out the lug teams, but there was so much chaos it was impossible to squash every skirmish.

Other floors began to flood as well as the entire plumbing system became clogged. Cracks and holes from E egressed water onto floors below but not so much water as to keep the water from rising rapidly. The same such cracks and crevices were depositing water from floors above, down into E.

The toilet-water had risen to a foot above the concrete floor and was still rising. The entire block was wading around as lockdown was thought to cause more problems than allowing them to find higher ground either in the cells or the rec area.

The opportunity was seized. Danny Mick had been up on a top bunk in a cell that was not his own. He was visiting a new-found friend while he waited out the flood. The friend was pulled out of his own cell by a couple of inmates and in all of an instant, Danny Mick was cornered in a cell with three others that were not his cellmates nor belonged in that one. Two others positioned themselves outside the cell to stand watch. Not that anyone would be looking at what was transpiring, there was too much else going sideways to worry about individual cells.

"What's going on boys?" Danny Mick knew what was happening, nervous jokes not withstanding.

The leader smiled, then shrugged his shoulders. "It is what it is, kid."

He was about to ask what his attacker meant, when the three pulled him off the high bunk he was using to stay dry. He didn't have time to scream or call for help. His face was shoved to the floor under the rising water that was geysering out of the toilet. The drowning was not a painful enough way to die, so the plastic cutlery that was given for the makeshift barbecue meal had been fashioned to a very sharp point, and then used to stab him too many times to count.

Danny Mick tried to fight back, but with three men holding him under water and his inability to acquire air, the fight was all but impossible. His lungs burned, desperately trying to tell him that they were in need of oxygen. That burning only being surpassed by the burning from each thrust that was being driven into his body, each stab adding to the agony. The jagged edge of the molded and flimsy plastic tearing his flesh both on the way in and out of his body. The water around him was turning pink from the blood and shredded meat escaping this thrashing body. Danny looked more and more like chum being submerged into shark-infested waters. The more he flailed, the more his heart pumped blood out of the increasing number of holes in his torso.

The thrashing and splashing was doing nothing to get him on the other side of the mortal danger he was in. He pulled at prison jumpsuits, dug his fingernails into what ever skin he could find purchase on. To no avail. The walls began to close in on the small room around him. His flailing waned. Only his bleeding increased.

When Danny Mick's body had gone slack, his head was pulled out of the water. As if by miracle he still had a very slight pulse. The lead aggressor dug the utensil into the jugular as far as the makeshift shiv would go and sawed the skin from jaw hinge to jaw hinge. The neck opened and the tongue was pulled out through the new hole to cover his adam's apple.

The grisly body was then pushed back into the crimson water. Hands were rinsed in the water's tide and the weapon was hidden as the attackers left the confines of the cell.

The group of assassins then receded into the crowd and commotion in the corridor. With their mission accomplished, they were free to wade through the water and wreak more havoc with the rest of the inhabitants on E.

7

MY MEMORIAL DAY WEEKEND THAT YEAR WAS PRETTY BORING. Lonely and boring. I was no longer dating anyone and I didn't have any plans with friends because I don't have many friends. The department was looking for volunteers to work because nobody wanted to work the holiday. Barbecues and such. Whether the detectives requesting the day off had someone to remember was a question I didn't care to ask, but I did volunteer.

What I mean by volunteer is that I agreed to work the holiday. They were going to pay me, and they were going to pay me big-time. The Massachusetts State Police have holidays, floating holidays, sick and personal days besides the vacation days that they give their employees. Memorial Day was a paid holiday for Monday. I worked the weekend and Monday which meant that I got twenty hours of overtime and double-dipped on Monday's pay. Time and a half each weekend day and on Monday, on top of a day that I was already getting paid ten hours for.

I needed the money. I still needed a new car. Three weeks and my insurance still hadn't come through with a check for a new one. I was thinking of upgrading anyway. The two-door sport coupe was way too small for me. Trucks and large vehicles are impractical in the city but they are roomy and good in the snow. I had my eye on the Cadillac *Escalade*.

The weekend was a washout anyway. It rained or was overcast every day. Temperatures never reached sixty. Why not get paid to be wet and miserable?

Saturday the twenty-ninth I spent a good chunk at the MMA gym in Brookline. When you grow up in Southie you learn how to fight early in life. Period. Even the dorks and homos fought. Call it a Darwin thing or whatever you want, but in Southie you either learn how to defend yourself or you don't make it out of puberty. I had picked up Mixed Martial Arts at a fairly young age, added to my street fighting abilities made me a pretty good fighter. I took several amateur bouts, a few semi-pro fights, and two UFC fill-ins as an undercard. That is where I met Kenny Florian.

Kenny was a Dover boy who was a natural athlete. He did the soccer thing and got a scholarship for it, Boston College I think. He had come up to MMA a few years back and made his debut the year prior. He was a black-belt in Brazilian Jiu-Jitsu like myself, so we sparred regularly. He was training for the Drew Ficket fight in July and I was training because I had a lesser known fight coming up as well. We were both light or welterweights, depending on the fight. He was a true lightweight, 5'10" and 145 pounds. He would gain weight to go up to welters. I was a true middleweight, 6' and 170 pounds but cut weight to make the fights. It was a good arrangement. We weren't friends so much as we worked out together.

MMA was just one of the ways that I made extra money on the side. When I got promoted to Detective in Troop H, they gave a lousy $5k bump. That amounts to two bucks more an hour, before taxes. Since I was never going to get promoted again, that meant that I was stuck at that pay scale ad infinitum. The only thing I had to look forward to was my yearly cost of living increase, which everybody knows doesn't cover the rate of inflation. Meaning that over the course of my career, I would progressively make less money. They wonder why cops go dirty.

My tenants on the floor above me and on the top floor of my three-decker paid my mortgage, which was kind of another way to supplement my meager income. Though I had to set money aside like I still paid a mortgage for when stuff needed to be fixed. When you live in a building that was built in the early 1900s, things tend to go bump in the night pretty regularly, and my tenants aren't exactly gentle on my stuff.

And yet another way to add a little coin to my pockets was to take on some PI work. Private Investigators sometimes get a bad wrap; but with the caseload that cops have, citizens often have to get someone who is a bit more committed to their cause. I had run into a couple of PI's and lawyers on some of my cases, and had taken on a couple of side jobs through them which paid very well. This was completely against Mass State Police rules and if I was caught, not only would I be sanctioned and probably fired, but I could face criminal charges as well. I never took a side job on one of my own cases so I figured criminal charges were a stretch. Also I knew specifically of many cops who were on the take in one way or another, so my secret was safe as long as I kept theirs. Of course my partner didn't know. I hoped he didn't at least.

I wasn't getting rich by any stretch, but I wasn't struggling like others within the department. I had to piece-meal a living as best I could with whatever talents I have, which made free-time and friends a pipe dream. Living in the city, or any major city I would imagine, isn't inexpensive. In Boston, houses were going to the yuppies. Southie has a ton of old buildings that get bought up because they are run-down. The buyers and flippers sell to those who can pay. Nobody can make it in the city on forty grand unless they are on the government tit.

I took Sunday off from the gym, but only because it was closed. Many things in the city were closed down for the holiday weekend. But not the bars.

Boston has a proud tradition of drinking, be it holiday or no. We are a proud heritage of both social and binge drinking. Add to that culture fifty-eight colleges and universities scattered about the city and you have yourself a time. If you throw something over your shoulder in Boston, it will hit a bar or a liquor store. On holiday weekends, the population as a whole hits the sauce pretty hard.

With alcohol comes drunken fights and nonsense. But otherwise crime is pretty low during long weekends. Major crime. The local cops handle all of the drunk and disorderlies, noise complaints, fake IDs, and the other petty bullsh. So while they are busy filling up their paddy wagons, detectives like me are bored. I had very little to detect.

One of the drunken assaults was pretty bad and the college chick who's college boyfriend got beaten-up was encouraging her lover to press charges. That is how I got involved. The city cops aren't allowed to handle major crimes. The guy who was roughed-up was in need of hospitalization. The crime actually fit the guidelines for attempted murder, so I went to the hospital to take statements. The boyfriend was embarrassed that he lost the fray and wanted to just lick his wounds and call it a weekend. Man-up. I kinda respected that. But the girlfriend was having none of the man-code and wanted to press charges. Only she can't, it has to be the person who was assaulted or else the charges won't stick. So around and around we went trying to figure out if I had a case to pick up or not. Technically, the state, meaning me or an Assistant District Attorney, could just make a call to investigate without the victim but let's face it — who adds work when they are already overworked and underpaid?

Investigating other cases that I had ongoing was an exercise in futility. Nobody wants their long weekend ruined by scheduling appointments with cops, so those were on hold. My partner had opted for the holiday off, so that was another hindrance on focusing on our open cases.

So that was my Sunday.

Monday was much of the same. Hangovers and late starts meant that even the phone calls into the station were sparse. I putzed around after going to the gym but that was about it. I should have felt a little guilty for taking the equivalent of double-time and a half for doing nothing but I didn't. Even Tits didn't come in on Monday, not that I complained.

I was waiting for the dial-up internet modem to finish connecting and squawking static at me when the call was patched through to my desk. I lifted the receiver to my phone, the receptionist told me I had a call on line 4. I was surprised that there were enough calls coming into the station to extend to the fourth line and thankful for something to do that didn't require the internet. I was no good at it.

"Detective Dennihan speaking."

"Your buddy didn't keep his end." The voice was low and muffled like they were trying to disguise it with something over the phone.

"My buddy huh? Who is this?"

"He wasn't gonna keep his mouth shut. Now it's shut for good."

"Who? What are you talking about?"

"He woulda squealed and begged if he hadn't drowned."

"I've got no time for pranks, guy. Either tell me who this is and what this is about or I'm gonna hang up."

"You should have taken better care of him Deni. Hiding him at Cambridge isn't hiding him."

"For the last time, what in the hell are you talking about?"

"Danny Mick didn't leave me a lotta room. Had to be done."

The caller had my attention. I had completely forgotten about Danny Mick, to be honest. Out of sight, out of mind. After my talk with Slopes, the subject never crossed my mind again. I had other cases, other things going on. I didn't even know where he was. I figured the ATF had hidden him somewhere.

"Who is this? What did you do?"

Click.

Thoughts ran through my head at about a million miles an hour. *What happened to Danny Mick? Why didn't the ATF move him out of state? Why wasn't he better protected? Who just called me? Was it Sean Teague that went after him? Why? The caller was right, Cambridge was no place to hide him if that's what the plan was. He shoulda been up in Berlin or Walpole. Why was he in Cambridge? Was he really there? Probably a prank call.*

I got on the phone and called the Middlesex County jail in Cambridge. The phone rang unanswered for what seemed like forever. When someone finally did pick up, I learned that it was absolute pandemonium over there. I had to give my name, rank and badge number several times to several different people before someone was finally allowed to tell me anything at all.

" .... these guys flood the place all the time but never this bad. The plumbing wasn't designed for this many — "

" — I'm not callin' for an architectural lesson, chief. I got an anonymous call that said a possible inmate there, Daniel McKennie, is in danger or has already been killed. First, can you tell me if he *is* there?"

There was some fumbling and rustling of papers that I could hear on my end of the phone.

"C'mon guy. Yes or no? Simple question, simple answer."

"It's very chaotic here right now. Give me a min .... uh, yeah. Here he is. Daniel McKennie. E block."

" 'Uh, yeah here he is' like you see him or 'uh, yeah here he is' on some piece of paper or on a computer screen?"

"Screen."

"Get him out of E block."

"You don't have any authority to demand that we move an inmate."

"Do you want the death of an inmate under your care tied to you? I am officially notifying you that there has been a threat against an inmate that you just confirmed is incarcerated there. If something happens to him because you didn't respond to that

60

threat, both you and the Middlesex County are in for some serious shit."

"If we moved an inmate every time someone was threatened, we — "

" — I'm on my way down there. So help me if anything has happened to him, I will make it my mission in life to make you pay for it." I might have broken the phone when I hung up.

WHEN I ARRIVED AT THE MIDDLESEX COUNTY JAIL IN CAMBRIDGE, the place was on total lock-down. Mine was not the only Memorial Day that was ruined. Higher ups had been called to come in as there had been massive flooding and riots were beginning to form on some of the various floors. Nobody had time for me until things were settled down.

I sat in the visitor's waiting area for hours as I watched modified school buses pull up and get filled with shackled prisoners. They were being moved to other facilities within the counties. Suffolk County at both South Bay and Shattuck, Middlesex County at Billerica, and even the minimum security at Roslindale were all going to be filled up with the three hundred ninety-four inmates that were housed at Cambridge. These facilities, like Cambridge, were already beyond capacity but the new prisoners would all be put in the hole if necessary. The solitary confinements of those other facilities were not going to be so solitary by the end of the day. Two and three inmates in a tiny cell designed to be just big enough for one. Those facilities would also now go on lock-down as they had to ensure that inmates couldn't commingle.

So I waited. And I sat. Then I waited some more. I scrutinized every inmate that was led onto a bus to see if I could spot Danny Mick. I did not. All of their jumpsuits were saturated and although it was raining I thought it unlikely that the light precipitation was the reason.

Three hours after my arrival, Deputy Sheriff Dominguez finally came to get me from the waiting area. Personally.

"I'm sorry to have kept you waiting Detective Dennihan. As you can imagine we have had quite a time of it."

"I see that. When I called they said there was a flood, everyone and their brother is soaked." Everyone except him. The Deputy was as starched as the ironing board his clothes were pressed on. His tanned skin looked darker in the white uniform. He looked Latin, of course. Puerto Rican maybe. His accent didn't give any hint of Spanish or Boston.

"It has gone beyond that, I'm afraid."

"How so?"

"We will have to investigate, but it seems that the flood was a diversion."

"Was my guy the cause of the diversion?"

"Come into the office over here so we can speak in private." We were already speaking privately but I followed him.

Deputy Dominguez led me to an office that was behind the empty reception window. There was no need to staff it, there was not going to be any visitors today. Once the door was closed I was offered a seat in front of a desk, the Deputy sat behind it. Whether it was his desk or not I didn't know nor do I know now.

"The plumbing is bad here, Detective. The inmates often flood the blocks to mix up the tedium of — "

63

" — yeah, I don't mean to interrupt but I already got the plumber's guide to the galaxy. What does that have to do with my guy? Where is he, and is he safe?"

"'Your guy' huh?"

"Deputy. You've had me waiting for an eternity and I'm sure that you know why. I called to ask about inmate Daniel McKennie, because I received a call sayin' that he was either going to die or already had. He's *my guy* because it was put on my plate. I'm sure you know all of this, so why are we having to go through the charade?"

"Who did you receive the call from?"

"I have no idea. His voice may have been disguised. Definitely unidentified."

"Do you have a guess?"

"No not really. My *guess* would be that Danny Mi …. inmate McKennie, decided to fess up who he was working for to the ATF, and whoever that was decided they didn't want to be implicated."

"You are not the detective working his case? Because you are listed as one of the two arresting detectives on his paperwork."

The pullover was a traffic misdemeanor, so LaDue would get credit for that but didn't for the felony arrest. He gets credit for the ticket issued for driving an unregistered vehicle. He might even share credit for finding a stolen vehicle. When the guns were found, however; the questioning and therefore the case was turned over to detectives. Hobbs and I were still listed as the cops linked to the case. When we turned it over to the ATF, they should have had their own investigators question McKennie and those investigators should have been the people listed. The fact that I was still on his paperwork was confusing.

"Wait. I'm still on his paperwork? So he really is still *my guy*. Didn't the ATF bring him here to hide him for pre-trial? We turned this case over to the ATF like three weeks ago."

"Yes but he refused to speak with anyone but you. The federal prosecutor tried to put him in protective custody but he wouldn't go. He refused to cooperate."

"That's wicked strange. I'm still on his paperwork even though my partner and I turned him over to ATF is odd to say the least, but whatever. Where is he now?"

"He is dead. Brutally attacked and killed."

He let that sink in and I was thankful for the moment of time. My mind raced as to how a suspect this big had fallen through the cracks. Jurisdictional Purgatory.

"Shit. I'm too late. What happened?"

"Either the flood was used as a diversion, like I said, or whoever did it seized the flood as an opportunity. He was stabbed more times than we had time to count so far. We will have to send him out for an autopsy, but at first glance he was drowned while he was being stabbed so nobody would hear him scream. Have you ever heard of a Colombian Necktie?"

"Ah Jesus. Yeah. Slice from ear to ear and pull out his tongue through like a necktie."

"Correct. That is how they treat snitches."

"That is how who treats snitches? I thought they normally get a buck-fifty."

A buck-fifty is referred to a large slice across a rat's face. The ensuing stitches to sew up the person's face requires a minimum of hundred fifty. When another felon sees the facial scar, they know not to trust the person because of the buck-fifty. That is why the slicing is done to the face.

"There are several ways to deal with a rat, Detective. Testifying in open court earns you more than a buck-fifty."

"So he *was* going to testify."

"That's just it. We don't have any record that he was. In fact, that is why he didn't get PC'd. He refused to testify. We still don't have a record of who he was working for. If we had known, at the very least we would have mandated stay-aways."

A stay-away is exactly that. It is a list of inmates and visitors that are to stay away from one another. Sometimes it is because they just don't get along. Other times it might be that they are witnesses against each other in the same case. There are all sorts of reasons to keep two or more inmates away from one another. Working in the same crew suspected of gun trafficking on an outstanding case definitely qualified. The trouble being that they had no idea from whom to keep Danny Mick away from.

"Then why the necktie? Why kill him? That's what the person on the phone said to me. He 'wasn't gonna keep his mouth shut'. That it 'had to be done'. Why would somebody think that? If he wasn't going to testify, according to you, who thought that he was?"

"We will investigate. But in all probability, with the chaos and rookies that we had on E? We are not hopeful in finding out, let's put it that way."

"So the kid is dead and nobody is ever going to pay for it? Have you questioned the Block? It had to be someone on E. We can look at known associates of everyone on his floor. Probably won't be long before we make a connection."

" You aren't listening. We've had a massive flood. Mini riots. We had all we could do to lock down the place, we certainly haven't questioned anyone yet."

"So the guy gets away with it?"

"I didn't say that. What I am saying is that it will be difficult if not impossible. We will do our best. We'll start questioning inmates in the morning, look at all the camera footage. But the hard truth?" He didn't finish his question. He didn't have to.

"I'm sure his sister will thank you," I mumbled.

"What was that Detective?"

"Nothing. Which Morgue is he going to?"

Three hundred ninety-four were being transferred out of Cambridge that night. Three hundred ninety-three to other cells, one was headed for the slab at Shattuck.

9

OUR CASE INVOLVING DANIEL McKENNIE had been over for weeks. I had forgotten about it, truthfully, and there wasn't any outstanding paperwork for me to sign that reminded me of it. Three weeks had gone by and neither my partner nor I had mentioned it or, as far as I'm concerned, gave it another thought. We were busy with other cases and he was the ATF's problem, supposedly. I never transferred him, but I assumed that Hobbs did. He was my senior after all.

Only Danny Mick, the poor prick, had never made it that far. I desperately wanted to go down to the Boston office of the Bureau of Alcohol Tobacco and Firearms and find out what in the hell was going on down there. How had they botched up a witness so badly that he was slaughtered in prison?

That is what I wanted to do. I had already stuck my neck out for the kid, beyond what was reasonable in the eyes of the law and my police department. I wasn't in any trouble, yet. But if I made a huge fuss over a dead witness from my neighborhood, that could very well change. What good would it do anyway? Danny Mick got himself involved with the Irish mob, Sean Teague A.K.A Slopes, and was now dead. My getting more involved was not going to change that situation. So what I actually did was nothing. I ain't proud of it, but the truth is the truth.

So I let it go with the exception of going to see his sister, Roxy. The County lock-ups don't send a Correctional Officer or anybody else to the homes of those that are survived by the deceased inmate. They send a kite, a form letter, to those that are on the inmate's contact sheet. They will also reach out by telephone to those on said sheet. If those provide no response, they may go so far as to look up the phone numbers of those that visited the inmate at the prison from the visitor sign-in sheets.

They do this not for humanity reasons, not because they want to notify next of kin. Not at all. They do this for budgetary reasons. They want somebody to claim the body so that the funeral costs could be deferred to the families that created the societal rejects. The hope was that the family member or loved ones would want better arrangements than what the county would provide. Cemetery space, or any land near the city, came at a premium. Plots were expensive. So the bodies were unceremoniously thrown into an incinerator. The ashes were then disposed of along with the other biohazardous material from the medical wing. More often than not, the bodies were not claimed, either the families couldn't afford better or they didn't care. So ziplock bags of human ashes were disposed of with used syringes, bandages, and other medical waste.

I know what Roxanne said the last time we spoke. I know she didn't want to see me. I didn't want to see her either. But I knew what would happen to Danny Mick if she was not properly notified. If the state could get through to her on a phone, which was a big if, it was a tough way to learn of his death. If she opened her mail, another big if as I had seen Roxy's apartment, it would be an even tougher way to find out. 'We regret to inform you' …. and 'hey by the way come pick you your corpse so we don't incur any further expenses for the taxpayer'.

68

Boston can be a hard city, with hard citizens. None more so than those who reside in Southie. But nobody deserves to hear that their brother was a human pincushion by form letter, no matter what the guy did. So I took it upon myself to go see her.

Tuesday, June first, I took some personal time and headed over to Roxy's place. I waited until later in the morning because I knew that she was not an early riser. Actually that's bullsh. The real reason was that starting off your day with that kind of news is almost as bad as reading it in a letter. But what time of the day is the best time to learn of a sibling's death? I was just avoiding it for as long as possible. In any case, I went to the gym, beat the shit out of some kid that wanted to spar with me, and headed over.

I was still without a car, so I was forced to use a Dodge *Intrepid* from the motor pool. It was unmarked but a five year old could have told you it was a cop car. Traffic parted for me like I was Moses, and those that were contemplating something illegal waited until I was out of view. There were some people in my neighborhood that worked, because there were plenty of places to park on the street.

The stairs leading up to Roxy's dump creaked and groaned as they had the last time, as I'm sure they did every time someone used them. But unlike the last time, she was not waiting for me on the landing at the top of the stairs.

I don't remember how many times I knocked on the door. Nor do I remember how many sets of knocks. I know that it was a lot. I know I waited for a long time in between, waiting for her to wake up out of her hangover or drug-induced coma or whatever. I remember that the inside of the windows to her front door were so dirty that she could have been on the other side of it and I wouldn't have been able to see her.

Through all of it, there was no answer. I was trying to decide whether I should wait out in the car for her to come home, or if I should just come back later. Those two choices were oscillating back and forth in my head long enough for me to take out the pins that I always keep in my wallet.

I might have mentioned that I used to do some shady things when I was a kid. Steal car radios, the occasional car. A few B and E's. When it comes to picking locks, I have a gift.

For those that have called a locksmith in the past, you know that they have a wrench and some specialized pins for lifting the tumblers inside the lock. I don't need those. I have titanium pins that easily fit into my wallet. I have a few in there as backups but I only use two of them at a time. One to turn the bottom of the lock, the other to lift each tumbler one-by-one. This is what takes most people the longest amount of time. There are a minimum of five tumblers inside the key hole, which is what the high points of a key hit to lift them. Each one has to be lifted and stay disengaged in order for the lock to turn. Getting each one to lift before being able to turn the lock open can be exasperating. You then have to do this for each lock on the door. In Southie, the front doors always have a minimum of two and a deadbolt can have as many as ten tumblers.

I was inside of Roxy's apartment in under forty-seconds. She had two deadbolts plus her door handle. The stink that wafted at me when the door opened was nauseating. It was the olfactory equivalent to a punch to the face. I guess that is what you deserve when you break into someone's home.

The kitchen was to my right as I entered the front door. Against every signal by body was sending to my brain, every signal that my brain was communicating back to my muscles, I continued inside. I was forced to bury my nose into the outside of my right elbow, my eyes were watering like I had been sprayed by a skunk.

It was unlikely that she had any dishes or glassware in her cupboards. They were all in her sink. Food had been left out on the counter. What it was would require a biology degree and a microscope. She wasn't in the kitchen, which is all I needed to know for the moment so I didn't enter any further than that into the doorway.

I turned around, heading into the apartment. The TV was on in the parlor but it was static. She either didn't have cable or it was shut off. The mess was the same as the day that I had gone there. The same exact piles of detritus that prevented me from taking a seat on my visit three weeks prior, had I had a notion to, were still where they had been at that time.

I moved my way down the hall toward what I assumed would be a bedroom. The first doorway I came upon to my left was the bathroom. I am unsure how one would call that a bathroom, except that there was a toilet and bathtub. I wondered how one could get clean in a place that was dirtier than the human that needed cleansing. Mold was growing in the grout between the tiles. Mold that was at a point of taking on a life of its own. There was no decorative shower curtain, just the liner that hung open as if to invite one into the sad excuse for a shower. That liner was also covered in mold. The toilet paper roll contained none, and every cosmetic belonging in a cupboard or medicine cabinet was strewn about.

Completely repulsed, and not wanting to touch anything, I continued down the hallway. My eyes burned like they had bleach in them. Bleach that the apartment desperately needed. Or a fire. I was going to need a shot of antibiotics when I got out of there. I made a mental note of it.

The bedroom door was open. The small bedroom was dark, the shades drawn to close out the already dark and rainy fifty-one degree day outside. The room was situated in such a way where you entered on the left side of the room, the bed and furnishings would have been feng shui'd to the right if the person occupying it cared about such things. The only furnishing in the room was a mattress without a box spring set onto the floor.

Roxy was on her back, on the bed, naked on top of the covers. It was cold outside and just as cold in the apartment. She was as pale blue-gray as the blanket that she laid on top of. The color of steamed bluefish. Her face turned away from the arm that had a needle sticking out of it.

I knew the answer before I had confirmed it, but I felt for a pulse on her neck anyway. She was dead and coming out of full rigor.

It had been in the fifties for more than a week, cold for this time of year but no freezing temperatures. Temperature affects rigor mortis, I didn't need the M.E. to tell me that. I also didn't need a Medical Examiner to tell me that she had been dead for at least twenty-four hours. Before her brother.

I didn't know if that was a blessing or not. But I mulled it over.

By the time the Medical Examiner and his team arrived, I had already gotten used to the smell. The team wrestled with the detectives who were assigned to the case about opening windows, spraying anything that would make the noxious smells more tolerable for the people who had to work in the apartment. The argument was based on whether the opening of windows or the addition of a fragrance or both would contaminate the crime scene. It should give you some idea of just how bad the smell in that place was. People who were accustomed to the smells of death were overpowered by that particular fetor.

Case assignments for Troop H are based upon case load and who is available. For lack of a better term, it is a macabre lottery. The fact that I knew the victim or that Hobbs and I had been originally assigned to the case involving her brother didn't even come up. If I was eliminated from investigating crimes involving people that I knew in the city, I wouldn't be investigating much. Hobbs and I were full, so our names were not up on the board. When I called it in, two other detectives from Troop H were assigned.

It was a case worthy of assignment only because of my insistence. By all accounts, it looked like a junky-whore overdose.

She had track marks old and new, she lived in squalor, had a history of prostitution and drug use. Everyone was busy, why investigate something that doesn't need investigating?

I didn't need a gut feeling to know that she wasn't likely to have overdosed prior to learning of her brother's murder. And there were a number of signs that I looked for, that were lacking. For example, where was her stash? Junkies have a stash-box with all of their paraphernalia and their drugs. None. So where did the needle and the drugs come from? Another thing that bothered me was why she was naked. It was very cold for this time of year and her heat had been turned off or shut off from what I could tell. Why get naked before juicing up?

Once the team started doing a prelim on Roxy, taking pictures and getting her ready for the move to the slab, the M.E. was starting to see things my way. Mark Bowman was the examiner who had been called out on the case.

"Deni I thought you were crazy on this one. Another junkie death, why waste time and resources? But I think you might be right."

"Ain't I usually? What brought you over to my side of things?"

"First, experienced heroine users know how much to juice up. When you are completely addicted, you don't want to use it all up in one dose. You want enough to get high, but there is always the next fix. Where ODs tend to happen is when they are forced to quit then start back up, or take time off for some reason and then start back up at the dosage they used prior to quitting. The point is that there is almost always a downtime prior to an OD. They do a short bid in jail, rehab or they try to quit …. so they go back to the same dosage that they were using before they stopped using. The other explanation for an overdose is if they get a bad batch."

"So assuming she uses the same dealer, you're sayin' she was probably clean for a while and went back to it?"

"I didn't say that. I won't know for certain until we do a tox screen, but judging from the track marks and needle holes I would say that it is unlikely that she had a recent break. What makes it strange is that she used enough to kill a horse."

"Suicide? How can you tell?"

"I can tell how much she used by the stains inside the syringe where the plunger drew in the fluid. Unless you can afford very good heroine, it usually leaves a coloration on the inside of the syringe."

"So suicide? You just said — "

" — unlikely. I know what I said. Again, experienced drug users know how to hit a vein. This one missed. She wasn't even close. There was enough in the syringe, I'm guessing, to do the trick without hitting one. If you wanted to off yourself you would make sure to hit a vein so you didn't wake up."

"Cry for help?"

"Possibly Deni. But added to the fact that you said her brother was killed in prison yesterday, and that he was possibly involved with the Winter Hills .... I tend to take your side in that she was murdered. At least helped along. I'll do a tox screen of course, but I'm guessing that what she was injected with was pretty horrible shit. Between the amount and the color of the juice .... "

"How long has she been dead, Mark? She's not stiff as a board anymore. I guessed at a day."

"Oh at least. I'll let you know for sure once she is on the table but I would say a day at a minimum. It takes three to four hours to start the chemical process, full rigor at twelve hours. The body gradually comes out of it, dissipating in another twenty-four hours. Give or take. Add it all up? I'd estimate it at about forty hours."

"So she was dead, probably killed, before her brother. Like I thought."

"I would say that it is a fact that she died before Memorial Day Weekend went into full swing. Saturday evening at the latest. When did her brother get killed?"

"Yesterday. Tough weekend for the McKennie clan," I said.

"I would say so."

"But why?"

"Not my department, Detective."

"Not mine either, I guess."

Part Two

The Old Men in the Mountains

July 2004

10

THE SECOND SESSION OF THE WAYLAND COUNTY SUPERIOR COURT, in Wayland, New Hampshire, was packed to the gills. It always was following a Fourth of July weekend. Independence Day was a time when people got drunk, and usually had or were around fireworks. Sometimes a bad combination however fun. Lots of arraignments and first appearances to get to. But that was not why the courtroom was full on Monday, July 5, 2004.

The courtroom was packed because of the press. Over the long weekend, there had been a murder. Murders didn't happen in New Hampshire very often, even in the southern part of the state just north of the Massachusetts border. The usual crime-beat reporters from the Wayland Courant would be there of course. The local FOX affiliate certainly in the majority Republican state. However there were CBS, NBC, ABC affiliates, and others that had traveled north from Boston also in attendance as well.

Sadly, the victim of the case was not what made the story newsworthy. The presence of the crowd trying to gain the scoop was there to follow the suspected ring of crime that surrounded and were believed to have perpetrated the murder. The headline was about the private compound up in the White Mountains that had been the target of many investigations over the years; rumored to have been involved in any number of crimes, but nothing that had ever stuck. They were older, gun-toting, 'Live Free or Die' types that secluded themselves against visitors with both man-made barriers as well as the natural mountains. They were referred to as 'The Old Men in the Mountains', though what they actually called themselves was anyone's guess. They rarely spoke to anyone.

On Saturday the third, just two days prior, a known member of this group was standing over the body of a man that he had shot in the face. Seven times. The victim was being monitored by the New Hampshire State Police for distribution of methamphetamines. Liam Breen was seen entering the building, gun shots were heard. Breen was arrested and brought to an interview room for questioning. They questioned him for several hours but garnered no confession. They wouldn't need one. He was caught virtually in the act.

The search of Breen's vehicle, which was allegedly used to drive down from the hidden compound in the mountains, resulted in the discovery of trace amounts of methamphetamine, heroine, cocaine, and an assault rifle with the serial number filed off. That weapon, along with the one used to kill the victim, were sent to the New Hampshire ballistics lab for testing. Breen's vehicle was registered to a P.O. Box not associated with the plot of land in the White Mountains.

The proceeds of the search of the vehicle were then used as probable cause in an application for a search warrant. That application was approved by a judge, the warrant issued for the entire property as it was purportedly linked to Liam Breen based on his comings and goings. That address was a gated property of over five hundred mountainous acres with one gated dirt road access.

It was a logistical and operational nightmare. Approach of the gate was met with gunfire. Backups were brought in, helicopters and all-terrain vehicles were used to secure the perimeter. There was a six hour standoff before heavy artillery was used to gain access and bring down the group.

The siege, a-la Waco, Texas, was plastered all over the news. Many different law enforcement agencies were brought in to help subdue the outlaws, but ultimately the ATF took the lead over the case. But not before two local police personnel were killed and seven law enforcement personnel were severely injured in the process. Tens of thousands of dollars were used and/or damaged in the name of justice.

Fourteen men over the age of fifty were apprehended and taken into federal custody. Several labs were discovered on the property. The men in the mountains were financing their enterprise with the manufacturing of massive quantities of drugs. They were a well armed enterprise as well. Assault rifles were a mere tip of the iceberg. Cases of weapons were opened including; HawkEngineering *MM-1 40 mm* revolver grenade launchers, Saab *AT4* rocket launchers, Russian *AN-94s* and *RPG-7s*, *TAC-50* McMillan tactical rifles, Heckler & Koch *G3A4s* and Armalite *AR-18* assault rifles, and hundreds of cases of ammunition. World War 3 could have started in New Hampshire. The war on drugs was not the only victory that day assuredly.

There were territorial pissing matches going on. The state of New Hampshire had seven vehicles that were either swiss cheese or had been blown up. They wanted a stake in the game or financial remuneration. The ATF wanted the case as it was a huge weapons boon. The FBI wanted the case because it was an unprecedented drug seizure on US soil.

Meanwhile, Liam Breen wasn't talking and had not been present during the raid. Neither federal government agency nor the federal prosecutor for the district needed Breen. They wanted him, but gave the lowly locals their low hanging fruit. The ATF took jurisdiction over the seized assets and criminals with the help of a federal prosecutor.

The Honorable Judge Grace McCaglia had a circus before her. This was only the first appearance for Breen and she already had a headache. This case was going to put Wayland, New Hampshire in the spotlight. And not in a good way.

Most preliminary hearings, such as the first appearance, are handled by lowly prosecutors or an Assistant District Attorney in a high-profile case. The DA, Timothy Cromwell himself, was present to handle the hearing.

"Mr. Cromwell. How nice to see you today. We normally don't have the honor of seeing you down here in the trenches." Grace McCaglia was a brand new Judge, had just sworn onto the bench that year in fact. She had worked in the District Attorney's office for several years, but at forty-one she had accomplished more and at a younger age than Cromwell. The two had worked together then, and the fact that Cromwell was jealous of her success was no mystery.

"This is very important case, your honor." He felt odd calling her 'your honor'.

She stared almost through him with her mystic blue eyes. Her black hair matched her black robe. She sat confidently at her post, if she was at all hesitant about her role, she didn't show it.

"It is. So let's get on with it, shall we? State of New Hampshire v. Liam Breen, yes?"

She turned away from Cromwell, taking in the well dressed defense attorney, Dan W. Forde Esquire. The dark gray, designer, Jones New York suit with light blue pin-striping screamed money.

"Mr. Forde, you are the attorney of record for this case?"

"Yes and no, your honor. I have two motions in front of you that I would like to address."

"This is first appearance, counselor. Motions already?"

"I have a conflict, Judge. I am the attorney for the enterprise that Mr. Breen works for. You may have heard of the case pending before the — "

" — save it counselor. I am aware of who Mr. Breen allegedly works for. I will dismiss you when a new attorney is assigned. Is he naming another attorney or is he seeking a public defender?"

"We have not yet gotten that far, your honor. We would need some time to assess that and get back to you."

"Fine but that will not delay this case. We move forward with you as the attorney of record until that is finalized. Next issue, or should I say the first issue …. "

"Yes your honor. With all due respect, I am asking that you recuse yourself from the rotation in the pool. That would eliminate any chance of this case being heard before you."

Wayland County had four judges on rotation with others that could be pulled from other courthouses in other counties if need be. Cases were heard before judges on a 'lottery' basis. This was deemed another way for the woman with scales to be blind. Forde had just asked her to be taken out of the rotation, meaning that there would be no way for her to hear this case.

"Pardon me?"

"There are several reasons listed in the brief your honor."

She took a moment to look over the document that the clerk placed in front of her. Lawyers can read lengthy documents at lightning speed, Judge McCaglia was no different.

"None of them good counselor."

"This is a very high-profile case and you are a freshman judge. Second is that the accused is Irish and will be using a defense that — "

" — stop right there sir. Are you saying that an Irish defendant cannot get a fair trial in the whitest state in this country? You must be joking."

"You are Irish, Judge."

"Are you referring to my last name? I think that I have heard enough — "

" — there are other reasons listed, your honor."

"Motion denied."

"It's an appealable issue your honor."

"One which the next attorney will take up I'm sure. Since the cart is before the horse, lets correct that shall we? Mr. Cromwell, the charges please."

"Murder one, your honor," he said. "Multiple counts of felony possession of a firearm, unlawful modification of a banned firearm, multiple counts of possession of an illegal firearm, three counts of possession of narcotics, and felony possession with the intent to distribute. We reserve the right to amend the charges."

"So noted."

"Your honor, I would like to address that this was a murder for hire," Cromwell added.

"One thing at a time, Mr. Cromwell. Next item up for bid is how the accused pleads."

Forde turned and whispered into Breen's ear. Then Liam Breen spoke.

"Not guilty on all charges."

"Very well. There is no need to discuss the issue of bail. Denied. I assume that is where you were going with explaining the murder for hire stipulation, sir?"

"Yes judge," Cromwell said.

She looked to her clerk. "We are going to set a date on *my schedule* for discovery and motions for sixty days out. I want to hear this case." She then turned back to the District Attorney. "Any dates off-limits Mr. Cromwell?"

"None your honor. I will free myself up on any date the court wishes." He said it directed more toward the press than McCaglia.

"First of all, you cannot hand pick cases Judge," Forde spat out. "If you are not going to take your name out of the pool, that is one thing, but hand picking the case for your docket? With all due respect, that is beyond your scope." He said 'with all due respect' like there wasn't any.

"Be very careful Mr. Forde. You are dangerously close to contempt. What is your second of all, counselor?"

"So we aren't going to discuss that you just slated yourself for this case?"

"No. Did you have anything else before we set a date?"

"I have some dates that might conflict," Forde said.

"Since you are dumping this case I don't need to hear them." She then turned back to her clerk, looking for the calendar date.

"We are looking at Monday, September 6, Judge," the efficient clerk said.

"Very well. First thing on September sixth in Session Four. I'll take a short recess before we get to the rest of first appearances so the courtroom can be cleared of the media circus. That is all." She then slammed the gavel onto the sounding block. Everybody rose as she stepped down and left the courtroom for her chambers.

11

IN THE BACK OF THE COURTROOM, amidst the press and other onlookers, were attorneys Jacob Grantes and Ryan Wells. The two partners had been watching the show intently, watching Forde bury himself before Judge McCaglia.

The two gentlemen were in their early thirties, having met in law school in Boston. They had become fast friends and practically inseparable since. Jacob Grantes, or JG as everyone called him, was an extremely talented defense lawyer. He was a hard worker, raised in northern Vermont by parents who had to toil for every nickel. He was the only child, the first generation in his family to get a college education. His friend and partner was not the only lifelong friend he met in college, he had also met his wife Anna.

Anna was also an only child, but her upbringing could not have been more different from JG's. Anna's parents didn't struggle to make ends meet. Their ends met and then some. Her father, Norman Craig, was an investment tycoon. He had started his own international conglomerate, responsible for other businesses and personal finances in the hundreds of millions of dollars. He provided financial stability but was rarely home. Anna's mother, Olivia stayed home and along with a staff, provided Anna with any and every day-to-day need.

It was the Craig's, JG's in-laws, that provided the seed money for the law firm just a few short years prior. They saw how talented Jacob was, how great he was to their daughter and what a life he could provide if given a solid foundation.

Ryan Wells could have been the brother that JG never had. They were alike in so many ways and yet so different. He also grew up hand to mouth. He too had to work while in college. Only he didn't have in-laws to pay off his student loans or give him money to start his own law firm. JG had asked Ryan to partner with him in his burgeoning practice and he was happily along for the ride. Ryan met his wife, Angie, when they opened the law firm. What started as an interview for a receptionist turned into a job and a recent marriage.

Grantes, Wells & Associates was formed after both had graduated law school, passed the bar exam, and a brief stint as public defenders. Both attorneys had left those jobs behind, as they were making no money, and became immersed in the new enterprise. Wells had no financial investment but was determined to provide as many billable hours as possible. Grantes took the big cases that were winners. Wells took the flyers. He was the 'hippie liberal' who was more interested in the spirit of the law than the black letter.

The two attorneys had been at the Wayland County Superior Court for other cases in other courtrooms at the Superior Court building. JG had the final criminal court hearing in a car accident, which would then begin the civil court phase of the defense. Ryan had to defend a violation of a restraining order. Once they were finished with their business, they rushed over to the Second Session out of morbid curiosity.

Neither of the two lawyers were getting rich because of the new venture, and the coffers of Grantes, Wells & Associates were all but bare. They would often hang around the courthouse to see if they could pick up a client. There was always someone without a lawyer. Public defenders were the last resort, they told their potential clients. They knew because they had each been one right out of college. Once it was determined that the client could pay, they were off to the races. JG was more selective, Ryan took everything with a bank account.

"What do you think?" Ryan whispered to JG as the Breen first appearance was about to close. Judge McCaglia was officially irritated. They had both been in front of her earlier that year and knew that once she started interrupting people, speeding things along, she was fed up and moving on.

JG lifted up his newspaper displaying a defiant Saddam Hussein in court to cover up the fact that he was speaking while there were ongoing proceeds in this courtroom. "I think Forde is digging himself a hole he might not get out of. McCaglia is fair but she has a long memory."

"No, I mean about the case."

"That's what I meant. She is going to make sure that she sits on the bench for …. whoa. You mean you want this case?" JG was shaking his head like he couldn't believe his ears.

"Yeah. You just heard him say that he has a COI and can't be his lawyer. They don't have one, at least not on record or they would be here."

"Ry, do you realize what kind of publicity this case is going to get? Hell, we are sitting here. This is going to take a bundle of cash to defend. Experts, subpoenas, investigators …. money the firm doesn't have. I'm not even going to get into the fact that if what is being covered in the news is accurate, this case is unwinable. The jury pool is officially polluted."

"Forde doesn't work for free, JG. He's getting big bucks from someone. He hasn't done pro bono work in years I'll wager."

"Why do you think he is dumping this case? No money in it. The feds have probably seized all the assets. I wouldn't touch this with a ten-foot cattle prod."

The entire courtroom rose, as instructed by the bailiff. The judge was stepping down from her perch and headed into her chambers. Breen was being taken away by the Correctional Officers for the holding cells in the basement of the courthouse. Forde was packing up his briefcase.

"But you're not me."

Before JG could protest, Ryan had already left the bench seating in the back row and was scurrying his way to the defendant's table. Grantes had never told his partner which cases he could or couldn't take, as long as he was bringing in money. Billable hours. The firm needed every dime to stay solvent. G, W &A were beginning to make a name for themselves in the area, but they were not Dan W. Forde Esquire. If Ryan did get this case, it was going to be a ton of work. If there wasn't any money coming in from it, that limited the number of other paying clients he could take. JG didn't need the personal income, he was rich through marriage, but Ryan did. If no money was coming into the firm, Ryan didn't get paid. Nor did Angie. JG and his wife Angie could continue to live their lifestyle without generating an income. Ryan and Angie were new to these social circles and might not continue to be in them.

JG told himself to reserve judgement until he had heard all of the facts. Maybe Forde wouldn't give Ryan the case. Maybe Breen didn't want the hippie lawyer in the linen suit. Maybe he had a nest-egg hidden someplace. Maybe this case *could* be won.

Yeah right.

"Mr. Forde. Hello. Do you or Breen have a lawyer in mind to take over the case?"

"And you are?"

"Oh, yes, of course. How silly of me. Ryan Wells. I am a partner in the law firm — "

" — ah yes. The boutique shop around the corner, across the street from Sully's Tavern."

"Right. We aren't directly across the street from them, but yes. McCaglia is a ball-buster huh?"

"She made a grave error, one that is reparable by appeal. By whomever takes over the case, that is."

"So you haven't got another lawyer lined up yet? I might be interested."

"Do you think your little shop can handle this case? I'm sure that other lawyers might be better suited. No pun intended." Forde ran his eyes up and down Wells.

"I don't follow. The pun I mean."

"You seem very nice, Mr. Wells, but this is a large case. A murder case tied to guns and drugs. The only thing that you are missing is the long hair and a 'peace, love & harmony' tie-dye shirt. This is not a good case for you. Breen is going to take one look at you in your wrinkled linen suit and send you packing. Save yourself the embarrassment."

"He should be the one embarrassed. He was caught standing over the body that he shot seven times in the face. Allegedly. Can he pay?"

"He says so."

"Then let me worry about whether he says yes or no. Will you support it? Put in a good word for me?"

"Sure. We can go down there together before they truck him back if you want. Why isn't your partner, Grantes, here with you?"

"Oh he is. He is sitting in the gallery." He looked over to where he had been sitting with this business partner. He was no longer there, nor anywhere in the courtroom. He turned back to Forde. "You know JG?"

"We've met at the club."

"I'm a member of the Wayland County Country Club also. I am surprised we've never met before."

"It's a big club. Maybe we can correct that at some point."

"Great. Will you give me ten minutes or so? I want to go find JG and chat with him for a moment. I'll meet you down in holding?"

"Sure. I'll set it up with the COs. Just prepare yourself for Breen to toss you on your ass."

"I'll keep it in mind. Thanks. Hey by the way, why are you dumping this case?"

"Didn't you hear me with the judge? COI. Conflict of Interest."

"I heard, but really why? Trying to separate him from the heard? That can be a double-edged sword. He tries to clear himself of the huge stand-off and the cop killers, but they could get the itch to make sure he doesn't testify. Is there any danger of that?"

"That is all confidential information with my actual clients, and you know as well as I do that I cannot be privy to, participate in, or assist in the cover-up of any planned criminal activity."

"Understood. If you want to punt this case you had better give me a glowing recommendation downstairs then."

"I stand corrected, Wells. You might be just the lawyer for this case."

12

LIAM BREEN WAS SITTING ON THE SAME SIDE OF
THE TABLE as Dan Forde when Ryan Wells entered the conference
room. They both looked about the same age, in the low fifties,
though Forde obviously took better care of himself. They were in
conversation when the door opened.

Breen's hair was disheveled and mostly white. His large
body was covered in tattoos, including his neck and the back of his
hands. He looked worse up close, Ryan thought, than he had from
far away in the back of Session Two. Ryan made a mental note that
if he were to lock down his client that costume makeup would need
to be applied to cover up the visible body art.

"Mr. Wells. We've just been discussing you."

"Excellent. All good things I hope." Ryan said this looking
at Forde. He sat in the chair opposite the two other men, setting his
leather briefcase down on the floor beside him.

"I got some concerns, " Breen said. He was cuffed and chained to an eye-hook that was bolted into the concrete floor.

"So do I Mr. Breen." JG had told Ryan that if he really wanted this case he was going to have to take charge. This group that had allegedly done all of this damage, been involved in so many criminal activities, were a hardened group. He was going to have to grow a pair, put Breen and probably Forde in their place if he was garner any respect.

"My first concern is that I get paid," he continued. "This is going to be a long trial and an expensive one, unless you want to take a plea. I'm not even sure what kind of time we could get everything reduced to, so at least for now we plan to take this to the hoop. $75,000 now and another $75,000 if this goes to trial. If we run out of dough before trial, we will need to fill the piggy bank. That is my concern, Mr. Breen. Money. Is my concern warranted?"

"I don't have it on me but I can get it. If I decide to go with you."

"Well it's time to make that decision big-boy. Mr. Forde here just told the judge that he isn't your lawyer anymore. Anything that you told him so far is still privileged, but just the same once we decide to go forward together we are going to part company with your former attorney."

"How do I know that you are any fuckin' good?"

"I guess you don't. You have to rely on your former attorney to set you straight. But you need to find a lawyer before you head back to the tombs, Liam. Can I call you Liam?"

He nodded.

"Good. So Liam, you have been down this path before I'm sure. What will happen is that you will have to meet with people at the Wayland County House of Corrections to determine if you qualify for a public defender. You will have to fill out financial forms, which you probably don't want to do. If you can afford my fees, then you probably don't qualify anyway. Meanwhile things are going to be happening with your case that you will be unaware of. Mr. Forde here will also be unaware of any progress because the prosecution will not keep him in the loop because he is no longer your attorney of record. The Honorable Judge McCaglia is a tough jurist. She made herself your judge. She likes to keep things moving. So while you are wasting away your days at county, without a lawyer, your case is still moving forward without you. Finally, when and if you do get somebody else that will take your case, they are going to have to play catch-up with very little time to prepare because she only gave you sixty days. What do you think that will mean for your chances of ever seeing daylight again?"

"I won't sell my boys down the river. You gotta know that goin' in."

Ryan looked at Forde and nodded like he understood.

"The so-called Old Men in the Mountains? We can talk about that when we sign some paperwork and free ourselves from the company of their attorney. Any other concerns?"

"Are you gonna look like a hippie when we go to court?"

"I don't see that as a legitimate concern of yours, but I'll address it. I am a defense lawyer with my own style. I like to be comfortable. I am not going to dress or pretend to be something I'm not. The jury will see right through it. My job is to make sure you look the part though. You could use a little peace and love on your side right now. Peace and love is good. Tree-hugging is good. Guns, drugs, and murder are bad."

"Ok. I'll do it."

"Good. Now, Mr. Forde. Thank you for your time and services but I would like to spend some time with my client please."

Dan W. Forde Esquire stood up with his briefcase. He patted Breen on the back with his free hand, gave a wink out of view of Breen. "Good Luck and remember what we talked about," he said. "And Mr. Wells, I will send the necessary documents that you will need to your office. Call if I can be of further assistance."

"Thank you again," Ryan said as Forde left the conference room.

"With that out of the way, Liam, we have to talk about logistical matters before I have you sign a form stating that I am your lawyer."

"What the fuck? You just sent him outta here sayin' that you *are* my lawyer."

"And I will be once I get the first seventy-five grand. I'd like to say that I trust you, Liam but we just met. You gotta earn my trust. How am I going to get the money from you when you are in jail?"

"The boys will send you — "

" — uh, uh, uh. No can do. First, that money has probably been seized. Second, they have their own case, in which they are probably going to separate themselves from you. That separation is good for us by the way. They can't be paying your bills and be separate. And last but not least, I represent you. The money has to come from you. Where you get the money doesn't mean a thing to me."

"Ok. Well that makes things a little more complicated. I gotta a girl on the outside. She can go get it. I can call her from lockup tonight maybe."

"Or you can call her now. Use my cell."

Ryan pulled out his Samsung S300 clam-shell flip phone, handing it to his client.

"But be quick, if they see you with it we are both in trouble."

"Can I make another call after?"

"Don't press your luck. Just call this girl of yours."

Breen started to dial as best he could with his hands cuffed. He then brought his head down to his hands so he could hear.

The person he called must have answered at that moment because he started talking into the phone. Breen was speaking in some type of code to her. He was saying it quickly, Ryan hoped that she was either a very good listener or was writing what he was saying down. And as quickly as the call was made, the phone was flipped shut and slid on the table back to Ryan.

"Is she going to give me the money in cash or what?"

"Yeah cash. You take cash right?"

"Cash and I are best friends."

"My ol' lady can meet you with the money later on tonight. Forde told me that your office is by Sully's tavern?"

93

"Yes, it is down the street and on the opposite side."

"Ok. Well she don't know where that is, but she knows Sully's. She will meet you there at five or so."

"Very good." Ryan retrieved an Attorney of Record form from his briefcase. " I am going to post-date this for Wednesday the seventh. Go ahead and sign it. If she doesn't show, Liam, I am going to shred this. But as long as she pays me, you have yourself a lawyer. I will give her a receipt for the money and put in escrow. As of Wednesday, if all goes to plan you will have a new lawyer."

"You better get me outta this, hippie. I done my part."

"Oh your part is just starting Liam.   That was just the finances. We will meet later this week or early next and we are going to go over every bit of this thing. You are going to tell me where all the bodies are buried."

"I told you that I won't give up the boys."

"You've said. But in order to do my job, I need to know every detail of every illegal activity you have committed or know about."

"That's gonna be a long conversation."

"I'm sure."

13

SULLY'S TAVERN WAS A DIVE BAR. It was not a charming dive bar that was trendy or kitschy. It was a pit. Ryan and JG went there because it was close to their practice, discussing repeatedly how much the establishment needed a makeover. Post work or post trial cocktails were consumed there often. The community went there as well because it was located on a main thoroughfare and the drinks were cheap. That thoroughfare was just three blocks away from Barstone, New Hampshire.

Wayland and Barstone shared a border, one that was delineated by a set of railroad tracks. The cliché was made real, clichés come from someplace. While the affluent of Wayland lived their lives, commuting on those tracks in and out of Boston for their daily work commute, the Barstonians lived on the other end of the spectrum. The Sheriff's department made sure that the debauchery of Barstone stayed on the appropriate side of the commuter rail.

Barstone shared the same county with the same name as the town that it was the stepchild to. Which made the Wayland County Courthouse abustle with Barstonians despite being located in the town of Wayland.

Grantes, Wells & Associates was specifically located in Wayland for its proximity to the courthouse, on the edge of Barstone which gave them the vast majority of their business. Ryan had picked up a few clients from Sully's. Defendants would tell of their woes to their friends over drinks, stories overheard by an eager attorney. Ryan's current case was the first time he had been hired by a client who frequented Sully's prior to meeting them there.

Ryan picked out his usual barstool, one that afforded him the best vantage point in the noisy bar. He could see those that were playing, or on the chalkboard waiting to play, pool. He could watch those that preferred darts hurl their projectiles toward the green and red wagon wheel. But that day he was most interested in the entrance.

He had a picture in his head of the woman he would be meeting. Liam Breen was in his fifties, covered in tattoos, had a long history as an outlaw, and was currently in a real fix for being involved with a tribe of men of the same relative age who ran guns and cooked drugs. Lest we forget that he had committed a violent murder. Allegedly. The woman that Ryan was envisioning to walk through the front door to Sully's Tavern could be summed up as a haggard, middle-aged biker chick.

How he would pick out that particular hardened woman who had spent a lifetime with hardened men was going to be the trick. The drinking establishment usually had its fair share of rough and tumbles. His linen suit stuck out like a toucan in the Sahara.

Ryan had been distracted by the fight that was about to break out between the pool players, both men wielding their respective cues as weapons, when he received a tap on his shoulder.

He turned around to a gaunt woman in her late twenties, dirty-blonde hair, and large loop earrings. She wore a brazen amount of make-up, especially around her eyes which glowed the

96

color of jade. The young woman's scant clothing was designed and cut to show off her tattoo-daubed endowments. Some of the artwork was inked onto her breasts, which were mostly available for view as well. Her stiletto heals were like stilts, how she could walk in the contraptions was a mystery to him. As was the person.

"You must be the lawyer," she said.

"For Breen? Yes. I'm Ryan Wells. And you are?"

"Maddy." She had an orange sling backpack draped over her shoulder, the strap ran down between her artistically decorated and propped-up breasts. She removed the pack and tossed it to him, which was unnecessary as they were but two feet apart. "Here's your money."

"Thank you. Let me sign this receipt." Ryan slung the bag over his shoulder and removed the folded, prepared carbon two-ply receipt from his inside suit coat pocket and signed his autograph. He handed it to her and said, "You don't want to give somebody that kind of money without a receipt. For future reference."

"And you should generally count the money you're given before handing someone a receipt for it. For future reference. So it looks like we both got shit to work on."

Ryan laughed while she turned to leave, but he stopped her by grabbing her wrist.

"Hey! You don't grab on me! Never." This gained the attention of several men in the bar.

"I'm sorry," he said with his hands up in surrender. "Let's go get a cup of coffee someplace and chat for a minute. This was not the best place to meet."

"What like a date? I ain't a coffee and muffins kinda girl."

"Not a date, Maddy. I need to go through this bag, and I also need to take a statement from you. It would be nice to get it out of the way now so we don't have to reschedule."

"Fine. But you put your hands on me again and I'll cut your throat."

"Understood."

97

The diner down the street was open but empty. The hour was too early for most people to eat supper, and happy hours were usually spent elsewhere. Even on a Monday following a booze-filled weekend. Ryan led Maddy to the back corner booth though the desire for added privacy of being in the back of the establishment was unwarranted.

Ryan tossed his briefcase and the backpack into the booth on his side and sat himself, taking up the end. He was retrieving a yellow legal notepad when the disinterested waitress came by to collect an order. He ordered coffee, and since the diner didn't serve booze Maddy didn't order anything. The woman rolled her eyes as the tip on a cup of coffee was not worth the time for her to pour it.

"Listen, we may have gotten off on the wrong foot here. I am going to do my best to minimize the punishment for your …. boyfriend?"

"Don't put a label on it, lawyer. I let him climb on top of me and he pays my bills."

"Sugar Daddy?"

"Why cuz he is older than me?"

"If I need a character witness, the nature of your relationship is going to come out."

"I ain't gonna be taken any stand or testifyin'."

"Why?"

"I wouldn't even make it inside the courthouse. I got outstanding warrants."

"Yeah, that wouldn't be good. What are they for?"

"Prostitution and larceny. It was from a ways back."

"How far back? You aren't very old. Mid-twenties?"

"It was before I met Liam. He told me to tell you whatever you want to know except about what goes on up in the mountains."

"We can work on your legal situation afterward if you like, but for now that is exactly what I want to know. What goes on up in the mountains?"

"Not a chance. I tell you and I'm dead. 'Sides, you don't wanna know or you're a dead man too."

"I already know what I've seen in the news or read in the paper. They are into guns and drugs. They provided him with the work and the weapon. This man that was killed, he did something to the men in the mountains and they sent Liam to kill him right? Those guys have their own trials to worry about. They are out of business. We need to focus on your …. daddy or whatever. Murder for hire is, among other things, a life sentence at best."

Maddy looked at him with pity. She shook her head while she spoke. "Why is Liam hitchin' up to your wagon? You don't even know what you got into." She paused, trying to decide whether to walk away from the table and the situation forever.

"Look, mister hippie lawyer. They ain't never outta business. They got eyes and ears everywhere. You think they don't know about that seventy-five grand in your bag? Liam is nothin' to them. And there will be a dozen more men to pick up where the others left off. Business is business and you stumbled into somethin' here that you ain't equipped to carry."

"Like what?"

"I've already said too much."

"You haven't said anything."

"Then that's the way I wanna leave it."

She got up and left the diner.

Ryan dug out his cell phone, saving the phone number that Breen dialed from the conference room into his contacts. He typed

99

M-A-D-D-Y into his phone, though he didn't know if it was a 'Y' or and 'IE' at the end. She was going to be a tough nut to crack.

14

IMMEDIATELY AFTER LEAVING THE BRIEF MEETING
WITH MADDY, leaving the diner, Ryan called the firm's primary
investigator. Cole Renner was a PI out of Boston but would work
anywhere within a two-hour radius. Ryan told him what had
transpired that day. How he had grabbed a high-profile case in
court. He gave him Liam Breen's name and his connection to the
recent news event in the mountains of New Hampshire.

He told Renner about Maddy. How she had put up a tough
façade but was obviously scared. Ryan wanted to find out more
about her, about Breen. About the entire situation. Maddy had told
him that he was now involved in defending a man caught in a
situation that was bigger than a murder-for-hire conviction. Which
meant huge.

Cole said that he had heard of the case, as anybody who was
up on current affairs would have, but didn't know more than
anyone else at that time. He said that he would get started on

Breen, the compound, and this girl Maddy in the morning.   He congratulated him on acquiring this big case and hung up.

On Ryan's way home to his wife Angie, Stephen Still's *Treetop Flyer* came on the car stereo. He liked the song but had never really listened to the lyrics. As Ryan listened, trying to clear his head, the words registered with him. *"Then some old boy walks up, and he says "Hey son" wanna make some fast cash?"* ….

He began to feel that it was a bad omen.   He wanted to change the station but decided to listen on.   The song continued, *"Well there's things I am, and there's things I'm not …. I am a smuggler and I could get shot …. I ain't going to die, I ain't goin' to get caught"* ….

The rain washed down on his windshield and he was suddenly filled with a chill. He turned up the temperature of his Jetta but neither the sixty-eight degree rain nor the internal temperature of the car was the issue …. *"I'm a treetop flyer"* ….

A bad feeling. He shut off the radio and tried to shake it off. Maybe this case was a mistake.   The rest of the drive home was done in silence.

The next day, after his morning routine with Angie, they both took their own vehicles in to work. They both worked in the same place, Angie was the receptionist for JG and her boss/husband at the firm. Angie liked to go in early to get things arranged for the day. And each day would often lead to Ryan heading off to court or in one direction or another, leaving Angie without transportation. She left the office daily at exactly 5:00 PM unless infrequently needed longer. Ryan's hours were less regimented. So two vehicles were taken every day despite their desire to be more green.

Halfway through his fourth cup of fair trade Arabica coffee, Ryan's office phone squawked with Angie telling him that Cole was on the line for him. He put down his coffee mug on his desk and picked up line one.

"I have to see you today. I'm in the area. I'll stop by the office."

"Hello to you too. What's going on Cole?"

"I'm on my way. I'll speak to you in a bit."

Ryan had other things that he had planned for the day but he agreed. Within an hour of that phone call, Cole was in his office. Resigning.

"You're just going to leave without notice? We have cases that are ongoing that we are depending on you for. I was depending on you for the Breen thing specifically."

"Yeah, and that's what I want to talk to you about too. You should quit that case."

"I can't just quit the case, Cole. Have you spoken with JG about this yet?"

"You've got other investigators."

Ryan got on his office phone and asked for JG to be sent in to Ryan's office. Angie relayed the message and a minute later JG entered the office wondering what the emergency was.

"Cole is leaving without notice."

"What?" JG looked stunned and pale. "Is this about pay?"

"Guys, this isn't about pay. Some things have come to light, and I just want to get away for a bit."

"Now? It's not a great time, Cole," JG said with an agitated tone.

"Why don't you use one of your other investigators?"

103

JG responded, "They do background checks. Criminal history. They aren't equipped for this type of .... "

There was a brief moment of silence while all three of them composed themselves. Ryan remained seated behind his desk, JG and Cole also sat on the other side of the desk but facing on another. Cole began again.

"I'm gonna level with you, Ryan. This latest thing that you have me on is not good. I poked around a little bit last night and this morning and you should quit the case."

"I've already committed to it. I've been paid. Paperwork has been filed with the court. I'm the AOR. I can't just walk away. Is that what this is about? This Breen case? What has you scared? The guys in the mountains? They are all locked up in federal custody."

Cole looked at JG, then back at Ryan.

"That's the tip of the iceberg. They run guns and drugs in and out of Boston and points west."

"So? That has nothing to do with my case. Just because he belongs to the same organization? He is being charged separately for murder one, among other charges."

"Ryan don't be stupid. The Old Men in the Mountains are Irish. They have been around a long time, not because they spread cheer and goodwill. They do business in Boston. Connect the dots."

"You're saying that the group that Breen works for makes drugs for the Irish mob to distribute?"

"They also house the guns that are brought in for distribution. And that is just the beginning."

"There's more?"

"Yeah. A lot more. The Winter Hill crew doesn't just run numbers and fix races anymore. Those Mc's are tied in with the real Mc's across the pond. I've already been told, in not so many words to back off."

"Who came to talk with you?"

"Like I said, in not so many words. My girlfriend's Pomeranian was stabbed and stuck into her purse. The dog was running around when we got up. I left to look into this Breen thing on the bright, like you asked, and she took a shower. She gets dressed and finds the dog. She calls me screaming saying that the dog was wrapped in a bloody resignation letter to GW & A. Meaning someone was inside my house, while she was showering. She didn't hear the dog bark, and it was stabbed to death and stuffed into her purse. They got in and out of a locked house and stabbed a fuckin' dog without a sound. She's freakin' out. I'm freakin' out. So here I am. She's been wantin' me to do somethin' else with my life for a while now anyways. I've been tryin' to fight it off, but now with this? I ain't gotta leg to stand on. She said it was either you guys or her." He placed the dried blood stained resignation letter on Ryan's desk. "I didn't type that blood-soaked letter, but I'll sign it if you need somethin' in writing."

There was another long pause as everyone in the room processed the information. They all stared at the soiled document in horror. Cole was again the first to break the silence.

"I've got a guy that I can call to help you out on the side," Cole said. "Maybe it can work into a full-time thing. He's fearless and he's not happy with his current work situation. I've used him to help me out on jobs in the past. I can call him if you want."

JG was finally out of shock and was regaining his color. He had a yellow lab and the thought of it being stabbed didn't sit well with him. "If you trust him Cole, set up an interview for all us to meet. You should be there too."

"I'm really sorry guys. I can't risk my life for this job. Or my girlfriend for that matter. I signed up to do background checks and stuff like that. I didn't sign up for death threats and mob investigations. This new guy is from South Boston, he knows all the players. I'm not saying that he will take the job, but he has been real good at heavy lifting for me in the past."

"It's ok Cole," JG said. "We understand. Thank you for your past work and good luck to you. Be careful."

Ryan added, "If you could set this interview up with him sooner rather than later, I would appreciate it."

"You're still movin' forward?"

"Yes. Will you set up the interview?"

"Uh. Yeah. Of course. Will-do." Renner shook his head in disbelief. "I will bring him up to speed on the other little things I have going for you both as well. It's been a pleasure. I'm really sorry. Hey, I'm just gonna say this one more time so you can't say I didn't warn you. You should get outta this, and like …. now. You really should quit."

After cole had left the office, JG had remained to discuss the latest development with his partner.

"So this case is already haunting us. I told you this wasn't a good idea."

"We now have $75,000 in escrow for this case. We needed the money, JG. I need it. This is a murder case that Breen is going to insist we take to trial, meaning another $75,000."

"At what price? I don't want to put my family or Angie or you in any danger with this. We just lost Cole. Do you know what your are doing? Get out. Give the money back. We don't need the money that bad."

"It will be relatively quick cash. Breen has already said that he isn't going to flip on the other guys. The feds don't want him, they have plenty already. I am pretty sure that Cromwell isn't going to be cutting any deals since Breen was caught standing over the body. He might be willing to drop some of the ancillary charges to avoid the cost of a trial, but this is a high profile case. The gun that was in his hand is probably going to confirm that it was the weapon used to make swiss cheese out of the victim's face. Breen is in all likelihood going to prison for the rest of his life and we will get a great payday out of it. I'll do the best I can but unless there is a major screwup …."

"Just be careful. And let me know if you get any threatening correspondence. And by the way, are you going to tell Angie what you've done or should I?"

15

THE CONFERENCE ROOM AT THE WAYLAND COUNTY HOUSE OF CORRECTIONS was booked for the lawyer and client to speak, but they were only given a half-hour. Other lawyers needed the room and the time as well. More than a week had gone by since the last time Ryan had seen Liam at the courthouse. Eight days was the soonest Ryan could get in to the prison to see his latest client. Between his other cases and the available times for the conference room, time was getting away from them. With everything that had happened, eight days seemed like an eternity.

Ryan had been led to the conference room and was waiting for quite some time. He was hoping that his half-hour time-slot hadn't already begun. While he waited for his client to be brought to the room, he organized all of his thoughts into bullet-points on a legal pad. The meeting was going to have to be concise.

Breen was eventually brought into the conference room looking no worse for wear. More often than not, incarceration took its toll on the prisoner. The volume of noise and shouting, the close proximity to your cellmate, the horrible food, lack of contact with the outside world, all have an adverse affect on the inmate's psyche which manifests into physical disfigurement.

Sunken eyes, a hunched back, and pallor were but a few of the tell-tale signs of depreciating physical and mental well-being. Ryan had seen it a number of times, the client that he had started the case with was not same person by the end of the trial. But not Breen. Breen didn't normally look great, nor did he in the conference room. But he didn't look like incarceration was having any affect on him at all. Just another day in paradise.

The CO who brought in Breen, apologized for the delay while locking the prisoner into the chair. "Sorry for the delay counselor. It's a zoo in here today. You're time will start when I get out of here. Just hit the panic button if you need us." He nodded his head toward the large red button housed in a clear plastic, flip-top box by the door. It looked like the big button that they showed in the 80s cold war movies. The button that would send off nuclear missiles toward the Soviet Union and would then destroy the entire world as we knew it.

"That won't be necessary, I'm sure, but thank you."

When the CO left, Ryan got right to it. "How are you doing, Liam? We don't have very much time and I have a ton of questions. It's already the thirteenth and time is moving pretty quick — "

" — it ain't for me."

"Nevertheless, I need you to be straight with me and don't beat around the bush so we can get through all of this. Good?"

"Yeah, sure."

"The compound where the big seizure happened, up in the mountains …. that's where you worked, correct?"

"You already know that."

"So what did you do for them?"

"Let's not go there, ok? We should focus on what I got charged for."

"We will, believe me. I'm getting there. I need to know all about the background of why you allegedly killed that man. The District Attorney is going to come up with anything and everything they can to hang you. They will turn over what they have to me, and I don't want to get ambushed by it. It's called discovery. But I'd like to be prepared before then."

"I know what it is. Allegedly? I thought you said that I could be honest with you. We both know I killed that motherfucker."

"I think you are focused on the wrong thing here Liam. And now taking the stand is officially off the table. I can't put you up on the stand to testify that you are innocent, which is what you have pled, knowing that you will perjure yourself.

"But let's get back to the compound," he continued. "Those men that are in federal custody lived there, yes?"

"Off and on. We all did," Breen said.

"And they found labs where you guys were making cocaine and methamphetamine and such. That was the main business, yes?"

"No comment."

"C'mon Liam. You've got to lay it out straight for me. My investigator quit because he has been intimidated. Someone doesn't want us snooping around to find out the truth."

"And I don't want to tell you either. I've told you over and over again that I won't roll on the boys."

"I won't have you testify about it. But it goes to supporting facts. If the guy that you shot in the face seven times was into your …. organization …. for money, or if he had stolen something from them, he has a very different expectation of surviving the act. It's the difference between a horrific homicide for hire on a random or specific victim versus mutual fray."

"Stop speaking lawyer and get back to English."

"It's like when two people get into a fist-fight. If you just walk up to someone and cold-cock them, you are guilty to a higher degree than if you and the other fellow decide mutually to take it outside and settle your differences like men. Obviously murder is murder, and much different than a fist fight. Especially if you were hired to do so. But the concept is somewhat similar. The victim didn't agree to let you use his face as target practice, but if he created the circumstance where violence to his person was inevitable, then that is mitigating. It's called the inciting event."

"So you could get me out of this?"

"No. I'm not saying that. Not at all. What I am saying is that I need all of the facts and time is wasting. So tell me if drugs are what you guys were doing up there in the mountains."

"That's some of it."

"And the arsenal that you boys had up there, that was to protect your enterprise? Protect the compound?"

"Yes and no."

"Liam?"

"You don't know what you are askin' dude. Seriously. Leave it alone."

"Liam …. why does everyone keep saying that? Maddy. You. My former investigator."

The struggle of how to proceed was visible on his face. The torture within Breen was displayed on his person as though the torture was physical. The silence was deafening.

"We used them for protection, but we moved guns too."

"Moved them where?"

"We were the housing and distribution for another group. We were like the middle men."

"For whom?"

"How does this help you get me out of here? This is like opening up that box that you can't shut. Whatever it's called. You know what I mean?"

"Pandora? Pandora's box?"

"Right. If I tell you what you're askin', you can't unknow it. There's no need to know it in the first place."

"Then just nod your head if I get it right. Irish mob?"

Breen did nothing.

"Boston?"

He looked at the ceiling and nodded his head. "Boston is who we work for. They have bosses too."

"Irish …. Ireland?"

He nodded again.

"Now we are getting somewhere. So what did your victim do to get himself killed?"

"He did something for us and couldn't keep his mouth shut about it. You see what I'm telling you? This thing is better if you just keep the reason he got himself dead out of the picture."

"I don't think that is going to be an option. Cromwell is going to want to prove motive as part of his case. They are going to look into it, and he may get evidence from the federal prosecutor to do it. Without your side of things, I don't really know what you expect me to do here, Liam. Why take this to trial if I can't tell the facts of the story?"

"Forde told me to plead not guilty. So I did. We go to trial to find a loophole, right? Isn't that what you lawyers do? That judge made a mistake, right? So she pays for it by lettin' me go."

"It doesn't work like that. This isn't the movies. She really didn't do anything completely wrong. It's in a gray area. Best-case is that we argue for a new judge. But you are still going to lose a trial."

"I can take a pinch. What kinda time can you get me down to?"

"There is nothing to bargain for. A federal prosecutor is dealing with your comrades in arms, they don't need you. That is why you are here and not with them. The D.A. can't get at them because they are being prosecuted federally, so you giving him information about other, bigger fish is pointless."

"So what did I give you $75k for then?"

"Because if you ever want to get out of here you are going to have to tell a jury that you were under their thumb. It's called coercion. Meaning that getting out was not an option. You feared for your life and so you had to take another life. That you did their bidding because you were forced to and under duress. That gets things down to the remote possibility of someday breathing free air. You are in your fifties and you have been a criminal, in and out of jail, your entire life. You've never been convicted of killing anyone before, which is really the only thing you have in your favor right now. Explaining your situation within the grand scheme of things is the only way you don't spend the rest of your life in prison."

"You don't know what you are askin'."

"I'm not asking you to do anything. I'm giving you your options. That's what you paid me for."

There was a loud knock on the conference room door. The CO on the other side of it was letting the two men know that their time was up.

"You think about it Liam. Let me know what you want to do. I'll be in touch."

16

SATURDAY, JULY SEVENTEENTH, was the first time that all parties were able to meet. Cole had arranged for his replacement to accompany him up to Wayland, New Hampshire, from Boston. Grantes and Wells were at their practice without their one and only associate, Angie. Weekends were sometimes necessary to catch up on work, however both attorneys had decided to minimize the extra workdays for their receptionist. It was deemed good for both moral and finances.

The two attorneys were amidst other work when the two investigators entered the firm. Cole knew that walk-ins were not being accepted on this particular Saturday, so he locked the door behind them. He knocked on each of the partner's office doors and led his replacement into the only tiny meeting room that doubled as a lunchroom. They had all jokingly referred to it as 'conference room one'.

Cole was obviously very comfortable with his surroundings as he was making a pot of coffee while waiting for his former employers.

"Hey Cole," Ryan said as he entered the room.

"I'm sorry for having to ruin your Saturday," JG said to Cole behind Ryan. Grantes closed the door out of habit more than necessity.

"No problem. It's the least I can do. This is Warren Dennihan. The man I recommended to take my position."

The tall thin man stepped toward them, pumping each of the attorney's hands with a firm handshake. He was ruggedly good looking, in his early thirties with dark blonde hair and bluish eyes. He looked a little more rugged than usual as he had a black eye, swollen cheek, and a fattened/split lip. Both attorneys looked at each other and then Cole.

"Call me Deni," he said to both of them.

"Ryan Wells. Uh …. are you alright?"

"Yeah. Sorry. I normally don't look like this. I had an MMA fight last night. Amateur bout. It went a little longer than I expected."

JG and Ryan exchanged nodds. The explanation seemed to appease them.

"I'm Jacob Grantes. With a name like Jacob I have several nicknames, but most people call me JG." With introductions out of the way, he continued taking the lead. "Why don't we all have a seat so we can discuss if this is going to be a good match."

Warren removed his sport coat, filling the shoulders of it with the corners of the back of the chair, then took his seat. The loose-fiber white tshirt that he was wearing did little to veil the tapestry of tattoos that covered his torso. Had the shirt been darker, none of his body art would have been detected. JG gave his partner another look of concern before continuing. The bad-boy look was complete.

"So tell us a little about yourself, Deni," JG continued. "You come with a recommendation from Cole which we value but know little else about you. Other than you participate in Mixed Martial Arts. Very brutal hobby."

"I get paid for it, so it's more than a hobby. But you're right, it can get interesting. I'm currently a Massachusetts State Police Detective for my day job, but I hate it. I been doin' side jobs for Cole here and there for a while now on top of everything else."

"Your accent is thick, Boston born and bred?"

"Southie."

"Should I be concerned that you are still in the employ of the state of Massachusetts and working as a private investigator on the side?"

"If you wanna be concerned, go ahead. I gotta make sure I can make a living doing the PI thing before I quit. I don't make much with them, but I can't just leave either. So for now, I'm gonna have to juggle whatever you throw at me and my regular job. If this works out."

Ryan jumped in because he was fixated on the fact that this Warren Dennihan was from South Boston. "If you are from South Boston you must know your fair share of criminals. That is a rough part of the city."

"Yeah. I know a few. Why?"

"I'm not sure what, if anything, Cole has told you about the reason he is leaving us. But we …. I …. have a case involving some people who have made it quite clear that they aren't interested in being implicated."

"From South Boston?"

"I believe so. My client has stated that his bosses work for an organization based out of Boston. That organization is well known for being in and around South Boston."

JG interjected. "Before we get into specifics, we need to make sure this is going to work out. This is an interview not a briefing. Confidentiality agreements need to take place once we decide to move forward. I am still concerned that what you know about our defendants is fundamentally at odds with your job in prosecuting these defendants."

"I can see that. Maybe this isn't going to work. I'm not gonna beg. All I can tell ya is that I have had my run-ins with the

Irish mob down there. That's what we are talkin' about right? I just dealt with them again not to long ago as a matter of fact. If you want to hire me for this one thing, then see where it goes …. I think I have some knowledge to bare."

It was Cole's turn to jump in. "I suggested Deni because he has done work for me in the past, off the books. He can't officially have a PI license until he leaves his current job. But because of that job he has a conceal and carry permit, and he knows how to handle himself. You did win that MMA fight last night, right Deni?"

"Yeah but you don't need to sell me like I ain't in the room." He turned to the attorneys. "If you don't want to work with me, no hard feelings fellas."

"We're not saying that," Ryan said. "We aren't saying that are we JG?"

"No. But I would like my concerns noted. If we decide to move forward you are going to have to sign some documents stating that anything that you learn about a client cannot be repeated. Criminal charges can be brought against you if you violate that confidentiality. We run the risk of disbarment, so we will cut ties with you and worse if that ever happened."

"I get it. No need to beat an already dead horse. Should we talk fees before I sign my life away?"

"Cole, would you give us a few minutes please?" JG wanted to talk about the financial arrangements without their previous investigator. He had served his purpose, it was time to move forward without him.

Once Cole had left the room, they discussed fees. It was a good thing for Warren that JG had begun the bidding. Warren was used to getting paid by Cole, which means that he had been taking a bath. Used and abused. The opening number was almost one and a half times what Deni was going to start with. But he wasn't dumb. He threw out much higher numbers and they finally agreed to double what he was expecting per hour, in addition to expenses.

For Warren, this was going to be a good deal. Even if it turned out to be just the one job, he was going to make more money per hour than he would for a full day of pay as a cop. In his mind he had already left the state police.

116

17

THE WAYLAND COUNTY HOUSE OF CORRECTIONS was a zoo again on Sunday, July eighteenth. Every Sunday was a non-contact visitation day, which meant everyone in the prison who was cared about by anyone on the outside of the razor-wire was corralled at various times of the day for visits. The visitation room was the size of a school gym. That room was then divided into two areas like two interlocking capital E's. The two long hallways which ran up the spine of each E had smaller hallways veering off of them lined with seats and phones. The prisoner would then sit in the non-private seat and speak to the visitor or visitors that were on the other side of the bulletproof glass in their corresponding E chamber.

Fights would always break out, which would set off the Ellis alarm and lug teams would interrupt visiting time. The fights were over anything and everything. It could be; another inmate listening in on a conversation, or checking out another inmate's scantily clad girl, not enough time to visit, a visitor wasn't allowed in because they were a felon, a phone doesn't work because it is broken and they cannot hear their visitor, or any number of other reasons. When somebody is confined in close quarters twenty-four-seven, it doesn't take much to set that somebody off.

There were a few brawls early that morning because the temperature of the prison was freezing. The Sheriff had mandated that the heat be turned off during the summer months. It was also deemed unnecessary for air conditioning to be operating as it had been an unusually cool summer thus far. It was not quite sixty-three degrees outside, not even sixty inside the prison. The coolness of the prison didn't seem to cool tempers.

Because of the number of inmates that get visits, on all of the pods within the prison, they have to be corralled off from their prison block by Correctional Officers. They are moved in a single-file line down to an enormous anti-room. That room has four cages inside it, with a hallway through the middle leading to the visitation room. The inmates are held in a cage with others from their pod within the anti-room until there is an available seat and phone in the visitation area. They are held there again once they are finished with a visit until a good number of inmates from the same block are ready to be corralled back into their pod.

On that Sunday, Liam Breen was brought down to the cage to await his visit. He was hoping that it was Maddy. He was hoping also that she was going to show off some flesh. Liam had been incarcerated for nearly two weeks at that point and had been without sex. He had not gone that long without it since the last time he had been jammed up. Maddy knew the drill. She would wear something that would barely cover her body, but just enough clothing where the guards would not turn her away. He would use the mental picture of her to jerk off in his cell, tiding him over until the next visit.

Other inmates he had come down with had already had their visits and were waiting to go back up. Liam had still not had his visit. The group that he had come down with were collected and brought back up to his pod, and Liam still waited. He asked any and every officer that went by, or who opened one of the other

118

cages to fetch an inmate, or to bring one back, what the hell was going on. He was ignored. Another group came down and were deposited into his cage without any indication as to why he was not allowed to see his visitor.

The new group, one by one, went out for their visit. They discussed who had come to see them with others when they returned. They would exchange stories with others who were in the same cage, or with inmates from other pods in the other cages. Back and forth, back and forth, inmate by inmate, until all of those prisoners had finished their visits.

And yet another group came down. Yet Liam remained. This group was not from his pod. They were of a different block completely, wore different color Bob Barker jumpsuits. This group remained quiet while the COs deposited them into the cage. Remained quiet while they waited to go for their visit. Liam continued to ask whomever passed in a uniform what was going on. Shouted it in fact. And each time he was again ignored.

Breen realized something was wrong when as one of the third set of inmates was removed from the cage to be led to the visitation room, he winked at him. The corner of his mouth turned up when he did so. Breen looked behind him while he held on to the bars of the cage to ascertain if the wink was for him. The others in the cage silently chuckled, looking down at their bobos. Something was up and Breen was nervous.

Within a minute of the wink, the Ellis alarm went off. This brought the lug team. Two or more inmates were going to spend some time in the hole. This kept the COs in the immediate area busy while they regained complete control over the situation. Various visitors would be asked to leave, inmates lugged. The distraction was set.

Two of the inmates in Breen's cage, one on each arm, grabbed him from behind. His legs were kicked out from underneath him, sending him onto his back. The two inmates on his arms, pinned his shoulders to the concrete floor with their knees while a third pinned his feet.

119

"Can't take any chances Breen. It's just business," a large white man said to him. He stood over Liam with his arms out like there was nothing he could do.

"Oh fuck."

The man who spoke to him, that was standing over him, lifted his leg and stomped on Breen's throat. His wide foot covered the entire neck from hyoid bone to trachea. There was an audible snapping sound before the onlookers cheered on the attack.

The stomp, or shot-foot as it is called, was powerful. The first shot snapped the thyroid cartilage. That cartilage is what forms the laryngeal prominence, or the Adam's apple. With that crushed, Liam would have a difficult time, at best, speaking as it houses the vocal folds. It also houses the air passageway leading to the lungs. That one stomp would have done the job if given enough time.

But the attacker didn't stop at one. The two hundred forty pound man came down with all of his strength and weight on Breen's neck again and again and again. The man stomped and smashed like he was trying to kick a hole in the white floor with the heal of his foot.

He smashed the larynx over and over again, collapsing the hollow passageway to both the stomach, and more importantly the lungs.

Shards of cartilage and bone and blood were forced into Breen's lungs. With his vocal cords destroyed and his air passageway collapsed, there was no fight left in him. The men who had been holding down Breen now had a very easy job. Liam's muscles were no longer getting oxygen as none were allowed into his lungs. No oxygen was getting into his blood. What began as a struggle to free himself, was now a resistance-free bag of bones. His heart stopped pumping. His brain ceased to function.

With the larynx crushed, the stomps then started to destroy the spine. The first cervical vertebra of the spine is the atlas, or C1. Stomp after stomp, the atlas was pulverized as well. The snapping and crunching after each thrust under the blood-soaked bobo could be heard over the cheers of the audience. The atlanto-occipital joint, the skeletal device that allows the head to pivot on top of the neck, was next to be destroyed and ceased to do its job. The head rolled

120

off of what was left of Breen's neck in the most horrific and unnatural of ways. Not much more than nerve chords and skin held the skull onto the rest of his body. Liam Breen lay dead on the linoleum floor staring at the feet that destroyed him. His lifeless eyes clouding.

The men in the other cages around them continued to cheer on the attack. It was the prison version of a UFC cage match. Only this fight was not sanctioned, all of the participants were not willingly so. Blood had spattered the concrete walls and was pooling under the dead inmate.

It took less than thirty-seconds to kill Breen. Twenty or so stomps. With all of the commotion in the visitation room due to the arranged distraction, the murder could have taken three times as long and nobody would have been able to stop them. The lug team dealt with the visitation room fight, hauled the inmates involved down to the hole and yet the Ellis alarm still whined and yelled. Radios relaying information and the teams then made their way to the anti-room.

By the time the lug and medical teams had arrived at the cage in the anti-room, Breen's body had already been kicked into the corner and his attackers having a laugh over it. They were carrying on, covered in blood, like they had not just collaborated in committing a gruesome crime. Like they had not just murdered a man in the most heinous of ways. In the coldest of blood.

18

THE SUMMER HAD FINALLY PROVIDED WEATHER that lived up to the bill. Summers are supposed to be warm, sunny, and spent on a beach if at all possible. The summer of 2004 in New England didn't provide much sunshine, nor many days on Hampton Beach or Cape Cod. That year there was an unusual amount of rain and oscillating temperatures. One day it would be sixty degrees and rain, the next it would be eighty-one and rain. Tuesday, July 20th, was a gorgeous day: seventy-five and sunny.

The people of New Hampshire, like everywhere else in New England, are used to weather fluctuations. The old saying, "If you don't like the weather, wait ten minutes" was true more often than not. Moods change with the weather. Sun brings out the best in people, rain not so much.

Nobody would have welcomed a change that day. Moods were lighter, people were happier. Southern New Hampshire had acquired the same tough exterior as the locals of the major city to their south. In Boston they would just as soon spit on your face as look at you, at least outwardly. But not on that particular day.

Ryan Wells was having a great day. He woke up and had his morning routine with Angie. Their lovemaking was almost always in the morning. Ryan was physically ready for the task at that time of day and Angie preferred it. That day, however, it wasn't just business as usual. Needs weren't just met, bodily needs weren't merely satiated, the experience was special. The sun is an amazing thing.

His coffee tasted better. It was the same fair trade Arabica coffee, from the same faux stainless steel Cuisinart coffee maker, but it was more delicious than usual. Ryan had a spring to his step. The perma-smile on his face would normally have attracted attention as he passed others, but they too seemed to be having the same stellar day.

At the office, JG was less frantic and demanding. Angie had the glow of a woman who was as content as any person on the planet. Ryan gave her a sly wink as he entered his office and closed the door.

There's not a whole lot on my plate today, maybe I can take Ang and sneak out early, He thought. *Maybe we can get over to the beach for the first time this year. This is going to be a great day.*

Until the phone call.

"Ry, honey, District Attorney Cromwell is on line two," Angie called out through the intercom on the phone. The green light next the 2 button was blinking. The two never mixed business at the office and home familiarity. But the day had gotten the better of Angie. 'Honey' was a slip that went by Ryan.

This really is going to be a great day, Ryan Thought. *He wants to put a deal on the table already?*

"Great Ang. Thanks. Hey what does your day look like? How about a half-day? Maybe we can enjoy some of this rare sunshine. Maybe the beach?"

"Sounds great. I'll see what I can put off until tomorrow." Her enthusiasm was palpable.

Ryan pressed the intercom button which ended the call with his wife slash receptionist, then lifted the receiver to speak with Cromwell. He sat back in his office chair and propped his feet up on the corner of the desk.

"Mr. Cromwell, I wasn't expecting to hear from you today. When can I expect discovery files on the Breen case? If you are calling to wheel and deal already, I'm afraid I cannot do that until I know what you know."

"The discovery package for that case was given to the courier yesterday, you should have it by noon today. But that isn't why I'm calling."

"I didn't realize that we had another case together. I have another case with your office, but to hear from the D.A. personally on them is a little — "

" — unusual, yes. I *am* calling about the Breen case, but not about where the state sits. There isn't going to be a deal, Mr. Wells."

"You're calling to play hardball? It's a little early for that."

"I'm afraid it is just the opposite. Breen is dead."

"WHAT?" Ryan put his feet on the floor and sat upright. "Is this some kind of joke?"

"Who would joke about something like that?"

"When did this happen?"

"Sunday."

"Are you kidding me? Two days? It took you two days to tell me?"

"I just found out myself. I sent out the discovery package yesterday, you will see the date and time when it arrives. Why would I have sent it out if the trial was moot?"

"How?"

"It's under investigation, but so far it looks like somebody doctored a visit. He sat in a holding cage waiting to see a nonexistent visitor. The right crew revolved into his cage and they crushed his throat. There is video surveillance of it. It is one of the most brutal killings I have ever seen, and I have been at this a long time."

124

"How do you doctor a visit?"

"Somebody shows up and says that they want to visit the prisoner. Their name goes on a list, the inmate is then brought down to a holding cell and waits for an available spot. Only the visitor doesn't stick around for the visit."

"Is there a record of who the visitor was?"

"Yeah, It's right here." Ryan waited while he heard Cromwell rustle some papers on the other end of the line. "A woman. Madeleine Truss. We are looking into her but we can't find her as of this moment."

"Maddy."

"Excuse me counselor?"

"The woman Maddy. She's his girlfriend."

"We figured. Some girlfriend. I'm not even sure how she was let into the facility. She has outstanding warrants. The correctional officers would make a phone call to the locals and snag her when she showed up for the visit. Somebody screwed up."

"Huh."

"For what it's worth I'm sorry. I heard you really wanted this case. Just disregard that package, I'll send the paperwork to McCaglia's clerk."

"This has never happened to me before. Do I need to be there for a hearing?"

"No. I send the NAP paperwork to the clerk, like I said. Then the charges are set aside."

NAP meant Not Able to Prosecute. This is rare. Usually the state either decides to prosecute the case or not. Sometimes they will hold off on moving forward until there is enough evidence to sustain an indictment and then possibly a guilty verdict. To NAP a case meant that there was sufficient evidence but for reasons such as dead witnesses, destroyed evidence, or in this case a dead defendant, there would never be a trial.

"Could you do me a favor?"

"Sure, Mr. Wells. If I can."

"Keep me posted on the girl."

"Will do. I was kind of hoping you could help *us* with that."

"I don't know much. I met her one time to arrange the payment of my fees."

"Where did you meet?"

"Sully's Tavern. That's where she wanted to meet. Well, that is where Breen said that she wanted to meet."

"I'll see if I can get someone in the Sheriff's office to stake it out. If she's a regular she will go back."

"Did you try her home?"

"We didn't think of that. You're so smart, Ryan. I'm the District Attorney for Wayland County, of course we did. Empty. We checked Breen's house too. The compound is locked down so she didn't go there. I don't really have too many man hours to spend on this. Whether she set it up or not, the doers are already in custody so I can't justify the expense on a conspiracy to commit charge. Just between you and me? If I was her I would put New England in my rearview and break it off. Never look back."

"That's probably what she did. Thanks for the call."

"I would say that it's my pleasure, but it's not."

"I get it. Thanks again." Ryan hung up the phone.

Thanks for ruining my day.

Ryan was lost in thought for quite some time after Cromwell's call. Nobody disturbed him. Angie was rushing around, trying to finish every bit of immediate work that had to be completed that day, and organizing how she would catch up on Wednesday. JG was busy with his own work, his own cases.

The courier package from the District Attorney's office arrived at 11:06 AM. Angie walked into Ryan's office after a quick knock. She had signed for the documents at the reception desk and was delivering them like she had done countless times prior. Documents would often come by courier from somebody in the D.A.'s office, another attorney, or sometimes the client. She noticed her husband lost in his own world.   His face and demeanor indicated that something was wrong. A one hundred eighty degree change from earlier. It was an aura that only a wife could perceive. Anybody else may have simply dropped the package and left the room.

"What's wrong?"

"My client was murdered in prison. This was the big case that I took from Dan Forde."

"Oh no. I'm so sorry."

"I think it's fairly obvious who did it, who had it done. But I'm trying to figure out why. He kept saying that he wouldn't flip on them.   I kept urging him to tell me about those men at the compound. I kept saying that it would be the only thing that could help him."

"You can't think that this is your fault."

"I don't. Well I didn't until you just said it. But what has me befuddled is who knew that I was trying to persuade him to talk about that criminal activity.   I'm certain that he wouldn't tell anyone, he knew what would happen which is why he didn't want to talk to me about it in the first place. And I didn't tell anyone, of course. So who could have known? And why kill him?"

"I don't mean to sound callous, honey, but is it your job to find out? You're a defense attorney."

"I realize that Ang. Thanks for the reminder," he snapped. "But this guy paid me seventy-five thousand dollars for a defense that's now unnecessary. His girlfriend actually gave me the money when she knew what was going to happen. Why pay me the money if she knew about the plan set in motion? And it's also bothering me that somehow I might have played a role in it."

She went around the desk and hugged him from behind his chair. Another familial act that was deemed inappropriate in the work place. Another act that wouldn't be highlighted. But like the sunshine, today was different.

"It's not your fault, honey. You were doing the best you could for your client."

"Which is why I owe it to him to finish the job. I think doing the best for my client at this point is finding out what in the hell happened. And by whom."

19

ANGIE DISGUISED HER DISAPPOINTMENT THAT THE SHORT DAY OF WORK was cancelled. She realized that it was a bit selfish to want to get out with her husband in the middle of the week. But how many weekends had he spent at the firm? And the ones where he didn't work, the weather had been uncooperative. The client was dead and without some serious smelling-salts that was not going to change. But she understood, forgave him for snapping at her. She went back to work, leaving her husband in his office.

Ryan had told her to hold all of his calls. He wanted to delve into the discovery package that the District Attorney had sent over. It was probably pointless, but he wanted to look it over anyway. Maybe there was more to this case than he knew. His former client was not a fountain of information that gushed forth. Ryan had to pry every tidbit.

Before he opened the package, he flipped open his cell. He scrolled down to the name Maddy, pressed the button with a green phone on it. The three-toned message from the operator said that the number was no longer in service.

She's gone, he thought.

He went back to the package, opened it and spilled the contents out onto his desk. The majority of the file contained crime scene photographs. They were very difficult to look at. There was a ton of blood and pieces of flesh strewn about with little plastic tents with numbers on them.

The state contended that Breen had not wasted any time when entering the residence of the victim. He went in blasting. The first shot, according to CSU, was to the victims chest. He had been standing in his doorway, the shot sent him back ten feet, where he fell onto his parquet floor. The victim then held his chest, probably in pain and maybe had the presence of mind to try and contain the immense amount of blood that spewed out so close to his heart.

CSU then determined that Breen fully entered the residence, walked up to the victim and stood over his body. The blood from the first shot was pooling around the body after being jettisoned from the wound, splashing the boots and pants of Breen. This was discovered by the splash pattern of blood on the clothing as well as how the blood formed under Breen's boots.

Standing over the body, Breen then fired seven .45 caliber mars short case projectiles into the victims face. These are rare, coming from an atypical weapon that is no longer manufactured. The Webley-Mars automatic pistol was fabricated in the UK but discontinued due to the large recoil and muzzle flash. This didn't stop Breen from making gunpowder and skull laced hamburger out of the victims face.

Pictures of the weapon were shown, footnoted and referenced to the ballistics report. The pistol, casings, and remaining ammunition was sent to Nashua to be studied and logged into the national database. Other weapons and munitions were discovered and logged from Breen's vehicle. Those too were sent to the lab.

The report that followed tied all of the weapons to Boston. It was a brief report that listed the history of the weapon. It mattered not that the serial numbers were etched off, the science of ballistics is unwavering. Ballistics is the scientific study of the mechanics of launching and flight behavior of a projectile. That projectile, once fired, has been marked with a fingerprint of sorts which tells the scientist which exact weapon it was fired from.

The weapons were used in various crimes throughout the years, all of which took place in Boston. This was the first that they were documented in New Hampshire. While Boston is a big city, and many weapons are bought and sold there, the information made the connection to organized crime that much more plausible.

The report was vague. It simply stated when the items were being examined, where and from what crime/case numbers they had been attributed to, and the serial number of the weapon if known before they had been filed off.

Ryan knew just the person he could ask to ferret out more information regarding these weapons.

"Hello?"

"Warren, er …. Deni?"

"Yeah?"

"This is Ryan Wells. Can you talk now?"

"I'm at work. Gimme a sec." The background noise changed for Ryan over the phone. Deni was taking the call on his cell phone and was audibly moving to a more private location to speak.

"I'm sorry to bother you at work, but that is why I'm calling."

"I'm at my desk, so I can give you a few minutes but I might not be able to say too much, if ya know what I mean."

"I get it. First I have to tell you that the case we hired you for, the trial run case, is finished. The defendant is dead. He was murdered in prison."

"Oh shit. There is a lotta that goin' around lately."

"What?"

"Never mind."

"Anyway, I am kinda thinking that he was killed so he wouldn't divulge any information about the combine in New Hampshire. But he did tell me that those good ol' boys were making drugs and housing guns for the Irish crime syndicate down there."

"Yeah I know, we kinda talked about that the other day."

"Right. So I received the discovery documents from the District Attorney. He sent them over before he knew that Breen, the client, had been murdered. See, discovery is when the prosecutor – "

" – I know what it means. I'm kinda in a crunch here. No offense but get to the point."

"Sorry. In that package is the ballistics report from the Nashua lab. They ran tests and entered all of the Breen weapons into the national database. They came from Boston."

"Stop the presses. A gun used in a southern New Hampshire crime came out of Boston? What are the chances?"

"I sense some sarcasm."

"I should hope so. I'm layin' it on pretty thick, guy. Listen, I'm really busy. If we don't have any more business together and I ain't gettin' paid, then I got work to do at the place where I am gettin' paid."

"You're on the clock. If I were to give you the data on this report from the weapons, can you get more information from the Boston ballistics team?"

"Not legally. But give me the information and I'll do it on the sly."

"I'll email you the report."

"Just tell me. I'm really not good with all that."

"You're not good with emails?"

"If it's a file I have to upload or download or whatever, then no. And I can't exactly ask someone on my end for help. Just read me the damned information."

"First is a Mars auto." Ryan read the serial number that was attributed to the weapon. "It's an old pistol and it has a long history of use, but most recently was five years ago."

Deni had hunt-and-pecked the data into his computer while Ryan relayed the information. "Yeah I see it here on my end. Used in a masked armed robbery on the North End. Bodega worker took a round in his shoulder for the trouble."

"Did they ever catch the suspect?"

"No."

"Hmmm. This might all be a dead end like you said. Another weapon was an assault rifle that they found in his SUV. H&K G3A4." Ryan again read the serial number from the report though the numbers had been filed off prior to the police discovering it at the scene.

There was a long pause. All Ryan could hear from his end of the phone was the muffled hustle and bustle of the police station in the background.

"Deni? You still there?"

"Yeah. I'll be damned."

"What's up?"

"Oddest thing. The last case number on this weapon, before yours, was my case. You definitely got your connection to Winter Hill down here."

"Winter Hill?"

"Irish mob. In this day and age, Irish mob in Boston and Winter Hill Gang are one and the same."

"That's great. Why is it odd?"

"Because it was part of a cache of weapons that were seized in a road-side bust a couple of months ago. That weapon is supposed to be held after testing at our ballistics lab in Maynard Mass."

"I don't understand."

"I don't either. You said this is the weapon this Breen guy had in his SUV?"

"Yes."

"The same Breen that was your client and killed in prison?"

"Yes, Deni. Why?"

133

"Because my case was the one where this rifle was seized. That guy was killed in prison too."

"That's quite a coincidence."

"I don't believe in coincidence. Especially when I know the crew my guy worked for. We've got a serious problem here."

"So let me see if I can connect the dots here, Deni. Breen worked for these red-neck yankees up here in the mountains that were into drugs and guns. The assault rifle that was taken out of his vehicle at his arrest was tied to the Irish mob down there in Boston. The same organization that my client didn't want to roll on. The same organization that is facing federal charges by the Department of Justice. My client from that group was killed a couple of days ago in prison. That assault weapon was supposed to be locked in a lab as part of a larger seizure from said mob. The suspect in that crime was also murdered in prison, presumably before going to trial since it just happened recently. Do I have this right?"

"Yeah. First in a long line of questions is how the fuck did that gun leave a secure state facility in Mass and end up in the mountains of New Hampshire within a couple of months?"

"I'm sure I don't know."

"And *I'm* sure as shit gonna find out."

20

WHEN I GOT OFF THE PHONE WITH RYAN WELLS, I was hot under the collar and dropped everything that I was doing. A not-so-old case that had been bothering me was just thrown back at me like a punch to the face. Danny Mick was murdered in prison, thus ending that case. His sister, a good-time girl that I used to have good times with when I was a teenager was also killed. Probably by the same people. Though that wasn't ever my case, they were linked by more than just family blood.

Those two murders were, in my mind, tied to Slopes. I had known that piece of shit almost my entire life and could have been in his crew back in the day. That crew being the Irish crime syndicate, or the Winter Hill Gang. They had been and were still the biggest of the gangsters in New England. And they were rumored to be doing the bidding of the real puppet masters in Ireland.

I had been hired to do a side job, some private investigative work, for these lawyers in New Hampshire. Their client was now dead as well, murdered in prison. They had at least one gun that was supposed to be under lock and key in a secure facility in western Massachusetts. It was supposed to be there because it had been tagged and put there pending examination in the Daniel McKennie case. I wanted to find out how that was possible, and I wanted to find out in that exact minute.

I got up and grabbed my jacket off of the back of my chair.

"Where's Hobbs?" I shouted it out to the general public, figuring somebody would respond but nobody did.

A runner was going by. I moved in front of her to stop her. She came to a quick halt, looked up at me with obvious annoyance.

"Sexual harassment is frowned upon in the workplace, Detective."

"Believe me, there would never be anything sexual between you and me. Look in a mirror. Have you seen my partner? Ricky Hobbs?"

"You're right. I'd go dyke before your dick."

"Funny. Have you seen him or not?"

"Yeah, he's in one of the observation rooms. Interview four I think. He's helping somebody out. And you should be careful with that Ricky thing, he hates being called Ricky."

"I know that't why I call him that. Thanks," I said as I moved out of her way.

She moved past me. "Don't mention it."

"Good luck with that lesbian thing."

I rushed down to the observation room and walked right in. Troop H records all of the interviews so it is customary to knock softly first so as not to disrupt the interviews. But I didn't really follow all the rules because sometimes they don't apply. Often they don't apply to me. Hobbs was standing there watching through the one-way glass while another detective was playing bad cop with somebody in the actual interview room. He held up his forefinger to his lips, the international call sign for be quiet. I didn't follow that either.

"C'mon we gotta go. It's almost one o'clock and we gotta get over to Maynard."

Hobbs looked annoyed with me, which was fine. He was my partner so technically wherever I went while on the clock, he was supposed to go too. He always wanted to adhere to that rule, but I never did. With the caseloads that we have, you sometimes have to divide and conquer if you want to get anything accomplished. Which is why he was in the observation room monitoring an interview while I was at my desk. In Hobb's mind we were still in the same place.

"What do you mean Maynard? I didn't know we had to head out there today."

"We need to check on the ballistics for the Daniel McKennie case."

"Oh. I forgot about that." The truth is he didn't remember the Danny Mick case but didn't want to admit that he had forgotten about an ongoing case. We didn't have an ongoing case involving Daniel McKennie. Not anymore. But the joke was on him even though he didn't know it. "I kinda told Foster that I would help him sweat this guy out."

"I can head down there solo. Gonna spend more time in traffic than at the lab anyway. You good with that?"

"Well no. Just gimme an hour and I'll go with you."

"Ricky. Just clear this up and I'll go out to Maynard. You forgot. It's no big deal. I'll watch your back you watch mine. Are we straight?"

"We really should go together," Hobbs insisted.

"Just relax and do ya thing here. We straight?"

"Uh. Yeah. Sure. We're straight. I'll tell Tits your in the bathroom or something if he asks."

Titanitaukis was a very hands-off supervisor as long as you closed cases. We didn't have the highest closure rate, mostly because of Hobbs, but we weren't on his radar either. He wouldn't ask.

"Good. I'll keep you posted," I said as I closed the door to the interview surveillance room. I wondered if Hobbs knew that in all likelihood our conversation was recorded in the background of whatever interview was being conducted in the adjoining interview room.

I wasn't lying when I said that I was going to be stuck in traffic. Storrow Drive both out and back would be enough to piss off The Pope. Route 2 west was going to be a parking lot. Not going there, most likely, but on the return because Route 2 was a heavy commuter route. I settled in for the long ride in my new *Escalade*. Traffic didn't bother me as much when I drove my new ride. The novelty would wear off, but it hadn't yet.

The twenty-five minute drive took me the better part of an hour. Goddamned rerouting at the end of Storrow messed everybody up. I wished, daily mind you, that they would make a public service announcement as to what they were going to destroy each day, so people could avoid that area. But they didn't. Not even to the police and rescue vehicles that needed the quickest routes.

When I arrived in Maynard and had gone down to the ballistics department, it was Willow who was working. Willow was a hot twenty-something that I flirt with every time I saw her or called her. She wasn't conventionally hot, she was librarian hot. She had this long spirally hair that was pulled up as not to interfere with her experiments or what not. Willow had pouty lips and wore glasses which added to her scholarly look. She had once told me that she was from Vermont and that her parents were hippies, thus the name. People used to call her pussy-willow behind her back. I won't lie I did it a time or two also.

Nothing had ever happened between Willow and I, but that didn't keep me from flirting with her each and every time we spoke. I think that she secretly enjoyed the attention, knowing that it was harmless and not going anywhere.

I was in no mood that day, however. I realized, of course, that she was the nerd and that she had nothing to do with security. She was not the reason that the guns that had been taken off of the street were back on them. There was no way that at a hundred and twenty pounds, and at five foot something that she would be able to stop someone in arming their own personal war. But guns had walked out of her building either before or after she had run tests on them and I wanted answers as to how.

"Just the person I wanted to see. What the fuck is going on down here?"

"Wow. No quips? No innuendo or double entendres? I was looking forward to a little rapier whit."

"I don't know what you just said but I'm not a rapist. I'm in no mood."

"All business today. What is it?"

"I've got some questions for you." I handed her a piece of paper with the list of serial numbers for the guns that were confiscated when Danny Mick had been arrested. I gave her a brief second to look them over.

"These were guns that were sent here for testing. What happened to them? Have you tested them yet? Where do they go after you test them?" I rattled off the questions and the questions seemed to rattle her.

"I - I - I - I send them over to be catalogued." She stuttered and typed a number or something into her computer. "See? Right here. I ran my tests, entered all of the data, and sent them to cataloging."

"And they get stored there?"

"I believe so yes. But I have nothing to do with them after I do my thing. What is this all about?"

"Lets go over to wherever they get stored, shall we?"

"I'm really busy here Deni. Just tell me what's going on if you want my help."

"At least one of these guns walked out of here and was involved in an another crime, in another state. How does that happen?"

"Uh, well, wow. Yeah?" Willow looked genuinely confused. "I have no idea. That doesn't make any sense. Are you sure?"

"No. I just wanted to spend my day in traffic to come down here and punk you. I was bored and Ashton was available. Of course I'm sure."

"Ashton is here?" She started to primp, looking for the hidden cameras, playing along with the sarcasm. Seeing that I was still in no mood for our usual banter, she stopped. "Fine. Let's go see what's up."

She led me down to the gigantic underground warehouse. It reminded me of Costco, only it was all below the frost level. Willow flashed her ID to several people, asked several others for the person in charge. I held back and my tongue which was unusual but necessary.

The highest ranking person down in the basement was this kid named Bryce. I hated him the second I heard his name. Bryce? Who names their kid Bryce? Yuppies who want their kid to get regular beatings from the normal kids with fewer options. These were the kind of people who were taking over Southie. What he was doing down there and where his career had taken a left turn into a toilet, I never found out.

Willow handed him the long list of serial numbers and yuppie-boy went to work on his computer. They were all stored together, because they had all come in and were tested together. So we left the front desk, got into this golf-cart type thing and went behind the floor-to-ceiling chain-link fence to find the lot number.

Bryce turned down one aisle and put the cart in park. Willow and I got out with him but he told us to stay where we were for a minute. He went to get a forklift. As I leaned up against the cart staring at the massive shelves in a long line, I knew what we were going to find. Or not find. There was a huge gaping hole where a skid was supposed to be up near the ceiling. I had the feeling that was where our lot used to be. I pointed the empty space out to Willow who understood what I was saying without having to say it.

I should have been a psychic. Bryce came back with the forklift, went to HH47, which was the shelving and catalogue code assigned to our lot, which wasn't there. He was confused, we weren't. He had just caught up to where we were.

"I gotta call my supervisor," Bryce said.

140

"You do that."

21

THAT WAS THE FIRST NIGHT THAT WILLOW AND I SLEPT TOGETHER. Or not slept. But not in the way that you think. We stayed at the lab in Maynard all night waiting for people with more responsibility to arrive. Supervisors then had to validate what everybody else already knew. They made excuses like they were probably just mismarked and in another part of the warehouse. So another team of people came in to investigate, which took most of the night.

By early morning my neck and back were killing me from sitting in a chair all night. I was overtired and the coffee that was in the area where we were waiting was terrible. It was from an old percolator machine and was the consistency of applesauce. In other words undrinkable.

I had been on my cell phone for a good chunk of the night, and it was dying. Willow had been on hers as well and it was dying. At least she had her phone charger which she had procured from her office.

Hobbs had offered to come out there. Insisted on it in fact. But I told him not to bother. I would let him know when I knew something. Which was kind of a lie. Either way I wouldn't be going to the station that day, which was fine with me. Hobbs would eventually have a shit-fit.

I told Ryan what was going on and he wanted to come down also, but I thought that was counterproductive. If a defense attorney was down there spouting off about misplaced evidence and the like, the searching would slow or halt. I wondered if he could get ahold of the federal prosecutor that was handling the old men case. I thought that he would have some considerable weight to bare and I wanted to rattle a saber that was bigger than little ol' me. He said he would try.

Ryan called back a short time later and said that the federal prosecutor was already aware and incensed. That was his word, because I thought incense was the stuff hippies like Willow used to make their house not smell like marajuana.

The federal prosecutor was so mad that he was going to be there, was on his way in fact. I knew his pants were going to be in a twist over the fact the missing guns from my case were the weapons seized in his. Ryan said that he didn't know that he was going to get that pissed or he would have waited until later in the morning to call him. He was getting in his car in the middle of the night and going to be in the little town of Maynard in the very near future. I thanked Ryan and asked if he was going to be down here also, to which he replied that he wouldn't miss it. He actually sounded excited.

When I informed the scurrying troops in the warehouse that a federal prosecutor was on his way down here to get to the bottom of what happened, people started to shit themselves. I may have ruined the element of surprise, but it was fun to see reflex-like finger-pointing and frantic calls to government officials.

It was absolute pandemonium. Willow was upset with me for making the issue so colossal, that there was a simple explanation that didn't require this level of exposure. She insisted

143

that she knew the people that she worked with. There was no way that I had uncovered some horrible conspiracy. Because of me people were going to lose their jobs, she said.

I just wanted to know how guns that were under the watchful eye of the state of Massachusetts could be involved in another crime, in another state within a few short months. It's not like we were talking about one gun. We are talking about two hundred guns. You can't just throw them in a back pocket and sneak out the door.

There was planning and stealth involved. There was somebody on the inside that had helped in the execution of that plan, or at a minimum turned their head while the deed was done. In my mind, this event couldn't have been isolated. If it could be done once, it could be done again. So how many guns had walked out the door? How many times had various cops like myself taken guns off the street just to have them go right back out again?

For these reasons I didn't care if someone lost their job. The very least that will happen to them will be losing their job. With the federal prosecutor for the district on his way, and Massachusetts State officials notified, there was going to be hand-wringing. Whomever was responsible was going to be publicly crucified.

With the fiasco that happened in New Hampshire making national news and guns being on the front page almost daily and in the front of the collective public's mind, the public was going to be wanting someone's head on a spike. Two more school shootings had just taken place in February. One in Washington, DC, the other in East GreenBush New York. The public was tired of gun violence. News of this was bound to make it into the press. And at the worse possible time for those involved. Since this scandal would be made public, so too must the punishment.

The fact that these guns had left Maynard only to end up in the New Hampshire storyline was about to be a debacle of the highest order. There were four deaths in Massachusetts related to these guns, which was bad enough. Then confiscated and supposedly secured. Now there were the dead and injured in the New Hampshire seizure with these weapons as well. I was relishing the implosion.

Walter Glibczieck, the federal prosecutor for the district Boston was in, a title in which there are only about ninety in the entire United States under the Department of Justice, and Ryan Wells were just two of the people in the massive influx that had come onto the scene. Walter had brought a team with him to assist in the investigation presumably. Other teams were called in by the state to cover their asses. Walter, Ryan, and I holed up in a corner to discuss what had happened and what was going to happen. Once introductions were made, and fortified with the applesauce-coffee that none of us took more than one regretful sip of, we convened.

"Mr. Wells tells me that you are a Massachusetts State Police Detective. You were assigned the Daniel McKennie case, yes?" Walter was a large, John Goodman type character. His presence in a room didn't go unnoticed. His physique and his title had everyone within view watching him, which is why we conducted our meeting in whispers.
"That's right Walt."
"It's Walter."
"Whatever. I had Ry call you because I wanted you to throw your weight around .... eh, bad choice of words, but you get it."

"I think what Deni is trying to say, Walter, is that things are getting a bit out of control. In the cases involving these guns, the suspects were both killed in prison and — "

" — yes Mr. Wells. As I told you on the phone, I'm aware. I know more about that case than you might imagine. Having access to federal databases, the ATF, DOJ, FBI, and US Marshals gives me a perspective on just about everything."

I freaked out and my voice rose above the whispers we had an unspoken agreement to use. "How long have you been following this? Suspects and potential witnesses are getting snuffed out left and right while you sit in some ivory tower doing nothin'? I'm not impressed, Walt."

"Mr. Dennihan — "

" — Deni."

"Turnabout is fair play. Just because I have unfettered access to information doesn't mean that I get that information as timely as I would like. Had we figured out all of the connections sooner, maybe we could have prevented some deaths. But we must look forward. We now know the connections to the Boston mob are real. The Winter Hills have a multi-faceted relationship with the group of men at the New Hampshire combine that were recently apprehended and now facing prosecution. We are also aware of the hierarchy of these groups. New Hampshire reports to Boston, Boston reports to the IRA who report to Sinn Féin."

"Who's this Sin Fine guy?" I asked for both Ryan and I. I could see that he didn't know who it was either by the look on his face.

"Simply put? Sinn Féin is to Ireland what Conservative Republicans are to the US Government. They are a major political party and the IRA won't wipe their own asses unless they are given the green light by them."

"So this Sinn Féin is a group that makes money from illegal activity here? That doesn't make sense," Ryan said.

"Why doesn't it make sense?"

"If the Republican party was making money by sponsoring illegal activities, the country would be up in arms," Ryan defended.

"There are differences in what is considered legal. Have either of you ever heard of The Troubles? Mr. Dennihan?"

"I seem to stir up a lot of trouble wherever I go. Can you be more specific?"

"You might want to brush up on Irish History. You are Irish and from Boston, yes?"

"I am Irish, yes. Is that why you are so pissed? This Sinn connection?"

"The reason I am here, the reason that I am so pissed, as you put it, is because with these guns missing from this facility — my case against the New Hampshire arm of this organized crime ring is out the window."

"I don't follow. They're the same guns. You have them now from the New Hampshire raid," Ryan said.

"My only leverage against them is the shootout at the O.K. Corral with those guns. The deaths, injuries and damage sustained from the raid. The fruits of the search once we eventually gained access to the compound are going to be null and void. Liam Breen is dead and he isn't going to be talking to anyone anytime soon, but his conviction and testimony could have been used to help our case.

The warrant to search the compound is likely going to be thrown out of court. Breen was suspected of being a member of that group, but nothing has ever officially tied him to the group, and the warrant was predicated on that connection. The compound was not his official residence. A warrant for his place would have been appropriate, but not the compound. The judge who signed the warrant was overzealous. Everything seized from that warrant is forbidden fruit. So the only thing I have tying guns from Boston to New Hampshire was Liam Breen. Without him the entire proceeds from the seizure are ill-gotten gains from an illegal search."

"So you were waiting to see the Breen testimony before making a motion to reinstate the proceeds from the compound warrant," Ryan said.

"Let's just say that I was watching your case very closely."

"Not closely enough, Walt. You didn't know that they were the same guns."

"Unfortunately no. You're right. I was focused on getting the weapons seized on the record and use them to nail the group. I was focused on the future not the past. Clearly I should have been more interested in if the weapons had a history. Once he was convicted of murder using the weapons that he did, they would be marked, exhibited, and on the record. The transcripts could then be used in federal court against the group. The weapons could be back-doored in when they deny having illegal weapons when they take the stand. If need be we could have reduced Breen's sentence once he was convicted by getting his sworn testimony. Now that I do know that these guns are from organized crime in Boston, I want to investigate how they walked out of this building."

"When were you going to fill me in on this plan?" Ryan was shocked by the now moot revelation.

"That's not the point. The point is that none of that matters now. I only mention it to show that I have a vested interest in finding out how these weapons left the custody of this secure state building and ended up in New Hampshire. That information could get the weapons back on the record and secure a conviction for the Men in the Mountains or whatever the press is calling them."

"Look at this place? It had to be an inside job," I said. "How many people know this place exists, and even if they did which crates have which thing that they want? Then gettin' past security?"

"Deni, what made you think to have Mr. Wells give me a call?"

"Once I found out they were the same guns, and knew for sure that they were taken from here, that it wasn't a mistake? I wanted to call down the thunder. Plus I thought you would wanna know."

He nodded his head. "Suffice to say that this is not a shining moment for law enforcement."

22

THE GUNS WERE GONE OF COURSE. Teams of people were still searching the underground warehouse that was supposedly secure, and the official spokesman said publicly that the investigation was still ongoing, but everyone knew that the G3s weren't in the facility. They were missing from one secure lock-up and housed in another the hard way. The National Guard was brought in to secure the sight, and assist in the search within the Maynard lab. They were going to comb through the entire building looking for them, which was going to take weeks. Each crate would be pulled off of the shelves, inspected and matched to the catalogue. It would be like going into Costco, taking each item out of each enormous case on all of the massive shelves and matching the SKU numbers to the store's database. It takes time and manpower.

If anyone on planet earth thought that those weapons were still in that warehouse, they were kidding themselves. The teams were going to go through the motions, however. Even that large of a cache was like trying to find a particular set of needles inside a needle factory.

I was now the personal pet of a federal prosecutor. Walter Glibczieck called my boss, Tits, requisitioning me to use my knowledge of South Boston for the good of his investigation. Walter used the justification that if he was able to amputate a huge revenue source for the Winter Hill crew, by securing a conviction for the New Hampshire combine, a huge portion of organized crime in Boston would be crippled. What he was really doing was looking at a bigger picture; and bringing down the IRA foothold in the United States, his district anyway, which would be a big boon for his career. The plan was not lost on me.

Titanitaukis saw the big picture for himself also. Politics drives me crazy. He knew that his helping Walter would give him a chip in the big game. He also knew that if he played a part in taking down the Irish mob in Boston, even if it was only financially, that it wouldn't look horrible on his resume. The Captain signed off on it as well. What he got out of this arrangement was anyone's guess. Another deal was made I'm sure.

So they had me do their bidding, like the minion that I was. If shit went south they were going to roll the whole thing up on me and choke me with it. I was told to go around Roxbury, Dorchester, Jamaica Plains, Mattapan, Charlestown, and of course Southie rustling up every known hoodlum in the hoods of Boston. The shakedown wasn't without precedent.

Tits reinstated Operation Ceasefire for this scheme. The project was first enacted in 1996 to curb the gun violence and gang activity. The police would hit all the hot spots in the city, shaking down all known criminals with relation to gun violations. Everyone and anyone with a gun infraction on their record was fair game. These raids produced results in two ways; by seizure of any and all guns that a felon possessed, and then the felon would roll on others who had weapons in exchange for leniency. Wash, rinse, repeat.

Technically Operation Ceasefire was still in use and had an annual budget, but it was rarely used. The budget was pilfered for

150

other initiatives every year, thereby making the shakedowns nonexistent. As long as there were guns coming off the streets year after year; there weren't any questions, the program considered a success, and tax dollars continued to be earmarked for an operating budget.

Whether the program was successful or not is debatable. There are as many strategies for eliminating gun violence as there are politicians with those strategies. Police the ammunition not the guns, ban assault weapons, enforce and make more strict gun sale laws, much harsher penalties for gun-related infractions, are but a few. Operation Ceasefire was just another strategy in a long line of programs utilized as much for political capital as they were for the root-goal. Numbers were skewed to make each and every pet project deemed successful, and therefore funded.

The new evidence was indicating that no matter how many guns were confiscated off of the streets, no matter which program was utilized to do so, those guns were finding their way right back out onto the streets from whence they came. This fact was going to put a great many of those politicians with strategies on the hot seat.

So off we went. My current cases were re-tasked, my focus was on the shakedown. Hobbs was partnered with other cops to collaborate on their cases and to gain help with his (formerly ours). I took the lead in the attempt to scavenge for every scrub in every borough until we had a bigger cache of weapons than the one that was lost. I was also attempting to glean as much information as I could about how the lot that was stolen had been accomplished.

In other words, I was trying to create a bigger headline than the one that was currently filling the media. Turn the negative into a positive. Spinning information to ensure that the people who were supposedly running things still had a job the next election. Did I mention that politics drives me crazy?

I didn't mind creating a stir in Roxbury or the other boroughs. I knew a lot of those people but I didn't live in their neighborhood. I didn't arrest as many as I was probably supposed to. I just took what I had to for weapons or information and had the uniforms go in with a paddy-wagon.

Where I treaded lightly was in my territory. Southie. I poked around more than anything else. I kept my ears open and my mouth closed. No big waves. The rumors had gone around about what I was up to. But nobody could prove it so the rumors stayed as such.

This went on for a couple of weeks before I was told, not too subtly mind you, that my footsteps were too heavy. I was stirring up things and people that need not be dredged up. Nobody said anything, but the message was received loud and clear.

I got up early on the last Friday in July so I could go to the gym. It was going to be a beautiful day weather-wise. Seventy-seven degrees with the sun shining. The only drawback to the day was that I had my usual detail of roaming the streets in search of someone with a gun in their possession scheduled for after my workout. I was able to find a phenomenal parking spot on the street in front of my place the night before. When I opened my front door to leave for the day I spied that the premium parking space had come at a price.

My new *Escalade* had a smashed driver-side door window. I had lived in that neighborhood my entire life and never did I have so much trouble with my vehicles being vandalized as I had that summer. People in my neighborhood knew what I drove. They knew I was a cop. Fucking with me was like asking for trouble. Live and let live kinda thing.

I approached the door and looked inside to see that nothing had been touched inside, but a few pictures were thrown on the driver seat on top of the shards of glass. I carefully reached in, retrieving the photos to see what the chicken-shit vagrant wanted to say but not to my face.

The first two pictures were of my old *Grand Am*. Smashed, beaten, and broken for my viewing pleasure. I had originally thought that it was my old girlfriend Jill who had been pissed off enough at me to have someone destroy it for her. I had stood her up, ignored her, and made her feel like a second-class citizen one too many times.

152

But the photos that followed made me realize that Jill had nothing to do with my car. The pictures that followed were of Roxanne McKennie at her worst. She lay there the way she was found in her apartment. Dead with a needle in her arm. One can only assume that the photos were taken before the police arrived. Before I arrived. Which means that the person who took them was likely there when she died. One can infer all sorts of things from that, none of it good.

The only reason to include those photographs in with the pictures of my car all fucked-up was to tell me a story. Bad things happen when I get involved with anyone who is even remotely associated with Sean Teague. Slopes. I had been asking around over the last couple of weeks, asking if anyone knew where I could get a good assault weapon for hunting game in the city. Asking if anyone knew how the Winter Hill crew took the guns out of a state holding facility. I was more subtle than that, and not in Southie, but the questions were asked. Those questions had gotten back to him. He was sending me a message telling me that inquiring minds get dead.

I had my *Escalade* towed to a garage to be fixed and got an *Intrepid* out of the motor pool. I told the guys who were going to fix it to take their sweet time. Everyone in the world could spot an unmarked police car. The curly pig-tail antennae off the back was a sure sign. Anyone who messed with that car, even in Southie, was foolish. And even if they did I could not have cared less about a car from the motor pool. My *Escalade* was safer in a garage for the time being.

Later that day, I received a call on my cell saying that the person had information about the Winter Hill crew. They wanted to meet. I did too, only I wanted the meeting to be in a very public place, and not in Southie. The informant agreed, so we met at a Starbucks in BackBay.

There were endless numbers of Starbucks in the BackBay area of Boston. Even with Dunkin Donuts being the majority favorite coffee by New Englanders in 2004, there was a Starbucks on almost every corner. This particular one was near Copley. I sat by the window waiting, watching for some sign that this was a set-up, but

I saw none. I spied the thousands of pedestrians walking under the tall buildings of the Prudential Center and the John Hancock Tower. The Westin Hotel and Copley Place Mall. The Boston Public Library and Trinity Church. As Dave Matthews said, 'Ants Marching'. None of them gave me a second glance.

"You're Deni, right?"

I turned to look over my shoulder at the tall man who was standing behind me. He was dressed in a Red Sox cap, t-shirt, and nondescript jeans. "Yeah. You wanted to meet me? You're Nate?"

"It's not my real name, but let's go with that. I'm only here because they did Danny Mick wrong." The green-eyed youngster moved in closer, uncomfortably close to the person occupying the seat next to me.

"What do you know about it?"

"We did some work together. I guess we were friends. Either way, I liked the kid."

"I get it. He wasn't half bad."

He took a seat next to me once the person that was occupying the stool got uncomfortable enough to leave.

"You're from the neighborhood. He said you aren't bad for cop."

"Great. So we are all good guys. What do you want, Nate?"

"I want Slopes, that slippery fuck, to pay for what he did."

"Slippery Slopes? Ha. That's a new one," I said.

He was not amused. "Business is business but this was excessive. He kept Roxy under his thumb so he could keep Danny Mick on the hook. Then when shit goes sideways he makes him out to be a rat. Has him killed like that."

"I know all of this. Well not the Roxy part, but most of this I know. Roxy was a junk-box for almost as long as I knew her. If she didn't get it from Sean, she woulda got it from some other shit-bag."

"Do you know that as big as Slopes is, he is nothing in the big scheme?"

"Irish?"

154

"As in *THE* Irish. Those Mc's across the pond have their hands into everybody and everything. That's how those guns got out of a secure state warehouse."

"And you can give me proof on that?"

"Fuck no. Course not. Slopes may be middle management, but he ain't stupid."

"Then what are we doin' here guy?"

"Slopes had to replace the guns from the pullover which were going to New Hampshire. Or get them back. Now that the whole shah-bang is gone from New Hampshire after the big raid? He's fucked. Those guns ain't in no state facility. They are in federal fucking lock-up. IRA may have their hands in a lotta pockets, but they haven't figured out how to get them guns back yet. So it's easier to just send over another shipment of 'em. At least until they can figure out how to get those others back, which rest assured they will do."

"So how exactly did the two hundred or so walk out of Maynard?"

"Don't know exactly. Somebody was paid off to get them out. My guess is that if you were to go into the guns that were seized from New Hampshire, you are gonna see those guns in there."

"Yeah. I know that too. The guns that were pulled off of Liam Breen were the same as from the lot that was supposed to be in Maynard. So obviously they were part of the same seizure in New Hampshire. You're not exactly sharin' the knowledge here kid."

"You don't see what I'm sayin'? That was just the tip of the iceberg anyway. One more small shipment to add to stock. That war chest up in New Hampshire was saved over time for one end user."

"Who?"

"New York, Chicago, West Coast."

"I thought you said one end user?"

"Same organization, but that ain't what you should be focused on."

"Oh really? What do you think I should be focused on?"

"The here and now. Those guns ain't there, not available. Because they got taken back again and put into federal custody. They gotta be replaced and all-of-a-sudden like."

"Where's the here and there? New Hampshire?"

"Try to keep up will ya? I'll make it simple. All of the guns were supposed to end up in New Hampshire so they could go elsewhere. Now they are in federal custody."

"You keep sayin' that. So fuckin' what? So they are going to bring in and move one large shipment to replace it?"

"Now you're startin' to see things."

"When? Where?"

"Don't know. But I know they are comin' in the same way they have been, only this time in bulk."

"How?"

"Ain't you payin' attention?"

"I know you better stop talkin' in riddles kid, or I'll beat that latte back outta ya."

"Irish guns are comin' in for Irish crews."

"Ireland? They come here from Ireland?"

"Fuck Yeah. Dublin to Boston Harbor."

Part Three

The Troubles are Féin

August 2004

23

I RAN OUT OF STARBUCKS ENERGIZED and ready to bring down the whole house of cards. Sean Teague was playing chess and it wasn't until I had received a little help that I understood the entire board. I needed to start making some moves of my own. I couldn't do much about New York, Chicago, and wherever else those assault weapons were supposed to eventually end up. Much less Ireland. The only thing that I could do was take care of my own. My own city. I needed to find Slopes.

The rest of Friday and all of the weekend and the following week was spent trying to find him. Search as I might, he was nowhere to be found. Nobody knew where he was. It didn't matter which felon I confiscated guns and drugs from, nobody knew where he was. Arrests were made but nobody was flipping no matter what they faced. Slopes was either in hiding or he was out of town. Operation ceasefire was creating quite the stir.

Monday, August ninth, ten days after my anonymous tip, another message was sent. This one suggested that I didn't understand the first one. The *Escalade* and photos hadn't achieved the desired affect. I was still investigating and Slopes didn't like it. I admittedly don't like to follow rules or instructions and I was never overly keen on school. I guess I do learn a bit slower than some.

I went home exhausted from the weekend search. My superiors were happy with the number of arrests, but they weren't too excited about having authorized all of the weekend overtime to come up relatively empty. It was late and I was beat, both with fatigue and in Sean's game. So far. I collapsed into my recliner with three fingers of cheap Irish Whiskey. And I passed out.

A couple of hours later I awoke after I heard a window break. Immediately I was breathing in heavy smoke. The smoke alarms were going off, piercing my eardrums. Flames were climbing up the walls and licking the ceiling almost immediately. The place was going up like a tinderbox.

I rolled out of my recliner and crawled along the floor. I was concerned about myself, but I was worried about my two tenants above me more. The flames were lining the ceiling, burning up. If they were trying to leave their beds on the second floor, they would burn their feet in the process. I needed to get out of my apartment and up to theirs and get them out.

Crawling toward the front door, I opened it and tried to get out of my burning powder keg of a three-decker. The moment I stood up outside after opening the front door, a blanket of automatic gunfire sprayed at me. Holes were being pierced into the siding on the front of my house by the dozens. If the bullets flying at me weren't enough, splinters of wood washed over me like hot shrapnel. I dove back into the fire. The front door was not an option. This was not an accidental fire, this was intentional. And if both sets of tenants upstairs didn't get help, it was going to be a mass murder.

Burning things were falling toward me from above, making my route to the back exit slow and winding. The building was old and going up quickly. I reached the back door off of my kitchen and slowly opened the door to escape while remaining low. Gun fire sounded off like taps on a snare drum. My service weapon was still attached to me in the shoulder holster, I fired a few shots of my own from my Glock-9. The breadbox on the counter housed my Sig Sauer P227, which I reached up for. A .45 caliber was better than a 9 mm but they continued their volley of automatic gunfire. I rolled back into my kitchen after I traded shots from my Glock with my left hand and shots from the Sig with my right for their sea of projectiles. I was trapped inside the fire. My lungs felt like they were already on fire.

Still in the kitchen I grabbed a dish towel and wet it from the faucet without raising myself high enough to be seen through the back window over the sink. Using the wet towel to somewhat cover my nose and mouth, I fashioned it around my neck and held it to my face by biting down on it. I sat on the floor to collect my breath and some quick thoughts.

I had to get out of there. This was obvious. But the way out was not as clear. All New England houses have a basement. The plumbing has to be beneath the frost-line or the pipes would freeze during the cold winter months. But going down there was only getting myself further under the blaze. The entire building would burn and collapse on top of me. But I felt it was my only shot.

Crawling on the hot floor, I made my way to the basement door. It felt like my skin was already burning. The towel covering my nose and mouth was heated and began to steam, burning my face and eyes. I half-slid down the unfinished wooden stairs to the basement. I only used it for storage and odds and ends. The boiler was down there.

Think Deni. Think.

Parts of the ceiling to the basement were on fire. I had bought myself a little time by being downstairs, but that time was fleeting. The bulkhead doors leading up to the small backyard wouldn't work. The shots fired toward my kitchen door proved that I would be going right into the lion's den.

I was turning in circles trying to find an answer. The east side of the house was covered with shrubs. There were basement windows on that side of the house, covered by the shrubs in order to hide an easy access for thieves trying to enter my house. The windows were very small, almost to the ceiling from inside the basement and just above ground level outside. I ran over to one of the windows, climbing on top of storage boxes to get at it. If there was a way to open the damned thing, I didn't know what it was. I used the wet, steaming towel to break the window as quietly as possible.

It was a tight fit, even for me. I was in good shape, the only fat on my body was from my booze habit. Slithering out of the basement and onto the ground above, I could finally breath. The shrubs were scratching me as I repositioned myself in them trying to assess where to go from there.

I could hear the screams of my tenants above, though for the moment I could do nothing for them. From the outside of the building, my house looked completely engulfed. The masked men ran from the back yard and into the front to join their accomplices. Satisfied that the job had been completed, they double-timed it right past me as I hid in the bushes. Once they were past, I darted into the back yard and up the back set of stairs to the apartment just above mine.

My upstairs tenants had obviously tried to get out of the burning building from the back exit as well. The deck, siding, windows, and back door were all peppered with the same gun fire as my place below. I kicked in the back door only to find what I had already feared.

Their bodies were cooking and blistering like a pig on a barbecue in their own living room. One or more of them were shot, because blood had been pouring out of them and onto the hardwood floor. The blood was bubbling as it boiled and steamed off the oak flooring. The crackling of burned and blood-soaked wood added to the horrible smell of burnt flesh.

There was no time to lament, I hurried up the second set of stairs to the top apartment. The same bullet holes lined their exterior as well but from a different angle. The shooters had shot from the ground level, sending bullets through the pressure-treated deck and into the siding. There was hope that the nice young couple hadn't been shot. As I did with the apartment below, I kicked the door in. The fire was working in this apartment but it was not quite as aflame as below. Yet.

The apartment was also boiling hot and it was all but impossible to breath. I made my way back into the recesses of the apartment calling to them. The young couple had lived in my apartment for a few years and had just been married that year. They were working on beginning a family. They didn't answer. I continued to move through the apartment, as quickly yet as thoroughly as I could. The top floor was now really starting to burn. *Please don't be home,* I thought. The floor was very hot and the rubber soles of my cheap dress shoes were beginning to melt and stick to the floor. The deeper into the place I went, the worse the flames got. The building seemed to burning from the outside in. I needed to get them out before there was no longer an exit.

When I got to the back bedroom, their door was closed. I reached for the knob but the heat was radiating off of it. I decided to kick the door in, which was a horrible mistake. The second the door opened an explosion like that of a grenade went off. Some sort of backdraft blew me back down the hallway, sliding down the hot, steaming floor. My skin continued to burn on the hot floor. I knew what was waiting for me inside that bedroom. But I had to go look. I tamped the flames that were on my clothes and went back into the room. They were curled up together, on fire while they lay in each other's arms on the burning bed.

One could only assume that they burned up instantly. There didn't seem to be any writhing in pain. Burning to death is the most horrible way to go. Maybe they incinerated when I kicked in the door. *Had I killed them instead of save them*? I hoped that they died from smoke inhalation before the blast but I didn't think about it very long. There was no time. No time to go toward them. No time to feel a pulse. For their sake I hoped there was no longer a pulse. They burned and blistered and charred in each others arms. The clothing they were wearing was singed and melted into the fiber of their seared bodies. There would be no family.

I was able to get out of the top apartment and down to the ground in my backyard before the building finally succumbed to the flames. I was hacking up creosote from my lungs and taking a physical inventory of my burns while I watched my life go up in flames. The things that I accrued in my life. For the moment I was still alive and able to accrue more bobbles and trinkets. I could not say the same for my tenants.

Their lives literally went up in flames.

24

TUESDAY WAS MOSTLY A BLUR. I had spent the rest of Monday night in the hospital. My burns needed to be treated, X-rays and things took place to make sure that the smoke inhalation didn't do more damage than indicated by the phlegmy soot that I was coughing up. I looked a wreck. The cuts, abrasions, burns, and singeing made me look like I had gone through a war. It felt like I was in the middle of one.

I'm not easily scared, but this ordeal had me rattled. I had been warned and I didn't listen. I was determined to take on Slopes for what he had done, and ultimately it wasn't me who had paid the price for it. But the battle wasn't over yet.

I had looked for Sean Teague all weekend after being tipped off as to his next plan. Those assault weapons were nothing but trouble. I had lost a car, had to replace a window on the second, and now my house. But it was nothing compared to what others had paid. They were dead. Danny Mick, Roxy, this Breen guy that the New Hampshire lawyers were pissed about, the dead and wounded from the compound raid, and now the six people who lived in the two apartments above me were all dead. I should have heeded the warning.

When I was allowed to leave the hospital mid-morning, I was taken to the station for questioning. I was upset and hopped up on meds so exactly how it went down is hazy at best. But I can tell you that after my statements to both police and fire investigators about the fire, I was handed over to Tits and Walter. This conversation was more clear because I was getting a lot of heat for wanting out. I wanted justice but I needed a break. I needed things to cool down. My skin for starters.

I was brought into Lieutenant Titanitaukis's office to have a chat. Walter was there and sat silently at first while things started off apologetic and cordial.

" …. Detective Dennihan, I am so sorry for what you have gone through," Tits finished after questioning how I was feeling.

"So you're alright? The hospital released you, so you must be cleared for duty. You probably look worse than it really is," Walter offered.

"Easy for you to say, huh Walt? I was burned and shot at in my own home. I saw the people that depended on me for a place to live burned alive. Cleared for duty? I'm taking a fuckin' vacation."

"Now?" Walter was having none of it. "Obviously you pulled at an important thread. That was an awfully big risk they took by burning down a State Police Detective's house and then having target practice on it. You can't give up now."

"Fuck you. I am."

Tits asked if I had any vacation time coming. He indicated that he might not approve the request if I had them to spare.

"I've got three weeks lined up. I'm takin' 'em. End of story."

"Why do you think they took a big risk at trying to kill you?"

"Because they know I was looking for them. Because somehow they know that I was tipped about the next shipment."

Walter looked perplexed by this. He was looking around the room, at both of us trying to determine where he had been left behind. I then realized that I hadn't reported this fact to Tits, so it was never sent up the food chain. My lieutenant was a hands-off kind of boss, and I didn't offer anything up until I had to. There wasn't a DD-5 for Operation Ceasefire.

"The next shipment? When? Why was I not told about this?" Walter seemed almost frantic.

"Because I don't know when, exactly. I got a tip last Friday, which I was going to report to Tit …. eh, my direct supervisor, if and when I could corroborate it. The tip is anonymous but seems reliable, but who knows? The person is pissed off about the way Slopes just kills with impunity. Friend of one of his victims, you might say. Guns come in to Boston Harbor directly out of Dublin. Slated for all points west from Boston now that New Hampshire is under wraps. God only knows how many stay here in the city. I know those assholes were using automatic rifles to trap me in my house."

"FRIDAY? It's tuesday. Why didn't anyone share this information with me?"

I didn't have the heart to tell Walter that I had received the information eleven days prior not four like he obviously thought. Tits already looked like a one-legged cat trying to scratch on a frozen pond. He was as white as a ghost trying to figure out if his career just hit the skids because of me.

"Because I felt that there was more information to gain before I reported on a wild goose chase. It was an anonymous tip. If I kept you apprised of all of the tips I get, we would all be running in circles. I have been scrounging up every cocksucker with a bottle rocket in every corner of Boston. What do you think I was doin' all week …. er …. weekend? Sean Teague, A.K.A Slopes, is in the wind. I can neither confirm nor dismiss this information about a big shipment."

"But you said that you think it's reliable. It's reliable enough to send you all over hell all weekend long. Reliable enough for them to take a big chance at killing you."

"Walt, it could be a trap. They lure us down to the docks and have open season on the police. Besides, how do I know that they know about this tip?"

"Then why try to kill you in your own home?"

"I guess I don't follow you there Walt."

"If the goal was to get a slew of cops down to Boston Harbor, then why try to kill him in his home?" Walter said to Tits like I wasn't the one who asked him the question. "There would be no need. Just kill him when he gets at the ambush. And for that matter, why not give him the date and time if it was a true ambush? Lieutenant, you have withheld some valuable intel on this project."

"I haven't withheld anything," he said. Backpedaling and distancing. I really hate politics.

"So you are saying that you have no control over your own personnel? That you don't mandate that information come through the chain of command?"

Tits was flummoxed. Between old Scylla and Charybdis. Any way you slice it, he didn't look good.

"Sorry to interrupt you two. But it seems like you two got a lot to discuss. So I'll just submit my vaca slip and be on my way," I said.

"I haven't approved your vacation time, detective." He was going to take his embarrassment out on me.

"Then call it medical, call it leave of absence, call it I quit. Call it whatever you want, I'm not going to be into work for a while. If I take this to the Captain, I'm not too sure you have a leg to stand on. I was almost killed for Chrissake."

I got up to leave gingerly. My medicine had officially worn off. It was early afternoon and I was in the mood for copious amounts of alcohol.

"Deni. Could you wait for me outside the office for a minute while I finish here with your Lieutenant? I'd like to have a private chat with you if that is all right with you."

"Yeah, I guess. Don't take too long. I need my meds."

I have no idea what the two talked about in Tits's office. I just know that it took a hot minute and I was ready to bail. I sat on the bench outside the office and every person that walked by gave me the stare. I looked horrible. I get that. Those that I knew would try to find out from me what they probably already knew from rumors. Troop H was like a high school. You couldn't have a hangnail without everybody knowing about it and giving advice as to how to avoid them in the future.

I was about to leave without speaking with Walter when he came out of the office. He asked me if I wanted to get out of there, which of course I did. We got into his car and we went to Parish Café, the one in the South End. I had been in there a few times. Swanky joint with high end comfort food. They make amazing drinks there as well, which is what I wanted.

We found a spot right at the bar. I normally don't go for elaborate concoctions, but when you go to Parish, it's kinda what you do. But nothing on the hand-crafted menu contained whiskey, it was all vodka or some such thing so I went with Jameson. Neat. Walter had some Belgian beer called Delirium Tremens. Food was not on my agenda, but he ordered two elaborate sandwiches called the Zuni Roll.

The conversation was going nowhere, but I didn't push it. I was on vacation and I wanted to drink. I couldn't drive the car from the motor pool while on vacation, and the *Escalade* wasn't ready yet because I had told them to take their time. Walter was someone to drink with and chauffeur me around, so I was going to milk it for all it was worth.

The sandwiches arrived and so did the moment to bring up the secret agenda and the reason that I was taken out on the town.

"What's wrong with a Sam or a Harpoon? You too good for local beer?"

"Belgian beer has more alcohol."

"Looks expensive for so little."

"So …. how well do you know these assholes that tried to kill you?" Subtle.

"I grew up with the prick. He's been in my house. We don't take windy walks on tha beach if that's what your askin'."

"I didn't say that you were in their pocket. I just mean that you think like them, right?"

"I wouldn't say that. I know how they think. Somewhat. If I really knew then I probably wouldn't be in this fix and I woulda found Slopes by now."

"Fair enough. I want you to stay on this case."

"You've only had one beer, slow down. Did you not hear that I'm on vacation?"

"And I'm asking you to not be on vacation."

"Look, guy. People are dead because I didn't know when to walk away. Every time I turn around I get further involved. Fucked deeper in the ass. I'm out."

"Where will you go?"

"What part of 'on vacation' is throwin' you for a loop? Two words, Walt. Look 'em up."

"Yes, Deni. I understand the concept of vacation. Where will you go?"

"I don't know, but it's going to be outta town. Maybe New Hampshire. I can pick up a couple of bucks pickin' up side jobs. Maybe go house hunting. You might have heard I'm in the market. Maybe my time in Southie has come to an abrupt end for good."

"What about Ireland?"

"I really don't like traveling too far. I don't like planes, I'm not much on …. " The meds mixed with whiskey had slowed me down. " …. wait …. you want me to go see if I can find out when the guns are comin' in. Go fuck ya-self."

"Do it for all the people who have been killed. Do it for the people that died in that fire. You owe it to them to get justice. You are a cop, Deni."

"I'm no federal agent. Get the ATF to do it. Or the FBI. Not me in other words. You seem to have everybody under your thumb, get some other slob. What am I gonna accomplish in Ireland anyway? I'm a Massachusetts State Police Detective. And I'm barely that."

"The ATF or FBI would have to be brought up to speed. I believe that they also have a leak. I don't want you to do anything more than just track them. Don't stop it, just get a vessel number and a crate number and come home. You don't have a place to live, and you need a vacation. Why not get paid to see the sights? You are Irish."

"Who's gonna talk to me?"

"You'd be surprised. Act like a tourist."

"A tourist with an inquiring mind about the IRA and this Sinn party?"

"Sinn Féin. And yes."

"Sure. That'll work. I don't know my way around to even know who to ask. This whole thing is fucked up. Did you come up with this? You been drinkin' more than those fancy beers?"

"I'll set you up with someone who has worked with our office before on investigations. You will be fine."

"And what if I come up with nothin'? What then?"

"Then you come up with nothing. But we both know that when you get on a scent, you're like a blood hound. A relentless blood hound in heat."

"Thanks for the imagery, Walt."

"And if you aren't properly motivated already, I'll sweeten the deal. While you are collecting your vacation pay, any information that you come up with that leads us to that gun shipment earns you a bonus, courtesy of Uncle Sam."

"What kind of bonus? A pat on the back?"

"Money. A bonus like I said. A sizable one. And I'll pay your freight. How can you say no to an all-expense paid vacation with a bonus?"

"Tits …. er …. Titanitaukis is never going to agree to this."

"You will be working for me. Under the direction and protection of the Department of Justice and the Attorney General's Office. One case, one goal. Find the new shipment of guns. Leave Tits to me."

25

I MUST HAVE BEEN DRUNK. Or the mix of booze and meds. Or Walter had caught me at a weak moment. Whatever the case, three days later, on Friday, August 13, I was on a plane. Friday the thirteenth. Talk about tempting fate.

I was trying to look at it as a free vacation. A good vacation for me was to head down to Fort Meyers to see Sox spring training, not go across the big pond. Spring training was long over and the Red Sox were having a decent year at 21-15 so far. I would have loved to take a week or two off and see Schilling, Lowe, or Wake on the mound. Pedro throw filth. I definitely needed a vacation.

But every time I would think about how great a free vacation to my ethnic homeland sounded, I dismissed the idea that I was getting myself in way beyond my depth. The thought of the fire and gunfire at my house and the increasing number of deaths would pull me back to the reality of it. This wasn't a vacation. This was leaving the proverbial pot for the fire. An even bigger one.

172

I wasn't scared.   We'll call it concerned.   Nervous maybe. Full-on uncertainty, certainly.

Walter had fortified me with a coach seat on American Airlines, compliments of the Department of Justice.   He also gave me some traveller's checks and said that he would have a contact from the Garda Síochána meet me at the airport.   The Garda detective was also a member of the anti-terrorist police task force, very familiar with the IRA, and had just been instrumental in the seizure of a trove of explosives and detonators in February of 2004. He would point me in the right direction, off the record, and help me to get situated.   His reward for hospitality and clandestine support was going to be the accolades from any arrest he was able to sustain from the leads I was investigating on the Ireland side of things.   Politics at work yet again on an international level.

While waiting to get on the plane in Logan airport, I had called Ryan Wells to let him know what I was up to.   We had spoken after the fire, and he said that if there was anything that I needed to let he or JG know.   They seemed like real nice guys.

"So I won't be around for a bit, Ry.   But I was only on a trial basis for the one job anyway right?"

"Right.   But this helps us with the Breen case anyway.   If we can further prove the connection to the Irish mob via the IRA through the guns coming over from Dublin, we can prove conspiracy."

"Okay but we don't have a case anymore, right?   He's dead."

"I found his girlfriend, Maddy.   Actually she found me.   She went into hiding and wanted to see about hiring us to look after her interests.   Seems Liam had a hidden stash of money."

"So .... "

"So she is definitely not the sentimental type.   Money and security is what makes this girl tick.   So if we can prove that Liam was murdered because of this large conspiracy, we have a civil case. We can sue the entities with deep pockets down the line.   She put down another retainer for a civil suit, for a shot at really big money down the line.   She also can't be on the run with so much cash, so she gave us money for us to set aside for her. She's on the run and scared."

"You're hiding money for her? Isn't that money from illegal activity, Ry?"

"Nobody can prove that. Besides, it came from her not him."

"So what are you sayin'? Cut to the chase. Am I on the clock for you too?"

"If we can get proof that Breen was murdered to shut him up, then yes. Money for time and a bonus on the back end if we win a civil suit."

"Deal."

"Good luck, Deni. Keep me posted."

Almost seven hours of being sandwiched between two other passengers without enough alcohol was about all I could take. My skin still burned from the fire and I was continually being touched by the people in the seats to the left and right of me. We landed safely in Dublin, but the pilot could have crashed the damned plane and I would have welcomed it.

I had a freakish feeling at the terminal because the building was held up with a suspension tower that looked exactly like the Zaxim Bridge they were in the process of constructing in Boston as part of the Big Dig.

The sign in the terminal for the baggage claim said *Bailiú Bagáiste Agus Sli Amach*, which I assumed was Gaelic, with English printed underneath it. I sincerely hoped that there weren't going to be any communication issues. I am Irish, but only to a point.

After claiming my bags and walking out the main exit, I stood on the concrete and brick kerb in front, watching the double-decker buses pickup and drop off. I again wondered how in the hell I had gotten myself into the mess. I was standing by the pickup area like an idiot waiting for someone who may or may not show up. I started digging into my carry-on for the name of the hotel I was staying at when a tall, thin man with freckles and ginger hair called out to me. Don't ask me what he said because I don't think it was English. He introduced himself, Detective Garda Cian

174

Daly, but I'm glad I knew it in advance because I never would have understood it otherwise.

He was nice enough to help me with my bags, speaking in tongues to me while we walked to his car. The only word that I could clearly make out was 'kerb'.

The white, elongated, rectangular license plate number K SF 2837 in black lettering was attached to a Ford sedan. It was a model I had never seen or heard of before. It was a *Mondeo Titanium V6*. I guess Ford has the market on police vehicles the world over.

We left the airport on Swords Road, through two rotaries and onto the M1, or Motorway 1. I wondered if Cian thought I was a mute, because he kept yapping away while I watched us negotiate another rotary on the left side of the streets from M1 to M50 in silence. It is an odd feeling being on the driver's side of the car without a steering wheel.

" …. bit whisht ain ya lad?" He looked at me to his left while he was driving on the right side of the *Mondeo* so I knew I was going to need to give him a response.

"I'm sorry but I don't understand a word of what you're sayin'."

"Ah. Taught you were a cod, der. Eh, touched. Not a bright one."

Not a bright one. Got it. He thought I was an idiot because I didn't speak. "I'm just going to need you to slow down a little, so I can understand you. Is that English or Gaelic?"

Cian spoke much more slowly which was still quite fast. He spoke to me the way people speak to retarded people. Loudly but not slowly. Like I was deaf instead of not understanding. Like no matter how slow he spoke, I was going to be a bit slower.

"English is the primary, everyone speaks Gaelic though. I'm told that yer the gurrier, but don't put a spanner in the works. Just make you're enquiries and turn it to me. If I you, I wouldn't touch Sinn Féin with a bargepole, I wouldn't."

I needed a secret decoder ring. But the gist was to not make waves. Just let him know what I found out. I didn't like the bosses

I had, and I had just inherited another. This one didn't speak English though he insisted that it was.

"I understand. I'm just here to find out when the shipment of guns is going out, hopefully get a vessel and a crate number. That's it. Technically I'm on vacation. Any help you can give is appreciated."

"Consider this a home from home. Put your oar in but don't get nicked, I can't help ya from that scrap," he said.

"Are you going to be with me every day? I could use a lay of the land. Walter said that you would point me in the right direction. Like I said, I could use the help."

"Aye. Though I've got me own urns in the fire. I'm a bit known here, so you mightn't want a sight with me. You'll be banjaxed and in the shore but quick."

The Garda Station was located about twenty kilometers from the airport near Pheonix Park. Cian introduced me around and took me to his work space. What I gathered from his explanation at his desk was that he had introduced me as one of his many distant relatives visiting from America, of which the native Irish all have large families and can relate, because we were going to be seen together on occasion for as long as I was in Dublin.

Cian opened up a few binders once we were alone and in a more private area, taking me through a show and tell session that was very much like Charades or Pictionary. I was able to learn a lot about Ireland and the IRA. He put various photos and mug shots out for me to put a face with the modern incarnations of Sinn Féin and the Irish Republican Army.

Two of the myriad photos were shadows. Pictures without any definition. They could have been Colin Powell or Colin Farrell. Cian Daly explained to me that these were important people within the organisation, but no clear photos had ever been taken of them. He said that they knew the two names and rank, that they knew they existed, but no witness had ever seen the men with their own eyes or had lived to describe them.

I began to ask a number of questions about these mystery men, but Daly said that he would get to that. First he needed inform me about a great many things that I was obviously unaware of. It is embarrassing, to say the least, of how little I had known about my own heritage. How little I knew of any european history, let alone the struggles of my own ancestral homeland.

The history lesson would begin.

In the 1920s the Irish Republican Army was utilised by a governmental elected assembly called Dáil Éireann after Easter Rising. The army was used to wage a guerrilla war against British rule in Ireland during the Irish War of Independence. The army was successful in that it held off the British enough to encite the Anglo-Irish Treaty.

The treaty allowed the Irish to police themselves but recognised England as the governing body. This is when the IRA split into two factions, those that supported the treaty and the majority of whom did not. Civil War ensued.

During World War 1 the unrest was still unresolved. Unionists illegally imported guns as the reliability of British forces were uncertain due to their use in the war effort. The unsupportive majority became yet more popular when public executions occurred by the British as a result of the rebels boycotting fighting for the British in the war. Because of the overwhelming rebel popularity, a new Irish Nationalist Party was formed, Sinn Féin, with the IRA at its beck and call.

Sinn Féin, who would best be assimilated to the staunch Conservative Republicans in the United States, after electing Éamon De Valera as their president, then created their own parliament after winning the forthcoming election. The now officially named IRA was the only army. The Sinns have been in and out of majority political power since, however they have never relinquished their power over the IRA despite having been sidelined as the official army of the Republic. The IRA was supposed to have been disbanded.

Once the IRA had been 'officially' set aside in the 1930s, they began their long history of doing what they must as a means to an end. From the 'Christmas Raid', where they pilfered virtually every last bit of ammunition from Pheonix Park, to attaining German weapons from the Nazis in WW2, to 'Operation Harvest', to the 'Long War', the IRA has done what it must under the direction of the Sinn Féin political party.

Even throughout 'The Troubles', the sectarianism between the Northern Ireland Protestants and the Southern Catholics, the Sinns have, " …. refused to criminalise those who break the law in pursuit of legitimate political objectives". Those objectives could be simplified into one phrase, "The vision of one true Irish Catholic Republic under an Irish Príomh Aire (Prime Minister)".

The vision not withstanding in 2004, the gun trafficking continued from Libya, the Middle East, and wherever else they could obtain assault weapons like the H&K G3A4s stolen from the Norwegian Police for the purpose of rearming under 'Operation Harvest'. The IRA continued to be engaged in paramilitary activity and were on the World Terrorist Watch list. Sinn Féin communicated their voted will to the IRA Army Council General, who then communicated to the vast number of illegal secret cells. The takings from their illegal activity, either from their own ventures or that of a myriad minion enterprises, went back to funding the political party that indirectly directed them. The Irish organised crime syndicate in Boston, Massachusetts was one of any number of enterprises sending money up to their puppet masters.

The faces of the top players in the hierarchy were on display in front of Deni. Finn Rourke, or Fin, was the IRA Army Council

General and a high ranking member of Sinn Féin. He was headquartered in Dublin and was virtually untouchable. No crime could ever be linked to either him nor his immediate neighbours on the council. His number one and number two 'Volunteers' were Darragh Kane and Aiden Dunne respectively. They had been tied to a number of small crimes but because of Sinn Féin had never spent one full day in prison. Never even arrested or pictures would have been taken.

Darragh Kane and Aiden Dunn were insulated from prosecution in Dublin, or anywhere else in southern Ireland for that matter. The vast number of secret cells spread out all over the world actually executed the dirty work. Any illegal activity that could be traced back to Kane and Dunn would then be handled by Sinn Féin, according to Daly. Evidence and people went missing. Every investigation was frustrated by this arrangement.

The number one Volunteer under Fin, Darragh Kane, was the first shadow-picture. He was essentially the direct report to the IRA Army Council General, and was an all-around mystery. This Kane was at the top of this illegal pyramid, and didn't have a face.

The number two Volunteer, Aiden Dunn, was the second nondescript picture. He was second in command under Kane, the second mystery man. Both of these men were responsible for directing the IRA secret cells. Whether their leadership overlapped was anyone's guess.

Cian Daley was excited that this was the opportunity to change that. Daley had been informed by Walter that this would be the devastation of an illegal network of unprecedented proportions. While the world was focused on Saddam and Bin Laden, other wars were secretly being waged. And the end was near.

Warren Dennihan was realising that he was up to his knickers in shit and he didn't have the shoes for it.

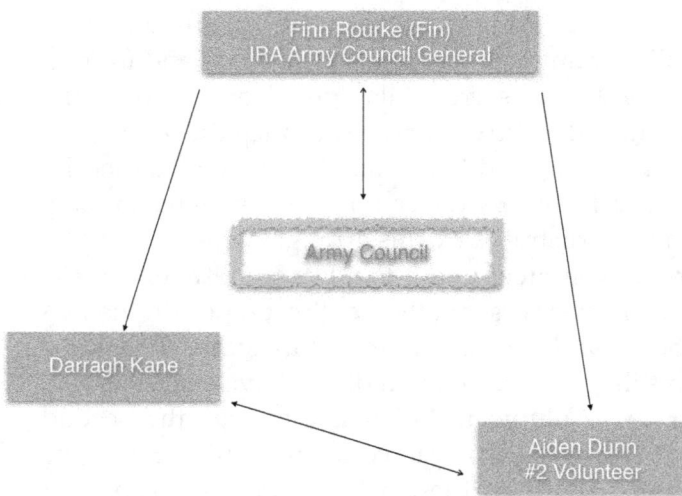

Sinn Féin

Finn Rourke (Fin)
IRA Army Council General

Army Council

Darragh Kane

Aiden Dunn
#2 Volunteer

IRA secret cells throughout the world

**countless
enterprises working
for the secret cells**

26

AFTER THE PICTURE SHOW AND TELL, Cian said that it was time for a 'rake of pints'. I'll translate. He meant it was time to get shit-faced. I checked into my hotel and met him at the public house which was close to both the Pheonix Park Garda station and my hotel. It was packed to the gills at half six san oíche. Happy hour was happy hour everywhere in the world.

I was starving and knew that food was essential with the amount of alcohol that was about to be consumed. He ordered me a 'Boxty' and a pint of piss-warm beer. I explained that I wasn't much of a beer drinker after tasting the pint. It was true that I am not a beer drinker, but I could have dealt with the Guinness if it had been cold. Cian made some comment about Americans and their beer having to be ice-cold because it had no flavor before he called to the 'landlord' to pour me a Redbreast 12 yr Irish Whiskey. His exact wording I can't recall, but that is what I received. The stuff was magical. I had never tasted anything so delicious in my life. It has become my favourite.

The food was another story. The plate that was put in front of me wasn't what I had been served every year on Ste. Patty's day. No cabbage on the plate as far as I could tell. It was a pancake-like thing made of potatoes wrapped around mystery meat and gravy on top. It was inedible, which I suffered tremendously the next day for not eating.

When I woke up on Saturday morning in my hotel room, it felt like I had been spit out of meat grinder. The Arlington Hotel O'Connell Bridge was centrally located in Dublin, but that is not why I was thankful to be staying there. I was thankful because Arlington is a popular street name in Boston and was easy enough to remember even in my drunken stupor. The three star hotel had either seen enough Americans go through their establishment or had seen me stumble in at whatever ungodly time I had returned; because travel packets of acetaminophen, vitamins, and a bottle of mineral water were waiting on the hotel room dresser on Saturday morning. They had just moved up to five stars in my book. The conversion from USD to Irish Euro was 1.2. At €70,50 per night, I thought the place was worth every penny. Especially since I wasn't paying for it.

Their coffee was shit though. I was forced to drink tea. I wasn't sure if tea had more or less caffeine than coffee, so I drank it like whatever I didn't consume was going to be dumped into the harbour back home. In any event, it worked to cure my Irish Flu. I pissed out the poison from the previous night and slept it off.

I met Cian in the lobby at 'half 'til noon' on Monday as was prearranged. Or meán lae. He drove north and east on M50 toward Dublin Port and the ferries to such places like the Isle of Man. We were going to do a little snooping and enquire how one would circumvent customs if they were moving cargo in and out of Dublin. Given that the IRA was considered a terrorist group and that both the US and Europe had experienced recent devastation as a result of terrorism, I wasn't the only one who was curious. Cian found it confounding albeit not surprising.

Cian had music playing in the *Mondeo* which saved me from having to understand what he was saying but was still an assault on my ears. I asked him what the music was.

"What are we listening to?"

"The Corrs. *Runaway*. Ye know them?"

"No, I don't *know dem*," I said emphasising his pronounciation. "It's horrible. It's like Enya trying to be The Cranberries."

"Easy lad. National treasures they are. They can't all be U2."

"Fair enough I guess." I turned the music down which didn't seem to make Cian happy. "How much do you think we are really going to be able to find out down at the port?"

"I'm on the anti-terrorist police task force, they see me a kilo 'til, but they won't be so cod as to mitch me or they'll be gettin' it in the neck."

"Was that English?"

"We'll be fine is all."

"Why couldn't you have just said that?"

We paid the toll through the Dublin Port Tunnel and drove in silence. I was glad he was driving. Not only is everything confusing with the bi-lingual signage, but traveling on the opposite side of the road was more daunting than I cared to admit. The car resurfaced above ground and we continued to Promenade Road, Tolka Quay Road, Bóthar Ché Na Tulchann, and then very slowly down Terminal Road South toward the water.

Dublin Terminal One holds ferries setting to sea for the Isle of Man, Liverpool, UK, as well as others on the southern face of the port. Along the northern side of port is a different type of sea. This sea houses storage units and a long line of enormous crates waiting for one of the I-beam cranes to hoist them onto the enormous cargo vessels. Each one of the crates was the size of an 18-wheel semi trailer or larger. Some of the containers were transported from the docks by those large diesel trucks.

The docks were beyond any word for huge. Cian used the word Brobdingnagian. I had to look it up, but even that word doesn't describe it. The number of crates would be like trying to count stars. If I had a map to the specific cargo container that was filled with weapons earmarked for my country, I still wouldn't have been able to find it.

Cian parked the car and we began to walk toward the end of the dock along the water's edge toward the end of the pier. When I say toward it, I mean it in the same way as if I were telling you that I had parked the car in the most satellite parking lot of Disneyland and was walking to the deepest part of the amusement park. It was going to be a fair hike. As he put it, I was lucky that I had my 'runners' on because we were in for a 'feckin stroll'. I was lucky that my Doc Martens were comfortable even though they weren't sneakers.

The water was rough and the tall Atlantic Ocean waves chopped at the sturdy support structure of the dock. The white-caps came nowhere near the top of the thirty foot high dock on which we were walking. The dock was nowhere near the decks of the cargo ships parked near it waiting to be loaded. The waves would have sent the breakfast of the novice seaman of a smaller vessel back from whence it came. Rocking even a moderate vessel into seasickness. But the titanic cargo vessels didn't move. They were as steadfast in the water as a skyscraper is on land.

As we walked along the edge of the dock, I had a strange feeling because the work area far ahead of us was busy, but nobody was paying us any attention as of yet. In my mind there was no way that we were not being watched. Not with the number of containers and being right on the port. But nobody revealed themselves. We continued to walk for what seemed like kilometers. Why we were walking instead of driving the rest of the way was a question I asked myself regularly as the trek progressed. We passed forklifts and other vehicles for conveyance that were obviously used on the paved pier. Cian was mumbling to me from ahead as he led the voyage. Even if he was next to me I'm not sure I would have understood him. I was slowly getting the hang of what he called English, but I still had a long way to go. It wasn't a horrible day for a walk, it was 21°c but the wind off of the Atlantic was cutting right through me.

I-beam cranes, forklifts and other heavy machinery were being operated all around the end of the docks. Monstrous cargo containers were being moved around like they were matchbox cars. Workers were everywhere but not making a bid to greet us or find out why we were intruding the area.

Cian was finally stopped at the Customs Security Building by the man that we had spent the better part of an hour to see. At least that was the man that we questioned. He was a short and thin man who looked to be in his late fifties or early sixties. The older gentleman was the equivalent of a Dock Supervisor and Customs Officer for the Dublin shipping hub. He wore a firearm at his side but it was difficult for me to determine which flavor because it was concealed by his holster.

Daly and the man were familiar with one another because they got on with smiles and jokes whilst I stood like the third wheel that I was. After all the playful banter was exhausted, I was finally introduced, again as his distant relative from America.

"Niall McCourt," he said as he stuck out his hand. His accent was as thick or thicker than Cian's. This was going to be slow and deliberate communication on my part.

I reciprocated with, "Warren Dennihan. Deni. Are you in charge around here?"

"I'm no Guv. You're the bobby ain't cha lad?"

"The bobby?" I looked to Cian for an explanation.

"He knows you're a policeman. You must have the fug about ye. It's ok, no need to yammer on the tale." Cian gave the nod to proceed.

"I am, yes. From Boston, Massachusetts. We're having some trouble with a group of criminals over there that seem to be getting stocked with supplies from here in Dublin. I was hoping you could help me find out how that's possible." I looked back at Cian to see if I had said too much and eloquently enough, said it slow enough to be understood, and that his nod meant what I thought that it meant.

"Anything's possible lad. Not as likely though. If I knew, I'd put the size twelve on 'em. You've go some neck on ye. Arrivin' at accusations. Any proof to go along with those jewels?"

"Definitive proof? No. But we have someone on the inside of the Irish mob over there that gave us the tip. There have been small shipments over time, but some of them have been seized. So there's supposed to be a big shipment coming our way in the near future. If it were to come off of this dock, how would they do it?"

"What's the meanin' behind 'they'?" Niall had a stern face and a cocked head.

I looked to Cian again for help, but none would come. "IRA," I said.

McCourt changed the position of his head from a cocked position to a nod. "If the army was movin' supplies through here boy-o, they'd have to have a ticket on the inside. I been here since I was wee. Seen a jumble or two. If you've gone down a trove from this lot, has to be a lad to slick the gears."

Inside. Slick the gears. Got it. "And how would you do that?"

"Wouldn't be me man." The stern face was back.

"I know that it's not you, but if it were. How would you do it? You've been around a long time, 'seen a jumble or two', as you put it. How would you do it? It seems like it would be more difficult in light of recent events."

"Easy is a state in yer mind. But it me? Army doesn't trade like that without feelin' worse for it. Not without the Sinns havin' a word in. Sinn Féin has a power in the government son. If it me, the container'd have the consulate seal. Container can't be touched and is put through."

Niall walked us between some cargo containers to his office. The office was essentially a container that was modified into a permanent office space. In that office, he explained after having to repeat himself several times so I could understand, that every container was locked and sealed. The containers were deposited onto the docks or filled there via what they called a 'juggernaut', which took some time for me to figure out that he meant a tractor

186

trailer truck. Once the cargo was verified, the container was locked and a thin metal tag was looped and contact-welded on the door. That metal tag had a series of numbers pre-stamped into it. There was no way to re-open the container without cutting through the seal. If the seal was broken, it was automatically seized. Since the stamped tags were randomly assigned at the time of welding, there was no way for a smuggler to know what tag number would be assigned to their cargo container with a proprietary serial number. The tag assigned would then be linked to the specific container number associated with shipper and receiver.

McCourt did admit that it was impossible for every single container that was to be shipped be thoroughly inspected prior to being sealed. Many times instead of the cargo being inspected prior to closing the doors, the container was sealed without the doors ever being opened for an official review. Containers to be thoroughly inspected prior to assigning and welding a seal were picked at random, by a randomly selected customs agent. It would be too risky or impossible to deliver contraband onto the docks with hope of slipping through without inspection, knowing which seal number would be randomly picked for which numbered container, and having the randomly selected agent in your pocket. The probability of not getting caught was astronomically slim, even if someone was paid off.

The only way to safely deposit cargo for shipment without risk of inspection was to have a governmental seal. If that seal was stamped onto the shipping manifest associated with that cargo, there would be no inspection and a tag would be welded on without delay. Those cargoes were immediately craned onto the vessel as they were deemed too important to risk tampering. But those governmental seals would have to go to another government agency on the receiving end.

Because containers with a welded seal that were attached to a governmental seal were protected with diplomatic immunity, there could be no inspection. This did, however, present another problem for the smuggler. Diplomatic 'pouches' were shipped from government entity to government entity only. Meaning that somebody on the Boston end would have to be blessed with some

187

government credential or another to be allowed to open said container. The containers full of weapons going to the US were clearly not ending up in the hands of the government, so there was a shell game occurring somewhere en route.

If this was, in fact, how they were doing it.

When Niall was finished with his explanation he looked to both of us with obvious pity. "Cian's been at the task for more than a tick a' the clock. You might be frettin' over the thuggery on your side a things, but my say is yer too light to be puttin' your weight about. Let be done what's to be done if ye care for yer health lad."

My take on Niall's laissez-faire approach to Sinn Féin and the IRA was that he was either a sensible older man who wanted a retirement, or he had inside knowledge and was protecting someone. The fact that he was saying anything at all to me swayed me toward the former.

"I'm just over here to find out what I can, Niall. I'm not planning on taking down an army by myself."

"Best not son. They're thick as thieves and yer a drunk lamb at a wolf party."

27

THE RIDE BACK INTO THE CITY OF DUBLIN PROPER
was a bit more comfortable than the trip out to the docks.
Comfortable in the sense that I was happy to be seated after an
eight kilometer walk, out of the wind, a bit less unnerved by the
roads and traffic, and the music was better. A song called *Sometimes*
by My Bloody Valentine was played on the car stereo that I would
have sworn was the Smashing Pumpkins if Cian hadn't informed
me otherwise.

My only unease was in the fact that I was dealing with an
organisation that had roots that were getting on a hundred years
old. This army had been at the beck and call of a major political
party and had committed countless violent acts for their
benefactors. They hadn't been stopped or slowed to a near crawl in
the entire existence of the institution. Cian had been seeking out
those roots for years and hadn't made a dent. I was meddling with
an entity that seemingly could not be killed but that most definitely

could get me killed. All I wanted was some information. But at what cost?

While the music was better and the ride comfortable, my thoughts wandered through the deaths that had already occurred because of the designs set forth by Sinn Féin. I had no illusions that this Finn Rourke had pointed to the Bostonians like a God and commanded his wrath upon them. Like any major organisation, the lofty figureheads have little knowledge of the trenches. The day to day. Or maybe he did and didn't care. But in my mind he was still just as responsible. He ordered his will be done full-stop. He needed to pay. I hoped this partnership with Cian would see to that.

This Darragh Kane and Aiden Dunn, according to Cian, passed down that will to the various sects of the IRA. The message had to be simple enough not to be misinterpreted or altered like the telephone game we played as kids. The story started on one end and barely resembled the same message on the other. That prime directive was then passed down to the likes of Slopes in Boston from one of these countless factions without waiver. Then he passed it on to his minions in the Winter Hill Gang and the geriatrics in New Hampshire.

This was a well-oiled machine that I was dealing with. The communications and networking ran deep enough where all parties knew their role, and all parties executed with a precision that had kept them in business for generations. Documents were forged. People manipulated. Salaries paid. Bribes divvied. And the collateral damage continued.

Danny Mick. Roxy. Breen. All Dead. Guns were stolen from the Maynard Ballistics facility. Guns and drugs were the business within the business in New Hampshire. All of these things were affecting my city because of the will of this organisation. How many other cities were also affected?

I knew that tracking those guns was not going to bring any of the dead back to life. Nor would it stop Sinn Féin. Nor the IRA. Nor the Irish mob. Nor all crime in Boston. But they had tried to burn me out. Bullets and fire had me scared at first. And while I might have been ill at ease riding in that car back into the heart of

Dublin, I was becoming invigorated at the thought of some justice. No matter how small.

The conversation in the car was light. All of our conversations were light because I had difficulty understanding Cian. He had been yammering on while I was listening to the music and lost in thoughts of retribution. When I had come around, determined to move forward with the next phase of the investigation, I enquired as to what exactly that next avenue would be. I was ready to run through a wall, I just needed to be pointed at it.

"So where now Cian?"

"Little else for today. Near impossible to get a formal word with a Sinn at the hour."

"It's still pretty early. Are you calling it a day?"

"Whattaya have me for? We go to the pub for a pint of the black stuff now."

"We just left the docks where Niall just told us that the only way he could see where the weapons that are plaguing my city can leave this one undetected is with governmental help, and you want to stall investigating that information? I'm not sure how things get done in Dublin, but in Boston we call that a lead and we follow that trail as quickly as possible."

"Easy lad. No need to be daft, now. All talks happen in pubs. Socialise and be merry. Get on with every toerag. Pay better attention without yer blood up. You'll be stunned with the handiwork. You lot seem to scrap yer way to stardom, we wet the tea and let it steep."

"Getting drunk seems to be the national pastime. Normally I'd be right there with ya. Our pastime is baseball which I am missing more and more of the longer I have to be here. Why can't we put pressure on one of your informants or something and get to the bottom of the lead? We know that Sinn Féin is behind every move the IRA makes. Surely they can get around the red tape. We need to find out how. If you don't want to help me, then I can snoop around by myself."

"Yer takin' a piss, Deni. You'll get nowhere with that talk and disposition. No need to be two sheets or spit drunken venom. Take heart. Spend the quid and filch your answers."

"I just walk up to some random guy in the bar and ask if he knows of any government official who might know about illegal shipments under the protection of diplomatic immunity? I know what daft means, and that sounds like it."

"No such random in this pub, sir."

"We're going to a Sinn Féin bar? Is that it?"

"Aye. Don't get yourself slain in the effort, boy-oh."

The Public House, O'Neill's, was the pub frequented by the political party and legal partners of Sinn Féin. It was packed from dark wooden, old-world wall to wall. It was early afternoon, not even prevening and the place was abustle. In the States it wouldn't have even been happy-hour yet and the occupants were many and merry. It was Monday mind you, and these boys weren't working. But the tarts were. My entrepreneurial spirit had designs on owning such a pub as it seemed to be a no-risk investment opportunity in Ireland.

The beer and whiskey soaked flooring gave off a sour odor that represented decades of consumption along with the fighting and merriment that accompanied such activity. The walls were covered with old paintings of aged men of whom I had no knowledge.   The establishment was like stepping into a time machine that could also transport you to a different place on the planet.   The culture was oozing from the porous wood with the same mystery and supply as the stale alcohol.   Each barstool and glass seemed to have an ancient story that I had not been privied to. The whiskey tasted better and the drunken stories seemed more rich. I felt as out of place as a karaoke machine would have been in that pub.

I was introduced to many people. Names became a blur. My coherence became a blur.   I tried to remain quiet and take in the people, interactions, and surroundings. Cian seemed to get on well with the crowd.   I was Irish and yet this tribe was a mystery. Detective Garda Síochána Cian Daly of the Anti-terrorism division was mingling with both men and tarts that he said were linked to or members of Sinn Féin. When it comes to drinking in Ireland, I guessed, love the ones your with.

As the delicious whiskey took hold of me, the more removed I had become from any and all conversation, the more agitated I became.   We were getting nowhere and we were getting there as quickly as I was becoming inebriated.   The trip to the pub was justified to me as part of an investigative tactic. The only things we were investigating as far as I could tell were the bottom of our glasses and the strength of our livers.

The decision to take the investigation to the next level was not mine.   The whiskey was doing the deciding and it was not soliciting any outside input. If my sense of reason was putting up a fight, it had lost like so many drunken battles that had taken place in that establishment before me.   I got off my stool, left my relatively empty corner of the crowded pub, and conducted my uninhibited interviews.

I don't know what was more reckless, my questions and accusations or the fact that I had no idea of the names and ranks of the men I was interrogating.   I was bounced around from one boisterous clique of men to another, making my enquiries with drunken abandon. I was most definitely getting noticed and not in a good way.

The boozy trip around the pub had left me with no answers, no leads, and thirsty. I looked for Cian to see if he needed another Guinness but he was nowhere to be seen. The pub was not that big and as crowded as it was, it took no time at all for me to give up on looking for him. He was either in the toilet or was taking a breath outside. I shrugged it off and headed to the barman to grab my next libation, but I never made it there.

A group of men encircled me before I could get to the bartop. Drunken Irish gibberish was thrown at me like a monkey throws his feces to articulate his unhappiness. They only word that I understood, 'cunt', came at me with venomous frequency. Then the shoving began. I sought sobriety and clarity as the situation dictated the necessity, but it would not come. They were corralling me toward the back door. Where that door led was a mystery to me at the time, but wherever it was, I was fine to let that mystery go unsolved.

Once they had me in the hallway leading to the back door, I was trapped. They were forcing me toward the back door from the pub end of hallway. The rage and volume intensified in the small space as I backed toward my doom. Any thoughts of trying to push my way back into the pub through the six or eight men that composed the angry mob was thwarted when the glassware was thrown at me. One such glass struck me on the side of the head, shattering and sending me to one knee.

As the alcohol-thinned blood began to flow from my head, flowing onto the sticky floor, a side door in the hallway opened up and I was helped through it. Blood and booze from the broken glass was stinging my eyes.

"Find yer own American! I want this one fer meself," said a female voice.

I searched my surroundings with my good eye. One of the tarts from the pub had gone to the ladies' room. In my sluggish stupor I had forgotten that the gents and ladies' toilets were located in the hallway that I had been pushed down. The ladies' was the last door before the back door that would have likely led to a beating or worse. The toilet was a one-holer, meaning that only one woman could perform a bodily function at a time. This particular woman who had helped me into the small space, entered behind me after calling off my aggressors and locked the door.

"Fine mess you've carved yerself," she said. "Let's see if we can clean it up."

She pushed my head into the filthy sink, turned the faucet on, cupped water into her hands, pouring it onto my wound. It stung at me while the crimson water cascaded down to the sink and into the drain.

"Thank you. Who are you?"

"A Catholic girl not wishin' to stand idly by while you get murdered."

"Well thank you Catholic girl."

"Let's not extend gratitudes yet. Yer not outta the furnace. Those lads are plottin' outside the door 'bout now, they are."

"So what's our plan fine Catholic girl?"

"We leave together. You'll be my prize for the evenin'."

"Listen if you're a whore, I'm not buying. You put yourself in harms way for me with thanks, but if you think getting me out of this jam gets you a john, you've misread the situation."

"I'm not bringin' you to a vice den for a slap n' tickle. I'm savin' yer life, lad. I'll bring ye to me flat. Yer gonna need a sew. I can't stop the bleedin' just now."

"I've got a hotel room."

"And they'll kill ye in the bed it's in."

"I'll argue with you later Catholic girl. First we need to get outta here."

"Best call me Rowena."

"Deni."

"I'd say it's a pleasure but I mightn't until it's certain neither of us is die'n today."

28

"IT'S NOT SQUALID YET BY NO IMAGINATION A PALACE," Rowena said as we walked up to her first floor flat. Which is a bit confusing because in Ireland the first floor is really the second floor. They call the first floor the ground floor. I was never the math whiz, but I think that would mean that if her apartment was on the sixth floor, it would really be the seventh.

She was right. Her flat was neither a palace nor palatial. But it was cozy and minimally decorated as though she cared about the limited space that was available. It was tasteful. Not kitschy or robust with knick-knacks that would make the confining space more so. There were just enough things in place to make one feel comfortable, to give a sense of personality without overcrowding or filling every bit of space.

The flat was clean and well maintained. If she was a prostitute, my immediate thought was that she must have been a clean one. The hardwood flooring was shiny, the area rug was clean and free of debris. The furniture in the parlour was tidy like it could be shown for an open house. Turning into the kitchenette, the tiny space was also clean and uncluttered.

Her apartment was a structural representation of her. She herself was very compact. She had the build of a skinny fifteen year old boy. She stood about 1.7 meters, or 5 foot 7 inches. She was the definition of lanky, the very picture of heroine chic without the dark circles under her eyes. She was not beautiful in the traditional sense, yet not ugly. What shape her body did have was angular. Her johns would be interested in purchasing time with her for her compactness. For the probability that her orifices were as tight as her body. For the male-ego fantasy of breaking her with their members.

Rowena grabbed my head and again shoved it into a sink, this time the basin in her kitchen. 'Bleed in there, not on me floors,' she said in a huff as she left the small kitchen space and entered another small room.

While she grabbed her sewing paraphernalia, I thought about how she had handled getting us out of the Sinn Féin pub alive. The back door led to an alley where other Irish men were waiting. Instead of them completing the job their comrades had started in the pub, they were told by Rowena that they were going to have to pay her to hand me over. I was money for her. In prostitution, money is everything. For Irish men looking to beat the life out of an American, money is everything also. They didn't want to part with one Irish Euro.

Rowena was allowed to take her foreign customer to whatever vice den the alley-men thought she worked in. She told me that the lads would either sleep off the drunken venom; or more probable, they would finish their handiwork on a later date. I was hoping for option one.

When she came back to the small space with her skin and clothing repair kit, she leaned into me as if she were trying to morph from two people into one. The space was small and claustrophobic, her adherence to me made it more so.

She poured some sort of alcohol on my head and it would not surprise me if the wound hissed, making a sound that would assault one's ears as much as it did my nerve endings. I must have pulled away or moaned but she was not having any of it.

"Quit bein' the mot?"

"What? Speak English. You all say you speak the language but none of you do."

"Girl. Quit bein' a feckin' girl."

"Is this why you got me out of that mess? You wanted to torture me yourself?" She started sewing my head, the numbing properties of the Redbreast whiskey I had consumed at the pub were gone.

"An American missin' er dead would make the dailies but it'd done nothin' for me cover."

"You're a cop? er, Garda or whatever?"

"I'm no Bobby," she said. "I'm no brasser either. I'm a pressmen. You lot say 'reporter' ye know."

"You work the Sinn Féin pub as an undercover repor — ow! Jesus Christ take it easy …. as a reporter?" She was stitching my head like it was attached to a torn teddy bear. "You sleep with these guys to prime them for inside knowledge? Kinda dangerous for a small girl like you."

"I'm in the wick! Nothin' of the sort, ye wanker. The lads get loose-tongued when their bolloxed on the black stuff. Their aims and ambitions get put in the dailies without a notion as to how. I lay with none of them, ye sap. Ye put quite the spanner in when you got a fifty and necked in. If I hadn't put me own diddies in, you'd be missin' and never heard of again. Those are officials, fella. Have a way of doin' evil works without spoil."

"Sorry to get you involved. Your diddies or whatever. " She rinsed off my head with more booze and stepped away. Which is to say that we were still very close.

"Jest an expression. Means tits."

"You don't have any of those do you?"

"Whisht! Shet yer gob!" She slapped my wounded head and I immediately regretted joking with her. "There's a towel in the press. Dry yourself ye ingrate." She pointed to the cupboard, which I opened to get a towel. She exited the kitchenette for the other small room. My skin was tender and swollen away from my skull. I opened another small door to find a bottle of Poitin. I pulled the top off and guzzled as much of the harsh poison as I could stomach. Alcohol at any cost.

When I followed her to the parlour she had a towel on the floor and pointed for me to sit on it and told me to strip. I must have had a confused look on my face because she explained that I was a mess and she wanted none of my filth on her furniture. The order to strip was so that she could put my clothes through the wash.

Once I was as naked as the day I was born, she tossed me another towel to 'cover my bits and body art'. Any man hates their genitals to be referred to as bits. It's emasculating. We prefer other terms that don't infer size; or if necessary, to aire on the larger size. As far as the body art, there was no covering that up. I was covered front and back, shoulders to thighs with the exception of my forearms and 'bits'.

I wrapped the towel around my waist and sat on the towel she had placed on the floor, but my tackle was still showing because she wanted me to cross my legs before her interrogation began.

"Quite the daft booze-hound to be strollin' into that pub for a pint. Have ya lost yer mind? Or are you eejit?"

After a quick moment of hemming and hawing, after deciding that she had a cover that needed protecting same as me, I decided to tell her my story. I felt that the reward would outweigh the risk. "If I tell you why I was in that bar, you cannot repeat it or print it."

"A fair prop. Go on."

I explained that I was a Massachusetts State Police Trooper from H, in the city of Boston. I explained that while I handled a portion of all major crimes against persons in the city, my specific area of expertise was in South Boston because of my background there. She learned about Sean Teague, and about how he was running an organised crime syndicate in Boston. After some interruptions for clarification, she also became aware of the gun and drug trade that Slopes ran into and out of the city via the compound in the mountains of New Hampshire. That the seizure of those guns and drugs was going to cause quite the headache for Slopes unless he was able to restock. I told her about the informant that linked the Winter Hill crew to a satellite sect of the IRA, which she already knew was run by the Army Council of Sinn Féin. She didn't know about Darragh Kane or Aiden Dunn specifically, only that there had to be top people to communicate messages from the untouchable Finn Rourke to the secret cells of Volunteers. I further explained that I was sent to Ireland to uncover information about the when and the where of the large replacement shipment that was to be sent via Dublin. I told her that Detective Garda Síochána Cian Daly was my contact here. That he was the one who brought me into the pub.

She said that she had covered many a story about the secret cells, as they are the ones who publicly 'claim responsibility' when an atrocity they execute needs a message tied to it. Rowena spoke about how the IRA always uses the name P. O'Neill when they communicate those messages through the press. How she had suspected that there was no such person which is why they continue to use the name. She continues to report on the political party and their agenda from the inside of a pub. She reinforced Cian's correlation of Sinn Féin to the Republican party in America. She said that Sinns bleed for the cause, hold their politicians in the highest regard. The mourning of a lost member was like the death of Ronald Reagan to Conservatives, which had just happened in June. She showed me a piece that she had written to ensure I got the point.

She portrays herself to be in the 'bugger trade' so she can uncover the mysteries and inner workings without suspicion. She has on occasion had to accompany an interested gentleman to a hotel room where she would 'give him a crack'. He would wake up the next day with a lump on his head thinking he got proper fucked, when in fact he had just been 'made hames of'. He had given the goods and his money without a release.

Rowena said that her stories were the scandal. Her reports were like no other pressmen in Ireland and many sought to find out

200

who she was. She had a fake name on her column, with a fake photo. She sent her columns to the paper by a courier who didn't know what he was carrying. Very cloak and dagger. If something was urgent she would contact her editor at the paper, her boss, but did so as rarely as possible.

When we both finished explaining why and how we were in the pub, she said that it was 'amadán' to have gone in there, and even more foolish for Cian to have left me there alone.

"I don't know if he left me there. He just wasn't there when I was looking for him. He might have stepped out. He might have been embarrassed or trying not to get killed himself."

"Aye. likely," she said. "On the toilet or no, he might have been a bit more cop-on."

"Cop-on? Like help me question people?"

"No. Cop-on. Eh …. have more brains in the way of things."

"Streetwise."

"Aye. That's it."

"If you all speak English, why is this so difficult?"

"It's less English as Gaelic, garsún. Gaelic used to be first language, English taught as a second in the south of Ireland. Now Gaelic is second, more the pity. Most of the Gaelic sticks though, so it's English in name only."

"That's what Cian said. It's damn near indecipherable if you ask me."

"I didn't."

"Fair enough. As a reporter, do you write the way you speak?"

"It's the accent most like. You'd be able to read better'n listen."

"A lot of words are different, so I don't know about that. Anyway …. so now what? Where do we go from here?"

"You keep me on the ticket, I'll let you settle here."

"You want me to stay here? What does 'on the ticket' mean? You want the story?"

"Aye. I help you. You help me."

"I don't know. This is supposed to be hush-hush. Low key. There's a big dog federal prosecutor at home that wants this under the table. I find out what I need and go home."

"Fine job of silence. 'pass the pitcher of mild, and while your at it do you know of any gobeen men?' About as subtle as an advert, that. All rights ye should be dead."

"Not my finest moment, but I don't want to be here forever and a day, Row."

"Rowena," she said. "Like most you have great grá for the whiskey. Let yer mouth run riot. Settlin' here in me flat will help with the death, but not if ye keep at it."

"Any suggestions?"

"If I you? I'd set an appointment with Finn Rourke himself, I would. He won't touch ye personally. Won't nothin' happen to ye on or after seein' him. Much the risk. His hands stay clean, you stay alive."

"You honestly think that he will tell me anything at all about his illegal maneuvers? He'll laugh me out of his office."

"Aye. But you'll have the sense of him. He'll know to take care and less like somethin' will happen to ye. A word with him means there's a link. A death tied to Fin would need an explanation. It's the politics of it." She left the room as she spoke, taking the bottle of Poitin with her. Returning a few moments later with a bottle of whiskey and two glasses.

"That might work. Cian will never go for it though. He has already told me he wants his involvement to be as silent as possible. Daly is on the anti-terrorist task force. He has been introducing me as his cousin or somethin'."

She poured the brownish liquor into the two glasses. "Then he'll not know. You go on like yer still in yer hotel, still takin' his cues. We'll confer when you come here."

We both shot our whiskeys back, set the glasses down on the table between us, and she poured another round.

"If I'm not to be touched after I meet with Fin, why would I need to stay here?"

202

"Amn't sayin' no harm will befall ye. I mean to say less like. And they know you're here and why, fella. The less predictable you are, the quicker you'll get what you desire. This is a story and I mean to help. You get yer guns, I get me story."

"How do I know that I can trust you?"

"I'm no slíbhín. I've me secrets and you yours. We keep what we must between us or the devil take us both."

She raised her glass to toast, I did likewise.

"Sláinte," she said. She was about to down her glass but she stopped. I must have a had a puzzled look on my face because she explained before slinging it back. "It means to our health."

29

FOR THE SECOND TIME IN UNDER A WEEK I WOKE
UP from a night of alcohol poisoning. Drinking or drunk would be
bad enough, but this was not just having too much to drink. This
was poisoning. It took me a few minutes to gather myself,
remember where I was. I was still drunk truth be told. I had been
nearly piss-myself drunk in the Sinn Féin pub. I had almost gotten
myself killed then finished polluting myself by getting hammered
with the woman who had saved my sorry ass.

My head was excruciating. Whether it was the hangover that
had not yet gone into full swing or the sutured wound from the
glass that was shattered on my head was anyone's guess. Maybe
both. I felt the tender stitching and winced as I did so. The thought
that there might still be glass in there was fleeting. It had certainly
felt like the woman was thorough in her cleaning at the time, even
in my inebriation.

Further personal inventory led me to the realisation that I was naked under my sheet. The question of how I had gotten naked was another in a series of notions flooding through my sluggish brain. My clothes were being washed. I had a towel. The towel was now gone. Rowena.

I turned to the other pillow, the other side of the bed. Speak of the devil. She was sleeping next to me. A slight lift and a peak under the covers revealed her naked body as well. She lay on her side, back to me. Her long slender body was motionless with the exception of the slow rise and fall of her midsection from her breathing. Rowena's body really had no shape other than where bone hinted through skin. The curve of her spine was the only undulation. She had been wearing a wig the night before, as the head laying on the pillow next to me had very short hair.

Rowena was already awake and pretending to be asleep, or the draft from the lifted sheet woke her.

"Don't have a blarney. I don't sleep in pyjamas or knickers."
"I got bombed last night. Did we .... "
"Feck no," she said. She slid her legs and feet off of the bed and headed toward a chair with clothes draped over the back of it. "I'll get us a fry-up."

There was no explanation as why we were both in her bed and naked, other than she doesn't wear clothes to bed and that we didn't have sex. When I sat upright to leave the bed, a massive bout of vertigo took over. I struggled with keeping what little that was already in my stomach settled where it was. With my feet on the floor to the side of the bed and my tender head in my hands, elbows on knees, I waited out the storm of spins and nausea.

I looked around the room once the sheet was pulled off of me and I was able to stand without fear of losing my balance. A mirror and a dresser. A long necklace hung from the corner of the mirror. The medallion looked like it was a religious token. Ste. Christopher. I remembered from catechism that he was the patron sainte of lost things and causes. I continued to look around, no clothes. None that belonged to me I should say. The waft of grease and food came into the small room from the small kitchenette. My stomach went into cartwheels but I was forced to go closer to the smell of breakfast to determine the whereabouts of my clothes. The flat wasn't big by anyone's standards, there were only so many places that they could be.

"Have you seen my clothes?" I stood in the doorway to the kitchenette, naked in want of garments.

"Aye. In the cupboard 'round the way." She stood over the pan on the two burner stovetop, pointing ahead of her with a spatula. I assumed correctly that on the other side of the wall against which the stove was situated was some sort of laundry closet.

Around the corner was a tall, narrow door which hid the tiny, front-load, convenience sized washer and dryer that stood vertically one over the other. "Should be done," she yelled from around the corner. I picked a door, the bottom one, and saw my dried clothes laying in the bottom of the circular bin.

My balance was still not back to normal so I sat on the floor to get dressed. I needed to go to a gym. These nights of drunken debauchery with no exercise was not good. I am a drinker, no question, but this was an entirely different level. I felt as though I was a little leaguer trying out for the majors. The fast ball had gone by me and I was waiting for the pitch.

Dressed, I reentered the kitchenette to see breakfast was being plated. It was unrecognizable. She handed me the plate and commented on what must have been an obvious look of apprehension.

"It's meat hash. Jest put in yer gob."

No wonder I don't play poker.

In truth I was starving. Liters of alcohol consumed with virtually no food. And no exercise. My body was freaking out.

The 'meat hash' was eggy mystery meat. The best way to describe it by looks would be Spam in an egg mixture and heated in grease. The best way to describe the taste and texture would be fucking gross. But I ate it. I needed the food, needed the grease, no matter what the flavor.

Over breakfast I asked Rowena what had happened and why we were in the same bed and if that was going to be the arrangement every night that I came back to her flat. She replied that she grew up one of eleven kids, that sleeping in the same bed was not just for married people. I thought it morally questionable to have siblings sleeping naked with one another, but I knew nothing of her upbringing and I knew that I was no sainte. Maybe she had the moral high-ground.

She also said that she would give me what she had and work her contacts to get me further background information on the current mainstays of Sinn Féin, and schedule an appointment for me to meet with Finn Rourke. She told me not to go back to my hotel under any circumstances, that she would go there later in the day to collect anything that I might need. 'Jest go to Pheonix Park like it's any other labour day.' Which meant just go see Cian and pretend that Rowena doesn't exist. I could do that.

I just wish I had a better poker face. With her at least. She was one of the few people whom I have ever met that could read me like the dailies.

"Wait. Row, isn't today Tuesday?"
"Aye."
"So is Cian going to pick me up at my hotel today? We didn't really talk about it. Maybe I should go to the hotel to see if he calls."
"Jest go to the Garda station. If he's not present, wait a bit."

Rowena gave me directions to a corner where I could grab a taxi to the Garda station. She said that it was not smart to grab one off of the street in front of her flat. This investigation and arrangement was likely going to take a few more days at the very least, and me getting into a cab every day would create a predictable pattern. I obviously knew that patterns were bad.

So I followed her directions and went to the corner of Paráid Lósaif and Plás Bhaile Coimín. The old stone buildings set on old narrow kerbs amidst old narrow roads between them gave me the odd feeling. And it wasn't the fact that I was still a bit hungover.

Boston has old buildings. These structures were ancient by comparison. Weather and years had warped and stained every surface. At night, I could have been in the North End of Boston. During the day, the history and age of the area hits you in a way that makes you feel small and insignificant. So much of the world has happened decades and centuries before and in other parts of it. If the structures could talk, I would have been there a while to hear the stories.

The cab rolled to me and stopped within a few short minutes of my waiting. The day was another 21°c and the sun was trying unsuccessfully to peak through the clouds. I didn't mind the wait. I was still lost in thoughts of old when the cab pulled up. It took a few extra seconds for the address to which I was headed spark in my brain and leave my mouth to the driver.

Cian was sitting at his work station, at his desk when I arrived. He hadn't looked up to notice me and seemed genuinely surprised to see me when I sat in the chair next to his desk as I had before.

"There he is. The bold boy of the minute."

"You seem surprised to see me. Wasn't I supposed to meet you here? Was I supposed to see you at the hotel?"

"Aye. But you had the piss in ye, lad. Thought you'd be sleepin' off the trouble you've caused. Are ye better now?"

"What trouble?" As if I didn't know. "You disappeared. I looked for you, but I couldn't find you."

"Stepped out for a fag. You the talk when I came back, ye were."

"Yeah. I might have ruined the element of surprise. I was asking questions I shouldn't have. I just got tired of sitting there and waiting to hear something that was never going to be discussed. Did you honestly think that I was going to stumble upon a conversation about a shipment of guns to America?"

"Naw man. But you mightn't let the world know you were searchin'. You could have met someone to point you straight. You could have heard a name."

"So now what?"

"Now I see if there's construction in the damage. Go phone yer mates."

"So you're going to call your Sinn Féin friends? Isn't that a little odd that you are tasked with stopping the IRA from committing acts of terrorism yet you are buddy-buddy with the group that tells them what to do?"

"Watch yourself bucklepper. Don't get yer parties muttled up lad. I keep enemies close. And not all of those lads are mixed up in the troubles. Some surely, not all. I let you here as a courtesy and you spit on me hand. I'll do my best to keep air in yer lungs, you mightn't want to continue workin' against me efforts."

I apologised and told him that I did appreciate his efforts to keep me alive. On the inside I wondered just what type of effort he was making. I could have died in that pub the night before and he was out having a smoke. But insulting him or his obvious political preference was no way to keep the peace.

Cian was right in that all members of a political party are not prone to evil designs. Even from what little I knew about the hierarchy, I had the sense that there was one man at or near the top, Finn Rourke. He was the Army Council General. The rest of the party was over and around him, and the army council was likely

209

unaware of maneuvers he sent down to his number one and number two Volunteers. The arrangement likely left the majority of the nationalists in the dark. While they might agree with the philosophy behind his actions, the deeds might not be what they had signed up for. Or maybe they had. Either way politics was not my business. In fact I hated it. The guns going into Boston were my business and I needed to stay focused.

I called Walter Glibczieck, the federal prosecutor, just to check in. Which was a giant pain in the ass. My mobile phone was not set up for international calling. 'Hellomoto' from my phone was useless other than fortifying me with the cell numbers that I needed to call. I then had to get the international code to dial the US and use the land line at the Garda Station. All just to make a phone call to an answering machine because he was otherwise occupied five hours behind Dublin time. He would be informed when he heard the message that there was nothing to report. I was no closer to attaining the shipment information a week in than I had been back in Boston.

While I had the phone handy I called Ryan Wells at his office in New Hampshire. I wanted to inform him that there was still no progress and see if there was any new information about Breen's murder, his old lady Maddy, or the other old men. Also forced to leave a message. I expected nothing less as it was still early morning there.

My last call was to Troop H. Tits and Hobbs had not been into the station yet, according to the receptionist/operator. Did I want to leave a message? No thanks, I was just checking in.

I was hungover and friendless. Kind of a thing with me.

30

AFTER MAKING ALL OF MY FRUITLESS PHONE
CALLS and after Cian had made his, we decided to take to the
streets. He said that he had someone that I should talk to. The
informant was someone that Cian used back in February when he
had made the big weapons and ammunition bust. He was located
up in Belturbet, which was inland and near the border between
northern and southern Ireland. The UK - Ireland border. The trip
would be just shy of one hundred thirty kilometers and take about
an hour and a half. One way. In other words the trip would eat up
the rest of the day.

I sat in what would normally be the driver's side seat of the
Ford *Mondeo*. We took Motorway 3 most of the way, then onto N3,
or Navan Road. Cian inserted a compact disc blaring the music of
Stiff Little Fingers. The music wasn't bad but at the high volume it
didn't help the hangover. The disc was repeated over again when it
was finished the first pass through. The only track that I remember

off of that CD, and still listen to on occasion to this day, is *Alternative Ulster*.

We took the right onto Upper Bridge Street and parked in Fitzpatricks Flats. The area reminded me of Lowell, Massachusetts. In other words it was beat up, mostly one way streets with lots of pedestrians, and of course public houses. The buildings were converted from townhouses of various styles and shapes, juxtapositioned side by side on both sides of the streets, into small businesses. The roundabouts and one-way streets were confusing and tightly spaced. The kerbs were only wide enough for one person and were not elevated off of the road. Traffic moved quickly despite the confinement, though both vehicles and pedestrians seemed to be used to it. I was happy to be inside the building where we were to meet the informant.

The ground floor was 'to let'. The space was empty and looking for a business to start paying the freight. This may or may not have been a cover to make the building look less desirable, but what I do know is that we were on the third floor walk-up which was called the second floor. The red door was cracked open and upon entry the flat looked like a crack den. The only living space that I had seen in that poor condition was Roxy's a short time back.

A gangly, spotted kid stood in the center of the room unfased by our entrance. Cian made the introductions.

"Oisin, this is Deni. Deni, Oisin Hanamy." We both nodded, neither of us making a bid to shake hands.

"American then?"

I hadn't even said a word yet.

"Yes I am. Cian told you about me?"

"You have the look about you. Shall we head to Duffy's then?"

"Duffy's?" I looked at Cian to see if he knew who this Duffy was. The look of confusion was obvious to both men.

"The pub across the way. We can use the back room over pints of the black stuff," Oisin said.

"Does anything happen here without alcohol in hand?" I had startled myself with that comment. Coming from me that is quite the statement.

"The day ye come into this world and the day ye leave." They both had a laugh at the younger man's witty response. I shook my head but followed them down the narrow back stairs anyway. We left through what could have been a kitchen and down a set of stairs attached to the outside of the building. Oisin was exaggerating how far away Duffy's was. Across the way meant the green building across the back alleyway that was no wider than a sub-compact car.

Pints of Guinness were being poured as we entered the pub. They took a minute to pour as the nitrogen gas creates what initially seems like more foam than beer. The foam cascaded into dark brown and then black liquid on the bottom of the glass, creating the elixir that these Irishmen craved. We didn't wait for the pints to be completed, we continued into a back room that stood empty until we arrived.

I didn't have the heart to tell them that I didn't want a pint of beer. I wasn't a fan of warm beer. Cold beer was a struggle depending upon the type, warm was like broken glass and turpentine. But I was still reminiscing about my lack of whiskey-soaked discretion the night prior and I didn't want a whiskey more than I didn't want a warm beer. So I shut my mouth, had a seat, and waited for my Guinness.

The pints didn't sit on the table long when they were delivered by the barman. They were hoisted into the air and what sounded like 'jeers' was said under their breath to one another. I was still grabbing my beer off of the table by the time they had already slugged a quarter of their ales as if it were milk. They had the white foamy mustaches to complete the simile.

Cian began the meeting. "Oisin here is what's dubbed a fountain. Seems to know a great many things about a many people."

"A supergrass," I said. "So what's the trick? How do you stay alive?"

213

"A super — what now?" The two native Irishmen looked to one another for the meaning of the term.

"Means you have a lot of people to tell on, Oisin."

"Aye. I'm a trusted lot," he said. "I pass on what I can when I can slide it through without suspicion." His accent was as thick as the beer he drank. No matter how many words he used that I was familiar with, I still strained to understand him.

"And this thing in February? That was a big deal. You were able to slide that by?"

Cian broke in. "That was a grand bit indeed. Made my year, it did."

"It was a rare bit but there were many who knew 'bout it. Not solely me," Oisin said.

"So are you Garda?"

"Naw. I get free of my indiscretions with a turn of word from Cian."

"So what turn of words could you give me about a large shipment of assault weapons headed for the States?" I looked around the table like I was finally glad to be talking with someone who could help me.

He had a look of mixed confusion and shock which he fixed on Cian. The young man was stunned into silence which he filled with the consumption of Guinness. Oisin drained his glass and continued his apparent look for help from Cian. It was also apparent how often he frequented that establishment because three more pints arrived virtually the moment he finished his adult milk. Cian also gunned his back and received his replacement. Mine was still full with a new one delivered as backup.

"I know nothin' of guns marked for the new world," Oisin said.

"What is this colonial times? New world?"

"Phrasin' matters not, fella. I don't know 'bout those guns." He looked scared. I had enough street smarts and had interrogated enough people in my short time in Troop H to know that I was being shined.

"Let me put it to you this way, guy. I've got a network of felons back home that have now been caught twice with their hands

214

in the cookie jar. H & K G3A4s a plenty, among many others. They are an Irish network. Not Irish like you, but Irish just the same. Anybody who might have known about the guns they got caught with is now dead. I also have information that those suedo-Irish are runnin' guns around my city and beyond to make money for your Irish. G3s are the assault weapon of choice for the Irish. The IRA. Especially after stealing so many in the Norway incident a while back. See what I'm gettin' at? Do you see where the dots connect? Now you, being the 'trusted lot', must know about when and where a new shipment is being sent over to replace all the weapons that are currently in a federal holding facility."

"Are ye mental?" Oisin's eyes were wild and crazy looking.

"I've been told that I'm insane a time or two, yes."

"If what yer sayin' is true, lad, that's a tall order to be filled. Trusted or no, they'll use only top people for that work. I'm not top people."

"I think Cian here can probably incentivise you to make more of an effort. I want to know the when and how. Those guns get through customs somehow," I said.

"Ye understand your not just putting me neck in, but me arse as well. Enquirin' minds tend to turn up missin'."

"They're going down, Oisin. How do you say? Nicked? You can be with them or not. Your call."

"And how does one live through such a plan?" He looked at Cian when asking the last. He knew any promise I made at freedom and sanctuary were wasted words. Another round of drinks were brought to the table. All of us were falling behind, me more so.

I told him how he could steer clear of the troubles with my unsolicited, sage advise. "The same way you have been. Don't get caught."

"Of course. I'm the only garsún breathin' free air. Couldn't be me who told tales," Oisin said.

"How did you do it in the past?"

Oisin again looked at Cian for help. "This lad is funny as rubber crutches, Cian. Where'd ye find him?"

Cian didn't answer. Instead the two swallowed the rest of the pints of black and began on the queued round. I was struggling to finish my first, two waiting behind it. I had a feeling there was going to be a third if I didn't man-up.

Oisin told me of the February affair, albeit with reluctance. The IRA had a warehouse in Newtowncunningham, near the border of northern and southern Ireland, near Londonderry. Just south of the United Kingdom. That warehouse stored hundreds of kilos of explosive material, bomb making hardware, Russian rocket launchers, and shoulder-fire missiles. He had been sent that far north on 4 February of 2004, with a band of other Volunteers to caravan out a small portion of the vast supply on lorries, namely the launchers and missiles. The trip back to Dublin with the large withdrawal was a success, only Oisin had spent the money he had been paid to execute the transaction poorly. He had been caught trying to turn those Irish Euros into more by investing and turning over large quantities of heroine. He was busted by Garda Detective Cian Daly on 8 February.

Oisin fessed up to both the Dublin withdrawal of weapons, which was long gone, and the Newtowncunnigham trove. By the time the anti-terrorism crew arrived at the Dublin location on 13 February, the safe house was empty. Cian and his group within the anti-terrorism division went north and succeeded in commandeering the warehouse there. The simultaneous raids had very different outcomes.

Much of the Newtowncunningham trove was outdated and in danger of accidental detonation. The seizure was deemed a success, however. Accolades abound for Cian Daly and his crew. 13 February, 2004 was a big day in Cian's career.

Not so much for the Dublin attempt. They had come up empty. Literally. The abandoned building had not so much as a trace of gunpowder or explosive material. It didn't even make the dailies as not to spoil the glory of the Newtowncunningham raid.

Oisin didn't spend a single day in detention. Cian let Hanamy go after the fess-up and Oisin watched in pretend astonishment when the raids went down. He said that he was able to get away with informing back then because there were many people who knew about it.

I was still nursing my second Guinness at the completion of the story. The queue of beverages was getting lengthy and I was receiving help on them from the other two gents who had caught up and were finishing theirs, and now mine, with ease. They weren't drunk, not even close. Not that I could tell either way. But they were feeling more affects of alcohol than I was for sure. Something wasn't sitting right with me, and I was sure it had nothing to do with the beer.

31

THE TRIP BACK TO DUBLIN WAS LACKLUSTER. Same roads, same Stiff Little Fingers CD. Cian told me that he wanted to go to the pub when we got back, which I had to spend the hour and change declining the invitation. He also wanted to drop me off at the Arlington Hotel, which Rowena specifically told me not to go near. I'm not usually one to follow rules or instructions, but she knew the city and this lot better than I did so I declined that offer as well. He dropped me off in front of the Garda station near Pheonix Park, where I walked several blocks zig-zagging to ensure I wasn't followed. Once I was sure, I hailed a taxi.

My failure to remember the address where I had hailed the cab to the Garda station that morning made the ride longer and more expensive than it had to be. I finally sorted it out, recognising some of the old buildings and got out of the vehicle €35 lighter.

Rowena was waiting for me in her flat, already tarted up in her uniform. She was 'dressed to be buggered' as she put it. But she didn't want to leave without hearing what had happened to me. I told her it was a long story, asking how her day had gone. She pointed to the corner of the small flat, where my luggage was resting.

She had gone to the hotel in disguise with my room key that she had pilfered when doing my laundry. She was a clever monkey. She said that she wasted no time in the room, threw everything that was possibly mine into the bag and got out of there within a few short minutes. She also said that if she had forgotten anything to let her know and she would go back, but only if it was worth the risk. Rowena had brought another disguise and changed into it prior to leaving my hotel room with my luggage. Essentially she had entered the Arlington one woman, and left a different one towing luggage.

I have to say, I was impressed.

She begged me to tell her what happened when I told her of the trip to Belturbet. I simply mentioned that I went, not who we met or what was learned. She desperately wanted to know but agreed that she should go to 'work' for appearances sake. I promised to tell her the entire story when she returned later that night.

I had no idea that later that night would only be three hours later. She had picked up a 'thick bockety' man as quickly as she could in order to get back to her flat. The drunk man had little whits about him, she said, and her low-ball offer was too good to refuse. He took her to a squalid kip of ill-repute where she 'fit him up' by knocking him out, stealing his money, and taking an indirect route back here.

When I asked her with a chuckle how that behaviour fits with her being a Catholic girl, she said that the money pays for all the drinks she has to buy on the many nights that nobody is interested in her pretend services. Stepping out on their missus was a sin and they should feel lucky for only a lump on the head and a few quid short. *Lucky for them*, I thought.

I explained to her what had happened at Duffy's earlier that day while she stripped out of her nearly non-existent outfit right in front of me. Only three garments and a wig. Row had no need for a bra. She might be Catholic but she was not modest. I'm a recovering Catholic but I didn't think immodesty was part of the ten commandments, apparently she didn't think so either. It didn't take her long to take off the three things she was wearing that could have been sized for an infant, and I was having difficulty focusing on the story while she stood in front of me in the nip.

"Focus on your dealin's and not on me gee," she said bending over to catch my eyes with hers.

"Can you get dressed? You don't have much to look at, but the part that makes you a woman is hard to ignore when your naked."

"Got a colleen back home?"

"Huh?"

"A girl. Do you have a girl waitin' for ye back home?"

"No. Not really. Why?"

"I'm the colour curious, ye cheeky devil." She left the parlour to go put something on. It was a normal sized tshirt, which means it was oversized for her. She was back in all of ten-seconds without her wig. "You look at me like you've not seen a woman in some time."

"I don't think we treat being naked quite the same way you do here. Or maybe it's just you."

"Oisin is the lad that feeds your Cian Garda Fella. Yeah?"

"Yeah. And as far as I can tell, he hasn't fed him anything since February. Meanwhile, he hangs out in the safe house and goes to work for the IRA when called upon. He also stays out of prison or jail or whatever you call it here. He's got quite the deal for himself."

"And you believe he'll fess up what yer lookin' for?"

"I'm not sure. Something doesn't seem right. He kept looking at Cian for the go ahead. Like he wasn't sure it was a good idea to talk with me. The February bust didn't seem to phase him, it was when I started asking about the new shipment."

220

"He's lookin' to his handler is all."

"Maybe Row. Maybe .... "

"You in your Row. My name is Rowena ye fugue. D e n i   i s
short isn't it?"

"Yes."

"Fer what now?"

"Short for Deni. Can we move on?"

She stared at me for a few moments before speaking.

"Cian gets recognised for the watered down lot, whilst the
Garda in Dublin are left with bell in hand, yeah?"

I sat up straight from the slouched seated position on the
small love-seat. "Yeah. That was lucky that he got that location
huh? It could have been him in Dublin with the short straw."

"Inside deal within inside deals, seems to me."

"Wicked Pissah, Row. Nailed it on the head, I think. That's
what's not right — what's been buggin' me. He and Oisin have it
worked out where he gets the .... wait you called it a 'watered
down lot'."

"Wicked Pissah?" She looked lost.

"Focus Row. 'Watered down lot'?"

"The old stuff that's like to accidentally detonate or is shite."

"Yeah Oisin pulled the real stuff out of the warehouse on the
convoy, which then disappeared sometime before the raid," I
confirmed.

"The business near Londonderry was a put up. Made to look
flash."

"Right. Oisin gives up the fake goods, so they can hide the
real ones. Cian got doped and he doesn't even know it."

"So if I'm straight, Deni, Cian is a fiddle. Oisin gives him
little or nothin'. You'll get nowhere 'til you strike yer own petrol."

"I'm attached to him at the hip. He says where we go and
who we talk to."

"You'll see him in the mornin' then?"

"I think I'm supposed to go over there. I bailed on him to go
to the pub tonight, but didn't make an official time to meet. Did
you see him there? At the Sinn bar, eh .... "

"O'Neills."

"Right. He was there when you went over?"

"Naw. Cian wasn't there."

"Hmm. I wonder where he went? I'll find out tomorrow I guess."

"Don't see him. Go to the consulate."

"You mean customs?"

"Naw. The American Consulate. The Embassy."

"You think I should just go home? I don't know anything yet."

"Naw, ye cunt. Ye go and see about shipments," she looked at me like I was half retarded. I could see the pity in her eyes. "If they hand pick the ports, how do they mean to get the guns out?" She said it slow like she was spoon-feeding me.

"But if I tip my hand, we'll never find the guns. They'll just find another way out."

"Aye. Force their hand, man. Think cheeky like. Tell them they come out the north. Dundalk, Belfast, Derry .... all searched high and low. Raise a fuss. The army gets word that ports are bein' sacked and it'll force their hand."

"You should have been a cop, Row. Fuckin' genius. They'll move quick and they might make a mistake. We know they plan to move them out of Dublin."

"More like they're stored here as well, Deni."

"Right. But where?"

"They'll not want to move them far. Near the port if I had guesses," she said.

It was at that very moment that I decided to hitch my wagon to Rowena. She was smart and had an investigative mind. Cian was lazy and foolish to wait for evidence to fall into his lap. She was keeping me alive both in the literal sense and in the mission. This partnership could work.

32

THE SURGE IN ENERGY IN THE INVESTIGATION called for a celebration. Rowena obtained another bottle of whiskey out of her press, which I continually called the cupboard but the cupboard was the closet which was confusing to me for some reason. She returned from the kitchenette with the bottle along with two glasses. I didn't ask where the old bottle went, I was afraid I already knew. I didn't get as shattered as I had the night before, but I still had some fuzzy spots in my recollection of the events after our successful meeting.

Again I woke up on Wednesday, 18 August, in a fog. Again I woke up naked in bed along side of Rowena who only sleeps in the nip. Again I snuck a peak to ascertain what I already knew as she lay facing away from me.

"You can stop starin' at me arse now." She didn't move or open her eyes as far as I could tell.

"Why are we always naked? I know you always sleep naked, but why am I? I could just sleep on the floor or something."

"You had designs of a sexual nature, but yer whiskey dick let you down."

"Now I know your full of shit. My whiskey dick has never let me down." I had a number of drunken one night stands on a number of occasions, and while the sex may not have always been earth shattering, there was never an equipment failure.

"Suit yourself. I'll get us fixed for breakfast."

I would have to have been more drunk than I thought to have tried any advances on Rowena. There was nothing sexual about her. Not unless I was a Catholic priest and she played the role of the preteen alter boy. She could win an oscar for the role.

By the time I had taken a shower in the undersized standup and changed into an alternate set of clothes that I had packed for the trip, she had challah toast with jam waiting for me. It was then her turn to shower, only she didn't close the door to the tiny bathroom. Instead she called out to me from behind the slender flap that made for a shower curtain.

"I'll come with ye to the consulate." The announcement wasn't an offer or question.

"Don't you have work today?"

"Nothin' to report. The story is with you."

"Is that really a good idea to be seen walking around with me? You said that it was dangerous."

"Consulate will be safe. 'Sides, word will get 'round that you've a meeting with Finn Rourke the start of next week. You'll live that long I expect."

"I have a meeting with Fin next week? When were you going to tell me that you set that up?"

"I told ye last night, Deni. Can't ye remember? Have ye always had trouble with memory? I didn' think ye was that pissed."

"No. And I wasn't 'that pissed'. I just don't remember everything from last night is all. I definitely don't remember you sayin' that. Anyway, you don't think he'll try to have me killed by then? What's to stop him from sending Kane or Dunn to take care of me before then?"

"He'll be interested in what ye know. Dead men don't tell tales, but they can't fess up what they've shared and with who neither. They'll keep tabs on ye, but you'll be alive 'til the 16th at least, I reckon."

"You reckon? Well that's comforting."

The American Embassy is located on Pembroke Road or R118, which is about ten kilometers away. We packed ourselves into Rowena's subcompact 2002 Renault *Clio* for the trip. There were four doors plus the rear hatchback but only two side doors were needed. My knees were in my stomach in the passenger seat and I wished that I could rip it out, sit the back seat for the added leg room. I am not a large man, Rowena was tiny. There is no way that the two of us should have had to logistically sort out where our arms and shoulders would cohabit. The twenty minute ride was an unhumorous two person clown car skit.

She punched a button on her car stereo and U2 came out of the surprisingly large speakers for the tiny car. I could tell it was Bono's voice as it's unmistakeable, but the song I hadn't heard before. The recording was from a live performance. The cheering crowd in the background was also unmistakeable. Row explained that it was a bootleg of *Sometimes You Can't Make It On Your Own*. They performed the song in a recent concert before it was scheduled to be released in a few months on the forthcoming album called *How To Dismantle An Atomic Bomb*. 'I never miss a show' she said. She also said that she 'wanted to have Edge's babies' and that U2 was 'The best feckin' rock band on the planet'. I just thought the music was good.

The round building looked more like an isolated hotel than an official embassy to the United States. The iron fence surrounding it looked more like the bars of a prison cell, only the vertical bars had spear-like ornaments on the top of each one meter column. There was a gate for cars, but ours wasn't allowed in. Maybe because the heavily armed security team didn't think that the conveyance we were in was actually a car. I had my doubts as well.

We parked on the street and were asked for identification prior to being let into the secure building. My passport was still being held at the Arlington, but I was let through with my Massachusetts driver's license. The guard may or may not have seen my badge.

Rowena had a more difficult time getting in despite having all of the documents one would possibly need to get in. Passport, Driving Licence, press documents, public health card, and the like. Everything but her birth certificate. She was eventually let in and we were escorted to someone at a director level, as per our request.

I was met with a cold stare upon my first request to speak with the Consulate General or some sort of Ambassador, but when I said it was an issue of national security to the United States we were led to a waiting area. Eleven September was still fairly present on the minds of those whose job it was to protect our citizens, even abroad.

Director Humphrey listened intently to my entire spiel after we were made to wait over an hour to speak with somebody high on the food chain. He was uncomfortable with the press being on hand for the telling of the story, but I made it clear that she would be present for the meeting or there wouldn't be one. That if there was no meeting and a catastrophic event happened, she would

226

make sure that the world knew that he refused the meeting that could have prevented it.

I played it straight for the most part.   I told of the circumstances that led to the deaths of Danny and Roxy. Of Breen. I explained that I was working with a member of the Anti-terrorist task force within the Garda Síochána to track the guns, but that detective wished to remain anonymous for reasons of cover. That the IRA was about to move an armament by boat to Boston. I left out any mention of Sinn Féin as Rowena pointed out that the supporters of the party were vast and hidden.   I also made Humphrey believe that the trafficking was going to come from an as yet unidentified port in Northern Ireland. In truth, I said that to him outright. Which was a big fat fucking lie.

Humphrey seemed to have his political appetites whet by the information. Enough facts were thrown in along with conjecture. I gave him the names of my US handlers. Walter. Glibczieck, federal prosecutor.   Lieutenant Manny Titanitaukis, my boss.   Even the New Hampshire lawyer, Ryan Wells so Humphrey could fact-check the Breen story. I urged him to check the names but quietly as this was a quiet mission.   He was willing to trade favors for the opportunity to advance whatever agenda he had rolling around his large, salt and peppered head.

Our favors were simple because we knew that they were not likely to find the weapons that we had told them they would find. Not in the wrong ports and cities. I wanted the crate number and cargo ship identification in order to have my bosses seize them when they arrived in Boston. Humphrey agreed. Rowena wanted to have exclusive rights to the information and interviews that was to be forwarded to the press.   She would be the first if only pressmen to have the story. He again happily agreed. He wanted to be the one to liaise with the United Kingdom and quarterback the search.

Only there would be no story. In the words of Row, they would be left with 'fuck-all'. While he liaised and quarterbacked, while the authorities were turning over every rock and searching every crevice in Northern Ireland, the weapons would be set to move in the South.

We left the meeting after declining protection or sanctuary. I told Humphrey that I needed to contact my Garda connection and re-acquire my passport from my hotel. I assured him that I would be fine and back on a plane to Boston as soon as I knew the information that he agreed to provide. He gave me a direct phone number to call him and I was to do so at a minimum of once per day. The 'information highway went both ways,' he said.

Rowena and I were pleased with ourselves.

So far, our ruse had worked.

33

OUR SMUG SATISFACTION WAS SHORT LIVED, however. The meeting with Director Humphrey had gone to plan, and we had another plan lined up for how to go about attaining my passport from the Arlington Hotel O'Connell Bridge.

Row drove us back to her flat to don disguises in order for the plan to work. Because of her various undercover reporting assignments in her eight years in the field, thirty on the planet, she had a wide array of costuming in her tiny home. She made herself into women of various sizes and shapes, sometimes even men.

The plan was to sneak into the hotel in costume, go up to the room and run through it one last time to ensure that there was nothing in it that I had left behind. I found it unnecessary since I hadn't spent but much time in there other than to sleep off hangovers since I had checked in, and Row had already been there, but I went along to get along. Rowena insisted that the hotel was at a minimum being watched, probably from the lobby, if for no other reason than to track my movements. I would then call down to the desk, informing them that I would be checking out. I would then politely request that the concierge bring my passport up to the room in exchange for the room key while she exchanged her original costume for another. We would then leave from an emergency exit on the side of the building unseen, an exit she had noticed when she had retrieved my luggage.

I didn't like my disguise. Row wanted to exploit the fact that I choose to have no body hair, save for my head. To put it bluntly, I made a muscular and ugly woman. The wig, hat and oversized sunglasses could only hide so much of my face. She said that they would be looking for me, a man. Women would garner little attention unless she was an attractive woman. There was no fear that I would get a second look.

She, on the other hand, did want to attract attention. Mostly to take it off of me as I insisted that nobody would think that I was actually a woman. Transvestite maybe. But not a woman. Row donned a blonde wig, large stuffed bra, and god only knows what to accentuate hips and buttocks which didn't exist. Rowena looked stunning, I have to admit. She could have picked up any man that she wanted, only to be disappointed if the evening crescendoed into sharing a bed. The hour glass figure was an elaborate hoax that would have fooled even me. She had the dimensions of Barbie. The fact that a bust, waist, hip proportion like Barbie was biologically impossible didn't diminish the unreasonable desire for it.

That night we called two cars to pick us up four blocks from Rowena's flat, as there was no possible way we could take her *Clio*. Her shapely disguise made it unlikely that she would be able to drive, nor would I be able to fit next to her with my new bust and big hat. Add to the logistical nightmare in the risk of someone getting the plate number off of her car and arguments 'pro Renault' were null and void.

Row and I arrived separately. Her car dropped her off at the front entrance first. She attracted all sorts of attention, which made my exit from my separate cab and entrance into the lobby completely unseen. She took the large formal stairs out of the lobby while I took the lift. There was no way that I would be able to negotiate stairs in heels. I could barely pull off walking in them on a flat surface.

I had to wait for the lift to arrive down on the ground floor, so we arrived on the top floor, which would be called the fourth in America, at the same time. We could not have planned it better.

The hallway was empty with the exception us. She was nonchalant as she searched her purse for a room key that didn't exist while I fumbled for the actual key from mine. I stopped short of inserting the key when I noticed the 'Do Not Disturb' sign hanging from the door knob. I looked both ways down the hall as I removed the hangar, showing it to Row. She gave a shrug of her shoulders which told me that neither of us had utilised the sign prior to or in the process of leaving the hotel room.

I used the key to gain access as quickly and as quietly as I could. Whomever was on the other side of the door needed to be surprised. In the police academy they teach you to enter low when gunfire is suspected. Armed suspects who don't want to be questioned or apprehended tend to aim high for the chest or face.

Turning the unlocked knob ever so gently, I crouched down leaning into the door with my side. The narrower the target the more difficult to hit, even low. With the door ajar, I slowly opened it while listening for any noise. I could hear none.

Upon the door opening wide enough to peer in, I knew why the sign was hung. Room service or any other hotel employee would have most definitely caused a commotion when seeing the room.

At a near crawl on the floor, I entered the bathroom which was the immediate left inside the hotel room. It gave me the opportunity to listen for any movement, get out of immediate gun range, and inspect the bathroom for occupants. No other human in the bathroom. I kicked off my heels, and charged left down the hall but nobody else was there either.

"It's clear."

Row entered the room and gasped. My hotel room, for lack of a better term, was fucked up. Somebody had lost weight destroying the place. This kind of damage takes energy and determination. What they were looking for was anyone's guess. Or maybe they were sending a message.

"Jesus, Mary. We've got to get out. Sharpish like."

"I'm with you. Let me call the desk." Only the phone was destroyed. Shit. "Can you call the desk from your cell?"

She dug into her purse and retrieved her mobile. She fiddled with the phone for a few seconds and handed it to me. It was ringing. The woman at the front desk announced the name of the hotel and stated that she was very eager to help. I believed her and told her what I wanted and that I was in a bit of a hurry. I had an imaginary flight to catch.

"Be right up sir," she said.

"Row, get changed and quick." But she was already on it. Unabashed, she stripped down to the alternate costume that was already underneath the Barbie disguise. I looked around the room amased. Full-on stunned. Even the wallpaper was shredded off of the walls. Curtains torn down. Mattress was knifed, pillows disemboweled. Desk and dressers were destroyed. Whomever had been in the room didn't like the program on the tele one bit.

"How'd they get in the room and do all of this damage without being heard, Row?"

"You've taken a piss in someone's shak shuka."

"I have no idea what that means, but if you're telling me that I've made an enemy I'd have to agree."

The knock on the door gave both us a start.

"Be the wife," I whispered.

"Aye. Let's get on with it."

"Who is it?" I quickly made my way to the toilet.

"Hotel Concierge sir."

I handed Row the key and jumped into the bathroom. With that door closed, she opened the main door to the room.

"Husbands on the toilet," she said in her least Irish accent and with the door opened only a crack. "Here is the room key. Are there any incidentals?"

"Eh, no. I'm only allowed to give the passport back to the holder, miss. Obvious reasons I'm sure."

I heard the concierge making trouble. I yelled out to him, nearly deafening myself with the hollow echo of the bathroom. "It's ok. I'm just going to finish my business in here, and then we will be on our way. We have a flight to catch immediately. Can you give my passport to my wife please?"

"I'm really not allow — "

" — and if you could call us a taxi and have them out front, that would be great. We are running very late and don't want to chance missing the flight."

After a mental wrestling match, the concierge agreed. "Of course. Thank you very much for staying with us." He handed my passport to Rowena and made his way toward the lift.

She closed the main door, opened the bathroom door and said, "Let's get the feck outta here. Now like."

We hauled ass down the stairs that Rowena had taken up. I was carrying heels, purse and trying to hold my skirt up so I didn't fall. One floor up, on the first floor, there was a large and open landing. One could see the entire lobby from that vantage point and either finish walking down the main staircase to it, or take the smaller side stairs to the emergency exit.

Rowena hesitated at the landing, looking around the lobby while I caught up to her down the stairs. She spotted what she wanted to see within a few seconds and guided me down the side stairs with a bit too much force. I nearly fell down the remaining twenty stairs to the base. The only thing that stopped me was the open railing on the right side of the stairs jammed into my armpit. I held myself from catapulting down the rest of the way like a gymnast falling onto one of the parallel bars.

"Hurry," she said. "They're charmin' up the lobby."

"Who's they?" I regained my balance and took the remaining stairs two at a time down to the exit.

233

"Sinns. Keepin' an eye on ye, they are," she said.

"Yeah? Charmin' the paint off walls I'm sure."

"Aye. I'd know them lads anywhere. From the pub. See them every night."

"Tonight would have been the last time."

"Aye. Means we're takin' the right path."

"I hope you're right."

34

THE IMMEDIATE THREAT WAS OFF OF US by the time that we had returned to Rowena's flat. We made sure that we hadn't been followed. We ran from the Arlington Hotel O'Connell Bridge as fast as possible, Row taking the lead with a novice transvestite in tow, running seven blocks where we shared a taxi back to another corner that was yet another six or seven blocks away from her flat. I was in great physical shape save for the past several nights of damage to my liver and the escape was exhausting.

We barely spoke during the trip back to the flat. Both of us were more concerned with the possibility of being followed. Watching every vehicle that followed our taxi. Scrutinising every pedestrian that noticed our harried travel. Once we felt safe, which wasn't until we entered the flat, the conversation came in the form of bouncing theories off of one another.

"The Sinns had to have followed me to the hotel," I said.

"When? Ye haven't been back to the hotel, have ye? Ye've been with me. Somebody knows who ye are, Deni."

"What is the possibility that it's random? American in the hotel .... "

"Naw. You're graspin'."

"Maybe somebody at the hotel is a member of party."

"Then the concierge wouldn't have come alone and without a fuss, hey? Who'd ye mention the hotel to?"

"I might have mentioned it to the dock superintendent. I'm not sure."

"We'll go see him tomorrow," Row said. It didn't sound like a suggestion.

"Why? Why go there if he was the rat?"

"See if he mighn't know somethin' or found information. We'll know by the look of him if there's a plot. Who else?" Row was waving to me like she was a traffic guard motioning me to move forward.

"Nobody. Cian may have told Oisin, but why?"

"To what end ye mean? To kill ye. Seems clear."

"Why would Cian want to kill me? He is working with a United States Federal Prosecutor. If I die, he'll have some explaining to do."

"He mightn't have been deliberate. Just in passin'. This Oisin'd get a chuff up if he gave ye to the IRA."

"Maybe. We should check him out too. Hey Row? Did you mention it to anyone you work with?"

"Me editor. But I doubt he gave your room a goin' through."

"No but he could have told someone else who could have done it. Like you said, nothin' deliberate."

"Naw. Graspin' again."

I paused to strip out my alter ego and think the situation through. The pile of large women's clothing next to the sofa was getting high. Row, ever the tidy one in her small space, picked the garments up off of the floor. She returned with a random selection of clothes from my luggage.

"Put some trousers on. We're not like to solve the mystery tonight. Might take care of yourself, however. Common theme is someone wants to make a hell on earth for ye. In the end, seems clear that neither IRA nor Sinns care for yer help."

"Yeah. Seems clear. They aren't really hinting, Row and I'm unarmed. I came over to this side of the pond to find out some information and get back on a plane. I can't go up against the IRA. That would be insane. Besides, that's Cian's job. I'll let him know what happened in the morning. I'll poke around a little more with you and Cian, but either way I need to get home. I'll meet Fin next week and see about gettin' outta here the next day."

"Sure that's wise?" She sat down next to me on her sofa. I was still undressed, the pile of clothes she gave me on my lap. The only cloak of any kind was the tapestry of tattoos under the cold sweat from the run on my skin. Her voice remained calm.

"Sure what's wise, Row? Going home empty handed or poking around?" My voice was not calm.

"If they are holdin' court in the Arlington lobby, Deni, they'll be holding court at the airport as well, I don't mind tellin' ye."

"So I can't leave and I can't investigate this without being chopped up and dumped in the Atlantic. Great. I'm all about busting some heads, but I'm defenseless. One on one I'll take on whoever they wanna throw at me. But a fuckin' army in another country? Fuck that. That's suicide and I ain't no martyr."

"We may be able to sneak ye out to Scotland or England. Fly home from there, hey?"

"In truth Row? I've got no home to go back to. Those assholes burned down my house with two other families in it. I watched them suffocate from breathing in all of that smoke and carbon, then roast like a fuckin' Christmas ham. I think I came here partly for payback and partly to get away from it all."

"A man without a country." She moved yet closer to me, put her skinny arm around me. She slowly massaged my shoulder with one hand and pulled me toward her with the other. My head rest on her bony shoulder. "We can sort this out."

Some time passed in silence, then she confided. "I've covered some bombings. Seen the devastation. Ye never get that smell outta yer nose. The burnt flesh. The sight of it. Haunts ye 'til death I imagine."

She kissed my temple, then pressed my head into her neck below her chin. She just held me in silence. I was thankful for it. It was a touch that I didn't know that I needed. Some time had passed that way, it could have been a year for all I know. I was lost in the moment. Lost in thought.

Rowena held on to me, kissing the top of my head every so often. The tiny woman was strong. Not so much in the physical sense, but in the spiritual. She was made of tough stock. Of strong fiber. Of durable faith and morals. But all of us have a breaking point, and that embrace was hers. That vulnerability.

She lifted my face from below her chin, raising it to hers. She stared into my eyes without competition. Row looked into my eyes as if to see if the feelings she had at that moment would be found in me. At least that is what I read in her pale brown eyes. Maybe I was trying to figure out why I was attracted to this woman. Maybe she was trying to figure out why she was attracted to me.

I don't have the same faith as she. I am a Catholic, same as Row. But the resolute knowledge of the difference between good and evil is not the same. Between sinner and sainte. Who determines what is right and wrong? Like between two lovers? We had not exchanged vows. But for that moment we both knew what was right.

The communication between us that followed was from touch and feel. No words were spoken, none were needed. Our mouths met, soft and gentle at first. Tongues caressed. Her hands moved from my jawline to the back of my neck. Mine tucking the wisps of her short hair behind her ear. The pile of clothes on my lap was no more, falling onto the floor between us. We kissed long at length, enjoying the feel and taste of the other.

A rush of adrenaline came back. This time not because I felt like I was in danger, but in a wanton desire. Our pulses were raised. I gently and steadily moved closer to her, on top of her. Row slid back on her side of the small sofa, head resting on the

238

pillowy arm. Her slim body lay nestled under me and between my legs. She warmed her hands on my waist, back and buttocks. I didn't mind. In fact I craved her touch.

Rowena's appetites and juices also began to flow. Realising that she was fully clothed, and obviously wanting to correct that, she pushed me up but not completely away from her. I went to my knees while she sat upright. She removed her blouse, then continued to kiss me. Row grabbed my hand and pulled me to follow her down the short hallway and into the bedroom that we had slept in but had not yet truly shared. She adeptly began removing what clothing she could along that short journey with her free hand.

She pushed me down onto the bed. It was her turn to be on top. To take charge. The remainder of her garments were removed, no longer necessary for the pleasurable task at hand. I lay there, watching her. Not because she was graceful. Not because she was putting on an alluring show. Quite the opposite in fact. The nimble woman was on a mission. That mission was me.

Her mouth was used for more than her gentle and passionate kisses. She tasted, caressed and pecked whatever she wanted. Row moved about my entire body, siphoning me with her lips and tongue from head to toe.

The lovemaking was gentle at times, animalistic at others. Rowena's spry body moved on mine or with mine as the positions changed. I didn't think about anything other than pleasing her, not even my own pleasure as it built to a geysering release.

I have been wrong about a great many things in my life. Stealing cars as a cocky preteen. Wrong to want to spend my career as Massachusetts State Police Detective. Wrong about what I thought made for an attractive woman. There was nothing immediately striking about Rowena. Nothing that conjured sexual thoughts or desires. I was never more wrong about this woman, though. She was gorgeous. A sexual Jedi.

35

NEITHER OF US SLEPT THAT NIGHT. Or the next. I could tell you that we spent the two days in torrid love. That we used each other to fulfill each and every sexual whim. But that would be a lie. We did spend some time doing that. Afterwards exchanging in post coitus dialogue with same fervor as we had the physical acts during it. The talk wasn't of our acts of love though. These passionate talks were of the mission. The mission to bring the illicit activities to light. To strategise. To find the cargo hold. It was as if each of our carnal releases had shed any and all of our apprehension or fear as well.

Rowena suggested that we go down to the docks. It was half 'til three on Friday morning. She knew from other investigations, other reporting, that the dock workers start their first shifts early. If this supervisor that I spoke with, Niall, was working, he would be present earlier than the rest of the workers to direct them once they arrived.

The drive to the docks seemed longer than it had when Cian and I went though it took a quarter of the time. For one, the tiny car was claustrophobic. All of the U2 in the world couldn't make the car bigger. Every turn in the road pushed me either to my right against Row or against the tiny passenger door. Second, Rowena was driving like a fucking maniac. *Bullet The Blue Sky* was blaring while we bulleted down Promenade Road. I don't know why she was in such a hurry, but she was.

Because of the size of her Renault, we were able to drive along the pier where Cian and I had walked. I was thankful for not having to walk on the north side of the Dublin port, but there were some tight spots that we encountered that I was sure Row was going to get us killed. At an early point we passed the small shuttle bus loading the dock workers in order to carry them to the same location we were traveling to, nearly sending us into one of the enormous containers. The tiny bus packed and carried the workers from the main gate along the north side of the port to their work area. It was the commuter equivalent of Row's Renault. We dodged in front of the parked lorry and left it in our dust.

The sun would soon illuminate the horizon of the ocean in the distance as far as the naked eye could see. Sunrise was just two hours or so away. It would become increasingly less dark, obstacles which were narrowly avoiding would become more visible. I had mixed feeling as to whether I wanted to see the near misses or live in the dark.

Row parked her go-cart sized car between two large containers. The doors were able to open just wide enough for both of us to exit the vehicle. I explained where I had met Niall McCourt the first time I had gone out there. On foot. The converted container that had been modified into an office was dark. The one window cut high into the container was too high to peer in, but it was obvious that no light was turned on. In the dark of the early morning, that meant that nobody was in the office or Ray Charles was now in charge of the Dublin cargo dockworkers.

I turned the knob and tugged on the office door, but it was as we assumed. Locked.

241

"I guess we wait for the bus that you passed to arrive," I said.

"Odd that."

"Odd what, Row?"

"Not a soul here to manage the workers. I've been here before, Deni. Someone's here to make work for the lads. Punch-ins. Give direction. Turn the feckin' lights on."

"So what are you saying?"

"I've already said what I'm sayin'. It's feckin' odd."

"Don't let the fact that we've slept together cloud your judgment, Row. No need to get snippy with me."

"How quickly you change from scared boy to bucklepper. I'm not causin' a stir, fella. I'm just pointin' at facts."

"I don't know what a bucklepper is, but I wasn't scared. I was just caught up in the moment. That's all. Don't get things twisted."

"Ah. Right then." She said that she understood, but the shaking of her head and staring out at the rising sun indicated that she didn't. I let it go.

"Maybe Niall is on the bus. Maybe he's runnin' late today."

After a long breath she turned and looked at me. "Help me stack a pile. I'll go into the office through the window."

"They'll be here in a few minutes. It'll take that long to pile up the crates and barrels. If the window is even unlocked." I went into my wallet and pulled out my pins as I went up the decking outside the office door."

Row was protesting, telling me it would take too long to try and pick the lock but she wasn't able to finish her argument. The door was unlocked and opened by the time she had closed the gap between us.

"Quite good with that kind of mischief, aren't ye?"

"In fairness this was an easy lock. I hope whatever they store in here isn't important."

"Let's not stand on ceremony. Carry on now," she said.

I entered the container/office first. The door opened outward swinging out and to my right. Rowena was on the stairs behind me waiting for the door to open past her, while I felt around the left side of the door for the light switch. The light came on, the fluorescents flicking their way to life. It took a brief second or two for my eyes to adjust to the harsh lighting. It took another moment for me to interpret what was before me.

"Don't come in here, Row."
"What's the crack, now?"
"Nothing good. Wipe down the door knob!"
"With what?"
"Your fuckin' shirt! Anything. We gotta get outta here. Now." I used my shirtsleeve to wipe down the light switch. She used the bottom of her cotton shirt to polish the knob out on the stairs. I tried to move down the stairs, past Row but I couldn't. "Is it wiped?"
"Aye. As best I can."
"Then let's get the fuck out of here."

I jumped over the wooden railing off the steps and onto the dock. Moving quickly back toward the car. I turned to realise that she wasn't following me. She couldn't help herself. She looked in before closing the door behind us. Row muttered a prayer while giving herself the sign of the cross, never completing either task. I should have turned the lights off when I wiped down the switch. Some things you just can't un-see.

Turning back toward the office, I raced back to her. I closed the office door with my elbow and tossed Row who was now catatonic over my shoulder. She put up no struggle nor said a word as I ran with her back to the car.

The dockworkers were always quiet during the morning lorry ride to the daily punch-in. Many of them would attempt, no matter how feeble, to get the extra winks their bodies required before the start of their shift. The first shift started early on the Dublin docks. In the winters, the sun wouldn't yet be awake until well into their shifts. Today the sun would be slowly making its way to the horizon when the time-clock would punch the all too early hour onto their manilla-stock cards. Hangovers abound most days. This day was no different in that regard.

The driver had cursed under his breath as the speeding Renault *Clio* weaved in front of the bus, nearly clipping the front as he was trying to load his lethargic workers. His day had just started and it was already terrible. Traffic was unusual on the docks at that hour. Especially going toward it. He continued to pronounce devilish outcomes upon the reckless driver under his breath as he made his way to the destination to avoid a stir with his slumbering cargo.

He was still spitting and sputtering about the incident when the tiny vehicle sped back toward him a short time later. The morning commute was nearly over, about to arrive at the destination, when the same vehicle raced toward him in a game of 'chicken'. The lives of the dockworkers were at stake, a head-on collision with the much smaller vehicle mightn't kill anyone but the occupant of the small auto but he couldn't take the chance. He immediately stuck the manual down, grinding the gearbox while simultaneously braking hard. The undersized bus quickly came to an abrupt stop, causing a small uprising with the men in the back.

The *Clio* dodged around the bus appearing to gain speed rather than slow down. The driver was too busy ensuring that his cargo was unscathed, the occupants of the bus too unaware to identify either the driver or a registration. In a matter of seconds, the offending vehicle had again disappeared.

244

The first dockworker to get off of the bus was the first to open the door to the office. As per usual, the light was on inside for the crew to claim their timecards to begin their day. Unusually, Niall the old sod was not out by the bus greeting everyone shouting demands. The lethargic docksman opened the door to the office, looking right to find his timecard in its usual home. The slotted holder held the usual contents which he removed, slid his card into the clock, stamped and replaced it in its proper spot. As he turned to exit, giving way to the next to start his day, he glanced left. His knees weakened. Bile from his stomach was rising and burning like lava spilling toward the top of a volcano.

"Jesus, Mary and Jos - " The vomit spewed forth despite his desperation to keep it down. The putrid liquid projected out onto the stairs toward his coworkers. He tried to regain his faculties after the first push. " — uuuuuuuuuuuuuuuuuhhhhhhh. Don't come up here, lads." He braced himself against the door-jam, looking out at the mess he created instead of the mess that was inside the office. Deep breaths.

What was left of Niall McCourt was spread out inside the office. The gruesome scene didn't illustrate exactly how he was killed, only that he was dead and in the most horrific of fashions. One could plainly see that he was tortured, pieces of him cut and torn off. But not how or in what succession. Not that anyone but the Garda detectives would want to know.

Blood was splashed about the inside of the converted container like a crimson paint can had exploded onto the files and binders and desk. Bloody bits of flesh clung to walls while the congealing liquid pooled on the floor.

Niall's severed head rest in the basket for outgoing post. His eyes plucked from their sockets. A knife had been used to cut them out. The same knife appeared to be used to cut open his face, enough to hurt him badly but not so much as to disfigure him to the point where he was unidentifiable. The torn flesh hung off the cheeks and jawline. The knife was stabbed into Niall's right ear as if there was no other place to hold it.

The older man's torso was tied to his office chair. His body had also been carved with entrails exposed to the fluorescent lighting. The freshly torn innards were pulled out of his abdomen, still hanging and dripping down onto the floor. His penis and testicles were removed and on the bloodred floor in front of where he sat.

Fingers and toes were strewn about the floor of the office. Niall's bloody nuggets snipped from the appropriate appendage. They lay under the desk and on shelves and on the floor waiting to be bagged for further identification. A toe rested next to a removed and cloudy eyeball.

The handle of a screwdriver was protruding out from the side of Niall's left knee. The business end of it wedged underneath the kneecap and had been used to pry it out. The right knee was not immediately present. Nor the leg from the knee down that it was supposed to be attached to. It was likely to be inside that death chamber somewhere, just as likely removed as part of Niall's horrific infliction of pain.

"Get the Gardaí. Feck. Phone everyone."

36

IT WAS MY TURN TO GIVE COMFORT TO ROWENA.
She said nothing in the Renault on the way back to her flat. She said nothing when we nearly were in a head-on collision with the lorry that carried the labourers to work. Row didn't make a move when I covered her face, and turned mine, in an effort to conceal our faces from the driver and passengers of the tiny bus as we passed them by. What I had originally thought was catatonic turned out to be reticent silence. She turned off the sound system in her car, no U2. The tears flowed as she looked out the left window, the passenger side of the *Clio*.

Row didn't comment or flinch when we were nearly involved in two other accidents on the trip back into Dublin proper. They would have been my fault, driving on the opposite side of the road on streets that are all but unmarked is not easy.

She got out of the car when we arrived back at the flat in the early morning. Row said nothing as we walked in, she just plopped herself on the sofa in the same spot where I had been sitting and in need of some comfort.

I am not a caretaker, nor a good caregiver. Like the typical male, I presume, it is not that I don't want to provide solace for those in need. It's just that I seem to be incapable. I never say the right thing or do the right thing or at the right time. When I get sick, I want to be pampered and soothed until the illness leaves my system. In the times where I had a girlfriend, Jill or any of the other transient partners, they had always expected the same in return but I could never give it. Not in the way they wanted. Not in the way that they had expected.

So was the case this time. I offered tea. No response. I sat down next to her and put my hand on her knee. She pushed it away. I tried to kiss her, touched her small breast in an effort to be intimate. She pushed me off like I was a rapist.

Rowena had seen, she said in our previous days, a great number of horrific things in her time as an investigative reporter. Bombings and murders, terrifying all. I understood the difference this time. I knew what made the sight at the docks so different from what she had seen in the past. A bombing happens in an instant. The poor prick that blows up has his brains and body spread out all over east Jesus before he knows what happened. People being shot sometimes suffer for minutes before either receiving medical care or die. A murder is more terrifying, more painful, but the dirty business happens in a relatively short time in order not to be caught in the act.

Niall McCourt was tortured. Torn limb from limb. He was cut, disemboweled, castrated, stabbed, and chopped. His demise took time. He suffered plenty. You didn't need to be a medical examiner or see the first three seasons of CSI to determine that. All it took was one look, one quick peek at the train wreck that you were told not to look at, peak through the fingers covering your face at a horror film, to take in the gruesome scene. If the smell of torched flesh from bombings was stuck into Row's brain, Niall's torture would haunt her for the rest of her days.

248

Since Row was inconsolable, had gone into her room with the door closed and locked, I decided that it was high time to contact my people back home. They were five hours behind, which meant that they were all sleeping at almost midnight their time, but I didn't care.

Tits was not in the precinct of course. He wouldn't arrive at Troop H for six or seven hours yet. He was the least important call anyway. I was working for the feds in conjunction with a local crime. I had already decided that I was going to leave the Staties anyway.

Walter Glibczieck, the federal prosecutor, was my second call. He didn't seem happy to be disturbed at that hour but he said that he was used to it and expected it with the time difference. He said that he received my message, that he had tried to call my hotel room a number of times but I was never there.

I told Walter what was going on. I told him that Cian was of little help. He was more interested in pubs than justice. Whatever the Department of Justice was paying him for support, it was too much. He had led me to two possible sources, one of which was just brutally tortured and killed that morning. I also informed him that I might need legal help if a witness placed me at the scene.

Walter seemed concerned when I told him that I was no longer at the hotel, that the room was destroyed and likely I would have been also if I had been in the room at the time of the breach. Again, I might need legal help if the Arlington Hotel went after me for the damage.

The fact that I was staying with Rowena, and investigating the whereabouts of the gun shipment with an investigative reporter sent Glibczieck over the fucking edge. "The mission was supposed to be clandestine," he said. "Your head is getting fucked up because of a piece of Irish trim," he also said. I lied and told him that there was nothing sexual going on, that she was plugged in and had engaged the very people that I was investigating. I knew what I was doing.

I told him about Oisin Hanamy, the informant Cian used up in Belturbet, and the fact that I didn't like the guy. There was something about him that was off. I asked Walter if he had access

249

to Irish crime files as a United States Federal Prosecutor. "On a limited basis, and only if it's important in a crime within my jurisdiction," he said. It would also tip our hand he pointed out.

In talking with Row, the idea that the February bust was a hoax had percolated in my brain. It seemed about right. I wanted Walter to see what he could dig up. He promised nothing and in truth I didn't expect much. If nothing else I just wanted another set of ears to hear what I was thinking, tell me if any of it made sense.

He seemed disappointed that I hadn't been able to uncover any information about the gun container as of yet. I reminded him that my only real source for information, Niall McCourt, was tortured and killed. That I had only been there about a week and clearly it was dangerous. I hadn't even met Finn Rourke yet, but when I did in a few days I would be sure to ask him nicely if he would give me the manifest information. I was sure he would tell me. Walter said that the sarcasm was noted.

Just as long as he didn't fuck me out of my bonus.

My final phone call was to Ryan Wells. The phone call with Walter had chewed up over an hour. Ryan was 'just headed to bed anyway' when I phoned him. I informed him of what was going on as well and that I was interested in being with Grantes, Wells & Associates on a full time basis. That I wanted to be an associate. This side job was partially for him. For Breen. That I wanted out of the Massachusetts State Police Department. He said that he understood, that he would talk it over with JG but that I was proving myself with this case. He reminded me that if they could prove collusion and conspiracy with a guard or guards through the Winter Hill Gang through the IRA connection, a civil lawsuit would be in order. That I needed to attain that information in order to get additional money from the firm as a result of winning a civil suit on the back end.

I said that I understood completely, and we hung up. I had added pressure in getting information that was proving impossible to attain. But I was going to need every dime when I got back to the states. I hoped that I lived long enough spend it.

Row was still crying or sleeping or whatever when I finished speaking with Ryan. I'm sure that I had rung up a significant international phone bill, but I would sort it out with her later. She was not answering and I needed to go.

I did my zig-zag for a few blocks and picked up a taxi to go to the Garda station near Pheonix Park. I wanted to catch up with Cian. I stopped the taxi a few blocks shy of the station, walking the rest of the way. The Niall murder hadn't just spooked Rowena. It had pissed me off as well.

"Detective Garda Daly is away on an investigation," the reception lady told me when I arrived and asked for Cian. "If ye'd like to wait I'd find out when he might be expected back. Yer name?"

I told her my name and I waited while she did whatever she did to get an answer. Pass it along to someone else? Call him on his mobile? Who knows? I just know that a few minutes passed before another, younger, prettier woman walked me back to Cian's desk. She told me that he was on his way back from an incident on the Dublin docks. I pretended like I wondered what that could be.

Nearly an hour I waited. But in that time I was able to nonchalantly snoop around his desk and work space. I didn't at first, but curiosity had gotten the better of me. A half-full bottle of

Redbreast 12 Year Whiskey was in his locked file cabinet. They don't make very good locks in Ireland in my experience. It was too early in the day or I would have put another dent in the bottle. But that wasn't the best thing that I found in the cabinet. A copy of what I assumed was the complete file for the 13 February, 2004 Anti-terrorism police raid was the treasure. And I struck gold.

I didn't know when Cian would be back, and I didn't want to get caught with the file. I tucked it into my pants along the small of my back and headed toward the door. I let the lady at the reception know that I wanted to go grab a quick mid-morning bite whilst I waited. She nodded like she understood, too busy to deal with an American I presume.

The café around the corner was busy and it had only one table left available. I didn't know how much time I had so I didn't want to go searching further away from the station. I quickly grabbed the last table, much to the dismay of the young gay couple that were looking to occupy it. I knew I was going to have to buy something in order to justify my being alone and taking up a two-top table. The couple already had purchases in hand, I had skipped a step.

From my position at the table I could see the sad looking things they were passing off as pastries in the case. Not interested. The bilingual menu, Gaelic and sort-of English, had only one thing on it that I recognised. One *Sweet American* coming up. I pulled out the thick file from my back, thankfully none of the contents had fallen out. Opening it on the table, I felt the weight of the two homosexual men staring me down. I think one was trying to convince the other to say something to me about stealing the table. I kind of wondered how uppity they would get now that their Irish was up. Hell hath no fury ….

"I'm sorry. I need the table, it's important," I said like I actually gave a fuck. I come from a city where people are not in the least concerned with their fellow citizens. The only people we are remotely kind to are tourists. I was a tourist, so they could fuck off — gay or straight.

The server brought me over an enormous concoction which she explained was a Nutella milkshake. It had mini-marshmallows on top. The *Sweet American* was called such, I can only assume, because of its over-indulgence. But I ain't gonna lie, it was really damn good.

Most of the thick file was a pictorial documentation of the weapons seized. There were many. All were outdated even to the naked eye. The explosives and detonators had been manufactured by Germans for World War II. Although the bust was large, it was not much of a loss for the IRA. You could have offered any of the seized material to a six year old from my neighbourhood and they would have told you that they were good; they could get better, newer, and more reliable stuff on the streets of Southie.

I read the reports that led up to the bust. The call came in to Cian directly. Detective Garda Síochána Cian Daly reported to his superiors on the Anti-terrorism Task Force that the call came in from a known and reliable source. The source, Tadhg O'Carolan, was said to be on the informant payroll. A subsequent investigation to find Tadgh indicated that no such person could be reached. Cian later testified that the informant had gone missing, probably dead after informing the Garda about the trove of weapons in Newtowncunningham. Cian had also been the one to pay Tadgh in cash.

Hmm. Why would the IRA kill an informant that gave the Garda almost nothing? The thought went through my head quickly, then I was on to the next document in the file.

The next set of documents were the records that stated that there were no records. The simultaneous bust in Dublin was just that, a bust. They found nothing. Same informant.

How could this missing Tadgh guy, a 'known and reliable source', be right about one thing and completely out in left field about the other?

I read on. An expense report for the housing and safekeeping of Tadhg O'Carolan. Dated after the seizure. He was being held in a Dublin safe house according to the expense report.

Who were they keeping? He was supposedly already missing by then. Is Cian the one that is making him 'missing'? Why is Cian hiding him from Garda? They are still paying expenses to house this guy.

Another document, listing all known informants and a schedule of payments, when monies were paid and received. No Oisin Hanamy listed.

Wasn't Oisin supposed to be the one who tipped Cian off? Both Cian and Oisin told me in Belturbet, in Duffy's, that he was the 'trusted lot' who informed on the troves. Yet there was no record of him. Cian just happened to go up to Newtowncunningham and become a hero based on the tip from a nonexistent informant? And the guy that is being kept in Belturbet as the real informant is off the books? Something is seriously fucked.

Four documents later, I thought I knew just what it was. As it turned out, I had half of it right. I was in real trouble. Rowena was in real trouble. And trouble was upon us.

I didn't go back to the station.   I bolted out of the cafe, running like my life depended on it. It did. Mine and Rowena's.

37

ROWENA DIDN'T WANT TO COME OUT OF HER ROOM. I ran most of the way back to her flat, getting into a taxi only when I was almost run over by it. I crossed Sráid an Teampaill and failed to look for oncoming traffic. Failed in that I looked in the wrong direction. The taxi stopped in time for me to be on the hood, which the driver called a bonnet. At least that is what I think he kept yelling. He definitely lost his bonnet. It was dented where my right hip and elbow made contact. He thought his Irish was up, but mine was in fighting position. And not in the old-school fighting position like the Notre Dame mascot.

Before it came to him getting a beating, the taxi driver said he would take me to Row's flat. She had told me that pickups and drop-offs in front of her flat were a bad idea. It was unsafe. We were beyond that now.

I didn't want to alarm her, make her any more scared than she already was. She was likely still in some level of shock from what we will call the Niall incident earlier the same day. But I did want her to come out of her room and I wanted it in all of an instant.

My gentle knocks were not getting the job done. My exaggerated calmness in getting her to open the fucking door wasn't either. I heard no answer, no rustling or movement. I didn't have time for her bullsh, so I picked the lock and entered. I wanted to kick the door in but thought better of it, as that would not do in keeping her calm. As calm as possible anyway.

She was sitting upright on the bed but she was passed out. Her chin was to her chest, drool had formed a line to her lap, forming a puddle there. She had an empty bottle of whiskey in her left hand, the top turned over onto her divan and what she didn't consume had been spilled, soaking through to the mattress.

"Shit. Row, you gotta wake up." I gently nudged her. Shook her. Felt her pulse. Her pulse was there but weak. She was beyond drunk. Hammered didn't quite say it either. After tapping her cheeks, her eyes opened but didn't focus on me.

Harder taps to the face. "Wake up. Up and at 'em. You picked the worst time to get fucked up." I lifted her up, attempting to get her to her feet. Her jeans were soaked. The Divan, sheets and mattress were as well. What I originally had thought was spilled whiskey was actually a combination of spilled bottle and spilled bladder. As much urine as booze.

Alcohol poisoning. I had seen it enough times with college kids. Boston is loaded with colleges and universities. Regardless of how accustomed to drinking Rowena was, the body can only process so much alcohol at one time.

The consumption and processing of alcohol by the human body is the exact same for every person, regardless of size. Bigger people can handle more, as are the bodies that are used to the presence of alcohol in their system, but the time it takes to handle the toxin is the same. Whiskey, in this case, starts soaking into the bloodstream right from the mouth through the lining. Without food to mix and aid in digesting, thereby slowing down the immediate uptake into the small intestine, it goes immediately there and into the bloodstream.   Once the molecules are in the bloodstream, it takes about 5 minutes to reach the brain, act as a depressant, and slow down all body functions. The whiskey is then transformed into sugars, for simplicity sake, in the liver.   It takes about 20 minutes for the molecules to reach the liver.   Once there, the liver can then only handle the breaking down of alcohol at a rate of approximately 8 milliliters per hour.

I don't know how many of the 750 milliliters Row drank, but even if she had only a quarter of the bottle, she was going to be drunk for about 23 hours too many.

The dead-weight of a hundred pound woman seemed like ten times that. I positioned her in front of the toilet and stuck my fingers down her throat. Bodily functions may have been slow, but eventually the gag reflex kicked in and the whiskey-soaked bile came up.   But not enough.   Three more times we repeated the process. Finally the dry-heaving began.

Satisfied that there was no more booze in her belly, I now had to deal with the poison that was already in her bloodstream.   I turned on the shower, using only the cold water. I peeled of her urine-steeped jeans and held her under the water. She could kick and scream all she wanted, this was happening.

We didn't have the time for this nonsense. We needed for her to at least get her thinned blood moving. Row went from one set of wet clothes to another, as the process of holding her up while I tried to dry her off after the cold shower were several steps we could ill-afford.   The new outfit clung to her like she had been caught in a mid-morning rain. In a way, she had.

I finally got her into her tiny car after throwing her over my shoulder. I was able to quickly throw a couple of changes of clothes for her into my luggage along with the file that I had taken from Cian. The bag took up what was supposed to be a back seat and the hatchback part of the vehicle, which I later figured out was called a boot. I thought she kept telling me that she *had* to boot, meaning puke, but I digress. Stepping on the petrol pedal of the *Clio* was like begging a dead horse for another mile. But it went. The small car wasn't peppy enough for my taste or immediate needs.

Rowena was conscious but speaking in tongues. She was of no use so I had to stop at a petrol station to buy a map. I had forgotten the way to Belturbet.

Oisin Hanamy's safe house was all but impossible for me to find. But miraculously I was able to find Duffy's. Stumbled upon it really. I parked the car to get my bearings and low and behold I was across the carriageway from the pub. The hour was late by the time that I found the place, so we slept in the cramped car until morning. It was not even noon on that Friday and Duffy's seemed busy from the outside. It was Tráthnóna somewhere in the world.

"Stay," I whispered. A bit like you would a dog. Not like Row was going to go anywhere anyway. She was snoring and sleeping.

After retrieving the file from my luggage, and realising that I had no weapon, I hustled quickly but carefully the back way toward Oisin's. I used the back stairs, same way that we had gone when the three of us went to the pub, only in reverse. My ears trained on every sound.

The closer I got, moving up the back stairs, the more sounds I heard. It sounded like someone was getting a beating. Muffled moans with thumps and undistinguishable commands. The outside staircase was giving audible moans and squeaks of its own.

I was hoping to be undetected, every strain of the old wood sounded to me like a cannon. Much like the teenager who comes home past curfew, thinking that every step could be heard two houses down. In the case of the teenager, the parents probably did know. In my case, I hoped that the sound of the apparent beating would mask my unstealth approach.

I've never heard anyone definitively say whether the slow squeaks over time attracted more or less attention than if the predator moved more quickly, or with one, louder, audible sound and closed the gap in less time. But I chose the former. By the time that I had reached the top landing, there were no more moans from the victim. Just the voice of the attacker, soliciting information that would not seem to come.

There was just a wood-framed screen door separating me from the kitchen, from the torture room that was as disgusting as I had remembered it. I popped my head above the bottom of the torn screen, at waist level, to take in as much of the situation as possible in the shortest amount of time.

A large kitchen and dining area. Devoid of furnishings save for the chair the victim was tied to. Center of the room. Bloody victim, unidentified. Large unidentified male standing before victim, back to me, handle of a pistol sticking out of his waistband. Mold, mildew, garbage bags.

I took it all in, exposed for less than two-seconds. I would have to cover 6 meters before the tormentor realised he was about to be attacked and reacted with his weapon. I hadn't trained in Brazilian jiu-jitsu in over a week; since I had been in Ireland, and I normally would train almost every day. Not that it would make any difference against a gun. I reached for the screen door handle, turning it as slowly as I could yet still turning it. It wasn't locked.

The door cracked open without a sound. I stood crouched and ready to pounce once the door was open enough for me to go through it. Looking through the crack, I noticed the large coil spring that was fastened in place to automatically close the door. It was rusted in the same manner of disrepair as the rest of the flat. Opening the screen door any further would not only let the occupants know I was entering, but possibly the neighbourhood as well.

If I thought about it too long, I would run the same risk of exposure as if I just did it. Rip off the goddamned plaster already. The ear-piercing screech of the coil could have awakened the dead. It may need to be put to the test.

The large, blond man turned and reacted quicker than I would have expected. It wasn't Oisin. He had no look of shock or confusion. He didn't assess the situation and call a meeting. He turned toward me, buried a large knife into the carotid artery at the base of the victim's neck, and reached for his weapon in a fluid motion. He was right-handed, that was his knife hand, and that was the hand he used to reach behind him to draw his pistol. He moved toward me, closing the gap.

I bolted through the door like a track star leaving the line. Only I had not yet heard the gun go off to start the race, nor did I want to. If a full second went by, that was long. His arm had not yet come around from behind him, which I needed to ensure stayed that way. By way of greeting, I raised my left knee into his abdomen, the momentum from my journey from the door and my strike taking the wind out of him. While making contact with my knee, I used both of my arms to hold his right arm behind him. The arm bar would only work if he was unable to spin out of it, which I tried to discourage with repeated blows to his body with my knee.

The mystery man was strong. As much as I tried to pin his arm behind his back, the more he struggled for the opposite. The gun went off, the victim in the chair was hit on his right side. I moved behind the man, which was a calculated risk. He would be able to spin out of the precarious hold if I didn't act quickly. I stomped on his foot and tripped him forward, tugging on his arm and wrist the entire way down. He broke his fall with his left hand. When he made contact with the floor, I heard the snap and felt the arm in my hands weaken. I had broken his right wrist and arm by putting pressure on his wrist and elbow, hyperextending them both. The gun fell to the linoleum floor. I kicked it away from the fray toward the screen door.

I tried to hold him on the floor, but he was able to spin. I had lost my grip on his broken arm. He was down on the ground facing me, ready to continue the fight with one hand. And two feet. He kicked me away from him, sending me into a pile of garbage. The man made his way toward the door, toward his weapon but I reacted and stopped him. He had managed to get to his knees, crawling toward the door when I was able to get a football kick to his ribs.

Without a cry, he rolled away from me and back toward the victim strapped to the chair. He had time to get up draw the knife out of his prey, who's bloody head sagged to his chest. There was no reaction from any of us when blood gushed out of the knife wound. The knife was wielded at me with a fully functioning yet obviously awkward left hand.

The thick file was still nestled in my waistband in the small of my back. I withdrew it and tried to roll it up as best I could. It was like trying to roll up a thick phone book. It can be done but not easily.

The knife came at me. I batted it away with the rolled file, sending an elbow to the striker's face for the trouble, then stepped back again. I could not let him circle me, could not allow him to get close to the door. Each time I tried to get close to the door to retrieve the gun, he would attack me with the knife. Again he didn't react like a person who was hurt and again he attacked. The knife deflected off of the file, slicing my outer bicep while I buried my left fist into his throat.

He stepped back but came at me again before I could assess the damage to my right arm. Before I could get the gun. I again batted the knife away from me with the file, this time it opened slightly as I was losing grip on it. He had lost grip of the knife and it was gone from his hand. This was my chance to end it. I used the thick file on his face, using it to shield his face. Pounding one side of it, the other side slamming into his face. He backed up into the refrigerator, trapped there. I worked his face with my upper body and elbows, smashing into the thick file which was compressing his face. I worked his legs by sending my bony knees into his thighs. Left, right, left, right. He tried to reach for me, reach for anything with his left hand, but the damage was being done and quickly.

The man fell, his tired and beaten legs gave way, no longer able to support him. He fell to the base of the refrigerator, I moved down on top of him. Adrenaline took over. Anger. I continued to beat him as I kneeled on his chest. The weight and strength of my entire body coming down onto his face. Smashing the folder into his broken nose. His broken cheekbones. He tried to move his head to one side or the other for air. For something else for me to pulverise. I regained my composure too late. Too late for the large blonde man.

A near death experience gets the blood racing. Fight or flight. I had been in many of them. Southie. In the cage. When you get into a situation where it is kill or be killed, thinking goes out the window. Instinct takes over or you are the one who gets dead. It's primal. That is why they have someone presiding over the MMA fights in the cage. Inevitably, all fights go to the ground, the pounding and beating won't end until too late. Someone needs to have their head about them to stop the fight, or one of the two men who voluntarily enter the fight will die.

My instincts took over in that safe house. It wasn't a safe house for me, and my life was in danger. And there wasn't a ref in there to call the fight. Kill or be killed. The man was dead. I beat the life out of him. I'd like to say that I am sorry about that, and the truth is that I am. But not for the reason you think. I'm sorry because I could no longer question him.

The man that was strapped to the chair was Oisin. I sat there trying to take an inventory of the situation, on the linoleum floor. His face and body was beaten so badly, so bloody, that it wasn't until further scrutiny that I was able to determine who my victim's victim was. Dead.

Oisin had been beaten within an inch of his life, that last inch taken by the knife wound. The bullet hole to his side was unnecessary and after-the-fact.

I wiped the outside of the bloody file on my victim's shirt while I searched him for a clue as to who he was. Why he wanted Oisin dead.

Mobile phone.

The message on the inside of the Hutchinson flip-top mobile phone said:

86 dunn

86 dunn? My mind raced.

The blonde man killed Oisin. *Did Oisin know where Dunn is?* I had gone there because he and Cian had a cocked-up story. I wanted to confirm what I had suspected. And what I suspected put both Rowena and me at great risk.

The term '86' originally came from the Irish. It was then carried over to the New World and then used in the Old West when settlers pushed westward across the country. The term has survived for use in restaurants. Every restaurant and public house in the world. Why? Because that is where the term was first used. 86 originally meant proof. As in whiskey. Whiskey was aged in barrels. The longer it aged, the higher the alcohol content. When a pub, or later a saloon, ran out of 122 proof — you were 86'd. In reference to the lower proof, the under developed stuff. Now, chefs yell to the waitstaff to '86 meatloaf', meaning take it off the menu. It is no longer available.

Somebody ordered to 86 Dunn, and I'll bet it wasn't a chef. Dunn. As in Aiden fucking Dunn, the number two Volunteer under Finn Rourke. Take him out. Make him no longer available.

Oisin wasn't on the books as an informant. He said the other day with Cian that nobody knew he was a rat, except Cian. That he was a 'trusted lot'. He kept looking at Cian for direction. Every word came with an approval.

I looked on the phone for the number the message was sent from. No number, just the contact marker 'K'. The situation was worse than I thought. The Sinns were ordering an IRA fire-sale.

Moving down the stairs, two and three at a time, grabbing the Hekler & Koch *Mark 23 9 mm* pistol formerly owned by the dead blonde guy on the way down. I raced back to the car. Row and I officially needed to be off the grid. My mind was still racing. I was going to be walking into the lion's den. The meeting with Finn Rourke.

Am I really going to take the meeting? If I do, will I leave the meeting alive? I have nobody to back me up.

When I got back to the car, I realised just how alone I was. Rowena was gone.

38

I AM USED TO BEING ALONE. I don't have many friends. Girls seem to come and go, sometimes with the seasons. No family to speak of. My partner, Hobbs, probably hates me. I know I hate him. I'm alone at home, alone in the cage, I was alone in Ireland. I could only rely on myself. My brain.

But my brain was playing tricks on me.   Questions and answers were being shouted at me like a schizophrenic. *They are following you. Who are 'they'? Everyone is dead. You're next. Danny. Roxy. Breen. You're tenants. Niall. Now they have Rowena. Forget her she's dead. Get out of Ireland. How? You're being watched. Get out of there. Now. Find a hotel ....*

The passenger door opened to my left. I pulled the *Mark 23* from between my legs and pointed it across my body at the intruder. Rowena.

"Feck! Point that elsewhere, ye cunt."

"Jesus Christ, Row. You scared the shit outta me. Where'd you go?"

"I needed a toilet."

"Where'd you go?" I looked around to see if she was followed or watched.

"Duffy's."

"You look like you're still drunk. Get in the fuckin' car."

"I am indeed. And added to it."

"Great. Listen Row. I need you to get in the fuckin' car. Now."

She complied but not without warning. "You'll watch yer tone."

"Row, I swear to Christ I will knock you back out. We are in some serious shit."

"Yer bleedin'. Y'all right?"

I hadn't had the opportunity to check my sliced arm as of yet. Adrenaline working over time. It was a scratch. A deep scratch that needed stitching, but they wouldn't get any. One of my tattoos was pretty fucked up.

"I'm fuckin' aces, Row. Are you listening to me? You can't just run off like that. And sobriety starts now. We are gonna need our whits."

"Can't just go into a pub and use the toilet. Patrons only. I had a quick bite of whiskey and returned."

"Who saw you?"

"Everyone in the pub. We're in no immediate harm, Deni. I've told you a thing or two about secrets. Where'd ye run off to anyway?"

I started the car and drove. Where to I wasn't sure. But I knew that we needed to get moving.

"Remember the informant Oisin Hanamy that I told you about?"

"That's his flat, hey?"

"How'd you know that, Row?"

"We're in Belturbet. The only garsún ye know here is him."

266

"Oh. Yeah. Right. Well that's not his name anyway and he's dead."

"Ye killed him?"

"No, I killed the guy that was sent to murder him."

"Who's that?"

"There are a lot of who's involved, Row. Let's just get to a hotel and I will explain the whole thing to you. What I know anyway. I've got to call Walter back home. I'd rather just explain it all once."

"No hotels," she said.

"We can't go back to your flat, Row. We need to lay low and think about the next move. We are literally going to be hunted, if we aren't already." I was flying around corners, driving aimlessly, being cursed as the devil from every direction.

"You'll need a passport for a hotel. Passports are faxed to the local Garda stations in Ireland."

"Yeah, no cops."

"I'll call me editor. He'll sort us out. Where's me mobile?"

I pulled over into a petrol station. Dug into my luggage, retrieving her mobile phone from the boot. She called her editor, told him we were near Northern Ireland but not where specifically. She was definitely still drunk, she would have failed a field sobriety test with her wobbling alone. But she was handling speech and communicating with her editor quite well considering. I was impressed.

While Rowena was checking in with her boss and getting us a place to lay low for the night, I was searching around to see if we were being followed. I did not believe that we were. She was taking forever, but I gave her the space she needed.

"We've a spot. We'll need to be tidy and brief. Only for the week-end."

"Whatever. Is it close?"

"Naw. But I know where. I'll drive."

"Yeah, fuck that. You're hammered. Just give me directions from the passenger seat."

267

"Sadly, I'll be better at the helm than you."

There was no arguing with her. She wouldn't move, wouldn't get in the car unless she had the keys. And I wouldn't have a place to stay without her. We were causing a scene, so I gave her the keys.

Once we were back on the road, she said something other than, "gimme the feckin' keys."

"If your caught with that gun they'll put ye ta death. American with a weapon? They'll proper feck ya," she said.

"I'm dead without it. So either way. I'm pretty good at staying alive, Row. I mean to keep that streak alive."

"Pun intended? I've been lucky as well. Maybe you tell me what scrap you've got me in."

"I told you I will. When we get to wherever we're going."

"We'll not be there right quick."

"The way you're driving, I doubt that."

Evening was upon us, but it was not yet full-dark outside. The house was a rural one very close to the UK/Northern Ireland border, off of L1506. The cottage was quaint and owned by an out of town relative of Row's editor. The spare key was placed under the potted plant by the back entrance. I unloaded my bag out of the *Clio,* grabbed a blanket from one of the cupboards and covered the car.

Row must have been hungry because she immediately started to cook something on the stove.

"Fess up. What's going on now? I'm not about to wait any longer. Call yer man after."

I put the file on the kitchen table while she stood above the pan. I emptied the contents of the folder, but threw the blood-stained folder itself away in the bin.

"I went to the Garda station by Pheonix Park to see Cian. To check in. After what we had seen at the docks, I wanted to report our side of things to Cian. We might have been seen by any number of people on that bus. He would know that we were there."

"Aye. And?"

"So they said at the station that he was still there investigating it. He was there for quite a while. I didn't know when he would be back, but I got to thinking. Why kill the old man? Why kill Niall? The authorities are aware of what I'm looking for, but they think it's up in the north."

"Only the IRA would know where the cargo is really bein' sent from," she interjected.

"Right. So how? Why? There are only two possibilities, Row. Somebody is plugged in at the embassy, or Cian."

"Aye. Cian brought ye to the docks. He knows who said what and who has eyes open."

"Exactly. So I start going through his file cabinet, and what do I find?" I pointed to the file on the table. "Cian is Anti-terrorism. He has a file on the whole shah-bang. Informants, who's alive, who's dead. Who got paid what and when...."

"And Oisin is listed."

"No. That's just it Row. He's not. Cian took me all the way up here to point out that he had a guy on the inside. Oisin was the one who ratted out the Newtowncunningham and Dublin stockpiles. Dublin was a bust, not literally, and Newtowncunningham was just old shit. Nothin'. But who got all of the accolades? Cian, in case you weren't paying attention."

"I don't follow."

"You will. Stay with me. So I'm digging through this entire file, Oisin isn't listed anywhere. Payouts made, list of all the tips and by whom. The biggest seizure so far this year and not one mention of Oisin. Not one Irish Euro spent to keep him in that safe house. The tip came from some other guy .... uh, it's right here .... Tadhg O'Carolan."

"Who the feck is he now?"

"He's fuckin' nobody Row."

"Maybe I'm still too drunk for this."

"Tadhg is Oisin. So why keep that a secret? An informant is an informant, right?"

"Aye?"

"Then I found this .... " I turned over a document, flipping it so she could see. Row took the pan off of the burner, moved over to the table. " .... look at the date of that document. Tuesday, 3 August, 2004. The day that I arrived in Ireland. It's a facsimile saying that this message was intercepted from DK to AD. Only look at the date of the fax on the top-right corner. It was post dated. I am named as a top-tier IRA secret cell operative. You are my accomplice. That you're my contact here. Your address is listed below."

"This is rubbish, Deni. I don't understand."

"You go to the Sinn Féin pub every night. That is no longer a secret. This document suggests that I work with the Sinns through you."

"Aye, but — "

" — aye, but nothin', Row. There are only two people who could possibly set me up for a fall. Only two people at the date of that document besides Walter back home and you."

"Cian and Oisin."

"Cian was the only one who knew that I was here, why I was here and that I was pulled out of O'Neill's by you. This is his file."

"Cian was settin' ye up for a fall, seems like."

"Right. So I know we need to get the fuck out of Dublin. We made our way here to see Oisin. He doesn't exist on paper, yet the two people who knew why I am here and what I am looking for, and who are top people in the Sinn Féin party under Finn Rourke do know. That document says 'DK and AD'."

"Darragh Kane and Aiden Dunn. But we just said that Cian and Oisin were the only ...."

"And Oisin was killed." I pulled out Oisin's killer's mobile, flipped it open. I handed it to Rowena.

86 dunn

She looked at the phone, then back at me. I continued with an explanation that probably wasn't needed. "DK sent somebody to kill Dunn. He couldn't do it himself because he was

270

investigating a murder on Dublin Port from earlier. You should have seen Oisin looking to Cian every time he spoke when we came up here."

"Oisin Hanamy is Aiden Dunn."

"Also known as Tadhg O'Carolan. I was onto the only person that could give up Darragh Kane. He had to get rid of Oisin or Aiden or whatever the fuck you wanna call him."

"But Deni. Cian was the lad who introduced you to Oisin. Eh, Aiden."

"I think the plan was to kill me. And You. Only explanation. You said that Cian wasn't in the pub that night that you went back. But we were supposed to go there after meeting Oisin. I bailed but Oisin slash Aiden could now put a face with a name because we had met. You were supposed to be there too."

Rowena was transfixed. Staring into my eyes. "Detective Garda Síochána, Cian Daly, of the Anti-terrorism Task Force in Ireland is Darragh Kane. The top Volunteer in the IRA .... "

"And when the mission failed, he needed to take Dunn out."

"What do you propose we do now, Deni?"

"Now I have to keep my appointment and see his boss, Finn Rourke."

"Ye can't still be thinkin' of takin' the meeting. You've lost the plot."

"You're not the first girl to think that I'm crazy."

39

NEITHER OF US SLEPT. Again. The first night crawled, every sound a call to arms. Rowena's hangover became so bad, her head pounded so brutally, she wouldn't have been able to sleep if her life wasn't in peril. The demise of Niall and Aiden Dunn were still locked into my mind. That was my future.

I am a recovering Catholic. Meaning that I haven't been to church since the last wedding for funeral. Which just so happened to be a mass for Daniel and Roxanne McKennie. But I prayed to Jesus that night. Then I thought about Jesus. He allegedly knew the night before his torture what he was in for. I bet he didn't sleep a wink either.

The attempt at sex to occupy the time was rejected like Row was a goalkeeper. I was batted away and reminded of her headache. I offered to find some sort of medicine in the cottage, find her enough water to supply a camel, but those too were rejected. Her heart wasn't in it, she said. I very much enjoyed it when she was in the mood, and I desperately tried to get her there. I failed.

We were told, meaning I was told by Rowena, that we were to leave the place as we had found it. We didn't really dirty anything, but we cleaned anyway. Wiping and undoing everything that we had done. Retracing our steps. The bloody folder was removed from the bin and taken with us. I asked how she would explain the missing food we ate over the course of the weekend, she didn't like my sense of humor. I didn't tell her that I was serious.

The appointment to meet Finn Rourke, the Army Council General, was scheduled for 10:00 AM sharp on Tuesday, 24 August. We came up with a game plan on the way back to Dublin. I don't know who was more nervous, Row or me. When I get nervous, I get quiet. When she gets nervous, she won't shut up. She chattered the entire way while Bono and Edge did their work in the background.

Row stopped at a postal annex on the way back. She made 2 copies of the file, one for her and one for me. Over €100. Like I said, the file was thick. I would eventually take the bloody originals, but not into the meeting with Rourke. If anything was to be confiscated, we wanted them to be the copies. And we wanted him to know that they were copies.

When we arrived around the corner from his office, we got out and split up. I had only the clothes on my back, her mobile phone with Dunn's murderer's mobile programmed into it, and a copy of the file. Row had the gun, both the original and her copy of the file, Dunn's murderer's phone, and my passport. If things went to shit, which I had every belief that they would, she had detailed instructions on what to do.

Rourke's office was more secure than the US Embassy building. I was patted and re-patted. Told I would not be allowed in without identification. The Council General, Rourke, was called to approve my entrance into the building.

I was led up to his office, where I didn't have to wait. His office door opened and closed behind me. The office was CEO-sized. Rourke's desk was larger than the car we drove there in. The man was slight, but I made no mistake of his power. He wore thinning, white hair. His hunter green eyes were almost an implausible colour. When he smiled I almost expected bloody fangs, instead his teeth were yellowed and crooked.

"Please have a seat Mr. Dennihan." He had a most definite Irish accent, but his English was perfect. "This is an impromptu meeting, and it was fit in. I do not have a great deal of time." We both sat down.

"Deni. Call me Deni. And I don't know how last minute this meeting is. It took me more than a week for you see me. How busy could you possibly be? Or you just thought that I'd be dead by now. Right Fin? Can I call you Fin?"

"No, you may not. Sir will do."

"Ok, there Fin. We have a big problem you and me." I decided to go on the offensive. I am not timid or meek when I'm nervous. Especially when I'm nervous. "We both know that you are the puppet master and the minions went rogue on you."

"I have no idea what you are talking about. This is going to be a short meeting if you think you are going to come in here and spout off with ridiculous accusations."

"Let's start from the beginning then, shall we?" I waved the thick, photocopied file like I was hot and I was in a Baptist church. You are a member of the political party Sinn Féin, yes?"

"Yes."

"You are the Army Council General, yes?"

"Also correct. Everyone knows this."

"I know a lotta things most don't there, guy. I'm here lettin' you know that I know."

He sat back in his chair, rolled his eyes and shook his head as if to say 'very well' but actually said nothing.

"You are the guy who tells the army what to do, the guy that takes the council vote and communicates that vote with the actual army."

"That is what a Council General does. Yes."

"You also control the IRA on behalf of Sinn Féin, yes?"

"No. That is not correct. The Irish Republican Army has been disbanded."

274

"We both know that's bullsh, Fin. You fucks have been documented as active, publicly, as late as February of this year. You are on the same terrorist watch list as those Al-Qaeda assholes."

"I am one of the top politicians in — "

" — and we just went through all that. I know. You have Darragh Kane, AKA Cian Daly doin' your bidding. You had Aiden Dunn, AKA Oisin Hanamy, AKA Tadhg O'Carolan as his backup until very recently. I was there. I got the motherfucker's phone who was sent to do it. Did that news make it up the flagpole yet?" I took the phone out of my pocket and showed it like it was a badge as way of proof. It was Row's mobile not the murderer's but he didn't know that. The phone went back into my pocket.

"Why are you here, Mr. Dennihan? You have no jurisdiction here. And I am too busy to listen to your rantings. I entertained this meeting as a courtesy to the press."

"And since then, you know that I'm not a member of the press."

"Correct."

"And you took the meeting anyway." It was a question, but I didn't project it as one.

"I was curious, and my curiosity has been exhausted." He rose from behind his giant desk.

"I wouldn't get up if I were you," I said. I opened the file in one of the clear spots near me on the outside of his monster desk. "I know about your gun shipment. I know that you are into a ton of illegal shit all over the world to pay for your political party and this big-ass desk. You had Niall McCourt killed. The guy you sent to kill him just so happens to be investigating the case. I'll bet that one doesn't get solved. I've got it all here in this file, Fin. These are photocopies of Kane's originals by the way. Kane being Cian the dirty cop or Garda or whatever you call him. I've got phone communications from Kane to Dunn, Dunn to Kane. Now that Dunn is dead, how long do you think it is going to take for Kane to cut a deal? He'll bury you in a heartbeat to save his sorry ass."

"Americans and their Hollywood."

"You don't wanna come clean, Fin? If what you do is so noble, why not own up to it?"

275

"I think that I've heard just about enough. Will you leave of your own accord, or shall I have you thrown out of the building?"

"I'm leaving." I got up to leave but turned to him as I opened his office door. "This is going to the press. This is an international incident you've got on your hands. 911 is comin' up on its three year anniversary, fuckface. We don't like terrorists, you are about to see just how much."

I played a heavy hand. I had no idea what, if anything, the US government would do. Officially. We were at war with the middle east, not Ireland. Walter Glibczieck wanted the guns to prove that he could get guns off the streets of America. I was here for that purpose only. There was nothing I could do to Finn Rourke other than make his life miserable. Titanitaukis would get his win. The state of Massachusetts would get their win also, a much needed win after the big Maynard Ballistics Lab fiasco.

Everything hinged upon what Rourke would do. Other than to have me killed, which I had seen enough in the short time that I had been there to know he would most certainly do. I wanted him to make a mistake. I wanted him to move the gun shipment quickly. I wanted the manifest information. I wanted to go home. Hell, I wanted a home to go to.

All eyes seemed to be on me as I left Rourke's office building. Call it paranoia, call it whatever you want, I was keeping my head on a swivel. Once I hit the kerb, Rowena came from around the corner. We met and walked toward her car without losing our stride. She nonchalantly slipped me my newly acquired gun and my passport.

"How did you make out?"

I shrugged my shoulders. Row had a grin on her face as I asked, indicating that she had made some progress. Progress was crucial.

"I think we know when and where, Deni."

"Nice! …. Well?"

"I'll tell ye in the car. Less ears." She looked around as we made for the car at a brisk pace. We were almost at the tiny Renault *Clio*.

276

"Toss me the keys, Row. I want to drive down to the docks again. We will have to walk it this time, I don't want anyone to recognise the car."

"Amn't a fan of your drivin'."

"I'm not askin', Row."

She tossed them, but tossed them like a girl. Or should I say not on target. The keys skidded across the kerb on the left side of the car. The keys fell off the edge and rested between the shoulder and the driver's side tire.

"Nice throw. You should play for the Yankees."

"Feck off."

I reached down to snatch the keys, when it caught my eye. A small, red, flashing light reflecting off of the pavement from under the car. It looked like a reflected, blinking, laser pointer. Paranoia? I went down to all fours, looking under the car. Black box with a blinking light under the driver's seat.

"Fuck! Run Row! Ruuu ….."

Everything went in slow motion. Her eyes widened to the size of an Irish Euro coin. Deer in the headlights. I went from all fours to like a runner off the starting blocks to full sprint. Hands and arms pumping. Legs propelling me as they moved. Knees to waist. Heels to buttocks. Slow motion like in the night terrors. The evil thing is upon us, and we cannot move fast enough.

Rowena didn't seem to move. Panic had rendered her immobile. She was on the other side of the car, in the road, and behind me now. *Should I go back to help her?*

The explosion was large enough to destroy a Humvee, let alone a subcompact car. The device took out the vehicles both in front of and behind the intended target. Metal shrapnel sliced through everything surrounding it like an infinite number of Ginsu knives, toward an infinite number of points from the center.

I was able to travel nearly ten meters prior to the explosion and was catapulted another ten plus meters. I was covered in cuts and scrapes. Sound was replaced by ringing in my ears. Clouds of smoke from the fire replaced sight. Debris falling like hail. Fiery balls falling like sparklers. What was left of the car and the surrounding area was more like a meteor crater.

When last I saw Rowena, she was no more than one meter away from the car. From the explosion. She was a petite woman. She wasn't as durable as any one of the structures that were now damaged or destroyed. She was human. She was tender flesh over tiny bones. And there was no way that she could have survived.

40

RYAN WELL'S OFFICE PHONE AT GRANTES, WELLS & ASSOCIATES rang after being directed from Angie the receptionist. The attorney was drafting a final summation for a trial the following day, Friday, involving a woman who had beaten her own child to death. The mother of three had lost her job, along with the third in the line of fathers of her brood, and didn't qualify for benefits. She snapped. Temporary Insanity was the defense Wells was going with at any rate. Nobody won TI defenses anymore. This one was the long shot of all long shots. New Hampshire juries are filled with mothers and fathers who have had tough lives. They may beat their children, but they don't beat their children to death.

Lost in thought on how best to spin the facts of the case, how to pull on enough heartstrings to attain a 'not guilty' verdict on murder two, nullify a jury, hope for probation on the reckless endangerment of the two other minors, while the phone continued to ring. His wife, Angie, knew he was in his office. She knocked on the door, pulling Ryan out of his deep focus, hearing the incessant ringing. He answered the phone without his wife having to enter his office.

"Ryan Wells."

"Ryan. This is Walter Glibczieck. The federal - "

" - I know who you are, I remember you. It hasn't been that long. How are you? What's going on?"

"Do you have a few minutes?"

"I'm sort of in the middle of something, but I can spare a few minutes."

"I'm calling with regard to our mutual friend. Warren Dennihan?"

"Deni. Is everything alright? Last I knew he was in Ireland for you." He omitted that Deni's efforts would help him in a potential civil suit as well. That he was there for the firm as much as for the federal government.

"Yes, well it helps you too, yes?"

"With the Breen case?" *Time to downplay it*, he thought. "It helps once we solidify all of the connections. Triangle trade all over again. Guns, drugs, and money. Once we can prove the conspiracy, we may have a civil case against several parties. Including the prison. But that is a long way off. A long shot at best."

"And bring criminal charges against his murderers."

"Prosecutions aren't my department, Walter. That's your gig. I just defend or sue the people you prosecute. So what is this about? Like I said, a civil case is a long way off."

"Have you heard from Deni lately?"

"A couple of phone calls, but it's been a while. I'd have to check on the dates to give you an exact amount of time. Why? Has something happened?"

"I'm not entirely sure, to be honest. I haven't heard from him. But he did mention a reporter the last time we spoke. I was against it, but he had already worked out a deal with the woman and he seemed to be getting further with her."

"And?"

"And her editor faxed me documents from her, at Deni's behest, indicating that the contact that I had Deni working with over there, the Detective Garda on the Anti-terrorism task force, is duplicitous."

"That's not good, Walter. You should get somebody over there who you can trust to get him out. I told you this was going to be too dangerous. You and Titanitaukis cooked this — "

" — save your righteous indignation, Ryan. There's more."

"More? Great."

"CSPAN is reporting a car bomb that went off in Dublin near the Sinn Féin and headquarters last Tuesday. Have you seen the report?"

"Nobody watches CSPAN, Walter. The people that produce CSPAN don't watch it. But let's not get crazy. So he hasn't checked in …. car bombs happen over there all time. Don't they?"

"The car belonged to the reporter that Deni was partnering with. The IRA has denied responsibility, but the experts say it is of the same type that is commonly used by them."

"Could be a coincidence."

"Ryan, the statement from the IRA came within the same hour of the bombing. They denied their involvement before the investigation. Before the authorities knew what type of device it was. Which is an admission of sorts. Sinns, IRA, the reporter that he was working with, the fax outing an insider …. those are a ton of coincidences."

"So you think that Deni is dead?"

"I'm not sure, that's why I'm calling you. I want to see if you have had contact with him since this happened."

"Since Tuesday? No."

281

"It's Thursday, Mr. Wells. We have to assume at this point ….
"

"I'm not willing to concede that yet. Why are you so quick to cut and run?"

"Because this was supposed to be a clandestine operation. Just information. This is turning into a complete cluster-fuck of the highest order."

"So are you going to send someone over to collect him? Investigate? Help him? The embassy should be notified."

"I can't. This was off the grid. This is about burying it at this point. We need to cut him loose. Cut ties."

"You are just going to leave him over there? Why are you telling me this Walter? You know that I can't just walk away from this. What you are suggesting is immoral, not to mention — "

" — I'm telling you this as a courtesy, Ryan. You might want to get yourself a new investigator. If you hear from him let me know. I certainly hope that you do. I hope that I hear from him. I'll of course let you know if I do. But if not, we have to assume the worst. This would be an international incident with a country in which the United States is an ally. I'm calling to tell you that if this goes anymore sideways, I am going to need you to be a friend. A friend that can be a very powerful one for you. Do you understand what I'm saying?"

"I do but I can't believe it. I am disgusted with you, Walter, but I know exactly what you are saying. What if I have enough friends? I wonder if someone above you would make a better friend?"

"I wouldn't do that if I were you."

"Are you threatening me, Walter?"

"Of course not. I'm merely saying that you can get further ahead with sugar than you can with spice."

"Well, I think that I have heard enough of what you think about how I make and keep friends. One of my new friends is in trouble, so you say."

"What I'm saying to you, counselor, is that you can never have too many friends. But you can have too many enemies."

41

SIRENS ECHOED THROUGHOUT THE STREETS OF DUBLIN. Only I couldn't hear them. I had a different sort of ringing in my ears, the kind from tinnitus, or ear drum damage. I imagined they sounded like European sirens. High, low, high, low, high, low. Pitch change after pitch change. Ambulances, fire brigade, and numerous other emergency vehicles cordoned off the area. One kilometer block by one kilometer block.

I tried to get up but failed. I tried to discern what was happening, but it only came in pieces. A slow strobe light if you will. Snapshots in time. Time that I was losing. All I can remember were all of the lights and all of the sounds that must have accompanied them. The gurney. The blood. Oxygen mask. Tubes. The ambulance. All of it coming in flashes.

The day I woke up, the day I really became aware of my surroundings, I will never forget. 31 August, 2004. It was a Tuesday. I rose in my bed into a semi-upright position. The hospital bed. Hoses and things were sticking out of me. Agitated would be the understatement of my state. Bits of the explosion came back to me. So too did the pain.

How long have I been out? Which hospital am I in? Rowena.

I started pressing buttons and yelling for someone to pay attention to me. I wanted attention. I wanted answers. Two security personnel of some sort were standing outside the private hospital room. They looked in, saw that I was awake and proceeded to flag some people down.

The doctor came in first, followed by a nurse who did little more than tidy up. The doctor was a short, rotund sort of woman. Glasses. Very librariany. She checked my chart and asked how I was feeling. I was able to hear her British accent. Her voice was muffled but I still thought it a minor miracle.

"I'm fine. How long have I been here?"

"A few days. A week actually. You had lost quite a bit of blood and you were very weak. You are lucky to be alive."

"Yeah, Yeah. I need to get outta here. Wait. Where is here?"

"Mater Misericordiae University Hospital. One of the finest in Dublin, I should think. Do you remember why you are here?"

"Car bomb."

"Yes. Precisely. Please don't remove your intravenous lines. You have had several pieces of metal removed from your body, many lacerations, two fractured ribs, and you were concussed quite badly. Not your first from the looks of things and I assure you that removing your medication is not in your best interest. The pain alone will be quite debilitating. Please do try and relax."

"I have to get outta here, doc. The motherfuckers that did this to me will be back to finish the job."

"That is why we have you under protective watch," she said. "Those hospital security men stationed outside have been there since you came out of surgery. I believe there will be a Garda

284

presence imminently. Your friend has the same level of protection outside the critical care unit."

"Friend? Rowena? She's alive? I want to see her right now." I tried to get out of the bed, but a surge of pain hit me, and one of the guards entered into the room in case I succeeded.

"She is hanging on. I can't say for certain for how long, or if she will ever recover. She sustained a great many injuries, some of which are to vital organs. The blast literally chucked her quite a distance, I am told, where she landed on her spine. She has undergone two operations to remove fragments in vital areas. More surgeries have been scheduled. She is unconscious and machines are helping her to remain stable."

"The blast …. I don't know how she made it this long. It's just …. she was so close …."

"About that. The Gardaí would like to have a word. They have been clambering all week to see you. Should I tell them that you are ready to receive?"

"No! Fuck no! I won't make it past the end of the day if you let them in here. Tell them I died. Tell them whatever you want, just don't tell them that I'm conscious."

"They are conducting an investigation and are arranging a more long-term security arrangement for you. I cannot impede that or I shall face criminal charges."

"How long can you give me?"

"I should think an hour or two would be reasonable to collect your thoughts."

"Fine. Where did you put my stuff? My belongings? And Rowena's?"

"They are in property. I cannot give those to you until you are discharged."

"I have evidence in there. I want to go through it, collect my thoughts like you said.   Then I will hand it over to them for their investigation. Then and only then will I be ready to have a chat. But I need Rowena's stuff also."

She gave me an inquisitive look before committing to a response. "I'll see what I can do." She nodded to the nurse who was still pretending to tidy up.

285

"Thanks doc."

Within a half-hour the nurse came back with the bagged items. The bags were large and sealed. I had to sign for them. I dug through them once she left me alone. The guards outside the door didn't seem to be interested in looking in through the large, narrow, vertical window that ran parallel to the door to the room. I was in the room. I was safe. Their job well done.

No clothes. They must have torn them off of us when we got here. Or the shrapnel did the work for them. My wallet was there, my badge and all of the euros present as far as I could tell. The files were strewn all over the inside of the bags. Some of it burned or bloody. I was trying to piece it all back together as best I could from all of the copies, who knows what was missing. Keys to the now non-existent car. My passport. Both mobile phones. No gun.

They either didn't want to give the *Mark 23* to me, which was understandable, or they didn't have it in the first place. Either way I didn't have it. Either way I needed it to protect myself. Probably the first reason. Row said that it wouldn't be good to be caught with it. Add that to the fact that the body in Belturbet housed a bullet from it. Another reason for the Gardaí to want to speak with me.

I had about another half-hour left before the Irish version of the cavalry would be coming through my hospital room door. I didn't want to be there for it. The machine that was keeping track of my pulse, attached to my forefinger, was plugged into the wall. Was. No alarms seemed to be going off, so I continued to disconnect things. I left the I.V. port in my arm but removed the lines to the bags that were hung on the rack. I put the medicine bags in my property bags. If I really did need the pain killers and whatever else they had me on, I would have it, but the doc probably just told me that to keep me dependent upon her.

With bags packed, all I needed were clothes. A hospital gown over my wrapped torso with my ass in the wind was not going to do. I needed clothes and a way out of the room. The two guards at the door were going to be a problem. I hoped that they were stupid. I opened the door to find out.

"The doc said that you guys were going to bring me to some sort of interview room? I have the evidence that I need to hand over to the investigators here in these bags. Care to lead the way?"

They looked at me like I had sprouted four heads.

"She didn't say anything to you? Go check it out if you want," I said.

The guard on the left side of the door nodded to the other and took off in search of the doc. One down one to go.

"Make sure he gets me some clothes too will ya? My ass is hangin' out. It's embarrassing. In the meantime, do you wanna just bring me there? I know what she said."

"Amn't bringin' you anyplace without proper authority. Go back in yer bed now."

"I gotta use the shitter anyway. This one is clogged. We can stop at a toilet on the way."

"Jest hold it a bit. He'll be right back. We'll sort ye out then."

"You want to pick up the mess? You'll have to when I tell the orderlies that you knew I had to go and you wouldn't let me. What's the harm in letting me use a working toilet?"

"Bollucks. Make it quick."

He walked me down the hall. "Why do you need yer bags?"

"I have evidence in here. I can't just leave it layin' around." He seemed satisfied with the explanation.

As I began to move for the first time since the bombing, the soreness took over. My body ached all over. The medicine was wearing off or my head and torso were in bad shape. Maybe all of the above. We took a left around the doctor and nurse station. Behind the counter there were several people talking in front of a large dry-erase board. I kept my head down and tried to keep the guard between the gathering and me. It seemed to work.

Further down the hall on the right was the individual restroom that the guards themselves used, he told me as we approached it. It was a large room with an oversized door for handicapped access. He opened his arm and pointed to it. It was at the end of the hall and across from the stairs.

"Quick like," he said.

As I turned the handle to open the door, I pretended it was locked and occupied. "Someone's in there."

"We'll go on to another then," he said.

I finished turning the knob. "Oh maybe not. Maybe it was just stuck."

"The guard gave me a concerned look, like I was playing games. Which of course I was. "Do you want to check it out first?" I opened the door a crack and let him come around me to look inside the one room.

He popped his head in just far enough for me to shove him against the door jam and slam the oversized, heavy door on the back of his head and neck. I looked back toward the nurse station, fifteen meters or so back, thankfully nobody noticed me. I slammed the door one more time for good measure. The guard began to slump when I reopened the door again, pushing him inside.

With the door locked, I was able to quickly change into the uniform that I removed from the unconscious guard. I swam in it, but it would have to work. Club and mace. No gun. That would have to work as well.

42

I FELT BAD FOR LEAVING ROWENA at the hospital. I didn't even get a chance to see her. But the window of opportunity for me to escape was small. There was no time. Mater Misericordiae would be on lockdown in a matter of minutes. Once the first guard came back to the second guard who was not at his post and missing, it would be all bells and whistles. Full tilt.

After descending one flight of stairs, I entered onto the second floor. I quickly meandered around that level looking for a lounge or a locker room. I needed another change of clothes. They would be looking for a man in a stolen guard uniform as soon as they realised what I had done. I had no other clothes, they had blown up with the bomb. I needed a change of clothes and I needed it before the hospital was completely sealed.

Nothing doing on that floor. Another staircase down, one more flight.

A group of doctors were headed into an area that said 'fostaithe amháin'. I assumed it meant employees only. Hoped. I followed the group in and there was a lounge on the left, to the right were two sets of locker rooms. I was met with odd stares as to my presence. Thinking quickly, I put on my best Irish accent. Mixed with my harsh Boston accent, it must have sounded odd to say the least. The stares didn't end after I spoke.

"Beg pardon. We have a patient thats gone missin'. He's a bit of a handful so ye mightn't want to be here for the moment." I looked around the area, all eyes on me. In keeping with the lingo, I might have been buggered. Nobody moved.

"Everyone out now!" I shouted. They all poured out. The club that was part of the guards uniform I then used to rattle on the men's lockers, those that had business in there quickly exited. I searched for any and all clothing that would fit, shoved it into a backpack that I took out of a locker. The evidence bags went into it as well. I thought about changing then and there but didn't have time upon further review. The call to remove the employees had created a stir outside in the hall.

Keeping my back to the wall in the hallway, trying to hide the backpack, I called to them.

"It's clear." I held the door open for the first few to re-enter then made a dash for the stairs again.

Out the front door, I turned to my right to see the car park. I ran as fast as I could toward it. My body weary and beaten, sore and protesting my every move. I wasn't yet to the structure when I heard the emergency alarm from the hospital sounding.

Once in the parking structure, I found a car that looked easier to steal than the BMWs and other luxury cars in the assigned spots on the ground floor. I settled on a silver Peugot *206*. I didn't know what year it was, I didn't even know the car existed before that day. It just looked like a four door piece of shit that I could steal.

Which I did. No car alarm thankfully. I had never stolen a car where everything was on the right side as a kid in Southie.

Certainly not as an adult. An adult police officer. But …. desperate times and all.

Car manufacturers think that they are slick by installing steering immobilisers in the column so if the car was to be stolen the thief wouldn't be able to steer it. The locking system is from the key ignition switch. But virtually every manufacturer as of 2004 had a very simple cylinder on the steering column. They made this so that locksmiths and local dealers could fix a problem if there was a lost key or the locking system malfunctioned. Pulling the wires down from underneath the steering column, connecting the 12-volt lead to the four other wires, and a lock-picking pin from my wallet jammed into the ignition and I was on my way. It took me longer to get into the car using my pins than to drive the car away once I was in it.

I pulled out under a flyover once I had left the hospital grounds so I could change. Again the clothes from the men's locker room didn't fit quite right, but close enough. Next stop, back to the docks.

It took me a hot minute to figure out how to get down to Dublin Port from the hospital. At first I went the completely wrong direction. I realised my error when I went by Boston College Ireland and Sainte Stephen's Green. Talk about weird. The fact that I had to drive by another hospital, the children's hospital, made me think that I was driving in circles in the wrong direction. I lost track at four times I went by that goddamned place. Or maybe it was a third hospital all together. At any rate, Seville Road empties out onto North Dock. From there I found my way.

On foot. I parked the stolen silver Peugot 206 like it was waiting for the Holyhead, UK ferry on the south side of the port and walked. And walked. To the other side of the port, where shipping is the industry not ferries to Isle of Man, Liverpool, or the like. Then along the docks to the containers.

The docks were shutdown until the investigation was to be completed. The doc said that I was down for a week and it was still on lock-down. I don't know what other evidence they aimed to collect but security was tight and no vessels were allowed in or out of Dublin Port. I found out from one of the underlings on the outside of the cordon that shipments in were either re-routed to another Irish port, or were anchored in queue out in Muir Éireann by the Poolbeg Lighthouse.

It was like a gigantic raft party like the college kids form on spring break. Only these were cargo ocean liners instead of rented Bayliners. Freighters are massive. They have to be in order for shipping internationally to be cost-effective. They range in size and scope depending upon what they carry; tankers, general, dry-bulk, reefer, etc., but can be 350-400 meters long. Another measurement used is TEU, or twenty foot equivalency unit, for measuring length. You know the thing is big when you use 20-foot increments to measure them. To put it in perspective, a Nimitz-class aircraft carrier is 330 meters long, or 4.5 acres. The aircraft carrier is 20 meters shorter than the smallest vessel in the bay. Weight is yet another category for measuring size. DWTs, or Dead Weight Tons. Each of the vessels in the water waiting to be loaded and unloaded could carry up to 400,000 DWTs on top of the vessel's empty weight. Now imagine about a dozen of them in one spot. It was a floating city.

I had to wait until dark to get further onto the docks. There was a small detail of security that night but nothing compared to when I arrived earlier in the day. There was lighting but not so much as to be spotted ten meters away like during daylight hours.

The sun had been mild yet baking my skin. I didn't want to go anywhere else while I waited for the sun to go down. I wanted to monitor who was let inside the cordoned area and who was made to leave. I sat in Irishtown Park for the rest of the day. I watched and I waited for night to come in order to make a move. And finally, it did.

43

NIGHTFALL CAME LATE, AS IT DOES EVERY NIGHT in the almost-autumn summer months. Of course it felt even later because I had been waiting and baking in the sun all day. Sneaking past the cordon and security was easy. I spent the first hour with my neck and skin against the cold steel trying in vain to cool it. Moving from crate to crate with as much stealth as I could muster down the long pier toward the office where Niall was carved up like an Easter ham.

I actually thought an hour was quite good considering. Sliced, bruised, broken, and then burned, I moved as fast as I could and as quietly. There were a few random guards meandering around the dock yard. They didn't look like they were looking for anything in particular, which suited me just fine. The office was where they had concentrated the majority of their numbers. The office and the cordon at the entrance to the pier.

And the office was going to be a bitch to get into if it was locked. I am good at picking locks. A fucking magician actually. But I'm not invisible. If it took 10-seconds to get in, which it could possibly take a few seconds longer than that, it would be 10-seconds too long. I studied the men that were watching the perimeter of the converted office space for a weakness, some way to get to the door unseen. There wasn't a way. Locked or not, I was not getting into the modified container through the door without being seen or taking some people out. There was no back egress. The normal two-door latch on the end of all 40-foot long containers was welded closed when it was converted into an office. The only door was the door that had been cut into the side, with a small deck and stairs leading up to it.

I climbed up on top of a nearby container to reconnoiter the surrounding area. I had been circling the docks, counting and ascertaining the best way to breach. If I had to take out some of the guards, I wanted to have to deal with the fewest number. They moved around with purpose. They were well trained. And they weren't wearing Garda uniforms. In my mind, that meant that without anything other than a club and mace, I needed to avoid engaging this particular enemy.

There weren't any lights on in the office. Meaning if I was able to get inside, I would be alone. As long as I kept the lights out or blocked the one high window and kept quiet, I would be uninterrupted for as long as I needed. I just needed to get in there.

The closest surrounding container was ten meters from the office. I thought if I could get on top of the converted container, I could jump down from it getting behind those that were guarding it. I couldn't jump that far. Olympians can't jump that far.

A crane had a line dropped above the closest container like a fishing rod into the sea. The heavy hook rested slightly more than a meter above my head, too high to jump. Delays delays. The obstacles were growing more aggravating. But it was not a time to get my Irish up. It was a time to assert my dogged determination. Affect my stubborn will.

The crane seemed far away. Especially since I had to avoid several guards, remain quiet while covering ground. This took more time. Climbing onto the top of the operator's cabin in my condition, then onto the long arm of the crane. Moving up and out on my tender ribs and belly using hands and feet in the rungs. All the way to the top. Moving up and out over the container. Dropping down onto the 9 cm wide, braided, wire rope cable from the jib. Taking breaks on the descent as the cable was cutting into my hands. All of this took time.

What began as mission just after dusk, was now close to one in the morning by the time I had lowered myself, hand below hand, down to the hook. My feet rested on the weld connecting the hook to the cable. My arms burned. My hands were bleeding. The cable was already swaying from my journey to the bottom of it. Back and forth like a pendulum. Moving me closer to the top of the office. The heavy hook now slightly heavier with me on it. Gaining momentum back and forth, slowly but surely.

Next was a crucial part of the mission. Silence. Dropping down onto the roof of the container could be noisy. *Would it echo?* *Would this adventure be finished before it began?* I was thinking and pondering these and other questions while fixing my gaze on my target. The roof. There was something sticking up from the top of the container. It was difficult to see what in the dark.

Do or die. Time to get off of the cable. Timing was key. Back and forth. Silently swinging in the night. I was separated from the hook and cable. Falling in the air like I was tire-swinging over Fresh Pond and jumping in off of the quarry ledge back home. Only this landing would not be so soft. Not by a long shot. The containers were built to stack on top of one another. For storage. For transport. The roofs were ribbed and welded in a grid fashion for support. While the landing was silent, it was hard and extremely painful.

After taking a physical inventory to ascertain if I had broken anything else on the fall; determining that other than my ribs and my head continuing to pound, my bleeding hands added to the rest of the dried blood and scabs on my body, my scraped knees and tender ankles, I was no worse for wear. The object that I could not make out on the roof was an open window. A skylight you could call it. It must have been opened to help with the smell of death.

296

Wide open. I couldn't tell what it was because the lights had been extinguished. Another drop through the opening and I was in. Finally.

My eyes were already used to the dark from being out in it for hours. But this was Stevie Wonder dark. I felt my way around. A hard hat. Clothing of some kind. A light switch would be out of the question at least for the moment. The smell inside the office could have gagged a maggot. A poorly ventilated morgue. Somehow it had gotten worse since I had last been in the modified container, even vented.

Whatever clothing or piece of cloth I had felt hanging on the wall, it was big enough to cover the small window. The window was high above the desk. I slid a lamp and something else that was tall over to the edge of the desk and used them to keep the cloth in place. In that blind search, I had knocked something on the desk over. I froze in place until I determined that only I had heard it. Fortunately nobody came to the door to inspect a noise, if they had even heard one. The clumsy error was serendipitous. The turned over object was a flashlight.

Nobody seemed to have made an attempt to clean the office. The walls and floor still looked and smelled like a crime scene a week after the event. They had gathered up all the evidence, all the bits of human remains that was once Niall McCourt. All but the blood stains and the smell was left to putrefy the office.

I searched every file. Every piece of paper in that office. It took all night. Every document. There had once been a computer, but it was gone. The chords lingered where the machine once lived. Every business that had anything stored there had a file in the cabinet I presumed. Every company that shipped something off of that port. Every boat that was parked out in the floating car park. Nothing pointed to Sinn Féin or the IRA. To the destination. The answer would be in the destination. File cabinet after file cabinet. Drawer after drawer. It was narrowed down to one of three vessels that would be carrying the shipment. Only three vessels from what I could tell would be headed into Boston Harbor in the foreseeable future. Which means it wasn't narrowed down at all. It might as well have been twenty. Each vessel had the capacity, depending on weight of each container, of roughly 1,500 containers. The three possible vessels meant having to search 4,500 plus, forty-foot containers for crates inside those containers holding weapons. Not gonna happen. If, which was a big question, they were still going move forward with shipping them out of Dublin.

Maddening. I felt like I was getting nowhere and time was running out. I wrote down the names of the three freighters that would be headed into Boston Harbor, and other related pertinent information on a piece of paper before deciding that I needed to get out of there. Dawn was coming.

I rose out of the top of the converted office no wiser than when I went in. Not realistically. Three vessel names. The light began to outline the shape of the horizon off to the east on the back side of the container. The top of the sun would soon peak out of the Atlantic Ocean.

Getting out of there was much easier than getting in. The back side of the office faced the water, to the left was the way I had swung in. To the right was a sea of containers. I would jump down from the office roof and disappear in those containers, making my way back to the park. From there I could leave the Dublin Port.

But go where? What now?

I decided that it was time to call Walter Glibczieck again. And once I got off the docks, that is exactly what I did.

44

"THREE VESSEL NAMES. THAT'S ALL I CAN COME UP WITH," I blurted from the confines of the stolen Peugot. It was a little past midnight on the east coast of the states. I had called four times from Aiden Dunn's killer's mobile phone. Walter let it go to voicemail each time, his voice requesting that I leave a message with a name and number, which I refused to leave. I just ended the call and dialed it again. He picked up the final time

"Who is this? It's the middle of the night." He sounded odd to me. Not pulled out of sleep. Just odd.

"It's Deni. I'm calling from a stolen cell. I've got vessel names. But that means close to five thousand containers. It's just about as far as I can go here, guy."

"Deni? I thought …. How do I know it's you?"

"It's fuckin' me. I've had some close calls but I'm alive."

"Prove that this is you."

299

"I'll tell ya what. When I do get back stateside, I'll beat the life outta ya with this cell phone. What the fuck do you want from me, Walter? Focus on the prize here."

"Okay, it's you. Uh, so .... three freighters?"

"That might be the best we got. Three ULCVs. Big suckers. The Annika Mærsk, The Cecil Mærsk, and the Giddeon Mærsk. All waylaid in the ocean just off Dublin Port. Those are the only ships headed to Boston."

"They all have the same last name? Mærsk?"

"Yeah I assume that this company, this A.P Moller-Mærsk Group out of Denmark names all their vessels with the last name. Is that important?"

"Remember the Heckler & Koch *G3A4*s that were stolen?"

"Norway.   Norwegian Police.   I'm not too up on world geography, Walt, but Norway and Denmark ain't the same country last I checked."

"No but there is a plant in Denmark. The *G3A4*s were designed and are manufactured there."

"I don't believe in coincidences, but I'm not seeing how that fits."

"Me neither. Did you say that all three of those vessels are parked in the ocean?"

"Yeah, it's very heated over here. The embassy knows I'm here and why, the Sinns know .... the contact that you sent me to .... he's like the IRA's number one fucking guy."

"Cian Daly?"

"Ya Mean Darragh Kane? They are one and the same. People are dying left and right, and I'm next."

"You said as much in the fax that you had sent over by the fucking editor of a major Dublin newspaper. You were supposed to keep this quiet, Deni. The US Embassy has been notified? You have this reporter on this. Car bombs? Not exactly going to plan, is it?"

"What do you want from me? I'm doin' the best I can."

"All this noise and we are still going to have to narrow the shipment down, Deni. I can't issue warrants to search those vessels with what you've told me so far."

300

"Let me spell it out for you chapter and verse, chief. They took out Aiden Dunn, the number two guy. They tried to blow me to the fuckin' moon, and that reporter that I was working with? She's probably gonna die or is already dead. I questioned this poor old guy, Niall, on the docks down here and they filleted him. Cut him limb from limb. Literally. These boys over here don't fuck around. If you piss in their Guinness, you wind up dead. You and everybody ya know. And in a very painful, very public way. I got in a tussle with one of these fucks up in Belturbet and he's dead. If I don't get the fuck out of Ireland soon, I might not ever leave. I'll be in the ground or worse, in a prison. Does that spell it out for you? Get me the fuck outta here, Walt."

"They killed somebody on the docks? The Dublin Port?"

"Everything I said, and that's what you picked up on? Yes. They tortured the poor prick."

"In Dublin."

"Walter. I know it's late over there but if you could fuckin' focus for — "

" — Deni. Why would they kill someone on the very shipping port that they mean to move their illegal guns out of?"

"Because they're sick fucks? Who knows?"

"Those vessels are waylaid because of the investigation. Correct?"

"Yeah Dublin is on lockdown. You think they aren't coming out of Dublin now? I was thinkin' the same thing."

"But they are the ones that killed this old guy, Niall, that you spoke with. You're sure?"

"I didn't watch them do it, but it seems real clear. Yes."

"I think that means that they are *definitely* moving the weapons out of Dublin."

"I didn't sleep all night. Walk me through that logic, Walt."

"They would normally have to go through customs to move their shipments, right?"

"I'm with ya. That was my guess, yeah. Well, Niall's guess in fairness, but we see how that worked out."

"So maybe they had some arrangement with this Niall, or maybe they didn't. But now that the port is closed, they won't need customs forms. No vessels in or out. So they are going to sneak them out of the closed port."

"That makes sense, Walt. The focus will be on every other shipping lane outta Ireland. They are gonna move the guns out right under their noses. They were probably going to create some sort of distraction to close this thing down all along. A shipment like that is too large to slip through customs like they have been doing in smaller loads, so they create a diversion. But that was a big splash. They cut this guy up really bad. Why go that big unless they were pumping him for information?"

"You tell me. You are the one over there. But if I had to guess? From what you've told me? They planned to shut down Dublin anyway. Niall talked to you, so they wanted to find out what he said. Like I was saying, maybe they had an arrangement with him and they wanted to find out if he had mentioned that to you. They killed two birds with one stone by creating the necessary shutdown with a murder, and pumped him for information at the same time."

"I guess. So how do they sneak a boat the size of Brighton outta Dublin?"

"Are all three of those vessels on their way in?"

"I don't know. There was a computer but it's gone. Those are the names of the freighters that are parked in Muir Éireann. They were listed on a random piece of paper. Looked like a loading and unloading schedule. I wrote down what I could."

"Were there departure or arrival dates on the ships?"

"Uh, I don't know. Let me see …. " I took out the piece of paper that I had written the vessel names and information onto.

"Which is the first to arrive in Boston, if you have it," Walter asked.

"The Annika Mærsk. Today is what, the first? So like two and a half weeks. Nineteen days. Says here 20 September. If I'm reading this right."

"Two weeks. That is about how long it takes to for the vessel to make the trip. It takes time to load those ships. Days. That's the ship. It's already loaded. It's already loaded and on it's way out."

"So once the port is cleared, the boat will float out with the guns. Still. That's like almost two thousand containers. What now?"

"Now I get with the DOJ and go through that cargo manifest with a fine tooth comb. We narrow it down and get the search warrants. Now we get you home."

"Good. How? And what about Rourke and Kane?"

"We can't do anything about that until we seize the weapons on this end. Then we pass along the information to the Irish government and move on. We deal with our guys on this end, they deal with theirs."

"The Sinns are the government here. The majority anyway. They don't really prosecute the way we do. It's complicated," I said.

"Our focus isn't on the supply of guns Deni. There will always be guns. There will probably always be an IRA, officially or not. But if we stop the demand side of things on our end, we've done our job. Rourke and Kane will be out of business in my district one way or another. Good Job. I'll call the embassy and get you out of Ireland."

"They are watching the airports. Row - uh, the reporter here, said that best way was out of Scotland or England."

"Fine. I'll contact someone to help you get to a safe spot and let me know where to get you a flight. Is this the number where I can reach you?"

"No. Don't call me, I'll call you."

"Deni, you need help. You can't just be out there on your own. Let me get you some help."

"I'm good. The last time you set me up with help, he turned out to be the fuckin' enemy in all this."

"I had no way of knowing that Cian was Kane. Or that Oisin was Dunn. But you are going to need help. You destroyed a hotel room, killed an Irish citizen — IRA or not — and beat up a hospital security guard. You're already a suspected IRA secret cell operative, there was a car bomb …. Listen, by now there isn't a Garda station in Ireland that doesn't have your photo. Let me help you Deni."

Huh. How the fuck does he know all that?

"Deni? Deni, you there?"

"Yeah. Yeah. I'm here. I gotta go."

"Just tell me where you are."

"I'm on my way home, Walt."

"Stay put. Tell me where you are so this doesn't get anymore out of hand."

"I'll call you when I get to a safe spot."

"Let me find one for you. What else do you need?"

"Just make sure my bonus is ready when I get home."

"Goddammit Deni! Deni?"

45

I SPENT THE REST OF WEDNESDAY, 1 SEPTEMBER getting back to Rowena's place and sleeping. I'm not sure if that was the wisest place to be, considering that either Finn Rourke, Darragh Kane, or one of the minions car bombed us. They put a device on Row's car hoping to kill me, Row, or both of us. Rowena had an unknown name and was in a hidden flat. Yet they managed to find her and me. But nothing in her flat seemed to have been touched. Not yet. So I stayed.

In truth, it was difficult for me to sleep at first. I made myself an American meal as best I could with what Row had on hand. Then a hot shower. My ears keen on every noise while I was wet. The hot water felt good on my beaten and broken body, but I was too skittish to stay in there for long. A dry-off with a thirsty towel but with nothing to wear. I raided Row's cupboard for something to be clothed in. Her space was entirely too small for the clothes and costumes that were packed and piled together. Knowing her there was a system to it, but I didn't know what it was. I settled for remaining in the towel, draped around my waist. Laying in Row's bed didn't rest my mind. It wandered and wondered. *Is she alive or dead? It was just a matter of time, even the doctor said so. Did her involvement with me get her killed?* There was no mention of it on the TV for the time that I had it turned on. I put on one of Row's many U2 CDs. I would have put on something else, but there weren't any other CDs as far as I could tell. The signature twang in Edge's guitar in the song *Bad* echoed in the small bedroom. Bono seemed to speak to me " .... Let it go .... and so fade away .... I'm wide awake .... "

I took a fresh bottle of whiskey from the press. " .... I'm not sleepin' .... " He kept singing, still speaking to me. Haunting me. It took almost a quarter of a bottle of the whiskey and the medicine from the I.V. bags to do the trick.

And sleep I did. Fuck you Bono.

I lost a few days. I woke up long enough to piss and hydrate. I was completely and utterly drained.

I woke up on Saturday, 4 September, feeling somewhat refreshed. It was evening and I was alive and well. Ish. Sleep didn't repair my fractured ribs. Nor did a fairy sprinkle magic dust on me in the middle of the night or morning to heal my stitched head and countless cuts and scrapes and burns. But I had survived so far.

Rourke and Kane had either thought the job had been accomplished or they thought that it was beyond comprehension that I would go back to Rowena's flat. I'm just stupid enough to be smart sometimes. Whatever the case may be, my enemies had let me be for the moment.

Several phone calls to Director Humphrey at the embassy went unanswered. 'Call me' he had said. I left messages to call me back at Rowena's flat, but he never did. Each time I stressed how important and urgent it was and that I desperately needed to speak with him. His help in getting out of Ireland would be crucial and urgent. But he never called back. And I didn't dare to go back there, I was certain that the embassy would be watched. I wouldn't make it to the gate.

The next morning I took another hot shower. This one was a long one. The I.V. port had to go. So did the stitches that were pulling on my head and body with every move I made. The wounds bled but they hurt less once I was finished fussing with them. Once I was out of the water, I wrapped my torso up with a new roll of tape. Partially to help clot all of the bleeding, partially to hold my ribs in place. Why Row had bandage rolls on hand was mystery. A pleasant one. Maybe she used them for some of her costumes. She had nothing to wrap up, nothing to hold in place. I missed her.

Thoughts of her and her well-being consumed me while I tried to find suitable clothes. There were none. I would have to don one of her myriad disguises. When I looked at the mirror in her bedroom, I was struck with an idea that I could not shake.

For laughs, I checked the washer/dryer to see if there were clothes in there. Rowena, ever used to having to remain neat in her tiny living space, had washed some of my clothes. They were wrinkled but dry.

I wish I could thank you in person, Row.

That thought added to the idea that I couldn't shake.

I put on the wrinkled jeans and Nirvana tshirt before grabbing the costume. Said goodbye to Row's flat for the last time. I'm just stupid enough to be smart sometimes.

The Mater Misericordiae University Hospital was no longer on lockdown. I learned in the police academy, and repeated many times to those I had partnered with, that criminals will often return to the scene of the crime because they can't help themselves. Often times that's how they get caught. It is ridiculously stupid. When I was boosting stuff as a kid, I did it outside of Southie. Mostly because the syndicates would beat the life out of me if I fucked up their gig, but it made sense to not be seen anywhere near the crime. I had just escaped from captivity and possibly being murdered, assaulting a guard and stealing a car in the process, and now I was going back.

I needed to check on Rowena. It was a need that I could feel in my bones. I would never be able to live with myself, always wonder what happened to her. She had helped to keep me alive, gave me shelter. The least I could do was see if she was still alive.

The taxi ride over to the hospital cost me nearly €20,00 but it was worth it not get caught in the stolen Peugot. I was finished with that car. In the unlikely event that I needed to drive again in Ireland, I could always acquire another one.

The trick to entering or leaving a secure building is to act like you belong there. If you look like you are trying to get away with something, then everyone assumes that you *are* trying to get away with something.

"Your badge sir," the security man said as I entered the employee entrance with the various second shift crews.

"Oh. Right. Let me dig into my pack …." I don't know if my accent was Irish or British or what. I took the back pack with my costume in it off of my shoulder, pretending to dig for an ID badge that didn't exist inside the accessory. "…. well this is a bit embarrassing. Surely you remember me." I looked him in the eye. "I'm here every day."

"Right. Name?"

Think, Deni, think. I blurted out the first name I could come up with. I didn't want there to be a pause. Who pauses when asked their name? "Smith." Definitely not an Irish name. Stupid.

The security man typed on the computer resting on the desk inside the employee entrance. He looked at me, then back at his screen, then back at me, before finally nodding his head. He handed me a green temporary badge with a clip on it. "Do see personnel about a replacement. This is acceptable for today only. You'll need them to make you a proper one for tomorrow, ye will."

"Thanks very much," I said. "Reckon I just left mine at home." *Reckon? Where'd you come up with reckon?* I walked away from the desk, looking at the temporary badge I was given. *Smythe.* The accent must have worked. Dr. Brannish Smythe. What a horrible name. But it would fit my costume. Better to be lucky than good.

I changed into the scrubs from Row's backpack, covering up with a long doctor's coat that I found in the familiar employee locker area. I didn't have a stethoscope or any other scope for that matter, just the green badge which I clipped to my left front pocket on the coat.

The lift was crowded so I utilised the stairs to the top floor. The critical care unit was located to the left, at the end of the hallway where I had escaped. I took the left at the top of the stairs, passed the restroom where I had knocked out the guard, walked slowly past the doctor and nurse station. Names were written on the dry-erase board, but I didn't want to linger in front of it or be seen staring at the board. The short, round, British doctor lady might have been there. I didn't want a chance encounter, costume or no.

Another hallway to the right would have taken me down to where my hospital bed had been located, the left would lead me to Rowena. Assuming she was still in there. She may have been moved to another part of the hospital. Maybe she was recovering. Maybe she was dead and in the morgue. I really didn't want to take a trip to the morgue.

The long hallway had rooms that were occupied on both sides. The critical care unit was down at the very end of that long

309

corridor. Since I wasn't able to really study the dry-erase board for fear of being recognised, I flew by the seat of my pants and resolved to look in on a number of patients until I found Row. But I could see which room was hers from the end of the hall by the two guards stationed outside the room. Hospital or Garda I was not sure, nor am I to this day.

At least she is alive. A flicker of hope.

The guards stopped me only to write down the name off of my badge. They didn't know what kind of doctor Smythe was, nor did I. When asked why I had not been there as of yet, why the name Smythe didn't appear on any of Row's other visits on their list, I simply told them that I was a specialist.

She looked terrible. She was always skinny and frail looking. She's Irish, so she's always pale. But her pallor was of skim milk. Grey-blue. Her breathing sounded like Darth Vader, more machine than anything organic. I imagined that NASA had less equipment than what was hooked up to Rowena. I don't know what I was looking for, but I looked at her chart anyway. It was all medical terminology for the fact that she was fucked-up and in a bad way.

The closer I got to the top of the bed, to her head, the less I wanted to see. The large neck brace holding her head facing the ceiling. The clear, plastic, fighter pilot breathing apparatus attached to her nose and mouth. The tubes tied together going into her arms were almost the diameter of her arms. She was somehow skinnier than she had been when I met her. One of the machines looked like an accordion was inside it, it moved up and down with the audible sound of her breathing.

Another machine had a digital spike and valley illuminated on the screen like the lines on a lie detector reading. The clear intravenous bags hung from the two racks like water balloons. Row was strapped down to the bed, probably to ensure that she didn't cause further spine damage by moving. Like she could or would move. It was horrible to watch.

I touched her hand, but there was no response. No movement. You see in the movies, hear people tell their miraculous stories, that they knew everything would be okay because of the blinking of the eyes or a squeeze of the hand. There was no blinking of the eyes. There was no hand squeeze.

"If I did this to you, Row, I'm sorry. I don't know if you can hear me, but if you can I want you to know that I never meant for this to happen to you. You're a good girl. I should have warned you that I always destroy good girls. I just came to say goodbye I guess. I'll see ya in the next life. Say a good word for me up there will ya? Not that I deserve it."

I reached into my pocket and took out her Sainte Christopher Medallion I had taken from her bedroom mirror. The patron sainte of lost causes would have his work cut out for him on this one. I put it in her hand, closing it around medal, and bent down to kiss her hand goodbye.

Just outside the room, as I was leaving, a man and another doctor were making their way toward Rowena. They stopped me, enquiries began.

"Who are you?" The doctor asked.

"Doctor Smythe. Specialist." I kept it short and sweet. I figured the less detailed I got, the less I could get hung up on.

"Right. The nerve specialist? How is she?"

I looked at the gentleman in tow with the other doctor, then pulled the physician off to the side.

"It's all right," the doctor said. "He is her editor and emergency contact. She is a donor, so we are keeping her alive with machines until it becomes necessary to turn them off. We hope for the best, but this is very bad. The Chaplin is coming up shortly to give last rights. I think it is a waste of resources to move forward with the other surgeries, don't you?"

"No. I don't." I said it a bit angrily. The tone didn't go unnoticed.

"She won't survive the surgeries. You must know that."

"We won't know that until we know it. If she doesn't survive, you can still harvest her organs. There is no downside to trying."

"As you know our resources are — "

311

" — what does the gentleman say?"   I pointed to Row's editor.

"He says to do whatever we can to help her recover."

"Then we had better get to it."

The doctor left me for Row's room. I left the hospital, never to return.

46

THE FERRY TO LIVERPOOL WAS A LONG ONE. And expensive. While the north side of the Dublin Port was closed for investigation, the south side was doing business as usual. There were several ferry lines doing business. With destinations to Isle of Man, Liverpool, Holyhead, and others; I could have taken a less direct route to England had I cared to part with more Euros. The Irish Ferries Company, P&O Irish Sea, DFDS, Moby, and a slew of others were all in the business of transporting people out of Dublin. I had a choice of who I wanted to give my money, compliments of the US Department of Justice and Joe and Jane taxpayer. But the various lines must have had an agreement, because they all fleece their patrons for the same fares.

The Stena Line was the last booth inside the Dublin Port South Terminal that I price-shopped, so that is the Ferry Operator that took my €49,50. It was also the soonest departure time on a

Sunday. I was forced to wait as many hours as the trip would take once it left Dublin.

Over the three hour wait in the terminal, and as we cruised by the Poolbeg Generating Station and the lighthouse, after we made way, I watched the freighters in Muir Éireann. They didn't move. They were all at anchor awaiting the lift of the temporary embargo. From the terminal I could not see The Annika Mærsk. Nor could I when we weigh anchor, nor as we set sail for Liverpool, United Kingdom. The large ferry sluggishly gained speed as we moved out of the harbour, floating past the parked vessels, slowly gaining speed to the 20 knots per hour that we would travel over the whitecaps. The freighter carrying the arsenal headed for Boston had already made way.

The powers that be of Stena Line had decided to turn a profit from the sale of alcohol on the ferries. Why I was shocked is beyond me, it was Europe after all. Nothing seemed to be accomplished in Ireland without being plied with alcohol. Why I was taken aback was because most people who take the ferry drive their cars onto it. I was one of the few people who didn't have a vehicle of some sort. Cars, scooters, even bicycles. The three hour ferry ride, with booze at the ready, was long enough to get a good buzz. Long enough to get drunk if one so chose. Then you arrived on the other side and were allowed to drive said vehicle off the boat and onto the streets of Liverpool. The logic is as dizzying as the heads of the consumers.

But who am I to judge? That's what I did. After I called Ryan Wells. Minus the driving of course. I used the mobile phone that came as proceeds from the scuffle in Belturbet.

"Ryan. Deni. How are things in New Hampshire?"

"Holy Shit you're alive. Worrisome. It's good to hear from you. I got a call from Walter Glibczieck saying that you were probably dead. Are you okay?"

"For the moment. I'm sneaking back to Boston. I haven't booked a flight yet but I'll figure it out."

"Be careful. You might not have as many friends as you think."

314

"I don't have many friends in the first place, Ry. Whattaya mean?"

"It might have just been political maneuvering, but when Walter thought you were dead he called me to let me know that he was cutting ties. He was trying to get as far away from you as possible."

"I spoke to him already. He knows I'm coming back. There is a ship already on the way to Boston with the load of weapons," I said.

"When was that? He called last Thursday, when he learned about a car bomb that you might have been involved in on that Tuesday. I guess he saw it on CSPAN. What's going on?"

"Yeah. These assholes tried to kill me. I was knocked out for a bit. So what? He said that if I was dead, that you guys know nothing about it?"

"Exactly. He has your boss Titani — "

" — Tits. What about him?"

"Well he has him on a leash, I think. And he was basically threatening me. Telling me that he was a bad enemy to have. You just might want to be careful. Does he know of your whereabouts? I'm getting a bad vibe about him. I don't like that you have hitched up to his star."

"No. I don't think he knows exactly where I am. I told him I would find my own way back. I was kinda getting the same feeling when I was talkin' to him. He knew stuff that I'm not sure how he'd know. I got a good knock on the head, and I'm pretty paranoid these days, but all I got are my instincts."

"Good. I think your instincts are good on this one. You might want to keep him in the dark for the moment," Ryan said.

"Thanks for the tip. He's probably just being a political douchebag, but you can never be too careful. He probably didn't want to have to explain shit going sideways. He wouldn't have sent me over here if there was something else going on. But with everything that has happened, it's better to be safe than sorry." I don't know if I was defending him or trying to allay my own fears.

"Do you still have my cell number? Call me day or night. I'll pick you up from the airport."

"Thanks. Will do. I am gonna need a place to stay also."

"We can figure that out once you get back. Day or night. I feel partly responsible that you are in this mess."

"It's not your fault, Ry. You didn't start it. I'll see you on your side of the pond."

When we hung up, I rested my elbows on the side of the ferry. I thought for few moments about what Ryan had said, and looked at the mobile phone. I looked around the vessel, nobody was paying me any mind. One last look at the device, then a toss over the side. If they wanted it back they could search the bottom of the Atlantic.

By the time we had made way into the sound in Liverpool, under the A59 flyover and moored onto the pier, I was more than buzzed. As a pedestrian, I was allowed off of the ferry first. I had thought that I would hail a taxi, which I did but not before taking the BusyBus over the River Mersey to the terminal. The terminal sits next to the Titanic Memorial and I was glad not to have surrendered to the same fate.

The taxi stand had a line of them waiting for fares. I chose the first one in line, just like I would in Boston, although I was unsure if the etiquette was international. I said, "The airport." I thought that meant that we were going to Heathrow. When you think of airports in England, do you think of any other airports? I didn't. I might have actually thought it was the only one.

Instead, we took Strand Street to A562, to A561. The roads had other names like Parliament and things like that, changing every few hundred feet but the numbers remained the same. Three roundabouts and thirty minutes later I was parting with another €40,00. I was going to need to cash in some more traveler's checks because I was running out of Euros.

John Lennon Airport. I shit you not. Those Brits are sentimental. And there were no direct flights to Boston. And none would get me there until Monday, 6 September. I thought the nice lady at the terminal asked me for cunnilingus. She seemed cute enough and I was still buzzed so I agreed. A few awkward moments later I realised that she was asking me if the airline Aer Lingus would be ok.   The Irish airline.   Meaning fly back into Dublin.

"No! Fuck no. Anything else. I'll go by carrier pigeon if I have to."

Icelandair it was. So I spent the night in Reykjavik, Iceland. But only in the airport. It cost me over €2000,00 for the privilege of sleeping in an uncomfortable position on a chair. Another country, another airport that thankfully had bilingual signs. Brottfarir and Hlið. I mean …. how would one even pronounce them, let alone interpret them? Phonics is not always fun.

The bank of uncomfortable chairs was next to a bank of ATMs or flight kiosks or some other popular machines. So even if I was able to contort my body a-la Cirque du Soleil into a comfortable position, the traffic to those machines would have made it impossible.   They made these god-awful digital noises when they spit out the tickets or money or whatever. The machines were as popular as Vegas slots.   Maybe they were spitting out money. I really should have checked instead of trying to get sleep, since it didn't come anyway.

The flight out of Reykjavik couldn't have come quick enough. The night crept along like an Icelandic Banana Slug. Which in case you didn't know is about as slow as slow gets. I didn't know it either until I read it on one of the illuminated walls littered with nonsensical indigenous animal facts in the terminal.

They called out the flight number at 5:05 AM on 6 September. But then we were made to wait before boarding. The magazine and book store employee lifted the garage style door and began placing racks for the daily newspapers out while we waited to venture on to the jetway and out of that frozen hellhole. The Guardian, a major newspaper out of London, was one such paper being put out on display. We were all forced to stand right in front of the kiosk and a

317

headline caught my eye. The one just below 'US Death Toll in Iraq Passes 1,000'. The headline was above the fold, the actual story below.

Suspected IRA Leader and Garda Detective Slain in Dublin

I threw money for the paper at the poor lady that was setting up shop for the day. I had no idea how much The Guardian cost, but I knew I gave her way too much. The boarding began and I walked onto the plane reading the front page article. It continued inside the front section, on page four while I found my seat and plopped into it. But to sum it up, Darragh Kane was dead. Rowena and I weren't the only ones who figured out that Cian Daly was also head of the IRA network of secret cells. What they presumably didn't know, because it wasn't printed, was that Finn Rourke was his overlord and was likely the reason he was dead.

Rowena was about to follow Kane into the afterlife if she wasn't already dead. I hoped they would end up in very different places if there was such a thing as an afterlife. Being a recovering Catholic, and in some cases simple logic, dictates that I have doubts. But I held out hope.

The only three people alive that I knew that had specific knowledge of Finn Rourke's nefarious deeds were now me, Ryan Wells, and Walter Glibczieck. And according to Ryan, Walt was a shady shit.

You're not out of the woods yet, Deni. Once Rourke knows for sure that I am alive, it won't take his new minions long to correct the mistakes of their predecessors. They have secret cells in their network all over the world. Slopes and the Winter Hill crew were brutal killers but very low on the international criminal food chain, though they were always looking to move up. Maybe they were looking to make the terrorist watch list. The Winter Hills tried to kill me by killing my home. They had already done so much damage, taken so many lives. Danny and Rox. Breen. My tenants. Imagine what they would do when Slopes was properly incentivised. Let alone if Rourke sent an actual crew over the pond to supervise the task. I might see Row in time for orientation at the pearly gate.

Part Four

Sometimes Life is an American Story

September 2004

47

HOME SWEET HOME. Logan airport, Boston, Massachusetts. Home of baked beans, clam chowder, and my beloved Red Sox. I wanted to kiss the fuckin' ground. But first customs and a pay phone. Ryan said that he would be a couple of hours, but he would be there. What else did he have to do in the middle of a Monday? So I had some time to kill. Thankfully I didn't have any luggage to cart around.

Speaking of clam chowder, I hadn't eaten anything resembling good food since I had left Boston. So I spent a couple of hours at the counter of Legal Sea Foods over in Terminal C. They didn't have Redbreast 12 yr Whiskey, but the food made up for it. Clam chowder, then the sashimi tuna, then the jasmine special. I pigged out. I drew the line at Boston cream pie. I was too full.

Ryan picked me up a couple of hours after I called him, just like we agreed. I met him out in front, we made small talk while he drove me over to pick up my *Escalade* from the garage that had fixed my window. He was nice enough to pay for my replacement window and storage before I followed him north to New Hampshire. The ride up was uneventful save for the U2 song that came on WZLX, the classic rock channel. *With Or Without You.* It reminded me of Row, and I was definitely without. It never would have worked out between us, but I didn't want her dead.

The hippie drives slow. If I didn't know any better I would have thought that Ryan was stoned and paranoid driving. I drive fast, partly because I think that the speed limit is more a suggestion than anything else. But also I was a cop. So being forced to do the speed limit or less meant that I had plenty of time to decompress.

Ryan and Ang were nice enough to offer me a room at their place. He and his wife Angie had already settled it, I found out when we pulled into his driveway. Ryan informed me as we exited our vehicles and were walking toward his front door. There was no thankfully declining. If I wanted a dime from him for my work, or the possibility of any future work, this was going to happen.

Angie was at their house in Wayland, New Hampshire, waiting for us to arrive. She was a nice lady. She was the efficient receptionist of Grantes, Wells & Associates by day, loving wife by night. She was very pretty and I had thought that Ryan had himself a catch. She was already home from work for the day and welcomed me in, showed me upstairs to the room that I could "have as long as I needed." She said supper would be ready in an hour, so I would have time to shower and change if I wanted. I didn't tell her that I was still full from Legal's and that I had no clothes to change into if I did take a shower.

She and Ryan caught up downstairs. The walls were thin so I couldn't help but overhear that there were a great many things that she had to reschedule in order for him to have blown off the entire day fetching me. She wasn't nasty about it. Didn't even seem irritated. Just the facts mister.

While listening but not listening to them, I made a list of all of the shit that I needed to do. Check with my bank. See how much money I had to my name and cash the few remaining traveler's checks I had. Call my insurance company. See if they had a check for me to rebuild my three-decker. Call Tits. My boss was probably wondering what was going on with me. Buy new clothes. New cell phone. New life. All would cost a fortune.

Supper came and went. Some sort of chicken and polenta thing. They were health nuts. I picked at it but was really not interested in eating. I had to be polite. So I did what all of the anorexic girls that I have taken out to dinner had done; pushed food around my plate to make a mess, take a bite every now and then to make it seem like I was eating. If Angie was offended, she didn't let on.

The three of us had drinks in their parlor. Angie with some sort of French white wine. The bottle said 'sincere' or some damn thing. Ryan had some sort of special dark beer. They had whiskey for me. The bottle was brand new so Ang must have bought it at the State Liquor Store on the way home. They really were very nice people.

"So Deni," Ryan said once drinks were poured and we were all seated comfortably. "All of your work is immensely helpful in the Breen civil case. "I've heard some or all of it, but I would like to hear about the case in full. Keep in mind that we will need to provide proof. Tell me everything, fact and theory. We can work on how to prove it all later. It might be a year or two before it ever sees civil court."

"You just want the stuff that relates to Breen? That's pretty simple and you know most of it. Breen was part of the old man combine up here in New Hampshire. They held guns and made drugs to make money for the Irish mob syndicate. The mob in Boston, works and distributes guns and money all over the country. All over the world." He nodded and listened to me, Ang also. But this was not what he wanted me to explain.

323

"So those guns that were confiscated here, and misplaced down in Maynard, are all part of the same supply chain that is coming over from Ireland," I said between sips of whiskey. "Those weapons are slated for distribution out of Boston to all points west. A safe guess is that they are for other enterprises that feed money through Winter Hill up to the IRA secret cells. Now they have to be replaced. Anybody that knew anything about the operation was killed so they wouldn't fess .... er, I was in Ireland too long .... rat on what was going on. My guy, Danny Mick. His sister, Roxanne. Breen. And of course they tried to kill me.

"Sean Teague, AKA Slopes, was protecting his Boston crew. The Winter Hill Gang. They are directed by the IRA because the army is supplying guns in exchange for money that they pay up to the Irish Republican Army Council, headed by none other than Finn Rourke, the Army Council General. Finn Rourke is also one of the leaders in Sinn Féin, a political group that is all about a pure Ireland. While they might have pure ideals, their deeds are not so much. Whether the Sinns as a whole know it or not is unknown, because the entire organization is so compartmentalized and this Rourke treats the supposedly disbanded IRA like his own personal security force. He *had* two guys named Darragh Kane and Aiden Dunn doing his bidding. Passing down orders to the secret IRA cells within the network to keep the money coming in. Funding the Sinn Féin party."

I let that sink in for a second while I refilled my drink. I told them I would be right back, went up the stairs to my room, returning with the copy of the The Guardian.

When I returned to the parlor, I put the newspaper on the coffee table between us. "Slopes was using the Finn Rourke playbook when he decided to take out anyone and everyone that stood in the way of moving product for cash. Even me. Those *lads* in Dublin decided to have a fire sale.

"I'm not sure if Ry told you this Ang, but Darragh Kane was also Cian Daly." I pointed to the newspaper. "Cian was the guy that Walter sent me over to consult. He was supposed to help me figure stuff out. Instead Daly was playing me for information and

324

tried to kill me. He wanted to know how badly the Boston shipment was fucked before they did the job. When it all went south, Rourke decided to kill everyone. I met this informant, Oisin Hanamy. He had a couple of names but he was really Aiden Dunn. He reported to Kane and Rourke. He's also dead. Kane outlived his usefulness." I was still pointing at the newspaper. "And now he is dead."

This too was given a moment to breath. To marinate. Ryan broke the silence.

"So how do we prove this connection to Breen?"

"When the guns get here. They are due into Boston Harbor on the twentieth. That delivery will tie up all the loose ends. According to Walter, he can't touch the Sinns or the IRA. But we can dry up their funding by cutting off the gun demand. By busting everyone who collects that shipment, we establish the connection."

"Connection is collusion. It's not a long leap from collusion to an elaborate conspiracy to commit murder. There's plenty of motive," Ryan said.

Angie leaned forward on the couch. "Maybe I'm missing something but from what Ryan has told me, why don't we think that this Federal Prosecutor, this Walter person, isn't involved? He sent you into the hands of this IRA guy. They tried to kill you. The mob here and the IRA over there. Why do we trust this guy? He thought you were dead and threatened Ryan to keep his mouth shut about sending you over there. Right Honey?"

"He did." Ryan was looking into his drink, nodding his head.

"Does he know that I'm back Ry?"

"I haven't told him."

"Fine. So he stays in the dark. You said that he has my boss, Tits, on a leash?"

Angie laughed. "Tits on a leash," she mumbled. "That's funny for some reason. I'm sorry." She tried to compose herself. Her laugh was infectious and we all joined her in the laugh.

I continued after the moment of levity subsided. "As soon as I check in at Troop H, they'll know I'm back and then it's going to be open season. I'll have to be careful. You both seem like nice people, I don't want you to end up like my tenants. I probably shouldn't stay here."

"And go where?" Angie looked concerned but determined. "You'll stay right here. We will all be careful."

"At Grantes and Wells, we protect our employees," Ryan said. "I spoke with JG and we want to hire you on full-time. If you still want that. You can work other cases or what have you, but we want to get first priority on our investigations. You said that you wanted out of the Staties, are you still interested?"

Ryan handed me a check with a fair number of zeros on it. "For your work so far on the Breen case. There is more down the line when we get our cut of the settlement. Breen's girl wants justice. By justice she means money. Just make sure that we nail this shipment coming in on the twentieth."

I was stunned to get a check that large. I knew what I was charging them an hour, but the check was much more than what I was figuring to bill them. This was a great start to getting out of the Massachusetts State Police Department. My days as a cop were officially numbered. With the pile of shit I was in, maybe all of my days were numbered.

48

I PUT OFF THE PHONE CALL TO LIEUTENANT TITANITAUKIS for as long as I could. It took me a couple of days just to get my own shit together, never mind taking on another helping of it. Tuesday and Wednesday were spent getting my own house in order, even though I didn't have one.

The bank was happy to see me. With the deposit of the business check from Grantes, Wells & Associates, of which I was now considered a part of, my account was looking pretty good. I went to the post office to find out what was happening with my mail. The mailbox that was attached to the three-decker was no longer in existence, so they just held onto my mail at the South Boston Post Office. My insurance check had come through. Along with my notice of cancellation. They had paid out for a replacement car and a home in the same year. They were done with me. I put the check into an escrow account with same bank,

Citizens Bank & Trust. The new house could wait until this case was over. With my luck, it would just get burned down again.

New clothes, check. New cell phone, check. Down the list I went in an attempt to get back to normal. All of these errands were done with the pedal to the floor and a thorough look in my rearview. As far as I knew, only Mr. and Mrs. Wells, and probably JG, knew that I was back in New England, alive and somewhat well. I wanted to make sure I kept them as safe a possible. They were kind, I hated to think of them of being in any danger of dying a horrible death. I hoped that they would break my current streak.

Each night I went back to their place in Wayland like it was my new home. Suppers were a time to catch up. Chat about everything. And nothing. I missed having someone to talk with. But how can you miss something that you've never had? Ryan and I would follow up after supper with drinks and NESN. The Red Sox crushed the A's both nights. They had a record of 84-54 and were still behind the goddamned Yankees.

I had called Tits after supper on Wednesday night. I was told to meet him the following morning in his office. Nine o'clock would be perfect. Perfect for him. Traffic out of New Hampshire into Boston at that hour was going to be an absolute goat-screw. The big dig would have shit torn up and diverted so horribly that it would take the normal bumper to bumper traffic and make it exponentially worse. I would have to leave at oh-dark-thirty to make the appointment.

Thursday, September 9th was already a terrible day by the time I rolled into Troop H in Downtown Boston. Three hours of traffic followed by detectives pestering me the second I walked into the station. "Where have you been?" seemed to be repeated over and over and over again. I wouldn't miss that. Eyes on your own paper.

I was surprised to see Walter Glibczieck in my Lieutenant's office as I entered it humming Warren Zevon's *Lawyers, Guns and Money*. It had come on the car stereo on the trip over, I had blasted it and it was stuck in my head. I wasn't worried per se, but seeing him made me stop humming rather abruptly. I expected Walter to be salty that I had not been in contact with him. And I expected that if Tits was going to sack me, getting fired would save me the trouble of quitting. It just surprised me is all. Less than twenty-four hours after I let Tits know that I was back, and Walter was sitting in his office awaiting my arrival.

"Walt. I wasn't planning on seeing you today." He stood and shook my hand, then sat back down. I repeated the ritual of pumping hands with my lieutenant before the entire room took a chair.

"I was wondering if you were ever going to call me," Walter said.

"Of course I was. I want to get my bonus check. I just needed time to get situated. In case you've forgotten, I don't have a house anymore."

"None of us have forgotten your sacrifice, have we Lieutenant?"

"No. Of course not. But we do have some concerns."

"I have some of my own, guys. Like what are we gonna do about Slopes? Ya know, Sean Teague and company?"

Walter appeared like he was trying to find the correct words. He was struggling. "The Mass State Police aren't going to pursue this any further. The ATF will take it from here."

"So I'm off this case? Just like that? I do all the grunt work, take a few attempts at killing me in stride? Just move on?"

Walter handed me an envelope. "Your bonus as we agreed. You've more than earned it. Thank you for your services."

"Lieutenant this fucking bullsh and you know it. The Winter Hill crew has been operating with impunity for how long? We get a shot and closing it down, after busting my ass, and we have to walk away?"

"Unfortunately it's a jurisdictional thing, Deni." Tits said my name like he was reminding me of my place in the world. Which he clearly thought amounted to the shit that is between the tread on the bottom of a hobo's shoe. "Hobbs is out in the field. You can catch up with him tomorrow after you've cooled down. You two can get caught up on his open cases. That's it for now."

"No. That's not 'all for now'." Eyebrows were raised. "Two weeks. I'm giving you my two weeks. I'm done with this shit."

Tits nodded like he wasn't surprised. He might have even been relieved. Maybe it was the goal. "Put it in writing."

"Fine. I'll give it to you tomorrow."

Walter's turn. "Deni? Keep in mind that if you go anywhere near this investigation, I will personally throw the book at you. Obstruction, interfering with a government investigation, misconduct …. you will be my personal pet project. There is an unsolved murder in Ireland that the Garda would love to close the book on. We can add that to the pile. And these are just off the top of my head. Imagine if I were to get creative?"

"I read you loud and clear. Are we done?"

Silence.

When I left the Lieutenant's office, I slammed the door loud enough for the suspects sitting on the bench on the other side of the precinct to jump like they had heard a gunshot.

"Ry, it's me. Almost exactly as planned. Although Walt was there."

"In the office? At the same time? Deni, did he give you your bonus check?" Ryan was somewhere noisy, he had to shout into his cell phone.

"Cash not a check. But it's all here."

"Deposit it. Right now. And don't lose that track of that deposit slip. Get a notarized statement from the bank that it was cash, and the numbers on the bills."

"How am I going to find a notary public that quick?"

"Your bank will have one on duty. They all do. At least one. Get them to count it, note the bills, make a statement and put a seal on it. Very important. Did they fire you?"

"No. I had to quit, but other than that it went perfectly. I was just a little surprised to see Walt there."

"Your Lieutenant might just be a pawn, but treat him like he's in on it."

"Will do. Walt made the threats. He wants me off of this. I'm supposed to check in with my old partner tomorrow. Not a lot of wiggle room."

"Can he be trusted to cover for you?"

"No. He's the king of all douchebags. If I go to the bathroom he's gonna want to hold it for me. But I'll figure somethin' out."

"Great. We'll talk tonight. I'm in court right now, and Judge McCaglia is in a mood. I gotta go."

"Knock'em dead. See ya later."

49

FRIDAY MORNING WAS A GIANT HEADACHE FOR ME. Rick Hobbs, my partner, was attached to me like a conjoined twin. I had to listen to him give me the rundown on what he hadn't accomplished in my absence. He was successful in that he had accomplished nothing. He had not solved one case. He had only taken more on. The guy was about as useful as tits on a bull. It takes talent to do so little and still have a job. I truly felt for his next partner. Poor prick.

Hobbs might have been a nice guy. Who knows? But I could never get past his uselessness. And how annoying he is. I had the constant desire to do the world a favor and choke the life out of him. His wife must be a saint.

He had requisitioned a *Crown Vic*, so he felt that he had the right to drive it. I preferred to drive in the *Intrepids* that were in the motor pool, but word had spread of my imminent departure so I

332

had no say in the matter. He also got to pick the traveling music. Fucking Chick Corea. *Hound of Heaven.* Jazz.

"Jazz is very intellectual," he said as way of counterargument.

"Then turn it up. You need all the help you can get."

"I never complain about what music you put on."

"That's because I listen to good music, not a cross between elevator Muzak and eighties porn."

"You don't have much longer to put up with it do you?"

"No, I don't. By the way, I was hoping to meet someone for a long lunch today. You can drop me off down by the Seaport District if you want."

"Where are you going? Barking Crab? Jimmy's?"

"Jesus, Hobbs. I'm not inviting you, so really it's none of your business."

"We're partners, so it does concern me."

"We're not married partners. We are investigative partners. Detectives. Though you haven't detected much while I was away have you?"

"Funny. We have leads we need to investigate today. Are you going to milk out the rest of your time? Cuz that is gonna suck for me."

"Because your clearance rate has been so high without me? Get over ya-self."

"I'm glad I'm getting a new partner. I've been asking for someone else since you and I were assigned together."

"Good things come to those who wait, Hobbs."

The rest of the morning was spent talking to two different people who were supposedly the last two people to see a woman who had disappeared. Neither of them knew where she was, only that she seemed in good spirits the last night that they had seen her. In other words, they were of no help. Wasted time and energy instead of doing what I wanted to be doing, which was namely to find Slopes.

333

Hobbs dropped me off on Congress Street on the western side of the Seaport Hotel and Conference Center at a quarter past noon. "Will an hour be enough time?"

"Better make it two."

"C'mon Deni. Really?"

"Tell ya what. I'll call you when I'm ready. You can pick me up right here." I didn't wait for a response. Instead, I slammed the car door and ran east on Seaport Lane, between the two buildings of the hotel. Halfway down the tiny street, past the cabs waiting for fares, I quickly entered the lobby. A right past the lounge, around to the left, past the bakery, and right out onto Northern Avenue. Congress and Northern run parallel, connected by Seaport Lane and others. I wanted to make sure that I had lost Hobbs. There was no place in my mind that I didn't think that he wasn't going to follow me and report me to Tits. He could just pull a bitch at the next one-way and watch me. When I crossed Northern Avenue, I looked both ways for the *Crown Vic*. Hobbs was nowhere to be seen.

On the other side of Northern Avenue is the Boston Seaport World Trade Center and on the other side of that was the Atlantic Ocean. Inside that building, among other entities are the Massachusetts Port Authority (MASS PORT) and Seaport Transportation Management. Those two entities report to the Bureau of Customs & Border Protection (renamed CBP after 9/11) and to the Department of Homeland Security all of the information about every vessel that comes in and out of Boston Harbor. Whether the boat carries people or cargo, these organizations know about them or other large boats with very large weapons get involved.

It was a beautiful day to be down by the water, sixty-nine degrees and sunny. I would have loved to spend the afternoon sitting on the docks and sipping beverages at the Barking Crab. But I wanted to solve this case more.

I circled the building from within, up flights of stairs and down. I wasn't followed. The MASS PORT office was on the eastern-most side of the building on the first floor. The actual first floor, not the ground floor like I had to deal with in Ireland. It took no time at all after the flashing of the badge to get cooperation.

"I want to see the shipping manifest for a vessel that is scheduled to dock on September 20th. The Annika Mærsk." I said to the gentleman in his early fifties behind a desk.

"Of course. If we have it. They are supposed to submit prior to arrival since 68 FR 68140 was amended. But this is only the 10th. We might not have it yet." He stood up instead of immediately typing the name of the ship into his computer terminal. He moved closer to me, his back to the ocean, Coast Guard boats and the bay behind him.

"68 …. FR …. whatever? What's that?"

"FR means Final Rule." He leafed through a folder, putting a piece of paper in front of me on top of the half-wall that separated us. Then quoted it verbatim while I read along. "Right there. 'The cargo information required is that which is reasonably necessary to enable high-risk shipments to be identified for purposes of ensuring cargo safety and security and preventing smuggling pursuant to the laws enforced and administered by CBP. These regulations are specifically intended to effectuate the provisions of section 343(a) of the Trade Act of 2002, as amended by the Maritime Transportation Security Act of 2002.' In other words, the information doesn't have to be listed on the Automated Manifest System until twenty-four hours prior to arrival. We are talking Bulk Cargo, yes?"

"Yes. But I don't understand. Somebody on the shipping end enters the manifest data in to this system — "

" — AMS, yes. A computer system."

"And it ends up on this end. But it can be well on it's way before having to be declared before it gets here?" I immediately remembered that there was a missing computer from Niall's modified office on Dublin Port.

"Very good. Yes. It is a very political and jurisdictional thing. Once it is at sea it is considered to be in international 'no man's land'. It is up to the nearest country's Coast Guard or Military to protect those waters. Once it is in port, then CBP or MASS PORT or other agencies get involved."

335

"So who has access to this computer transmission? It can be altered prior to reaching the destination, am I right?"

"Theoretically. But only a bonded transporter or a third-party AMS service provider would have access to the specific manifest entry."

"Explain. I'm not good with computers. So use small words."

He laughed and slowed his speech like I was mentally challenged instead of technologically challenged. "For example China. Believe it or not, even here in 2004, there are still some bulk shipping companies that still only use paper manifests. Since 9/11 the AMS, the computer system, has been mandated. No more loose paper manifests. So these companies that are behind the technological times utilize a third-party to transfer their paper manifests onto the AMS."

"Seems very risky. Some random company can mess up or completely omit cargo from a freighter that sails on into a port. After everything that has happened that seems very dangerous."

"Again, they have to be bonded by the CBP. They would have to be a vetted and trusted enterprise or they are not allowed onto the system or into the port. But you are correct. It isn't perfect, but when we are dealing with international organizations it's the best we can do at the moment. If it weren't for these ships, virtually no international commerce would take place. Imagine the number of planes it would take to move the amount of cargo that these vessels move. Airports would be at a standstill."

"So do you have the manifest or not?"

He moved back behind his desk and typed into his computer. "It's here yes. The Annika Mærsk. What do you want to know?"

I went around the half-wall that we had been speaking over, through the saloon style half-door and stood over the gentleman's shoulder. His computer screen was blurry. The dark blue border with the yellow background was harsh on the eyes. Only a government agency would make something that needed to be studied at length so difficult to look at.

"How do you read this ….. er ….. I'm sorry I don't even know your name?"

"Glen. And they can be hard to read. Unless you know what you are looking for it's like trying to drink water from a fire-hose. So what are you looking for?"

The vessel ID, vessel name, time and date of both departure and arrival, house bill, ocean bill, and voyage number were all in white boxes lined up on the yellow field. And that was just the information at the very top portion of the window. One could scroll down at all of the information, every container, for seemingly days. Container number, cargo type, both port codes, U/B, Dec, status. All columns with endless numbers and letters underneath them.

"How can I tell who sent what to whom off of this, Glen?"

"That would take some investigating, sir. There has be over a thousand containers on this manifest."

"More like fifteen hundred. And even if we found the container or containers I'm curious about, who is to say that what is inside is what is listed? Right?"

"Sort of. Theoretically all containers are inspected and have a seal on them."

"Yeah well I know for a fact that they aren't all inspected on the shipping side of this equation. Are they inspected on this end?"

"Not unless they are suspicious. I see warrants for containers all of the time. But, no offense, you seem to be fishing."

"I know what is in at least one of those containers. I just don't know which. Can you look into this? Give me a list of the companies that shipped the containers, how many, and who they shipped it to?"

"I'm kinda busy, here officer."

"Detective. And I'll make it worth your effort. Can you do it?"

"It's not coming in until the 20th. How long do I have?"

"As quick as you can. The sooner I get it, the more worth your effort it will be. Do we have an understanding?"

Glen smiled. His entrepreneurial spirit had been kindled. "I think we do detective."

337

There were more things that I wanted to do in my allotted two hours. Find Slopes. Find some lunch. But I didn't have the time. Other than getting Glen on the case, I went through an old cell phone bill I had collected from the South Boston Post Office to determine the phone number of the informant that I had met at Starbucks in Backbay near Copley. He had proven very helpful thus far. I wanted to thank him and see if he had any other bits of useful information. Like maybe if he found out more information about the shipment that could help me isolate the container or containers. Maybe he knew where Sean Teague was. But I would never find out. The number was disconnected. Something told me it wasn't because he had failed to pay his bill.

50

LUCKILY IT WASN'T OUR WEEKEND TO PULL OVERTIME. I had only been back working with Hobbs for one day and I already needed the break. And some space. I heard nothing but the third degree on Friday when he picked me up where he had dropped me off at the Seaport Hotel. I didn't share any information about my 'lunch date', nor did he share any information about how he had spent the time. Suffice to say that in terms of our mutual caseload, about as much got accomplished at the end of the shift as in the beginning of it.

Saturday was spent scouring Southie for Slopes or any of the Winter Hill crew. I combed the streets all day. I went to the abandoned warehouse on Washington. It was under construction, nobody other than some Shawmut workers were in or around the building. So I continued to scour, turning over every rock, questioning every kid that was playing stickball in the streets or was in the process of mischief until they spotted me. They all knew the drill. They all knew me, and they knew who Slopes was and what he was capable of. If they had any information, they knew to keep it to themselves.

I hit every seedy dive bar in my neighborhood that night. And there are many. Too many to hit in one night, so I concentrated on the non-gentrified watering holes. Like Croke Park, Whitey's old hangout. The Corner Pub. The Blackhorn. The L Street Tavern. And my actual hang out, Murphy's Law.

I questioned no one. I just drank and listened. I did learn something from my time in Ireland. People came over to catch up. Find out how I was doing since the fire. Where I had been. Whether I was going to rebuild. Only one guy that I knew well from Murphy's had the balls to ask me what they all really wanted to ask me, which was — who did I piss off bad enough to warrant being burned out and about a thousand bullet casings out in front of the fire on the street? Like they didn't know.

Slopes was laying low. Nobody was talking about him. I didn't recognize anyone from his crew in any of the dives. Except The L. Of course it was the last place I had hit for the night. It was the last place that I would think to look for a mob guy. The L Street Tavern was one of the bars *Good Will Hunting* was filmed in. Pictures of Matt and Ben and Robin were everywhere. The place was cheap and divey, but in a hipster kind of way. The new folks in the area who were gentrifying the neighborhood love it because of the recent history and prices. Tourists love it like they love Cheers.

Of course I was half-buzzed by the time I saw him. Shey Brenner. Mindless kid who was way down on the Winter Hill hierarchy. An idiot who was faded in the back. Swaying like a Weeble. He weebled, he wobbled, but he wouldn't fall down. He was yelling at one of the many TVs while the Red Sox killed the Mariners. Nobody had the heart to tell him that it was a west-coast day game and NESN was replaying it 'in two'.

I waited until he stumbled his way outside in front of the bar for a smoke to corner him.

"Shey Fuckin' Brenner! Slummin' with the yuppies and tourists tonight, huh chief?"

His eyes tried to focus. His mind tried to focus. Then bingo. "Deni? Tha fuck are you doin' down here?" If you think my Boston accent is bad — try this drunken idiot's on for size. If I wasn't from Southie I wouldn't have understood him.

"Lookin' for the big kid. Where you been, Shey?"

"I been around. Everyone wants to know where you been though."

"I've been around too."

"Why you lookin' for me?"

"I wanna know if you were the one who peppered my house and burned it?" I helped him over to the 8th Street side of the bar. Leaned him up against the wall so he wouldn't fall, though he probably wouldn't. He might have been in his early twenties, but he had been drinking for years longer than he was legally allowed to.

"Don't start shit again, Deni. You know tha drill down here. Live and let live. Until you don't."

"So it was you? Are you still lookin' for me? I'm right here."

"If it was the crew, you know they wouldn't put me on somethin' that big." He lit another cigarette off of the first. Only he lit the filter instead.

"So who was it?"

"No fuckin' clue. Lemme buy ya a beer. Stop askin' stupid questions."

"I help you out Shey, and you help me out. It's deal time."

"Yeah you don't seem to be helpin' out the neighborhood so much these days. You tryin' ta make captain or some shit?"

"I'm done as a cop. But big shit is coming down. And it's comin' your way. You don't have many beers left, Shey. It's gonna be Walpole for you. So whattaya gonna do?"

"Are you fuckin' with me?"

"Nope. Why would I fuck with you Shey? You burn down my house? Fuck it, I got my insurance. Like you said — 'Live and let live'."

"What do you want from me?"

"The guns."

341

"Fuck you, Deni. You don't even know what you're askin'."
He lit a third cigarette properly this time.

"I know things are about to get real bad for Sean and the
crew. Raids. Details. I don't give a shit about my house, Shey. I'll
rebuild. But my tenants were killed. Murdered. Those murders
are still on the books. Investigation is still open. I start pointing the
finger at you guys?"

"Everybody already knows who did it. But nobody can
prove it."

"You boys peppered the house from the middle of the fuckin'
street, Shey. People saw you assholes. Those guns that you used
were the same ones from New Hampshire. Same ones that went
out of Maynard Ballistics lab as quick as they went in. Same types
that are on their way over here from Ireland right now."

"Nobody is talkin'."

"Not yet. But like I said, shit is going down. You have time
to get out."

"And do what Deni? Last I checked the fire department ain't
hirin'."

"You only set fires anyway. You have a choice here fuck-tard.
You can spend the rest of your life in Walpole, or you can be a free
man."

"You can't make deals anyways. You ain't a cop anymore
you said."

"Two weeks left. Little under. I file you as a CI, give you
immunity and you skate."

"Fuck that. I ain't no rat. You know that."

"Rats are survivors. You wanna survive? All I want to know
about are the guns. I already know when they are comin' in. I just
want a container number."

"Fuck that. We got a system. We're straight. It's a lock.
'Sides. I don't know what you're talkin' about."

"That's what you're goin' with? Down with the ship?"

"Whatever you say, Deni. We done?" He flicked his butt
onto the empty 8th Street.

"I guess so. You realize I'm gonna make you pay right? This
was a one time offer. All of those deaths. Danny Mick, his sister,

Breen, my tenants .... You had a chance to make it right, but you wanna play games. So now I'm gonna make you pay. You and the whole crew."

"My advice for you Deni is to disappear. Go back to wherever you was hidin'. People who fuck with Slopes tend to have accidents. You get the bagpipes and a parade if you're a former cop who has an untimely demise?"

I wanted to kill him right then and there. With my bare hands. He had more than my Irish up. The motherfucker was egging me on. He knew that I knew what he had done and was going to do. And he was basically laughing in my face. Killing him didn't get me the result I needed. Killing him wouldn't put Sean Teague or his crew in a panic. Wouldn't make them come out of hiding and make a mistake. I wanted Slopes to know that I knew that the guns were coming into Boston Harbor, and that I knew when. I wanted him to think that he was fucked. Not delivering those weapons meant certain death. The syndicates would see to it. Getting caught with them was a slower and more painful death. Prison and out of business, then the Irish would get to him on the inside.

"I don't think I'll have to worry about it. Go back in and have your beer. By the way the Sox win 9-0 asshole." I wondered if he would ever know how I knew that, and what else I possibly knew.

51

SEPTEMBER 11, 2004 WAS UPON US. CNN ran an all-day remembrance. All 2,749 names of the deceased from the towers were read aloud at Ground Zero. The lights of the Empire State Building were extinguished at 9:11 PM. George W. Bush made his appearances and speeches. Iraqi interim Prime Minister Ayad Allawi also issued a statement of condolence not only for the victims of the September 11 attacks but also for all victims of terrorism.

"Three years ago, the hand of terrorism claimed the lives of thousands of innocent people at the World Trade Center in New York," Allawi said. "Terrorism did not stop at its mean act but further wreaked havoc in several spots of the world, with no discrimination between one religion and another and one people and another."

US Embassy officials all over the world also laid wreaths in honor of the global victims of the attacks. British citizens were conducting business in both New York and Washington, DC. The Irish. The Swedish. While most of the devastation was suffered by Americans, on American Soil, the world over joined us in our continued mourning.

But while Americans paused to remember fallen loved ones and where they were when the towers fell, life went on. Businesses were open. American Airlines still had flights by the thousands taking off and landing. The Red Sox still had a game at Safeco Field, albeit with a different result than games one and two of the three-game stretch.

I had been out all night trying to learn more about the logistics of the container or containers that were coming off of The Annika Mærsk. They were going to need more than an *Econoline* van to move them out of Boston Harbor. Shey was of no help. It took until the wee hours of the morning to come to that truth. Then the drive back up to New Hampshire. I took a very circuitous route to Wayland to ensure that I wasn't being followed. Shey was drunk, but not too drunk to make a phone call.

My morning start was a late one. Meaning it was late afternoon by the time that I got my ass out of bed. Neither Ryan or Angie said a word about the time when I descended the stairs. "Good Afternoon" didn't even seem sarcastic. I wondered how many September elevenths would go by before people went back to being who they really were the rest of the days of the year save for Christmas.

Angie said that she had errands to run. A grocery run was one such errand. She asked me if there was anything in particular that I wanted. She also said that she would be doing some cleaning, asked if there was any laundry that I needed done. Sweet woman. Although this was a new-age couple, she still seemed to take on the more domestic roles. I wondered if Ryan mowed the lawn and the like, or if he got out of his chores because of his workload. Ryan was in his office, presumably tackling his pile of work, when my cell phone rang. It was Glen from MASS PORT.

"Working the weekend Glen?"
"When else was I going to get this project of yours done?"

345

"It's done? Pissah. What'd you find?"

"I don't know. Probably nothing. But I put together a list of businesses sending and receiving cargo on The Annika Mærsk."

"That was fast."

"You said you would make it worth my effort. I worked through the night after my shift and all weekend so far to get it done. Do you have a fax number I can send it to?"

"Hold on." I went into Ryan's office. "Hey Ry, do you have a fax machine here?" He was sitting behind his desk doing something when I interrupted him.

"Of course." Ryan gave me the fax number in the 603 area code.

"Thanks. Glen? You still there?"

"Waiting."

I repeated the number and he said that he was punching in the number on his fax machine as we spoke. "You should have it in a few minutes. It's six pages, so it might take a second."

"Thanks Glen. Lemme know if you come up with anything else. I'll take care of you Monday. Tuesday at the latest."

"What was that about, if you don't mind me asking," Ryan said after I flipped my cell closed.

"Guy at MASS PORT is faxing over a list of the parties that are shipping and receiving on the incoming freighter. I'm hoping that I can narrow down the search to specific containers by picking out the sender or receiver."

The fax machine was making its hums and noises, indicating that it was deciphering the incoming message in order to spit it out onto paper.

"Deni, do you think that they are going to be stupid enough to list Sinn Féin or Winter Hill on the shipping manifest? These people have been conducting illegal business for generations. They haven't been doing business this long because they make those kinds of stupid mistakes."

"Well according to Glen they have to put something down on the manifest. They have this computer system called the AMS, or something like — "

" — yeah I know. I get it. Unless they just get the cargo on the freighter without the paperwork. Or have a legitimate business list the items they mean to ship then switch the cargo before the ship takes off. Or have diplomatic seals on it."

"I didn't take you for a glass is half-empty kinda guy. From what I understood, not having paperwork or the seal on the cargo raises more eyebrows than just providing false information. They can't switch it without breaking the seal. And they can't have a diplomatic seal unless a government official is on the receiving end. They aren't sending to the embassy, cuz the US Embassy in Ireland is aware of what's going on. So my guess is that at least one of the entities on that list coming out of the machine right now is phony. I have to give the guy money, so we might as well look it over."

"I'm on board. But I hope that you aren't spending too much money, because I think that you are going to pay this guy for nothing."

The facsimile was finished. The beep at the end announced the fact. We each took three pages of the list of shippers and receivers. Ryan seemed to scan through his three sheets very quickly at his desk. Lawyers have the ability to take in large quantities of information very quickly. They have to read through piles of legal documents and statements of various types on a daily basis. Statutes and briefs which are never brief. Speed reading comes with the job description.

I was taking longer sitting comfortably with my feet propped up in the corner of his office. Much longer. I scanned each name, let it rattle around my skull. When nothing in that name rang a bell, I moved on to the next. It took me an hour to go through my three sheets. I think Ryan went back to whatever he was doing before I stormed into his office asking for his fax number. I came up with nothing.

"Lets switch," I said. Ryan just shrugged, handed me his list after I made the journey from my seat to him. I could see by the look in his eyes that he thought this was a big waste of our time. Definitely his. "I don't want to hear it. You might have missed somethin', or I might have," I said. "You went through your list pretty quick. You probably did miss somethin'."

"Because I can read fast? You think I missed something because I can read fast?"

"No. I think you might have missed somethin' because you skimmed it lookin' for somethin' obvious. You didn't appear to be puttin' any thought to it. Like you said, they haven't been able to get away with this for as long as they have by bein' obvious."

We reviewed each of the other's list. I returned to my chair, settled in for another lengthy and fruitless search. Halfway down the second page, about thirty minutes later, about when I started to lose hope, I saw it.

"P. O'Neill Inc! What did I tell ya?" I shouted it across the office.

Ryan was already finished reviewing my list and was onto something else. He looked over at me stunned as my shout had scared the shit out of him.

"You found something?"

"P. O'Neill Inc. That's it. That's them. To and from."

"I must have missed something."

"You sure did. You missed it big time."

"Enough Deni. Who works for whom here? I missed it because I don't understand how P. O'Neill has anything to do with our guns."

"The IRA, Irish Republican Army, they always use the name P. O'Neill on every thing. They have for the past 40 years. Public Statements, Public Houses, you name it. I'm not sure who this guy was or is, but they use the name for everything. Some people think that it's the nick name of the committee of seven on the Army Council. Whatever the case may be, we got 'em."

"So you think that they are moving guns under a dummy company that has the same name as the one they use as a signature for all of their misdeeds?"

348

"They don't see them as misdeeds, Ry. They see it as a means to an end. They avoid prosecuting illegal acts if they are done in the name of the Republic, for the good of Ireland."

"Isn't it a little obvious?"

"You're a lawyer and you missed it."

"Let me see that list, would you?"

I handed him the list. The contact information for P. O'Neill Inc. on both sides of the pond was listed. +353 1 803 2215 for Ireland. 617-703-2215 for Boston.

"Hmm," Ryan said while rubbing his chin.

"What?"

"Look at the cargo container number." He handed the paper back to me.

"PONU0322155. So What?"

"Do you know anything about international cargo shipments, Deni?"

"I went to the Dublin Port and Boston Harbor. I know about as much as what I've told you. What are you getting at?"

"I happen to know a decent amount because I had to defend a client once that was in business as an importer-exporter." He took back the piece of paper and motioned me over to his desk.

"Good for you, what's the point?"

He ignored the jab and went into his explanation. "The first part — 'PON' is the owner code. Makes sense. P. O'Neill .... PON? Then the next letter is the category identifier. In this case 'U'. Which means that it's a 40 ft. container instead of a reefer or trailer. Then the next six letters are the serial number, '032215'. The last '5' is just a check digit. Look at the serial number and then look at the two phone numbers."

Ryan slid the paper on his desk to his right, giving me a better view.

"Both phone numbers have the last six digits of 03-2215, which matches the cargo container serial number," I said.

"They wanted to make it idiot-proof. But that isn't the best part."

"That's pretty fuckin' good, Ry. What's the best part?"

349

"Do you recognize the Boston phone number? It's a cell number. Who's cell is that?"

My eyes lit up like a Christmas tree. I looked at Ryan who was already nodding, already steps ahead of where I was. We both said the name at the same time.

"Walter Glibczieck."

52

THERE WAS AN EMERGENCY, ALL-STAFF MEETING Monday morning at Grantes, Wells & Associates. When a law firm has an emergency, all-staff meeting it sounds like there was a great many people, hunkered down in a room for serious business. While there were only four people in the small conference room, the discussion was serious. Jacob Grantes, Ryan Wells were the fountainheads, and Angie Wells and I as associates were all hunkered down to discuss recent revelations.

I had taken a personal day, calling Troop H and leaving Lieutenant Titanitaukis a message. He called back later which I let go to voicemail. He called again, which I also didn't pick up. Neither of the messages were happy in nature or tone. He wanted me to know that calling out for the remainder of my days would jeopardize the money in my pension account. I didn't see how that was possible but I wasn't going to call him back to argue the point either. Nor did I choose to speak with Hobbs when he called and left three messages.

Ryan filled in JG on what was going on with the investigation, and how it related to Breen. They had received a $75,000 retainer for a defense that he no longer needed, and another retainer for a forthcoming civil suit once we proved collusion. Finding the weapons in container number PONU0322155 was a key piece in that case. The rest of the information was given to JG in waves as he walked around the conference room table digesting the information. I would fill in some of the gaps as I saw fit, Angie was silent as she took the minutes.

"So let me see if I have this right," JG said when we completed the briefing. "The federal prosecutor, Walter Glibczieck, is in bed with either Sinn Féin, the IRA, the Winter Hill organized crime network including the enterprise on the compound here in New Hampshire, or all of the above? The missing guns out of the Maynard Ballistics Lab? All him?"

"*All* him?" I looked around the table. JG sat down in the only remaining empty chair. "I don't know for sure if it is all him, but he has to be involved."

"Walk me through it."

Ryan spoke up. "The Irish move guns into the United States as one of the many illegal activities the army conducts with their secret cells. That is fact. They do this in order to supply their countless enterprises like the Winter Hill crew and Men in the Mountains with hardware and salable merchandise for all of their enterprises west.   Proceeds from the drugs and other illegal activities fund the various groups and are used to buy guns which feeds the IRA with money which then feeds the Sinn Féin political party. And the cycle continues."

"How do we know that to be fact, Ryan?" JG was playing devil's advocate.

"That cargo container ends up in the hands of …. what's his name, Deni?"

"Sean Teague, or better known as Slopes."

352

"Right. So when they get busted with those weapons, that proves that connection. As you know, parties who are participants in an illegal activity have an implied collusion under Title — "

" — yes, Ryan. I know the law. But that only proves the IRA — Winter Hill connection."

"JG, when the ATF goes in for the kill, grabs up all the weapons and remaining evidence, how much do you want to bet that those weapons will match the type that were stored in Maynard and New Hampshire? The weapons seized from the New Hampshire compound have already been proven to be the same as those missing from the Maynard Lab, from Breen. Thus proving the IRA — Winter Hill — New Hampshire connections."

"All of the members of the IRA secret cells are called Volunteers. They lead a meager existence in order to send money up the chain, " I said.

"Good. Go on," JG said. He was thoroughly engrossed and writing on his yellow legal pad.

"Deni going over to the other side of the pond created quite a stir, everyone and anyone that could possibly testify against this …. "

My turn again. "Finn Rourke …. "

"Rourke …. is now dead. And there is really nothing we can do about them anyway, that is for a federal prosecutor to sort out. They would need to make a deal with Ireland for extradition. Which Walter won't do if he is involved."

"Which you still haven't proven, guys. Why would the federal prosecutor send Deni over there to solve the case if he was involved in the enterprise? That's counterproductive."

Ryan had not yet told JG how we connected him to the weapons distribution, only that he was connected. He slid the list from the fax machine over to JG, along with an itemized phone log for both his cell and his office phone compliments of Angie. He then walked him through the connection that he had made the day prior.

" …. and as far as sending Deni over there? We think to kill him. They tried. He sent Deni right into the hands of the number one and number two Volunteers and when they failed they were killed." Ryan slid The Guardian newspaper that I had given to him across the table.

"Wow. This is unbelievable." JG was shaking his head, trying to make room in there I guess.

"So what do we do?" I asked the room, but really I wanted to JG to say it. Ryan, Angie and I had discussed it at length in his home office on Sunday.

"We are not prosecutors. We are defense attorneys. We don't help the prosecution. But we need this container seized in order to prove conspiracy and collusion, which gets us a prima facie civil case for our deceased client Breen." He stood back up and paced around the small lunchroom/conference room. He paused to think, I broke the silence.

"Which means we need to out Walter. When what I really want to do is kill him."

"You can't kill him Deni," JG said.

"Obviously. So then what do we do?"

"We get the ATF involved."

"We don't know how deep this goes," I said. "What if we report it to someone who is working with Walter?"

"There has to be a record of people who he has worked with in past cases. We *don't* notify any of those people. We go around his inner circle."

"Great. So how do we find that information out without tipping him off that we are snooping around?"

The two attorneys looked at each other, knowing the answer. But Ryan answered me. "All court filings, even federal court, are a matter of public record. As an attorney, I can have that expedited through a clerk. Within a couple of days we can have transcripts of his last few federal cases with regard to gun trafficking in the area. We make a thorough list of all names in those cases and avoid them like the plague. Then we set up a meeting with anybody but those people from the ATF."

"All this goes down on the twentieth, don't forget," I said. Today is the thirteenth, so that leaves us a week to get ready. At the most."

Everyone knew what we had to do when we left the table. Unfortunately I would have to do double duty. Go into the precinct each day to work with Hobbs, and try to find Slopes by night. Then drive all the way back up to New Hampshire to report any news and get some sleep. It wasn't so much the distance, it was the traffic. People from Wayland commuted into the city every day, they just usually did it by commuter train. It was going to be a long week.

JG and Ryan didn't have it any easier. They had other cases, other demands on their time, while trying to get copies of all transcripts and evidence to their office as quickly and quietly as possible. They would then have to go through all of the data and make comprehensive lists of all persons whom had crossed paths with Walter Glibczieck. I had a hunch that much of the tedious work was going to be passed onto Angie. But she was a sweetheart, she probably wouldn't mind it one bit. And she was also very efficient.

On the way out of the office after the meeting, a very attractive woman was waiting in the reception area of the law firm. She screamed money from a mile away. She wore a pink tennis shirt that had an alligator on it, a short white skirt that didn't have a single wrinkle nor did it leave much of her legs to the imagination. She had a tennis bracelet on as well that looked like it was worth more than my *Escalade*. Why they linked those bracelets to tennis I had no idea, who plays tennis with something that expensive? Whether she was about to play or not, she looked like she participated in a regular exercise regimen of some sort. Her thin body was hugged nicely by her expensive clothing.

I couldn't help but notice her, I doubt she could walk into any room and not be noticed. She was staring back at me as much I was staring at her. I wondered if I had met her before when I realized that JG was behind me, she was staring at him.

"Deni," JG said. "This is my wife Anna. Anna, this is Warren Dennihan. He is our new investigator."

"Pleasure," she said.

"Yeah. Pleasure is mine," I said. "Ya did okay for yourself there Guy." Everyone in the room laughed but I didn't know why. I thought I was stating the obvious. I wanted to be a lawyer, apparently they get all the girls.

She recovered from her demure giggle and said, "We both did okay for ourselves. Babe, are we still on for lunch at the club?" She looked at her husband and pointed to the clock on the wall of the reception area.

"I'm sorry, no. Something has come up and I am going to be busy. Raincheck?"

The look of disappointment on her face was short-lived. "No worries. I'll call Chamille and see if she is free."

I walked out of the law firm thinking about Rowena. She would not be categorized in the same class as Anna, but I didn't know why. She might not be as attractive or as rich, but she was a beautiful person. I was lucky to have known her.

53

ISOLATING AND VETTING COLLEAGUES AND
WITNESSES for a federal prosecutor under the radar is tricky.
And time consuming. The documents were requested and sent
over in a cardboard file box that was the size of a case of copy
paper. There are only about 90 federal prosecutors in the United
States, each covering a specific district. So they have a lot of work
and a great many contacts.

The documents weren't sent to Grantes, Wells & Associates.
One phone call and the jig would be up. They were sent to the
Wayland County Superior Courthouse, then brought over to the
firm. An intern in the records department of the court was the
daughter of country club friends of JG and Anna. She loaded the
heavy documents into her newer VW *Beetle* and carted them over.

Names were then highlighted from over 3,000 pages of court
documents. Those highlighted names were every witness, suspect,
ATF agent, prosecutor, court clerk, DOJ employee, and judge that

had been involved with Walter Glibczieck. The highlighted names were then compiled onto a list, categorized and prioritized in order to then move onto the next step. Vetting.

That is where I came in. When I wasn't combing the streets of Boston every day with Rick Hobbs the one trick pony, I was investigating the names that had been compiled onto lists. Angie would give me a fresh set of names every morning, I would do my best to get as much information as I could by the time I rolled back to the house late in the night. Looking up jackets, parking tickets, registrations, and such of the names and family members on the lists was difficult. Made more so by the fact that Hobbs was always attached at the hip. When I stayed late, he wanted to join me. I was running out of excuses to shake him.

All of it took time. Days.

Slopes and his crew had gone into hiding. Boston is my city. I know it like the back of my hand. They had obviously moved out of Southie. Other than my encounter with Shey, nobody had seen or heard from the Winter Hill crew in what seemed like ages. Normally that would be a good thing, but I wanted to set up more permanent surveillance. In order to surveil, I needed to find them. Allston, BackBay, Bay Village, Beacon Hill, Brighton, Charlestown, Chinatown/Leather District, Dorchester, Downtown, East Boston, Fenway Kenmore, Hyde Park, Jamaica Plain, Mattapan, Mid Dorchester, Mission Hill, North End, Roslindale, Roxbury, South End (different from Southie), West End, and West Roxbury. Vanished. Nowhere to be found. Even Shey was gone. They had taken laying low to a new level.

On Friday the 17th of September, JG and Ryan decided that we had to set up a meeting with the ATF. With only three days left before The Annika Mærsk came floating in, the authorities needed to be notified. An eager young agent was chosen as he was not on any of the lists of names associated with Walter and he was vetted by me.

Jamaar Dennard made the trip from Philadelphia. He was working on another case when JG made the call. Grantes had chosen him because he was the hot hand, had made his bones the hard way, and conducted himself like he always had something to prove. He grew up an African-American from a single mother in the projects of Mattapan, so he knew Boston. Jamaar had to fight all odds at every age. At thirty-two he was still fighting to be taken seriously, fighting to get what was due. He took a train from Phili to Boston, then the purple train up to Wayland where I picked him up in the *Escalade* and drove him to the firm.

"Thank you for making the trip Mr. Dennard," JG said.

"Jamaar. And you seemed to leave me little choice." All of us were there and pumping hands, making introductions. Angie had set an extra chair for him at the conference table, we made our way in to begin the meeting.

Once we were all seated, JG took the lead. "It may seem odd to you, Jamaar, that defense attorneys are contacting you with regard to an illegal gun shipment coming into Boston. But this situation is complicated and those weapons being seized are very important to a pending case that we have as well. It is in our mutual interest to see that this is dealt with swiftly and publicly."

"You said something about corruption in the ATF, the DOJ specifically in the Attorney General's office? I would ask that you provide proof of that before we proceed." Jamaar had either been educated or he had taught himself to lose the typical ebonic accent that is commonly found in Mattapan. His diction was overly perfect. He said "ask" instead of "axe" for example. "I made this trip on good faith, but I assure you that I cannot nor will not move forward without something more tangible."

"We will get to that. And it's one federal prosecutor for certain, not the Attorney General's office on the whole. But first I have a document which I would like you to sign. It clearly states that all of the information that you are about to receive is off-the-record, confidential, and any admission to a crime or crimes will be granted immunity from prosecution." JG was taking the lead and being very lawyerly while he was protecting me.

Jamaar skimmed through the document and signed it. He too was a fast reader.

The next hour and a half was spent going over the entire case. We all took turns telling our portion of the events leading us to that

359

very meeting. Jamaar would interject for points of clarity, questions or requesting some shred of proof to what he was hearing.

I spoke of the stolen van driven by Danny Mick that was pulled over on Storrow Drive. The confiscated weapons sent to the Maynard Lab for testing that were stolen allegedly by Walter or his associates, which we couldn't prove, but somehow made it out of the facility and into the hands of a group of men nestled in the White Mountains of New Hampshire. I told of how Danny Mick was killed in prison, his sister Roxy taken out with a staged overdose of the poison that plagued her for most of her life. Ryan told him the details about the Men in the Mountains, the manufacturing of drugs, and the trove of assault weapons originally from the Maynard facility, which Jamaar was already familiar with. How those weapons had matched the type if not the exact weapons from Danny Mick pullover. How his client, Breen, was one of those men and who was also killed in prison. I told of my trip to Ireland after being burned from my home at the request of the federal prosecutor, Walter Glibczieck. How my tenants were burned alive. Of how Walter had sent me into the arms of Sinn Féin and the IRA for the only logical purpose of finishing what Slopes and company could not. How Rourke had ordered the killing of anyone and everyone that I had talked to over there, including an investigative reporter that had been looking into them with me. Agents and double agents. Moles. The phony seizures of weapons. Niall, the dock foreman. The entire story, everything, was laid out before him. Documents, newspapers, phone numbers, and other evidence was set on the table before him as the facts were divulged.

"The Annika Mærsk comes in on Monday. PONU0322155 is going to be a forty-foot cargo container filled with assault weapons that will wreak havoc on not only Boston, but cities all over the US," I said, finishing my portion.

"I'm going to need time to look into this," Jamaar said.

"You don't have time. We are into double-digit murders on this and it will get much worse once those weapons are distributed. Walter was handling this, but as we have pointed out, he is complicit in how they have gotten away with this for as long as they have," Ryan said.

"My boss will need to verify — "

" — we came to you because there are very few people who can be trusted. We checked you out. You need to act," JG interrupted before Jamaar could finish.

"Why didn't you come to me with this sooner?"

"Because this story has a lot of twists and turns. It's fantastic. Without proof, you wouldn't have even gotten on the train," JG said.

"I'm going to need a team down there on Boston Harbor. I have to get clearance to move a team. That could take days."

"Do what you have to do, Jamaar. But keep in mind that they have moles everywhere. A leak and this all goes sideways. And you don't have days," Ryan was emphatic.

I added my two-cents. "And the Winter Hill crew is on lock-down. You won't see them coming until they pick up the goods. A tip-off and they could stay hidden."

Jamaar scratched his chin. "So we sit on the container until they show up to empty it? They could wait days, weeks to empty it."

"They won't," I said. "They need to get these things off the pier and in distribution. Especially since everything that has happened. But I say we let them do all the work."

"I don't follow."

"You will. We just need some help."

"*We* Mr. Dennihan? Thank you for your offer but we will take it from here."

"All that I have been through with this and you are going to shut me out?"

"It's a jurisdictional issue now. As well as one of liability. I can't have an outgoing Mass State Trooper getting killed during an ATF raid. My ass would be in a sling," Jamaar said.

"I'm gonna be there one way or another. I'll sign a waiver or whatever."

Jamaar stared into his hands which rested on the table. "I hope I don't regret getting on that train."

54

THE NIGHT WAS BLACK. Not Jamaar black, blacker. There wasn't a moon on Monday night and the clouds were thick. It was only fifty-eight degrees and the wind was gusting. While the wind helped the balls leaving Fenway Park for the Orioles, it did nothing to help us in our reconnaissance. We couldn't see shit, nor could we hear anything more than wind, ocean, buoys and bumpers rattling off the docks.

We had been there all day. The Annika Mærsk docked very early in the morning, the cranes began unloading it a few hours after that. An ATF presence and I watched from a distance, using binoculars. They stayed hidden throughout the day shift on their post, into second shift, and I stayed in mine.

Glen was happy to have gotten paid handsomely for his previous help. So much so that he gave us information on how the docks are unloaded, how they sort through the containers in the hopes of getting more. With thousands of containers from that and other ships, there was an elaborate system as to how they are unloaded so the receivers can find their shipment. The cargo is unloaded by container type. The forty-foot containers that are not subsequently loaded onto large trucks for further transport are unloaded into a specific holding area. Within that area on Boston Harbor, the containers are then divided by alphabetized serial numbers. PONU0322155 was dropped by a Super-Post Panamax into the 'L-Q' storage area. We watched and waited all day but nobody came to open it.

Until that night. The docks were closed after seven at night unless you were one of the unionized crew on second shift working the docks. The Big Dig had taught us that unions can be bought. Somebody was paid to let the white International *Workstar* truck through the gate. They were nice enough to use a white truck. Had it been a darker model we might not have been able to see it as well in the darkest of nights. A horde of men came out of the back when the two men from the cab opened it. The back of the truck was parked but a few feet from the double-doors of cargo container.

"He we go boys," someone from the ATF said over the radio. We all had earpieces so the transmitters wouldn't make noise, but with the wind it wouldn't have mattered if we were shouting into the radios and the volume was turned up to ten.

"Let them load it like we planned," I said over the line. "We will just take the truck once it's loaded, let them do all the work."

"Roger" came over the radio, one by one.

The horde of men in the enclosed back of the truck was actually eight men. Ten total. They snapped the thin, metal seal off the container and began to load the *Workstar*. Large wooden crates were hoisted from the cargo container into the truck systematically. They appeared to have a rhythm, like they had executed the task before. The twenty-foot bed of the truck was nowhere near the length or height of the cargo container. From my angle I could not see if another trip was going to be necessary, or if the forty-foot shipment container had been filled in the first place.

363

It took almost an hour for the ten men to load the truck. When they were finished, the double-doors of the cargo container were shut and latched. Even with the wind, we could hear the metal-on-metal.

"Now," came over the radio. Then, "Deni stay put."
Fuck, I thought to myself. I may have even said it out loud.

From their posts came more than a dozen ATF agents as flood lights were turned on. My eyes were blinded as they had become accustomed to the pitch black. Someone over a bullhorn announced that they were from the ATF and for everyone to put up their hands. I blocked the blinding light with my left hand, looking away. I heard gunfire. And more shouting. And screaming. People were being shot, I hoped it was the bad-guys from the Winter Hill crew.

As I looked in the opposite direction, away from the blinding light, hidden at my post. I saw movement in the darkness twenty yards behind us. Then more movement. It wasn't one person, there were several.

My mind raced as instincts took over. I ducked down and yelled into the radio, "It's an ambush! Behind us!"

I moved around containers heading back to where Slopes's back up was moving in. More gunfire came from them. The ATF was caught in the middle. The detail from the truck and the backup were firing automatic weapons toward the middle. Shouts of "man down" and "I'm hit" were shouted over the radio into my earpiece. I continued to move back, trying to get behind the backup team. My Sig at the ready. I was thankful for my presence of mind to bring a step up from my 9 mm mandated Glock service weapon.

As I rounded the corner of one container, a man with an Israeli Tavor Tar-21 turned toward me. Two shots landed on him. One through his neck, one through his left cheek on his face. Blood spouted as he fell, firing dozens of rounds into the air as the gas-operated rotating bolt was activated by the reflexive finger on the trigger. When the man fell, the rifle was dislodged from his hand. I moved toward him, my eyes oscillating between the wounded man and my surroundings. I thought of picking up the weapon, as it would have been a marked upgrade, but decided against it so not to be confused as one of them by the ATF.

He had virtually no pulse. Blood covered my left hand as I pulled my fingers from his carotid. No idea how many there were. I popped my head to my right, looking to see if another assassin was lurking around the next container. None. I stood crouched, thinking, listening.

A sound of gravel behind me. How I heard it over the wind is a mystery. I turned in time to see another man backing up slowly. He didn't see me, as his back was to me, his weapon aimed in the other direction. Slowly he backed toward me. I returned my Sig to its holster, stood up and with one swift motion braced the rifle toward the ground with my left hand and choked him with my right arm. His Adam's apple was pressed against my right antecubital fossa, or elbow pit, my right hand clutching my left shoulder to choke him out. Pulling upward and arching my back, he had no leverage, his body weight adding more pressure to his throat and cutting off his oxygen. I continued to look around for more aggressors until he passed out.

Gunfire and screams near the truck could still be heard faintly over the wind, frantic yelling through my earpiece.

And voices behind me. I grabbed my gun from the holster, turned behind me. Two men running right at me. Six shots. Knees, thighs, and groin were hit between the two men. I dove behind a short crate as they fired back at me from the ground. After trading clips, I popped up and fired four more shots. They didn't return fire. Slowly moving toward them, gun trained, and looking through the pitch black night to determine if I was hunting or being hunted.

The two men were alive but hit and struggling. I kicked both of their Heckler & Koch G3A4s further away from them. I squatted to question them.

"How many of you?"

Neither answered me. They just stared at me as I looked down at them.

"Where's Slopes?"

365

Again they stared at me with pained looks, remaining silent.

"I'm right here."

I stood up but didn't recognize him in time. Slopes moved toward me. I raised my gun, but also not in time. It felt like a shotgun blast to my chest. It must have been instinctual, but I emptied my clip as I fell to the ground.

The rest comes in waves. It was difficult to see in the dark. I couldn't breath. Air, anything for air. The pain in my torso cannot be described. I lay there, eyes toward where Slopes was. He was gone. Still no air. Gun shots, somewhere in the distance. More screams. Can't move. Somebody crawling toward me. Out of bullets. Slopes. Gurgling and bleeding. Face and chest covered in blood. Then total darkness.

55

THE ENTIRE FRONT PAGE OF BOTH THE HERALD AND THE GLOBE were dedicated to the colossal event. The city had dubbed it the 'Boston Harbor Bust'. The headlines were many, several writers with their various takes on the many angles.

Irish Mob Forever Silenced. The Department of Alcohol, Tobacco & Firearms have been long collaborating with Boston Police following a lead about a major arms shipment.

Federal Prosecutor Arrested In Scarsdale Home. The article went on to say that he had alleged ties to the recent political catastrophe in Maynard, and in the mountains of Wayland County New Hampshire.

IRA Has Not Yet Claimed Responsibility For Arms Shipment. Despite evidence and statements, the Irish Republican

Army has refused to issue a statement regarding their involvement with the arsenal of assault weapons seized in Boston Harbor.

Organized Crime from New York, New Jersey and Providence Move In On Whitey's Old Turf. The Winter Hill Gang, named and successful since Whitey Bulger's days, has left an open market ripe for the picking. Other Area's crime syndicates have already staked their claim not twenty-four hours after the famed Boston Harbor Bust.

Will Whitey Come Out Of Hiding? The article was complete speculation that Whitey Bulger would come out of hiding to reclaim his thrown and his territory.

Sean Teague, A.K.A. Slopes, Shot And Killed. Famed leader of Boston's Irish Mafia, The Winter Hill Gang, was shot and killed during arrest. A mug shot from a previous arrest provided.

ATF Agent, Jamaar Dennard, Receives Commendations. Governor Mitt Romney and other officials will be holding a public news conference to recognize the ATF agent for his role in taking assault weapons off the streets.

Undercover State Trooper Shot During Boston Harbor Bust. *A* Massachusetts State Trooper out of Boston, who was working closely with the ATF, was shot during the apprehension of the suspects. He was in his final days as a detective, and is listed as in critical condition in an undisclosed hospital.

The famed Boston Harbor Bust concluded with 9 dead and 7 wounded, other articles went on to say. The mix of dead and wounded were on both sides of the skirmish. The seizure was considered a success, however, as an arsenal was taken out of distribution. HawkEngineering *MM-1 40 mm* revolver grenade launchers, Saab *AT4* rocket launchers, Russian *AN-94* and *RPG-7s*, *TAC-50*, McMillan tactical rifles, Heckler & Koch *G3A4s*, older Armalite *AR-18* assault rifles, and hundreds of cases of ammunition were reported to have been taken into custody. The Irish

Republican Army could have started another army with the hardware shipped.

Other major news from around the country and the world were relegated to other pages, other sections. **Democrats Say GOP Playing to Terror Fears** was buried. Though world news did beat out local headlines in the sports section. **Europe Roars to Another Ryder Win** beat out the story that although the Orioles had beaten the Red Sox at Fenway Monday night, at 89-60 Red Sox Nation would likely claim the Wild Card Spot.

As usual, the newspapers had some of the facts wrong. I was shot in the chest, that was true. The Tar-21 felt like a shotgun blast to the chest because of the number of rounds that hit me. But I had been wearing a Kevlar vest at Jamaar's insistence, so I had more broken ribs but thankfully nothing had gotten through. And just as thankfully the recoil from the automatic weapon didn't pull the barrel up far enough, or quickly enough to send a dozen rounds into my face. I had lost consciousness because I had hit my head on the side of a container when I had fallen backward after being shot. The bust was late and the papers wanted to get the stories in before the competing rag covered it first. So while I was being treated, I was not in critical care. In fact I was released before noon on Tuesday, broken ribs and concussion-like symptoms not withstanding.

In the cab from Beth Israel to Troop H, my phone rang. That wasn't a big deal, since the bust which occurred just hours prior, my phone had been ringing incessantly. Everyone in Boston wanted a word from me. But the number struck me. It was a longer sequence starting with +353.

"Yeah."

"You've gone an made yerself famous now, haven't ye lad?"

I couldn't believe my ears. "I never thought I would hear from you again. How did you find me?"

"T'wasn't difficult. Especially since you've made quite the splash. I wanted to thank you for the gift?"

"What gift?"

"Had to be you that left it."

"How do you figure?"

"I'm an investigative reporter, it's my job to figure. I didn't reckon you were the true Catholic."

"I'm not Row. But I hoped it would help. How are you doin'? You sound different."

"Aye. And I believe that it did help. They say I'll live. What will you do now that you're no longer a Bobby?"

"I've got work lined up. What are you gonna do? Still gonna dress up like a whore?"

"I might. Someone's gotta do it."

"Just take care of yourself, Row. I'm glad you made it, but you can't cheat death more than once."

There was a long pause, music was playing the background. I couldn't tell what it was but it didn't sound like Bono.

"Is that the new U2 album, Row?"

"Naw. Tears for Fears. *Everybody Loves A Happy Ending.*"

"We both know that it's almost never a happy ending."

"Don't carry a worry about me, Deni. Sometimes life is an American Story."

EPILOGUE

NOBODY WOULD HAVE NORMALLY GIVEN TWO SHITS about Tuesday, September 21st being my last day. But when I arrived to turn in my badge and Glock, my desk was swarming with people. Not because I was now semi-famous or had gone out in blaze of glory or some other such nonsense. Boston isn't as big as New York City, but it is a city nonetheless. Famous one day and a nameless loser douche the next. The reason why I was popular was because Jamaar had used his newly found influence to send me a row of tickets to the Red Sox game Tuesday night. He sent them to Tits for me and whomever I wanted to take with me as part thank you for standing by the 'working with Boston Police' story. Part gift for me on the job well done and part congrats on getting the fuck out of civil service. Jamaar had called me on my cell while I was on it with Row. He wanted to make sure that I went to claim them. Why I listened to that message instead of the countless other messages left by the countless other people wanting to hear my side of things is beyond me, but I did. The people in the precinct were loitering around my desk waiting for me and wanting a seat to the game.

In a stadium that seats only 35,000 people, Red Sox tickets are nearly impossible to come by. They sell out every game although they never win when it counts. But whether a good season, when we just miss the ALCS; or a bad one, when the lowly Blue Jays and Orioles have better records, you can't get a seat.

I moved around slowly with my broken ribs and fuzzy brain, clearing out my desk while trying to clear out my twenty-five new best friends. All things considered I was in a great mood. I was no longer going to be a political pawn. I had ended my career as a Statie with a bang. Row was alive and well for the moment. And I was about to tell Hobbs he could go fuck himself.

Hobbs approached my desk, hand out. Whether we wanted a shake or a ticket I have no idea. But he got neither. Not from me anyway.

371

"Listen Hobbs, I want you to take this very personally when I tell you to kick rocks. Okay?"

"Why are you always an asshole? I just wanted to say good luck."

"I want to say go fuck ya-self. I feel bad for your next partner. Do you know who it is yet?"

"Yeah. Sheed."

"A girl? Ugh. That poor woman."

From deep into the crowd around my desk I heard her say, "I know right?"

The crowd moved around me as I moved toward her. "Take two tickets, go have fun. I feel bad for ya. Tits has 'em."

People started clambering for their seats both physically and verbally as they followed me on to Lieutenant Titanitaukis' office. The door was open. I set my badge and 9 mm on his desk.

"Sheed gets two tickets. She is gonna need some fun after getting the horrible news."

"You have any other thoughts on who you would like to go?"

"Nope. I'm done. Give 'em to whomever you want."

"You're not going to go? After all of this?" He pointed to the newspapers on his desk.

"I don't want to hang out with any of these people."

"What do you have against them, Deni? You think you're better than them?"

"I just don't like them. I don't like politics, and I really don't like office politics. You got yourself out of this pretty clean, by the way. How'd you swing it?"

"I don't know what you mean."

"You and Walter were pretty tight. He's arrested and you aren't. Lemme guess, you're saving your ass by testifying against him."

"I'm not at liberty to say."

I shook my head, walking toward the door to his office. "And they let you keep the badge. I won't miss a fuckin' day of it." With that, I left Troop H as an employee forever.

372

Over the course of the next few months, more about case came to light in the press. Bringing the story back to the front of the minds of those that cared to know about it. Walter Glibczieck was responsible for the guns disappearing from the Maynard Ballistics Lab, just as we suspected. The FBI had jurisdiction and originally wanted both the Massachusetts and New Hampshire cases, but the ATF took control thanks to Walter. He made sure the ATF handled all of his cases as a federal prosecutor, as he had several agents in his pocket.

He was the person who organized which prison Daniel McKennie would go to, and the block he would be housed in. The inmates therein had carte blanche as to how he was to go away after being given a false 'rat' story. There were pictures of Walter confessing in court, the John Goodman look-alike on the front of every paper. But he would never be heard from again. Probably because he ratted on the Winter Hills to save his own ass, but that is pure conjecture.

Everybody knew what happened to Roxanne McKennie. She was a junkie. A junkie from Southie. It could never be proven and Walter didn't confess to it, so it was never solved. Her file is still sitting among the cold cases in Troop H.

Maddy went on to win her civil case, almost two years later. She wanted Walter to pay. She wanted the guards and inmates who were on Walter's arm to pay. Breen was her man. She learned how to be sentimental. There were a great many 0's to lose if she wasn't. Who ultimately paid the punitive damages was the state of New Hampshire. The department of corrections therein would never be the same.

She told on the stand that she had received a phone call saying that Liam Breen was requesting that she visit. When she saw the ATF hanging around, which turned out be Walter's cronies in the visitor's lounge, she fled in fear of being arrested herself. That was what had gotten Breen out of his cell and made vulnerable for his murder. Whether it was true or not, the proof was that Liam Breen was dead. Maddy left the area a very rich woman and was never heard from again.

The IRA didn't make any more or less headlines than usual that year in the United States.   The occasional car bomb.   An assassination attempt.   De rigueur.   Not until 2005 did they officially announce the end of their campaign.   But that story had been told and heard before.   The press release was signed by P. O'Neill.

But not Sinn Féin. They continue to be a strong political force in Ireland to this day.

Drunk one night I tried to call Director Humphrey at the embassy to inquire about what if anything happened on that side of the pond. He never returned my call. Nor did Rowena.

Everyone had moved on. So I did as well.

I went down to the game that Tuesday night after leaving the precinct, but I didn't sit in the stands with my so-called friends. I sat practically in the belly of Fenway Park, at Cask 'n Flagon. The bar sits on the corner of Landsdowne and Brookline. Anybody who has been to Boston or Fenway knows where it is. The owner owed me a favor or two. So I sat there that night, watched the Orioles lose 3-2. I was there on Sunday the 26th too, final home game of the regular season. We beat the shit out of the Evil Empire 11-4. I was there again when we swept the Angels, the only game of that series in Fenway, on October 3rd.

But on Sunday the 17th, when the Sox came back to win their first game of the series, 6-4 in twelve innings in game 4, it was fucking amazing. I sat there drinking Redbreast thinking we were out of it. Crying into my drink, though I had been used to it. This is it. Done. Then we weren't.

Then we won again. And then again on the 19th in the forty-eight degree rain.   And one more time on the 20th to send the goddamned Yankees home for the year. Four in a row with their backs against the wall.

A flicker of hope. Sweeping the Cardinals, Schilling's bloody sock, and winning the World Series for the first time in 86 years confirmed why Bostonians believe even in their dying breath. When their heads tell them one thing, their hearts something else.

Past sins had been forgotten. Trading Babe. Penance was the curse of no Pennants. But the curse was lifted and sins forgiven. The slate was clean.

Although I never heard from her again, Row was right. Sometimes life is an American Story.

AUTHOR'S NOTES AND ACKNOWLEDGEMENTS

The previous work is one of fiction, any resemblance to specific and true incidents is purely coincidental. Some of the places, laws, crimes, procedures, news stories, and experiences are based upon real research, however. They were used to add a legitimate feel to a completely fabricated story. Without the help of the people and entities listed below, this book at worst doesn't get written, at best isn't nearly as rich and believable.

There is no such place as Wayland, New Hampshire. Not that I am aware of. Though there are many townships that this fictitious place emulates. Nor is there any Waco-esque combine nestled deep in the White Mountains that I know of. I grew up in northern Vermont, have had the privilege of traveling about New England extensively. The number of times that I have driven through a New England State, been seemingly in the middle of nowhere and stumbled upon a community like Wayland can't be counted. In my experience, always friendly.

The history of Whitey Bulger and the Boston mob is well documented. The history behind my take on it here is legitimate, my spin is arguable. I have listed references below backing my belief in the historical connection between the Irish mob in Boston and the Irish Republican Army. Once upon a time. The Winter Hill Gang/Crew is still in existence, but I believe the myth and hype is bigger than their presence.

One may have noticed my use of Queen's English and British spelling in the *Troubles are Féin* section of the book. My use of the metric system and temperatures in celsius as well. I struggled with this but ultimately found it the best way to attain the feel of where the story was unfolding. The difficulty to sort out Deni's point of view with where the story took place was one that I hope the reader doesn't experience. That they added a level of mystery and confusion, the way Deni would have felt.

I would like to thank the people of Ireland. They are warm and opened themselves for anything, especially a laugh. I have portrayed a darker side of their culture, taken out of their history. While it makes for a fantastic story, it might not seem overly fair. How many of us would like a page taken out of our history, only to have it exploited and twisted to create a macabre picture? Ireland is a very beautiful country, a very proud country. I was lucky to have been a part of it if ever so briefly.

When I speak of Ireland, I speak of the south. I didn't explore the Northern region for this particular novel. While Northern Ireland is yet another fantastic place on this planet, the culture and politics of sovereignty of the south suited this novel best. The Gaelic. The idioms. The Sinn Féin headquarters is also located in Dublin.

The political party Sinn Féin which I used in this novel is real. The history that I have outlined herein - also real, to a point. Facts were picked out and exploited, which is the beauty of writing fiction. They did use the Irish Republican Army, kept them at their disposal, again once upon a time. As I have said many times, in every legitimate group, there are always the outliers that take themselves a bit too seriously. While these particular outliers are not technically still operating, the IRA did exist and they were on the World Terrorist Watch List. Thankfully times have changed.

I would like to thank the Arlington Hotel O'Connell Bridge in Dublin, Ireland. They not only housed me, they treated me like a visiting family member. I asked many questions, no matter how ridiculous they never made me feel anything less than welcome. I miss those Nutella milk shakes and cannot recreate them.

To my friends, family and acquaintances who are a part of this novel in spirit. I hope that you can see yourselves in some of the characters, as I drew upon the nuances of your characters that make you who you are, to make mine

377

come alive. Thank you for being a part of my life and part of the fabric of this work.

Thank you to the Boston Red Sox organization and Major League Baseball. Not only did you help me to get the scores and highlights straight, but allowed me unfettered access. I have been a fan my entire life, thanks for exceeding my every request. This is an extremely classy organization.

The City of Boston. This book is dedicated to you. You were my home for many years. I love and miss you. The heartbeat of New England. And I hope I have done you proud.

Finally, but most importantly, I would like to take the time to thank those that took the time to speak with me. I am just a guy trying to spin a good yarn. Without your insights into the history, culture, politics, policing, how the embassy works, cargo shipping, and many many more topics, this is a little yarn that never gets spun. If you enjoyed this book, it is largely because of them.

Thanks for your time and I hope you enjoyed the read.

-sw-

REFERENCES

A Criminal and an Irishman: The Inside Story of the Boston Mob - IRA Connection. **Nee, Patrick; Farrell, Richard; Blythe, Michael** Hanover, NH.: Steerforth Press. (2006).

CNN World News Reports. 2004.

Boston Red Sox Statistical Archives. 2004.

Major League Baseball Statistical Archives. 2004.

378

National Weather Service. *Precipitation Data.* 2004.

Interview. *Massachusetts State Police Detective.* Anonymous. December, 2013.

Mass Turnpike Authority. *The Largest Construction Project in the United States.* (http://www.nap.edu/openbook.php?record_id=10629&page=14).

News. *The Boston Herald.* Daily Archives. March 2004-October 2004.

News. *The Boston Globe.* Daily Archives. March 2004-October 2004.

News. *The Guardian.* Daily Archives. June 2004-September 2004.

Brutal; *My Life Inside Whitey Bulger's Irish Mob.* Kevin Weeks and Phyllis Karas, Regan Books, 304 pp., ISBN 0-06-112269-6

Reducing Gun Violence: The Boston Gun Project's Operation Ceasefire. Kennedy, David M., Anthony A. Braga, Anne M. Piehl (2001).

ABOUT THE AUTHOR

Photo ©2013 WWPGroup

Scott Wellinger is a well-traveled editor and novelist. His writing features, among others, the fictitious private investigations of Warren Dennihan. A native of New England, he was born in Vermont and was educated in Boston, Massachusetts. He holds a Master's Degree in Applied Economics and when he is not traveling, he is on a golf course.

Also by scott wellinger:

CRASH
A Warren Dennihan Novel (first of series)

Venom

A Warren Dennihan Novel (book 2)

A sample of the bestselling novel **CRASH** follows (unedited). The full novel is available for purchase on amazon.com, iBooks, www.WWPGroup.webs.com, Google Play, and wherever books are sold.

Scott Wellinger

CRASH

A NOVEL

PROLOGUE

THE NIGHT HAD DRAWN DOWN like a blanket over the small New England town, tucked in the mountains of southern New Hampshire. A cloudless, late summer sky made the bright stars the only form of illumination, which were little more than pinholes of light off in a distant universe. The pine forest that shot up from the fertile ground gave off a rich perfume reminiscent of Christmas, which was less than half a year to come. Above the tree-line, the natural rock formation known as *The Old Man on the Mountain* was a slight, silhouetted backdrop bidding the tourists a final goodnight whilst he slept. The narrow, windy roads meandering through the hills below that watchful cliff north of Boston, Massachusetts, were fortified with guardrails and graveled pulloffs to accommodate the looky-loo tourist vehicles. The fall foliage leaf-peepers were still a month or so away, but the hiking and camping season was still in full swing. The heavy traffic from the visitors trying to get a last trip in before the arrival of colder nights, was nonexistent in the hours after dusk. The hikers, campers, and naturalists had long since ventured home for the night or abandoned their parked vehicles on one of the pulloffs on the side of the road, as they made camp somewhere in the darkened forest.

The *Old Man* was the sentry for several communities below his perch on the White Mountains; the county and township of Wayland, New Hampshire was by far the most affluent. The old and new money was drawn from the financial hub of Boston in the form of large salaries. The town flourished as the commuters preferred to spend their ample earnings in the sanctity and "tax-free" state of New Hampshire over the Metropolis of Boston which fed them to the South. Another form of income for Wayland was the tourism, but the affluent of the community was torn in that while the outsiders boosted the economy, they trampled over their turf. The people of money from Wayland did appreciate the financial relief from tourism, which was their dilemma in refraining from ousting their numerous intruders. The visitors should be felt yet not seen.

The winters were the most difficult for the citizens to avoid the onslaught of outsiders. The skiers would come from the flatlands to trample the towns and, in their opinion, the face of their great State.

Throughout the rest of the year, they spent their time and income away from the flatlanders at the Wayland Country Club. Golf was just one activity taken in there, and in truth many claimed to play more often than they had a tee-time for. The sanctuary was more for camaraderie and companionship than the activities the club promoted. A place for the wealthy to rub elbows with others of their kind in the same area.

This particular night, those with money were keen to show off just how much they had and were willing to part with. The Gala and Charity event that was taking place in the pavilion was under way, all of the who's-who in place and opening wallets for the silent auction, though whom or what charity would be receiving these sums was anybody's guess. While the sprinklers were misting water over the lush back-nine of the manicured golf course, which could be seen out of the large windows, elegant gowns and tuxedos flattered the bodies of the occupants in the club. Live, light jazz music and the mumbled conversations of the local power couples mingling under the giant chandelier could be heard faintly in the distance, while the rest of the community went about their Saturday night. The well-to-do's had their evening festivities, freeing their assistants and staffers to have theirs.

Arelia Diaz had made her plans weeks prior, when she learned that she would have a rare night off. She was a live-in maid for one of the rich and beautiful, though she called herself a caretaker, and was looking forward to blowing off some built-up steam with a night of dancing with her girlfriends. The initial response from her friends at her invitation for a night out on the town was a jealous decline, until they too were informed that they would have the night off. Her friends in the area were also in the employ of other event attendees and would also have the night free from; babysitting, nannying, serving, cleaning, maintaining, cooking, or the myriad other tasks their employers were too important to perform. A night of dinner; gossiping over the comings and goings of their respective power families, and certainly dancing would be just the cure for the tedium that ailed them. Only one friend, Marina could not make it. She was told that she would have to take care of a child, though her employer didn't have any children.

Arelia was a mid-thirties Brazilian woman who had left her own family back in Recife. Other than her gaggle of female friends, she was alone in the United States. She had no spouse or children, which was the mainspring for many nights of tear-soaked cheeks and a saturated pillow. The oldest of four daughters, she saw limited opportunities in her native village and networked into an immigrant sub-community tucked into the American Northeast almost ten years prior. Alone but not alone, she was content in managing a dream household, though it was not her own.

Ms. Diaz did not consider herself to be what the Americans called a *cougar*, she was too young to be considered for the part, but she was going to be on the prowl this night. All women had needs, this was a rare opportunity, and she was going to make the most of it. She painted on a pair of the most expensive jeans she could afford, her ample bosom bursted out of the front of her new, sparkling, black-yet-shear blouse, exposing her black push-up bra, and donned a pair of high heels which lifted her four inches higher than her usual five-foot-three inch frame. With her raven hair done (in what was coincidentally called a Brazilian Blowout), and her makeup accentuating her big, beautiful brown eyes, she would be turning some heads. She still had what it took to bag any man she wanted, despite her lack of practice.

She would not be bringing anyone back to her suite at her employer's palatial home, this was not allowed, nor did she have any intention of staying with an interested gentleman. Her duties would resume bright and early in the morning. Her employers would likely be as moody as usual, as demanding as usual. Maybe they would even be a little hungover, though they would never in a million years admit that to the help. The agenda for the night would be dinner, *Forró* dancing, and a copious amount of flirting. Unfortunately the line would have to be drawn at flirting.

She was given an older, red, Honda *Civic* to use in her daily errands, which she was using while on her way downtown to meet her girlfriends. It was a small yet able car, in spite of the age, much like Arelia believed herself to be. She had plenty of life left, this was just a means to an end. A way to go back to Brazil with enough money saved to provide for a family she would make, and their family after she was gone.

Diaz was used to the car and all of the idiosyncrasies that came along with it. She loved the limited freedom that the car provided her, but she loved the stereo system the most. In the ten years of being the caretaker, she was never allowed to listen to her music loud enough to be heard by anyone in any part of the house. Nor was she allowed to use headphones as she was always on call. Always. Failure to hear, much less respond to a call from the main house would mean an immediate end to the life she had built here. Relegated to vehicular sonic therapy, she would blast her beats as loud as the car stereo and tiny speakers could muster.

She had the windows down, feeling the night air through her already blown locks of hair. The outside sounds were competing between the crickets, the sounds of the Country Club in the distance, and Arelia belting out the Portuguese lyrics over the loud music of her favorite band *Falamansa*. She was blissfully unaware that this would be her final concert.

As she rounded a sweeping blind turn on Wayland Country Club Road, the singing and car-dancing was immediately interrupted by the harsh LED, high-beam headlamps glaring into her eyes from seemingly nowhere, yet everywhere. She knew nothing of candlepower light measurements, but the retina-burning headlamps blinding her surely could have illuminated Fenway Park. Diaz could not see anything, much less navigate the rolling left turn. She could not see the lever protruding off of the steering column to flash her own high-beams at the offensive driver coming towards her. Could not see her bearings on the road. She was desperate to see a yellow line. A white one. Anything to pinpoint if she was in a lane. There were no vibrations from the warning grating on the side of the road, because there wasn't any grating on the side of the road. No reflectors, not that she would have been able to see anything being reflected in the already blinding light. She would have welcomed the grazing of a guardrail, just so she could sort out where she was. Everything was happening so fast. Brakes were unused. The stereo remained at full, deafening decibels. There was no time to turn it down. No time to think. No time to sweat. Was there somewhere she could pull off? But that question did not register in the time it took her to sail off the road.

The little-Civic-that-could missed the end of a guardrail, grabbed the bit of gravel just off of the pavement, bulleted her through the small pulloff. The car continued, severing a maple tree that was contemplating the changing leaf colors soon, continuing on to impact the base of a large rock formation. The car came to an immediate halt from the forty-plus miles per hour it was traveling just seconds prior. The rear of the car was the last to learn of the immediate stop being insisted upon by the fixed and rooted boulder. It had no choice but to follow the rest of the cars' lead and jetted into the air, rear tire spinning as it tried to continue beyond the mess. It failed.

The sound of the dance music halted, replaced by the sound of mangling of metal and the pulverizing of bone. The jagged metal sliced through flesh which added to the cacophony of horrific sounds. The macabre series of sounds lasted but a beat, but the devastation would be permanent.

Nothing would be continuing beyond the crash. Not the maple tree, not poor Arelia Diaz formerly of Recife, Brazil and more recently of Wayland, New Hampshire. Where her body existed in the cab, where she was car-dancing to her favorite band, singing as loud as her beautiful lungs could project, was a sick sculpture of metal, plastic, glass, rubber and human organs. The front of the car no longer existed. It was impossible to discern car from body, where the red paint from the Honda started, through all the blood, and the end of the former occupant. Her lifeless face rested, burning on part of the steaming engine; searing what was left of her beautiful features, her head and neck was now where the backseat should have been.

The offending headlights stared onto the wreckage for a time, determining what was already known. The lights crept slowly toward the destruction, attached to the black vehicle that was camouflaged by the dark of the night. They would abandon the devastation they had caused. The upbeat, accordion-based dance music and singing, followed by the horrifying reverberations of the crash were no more. The sounds were replaced by the ticking of the cooling, destroyed engine; the sizzling of flesh; the acceleration of the fleeing murderous vehicle. And crickets.

1

UGLY. THE IMAGE APPEARING back at him in the makeshift mirror was ugly. No other word could summarize the reflection and the atmosphere surrounding it; his every thought and emotion. The stainless steel metal above the all-in-one, Willoughby sink-toilet reflected pure ugliness. The image itself superimposed upon the backdrop of the institutional beige walls, the florescent lighting, the grey concrete floor.

Jacob Grantes had never been considered a hunk, nor an Adonis, he was not a physical specimen for which to lust. He had never been compared to the likes of George Clooney but he had been somewhat attractive, smart, confident. His six foot one inch frame, his square jaw, his sea-green eyes were some of the features that admirers had named when defending him as 'a catch'. The image that had once stared back at him, however, had disappeared, morphing into the figure that was reflected back at him in the polished steel. He was splashing water on his face, one push button at a time, but no matter how much water he applied, how much he washed, and how much he scrubbed his face, he could not cleanse the ugliness inside or out.

Grantes, inmate #437261, had been a guest at the Wayland County House of Corrections for the past six months, having been denied bail. He had not been in trouble with the law prior to the events leading him to this very moment, which made the denial pending trial quite unusual. Jacob was accustomed to living in a large home, family, and the picket fence; which made the current accommodations all the more intolerable. His cell was an eight by twelve foot concrete room with a double bunk, a small desk and a sink-toilet which he had to share with his celly. The space was tight and the nerves were stretched even tighter. Twenty hours per day were spent in this tiny space. Best friends could be put together in such a way and it would not take long to become mortal enemies. To make matters worse, the door to the cells lacked bars, it was a solid door, which allowed little air flow, with a narrow, horizontal slot at waist-high for food trays to be passed through, or to be handcuffed prior to exiting. The small, vertical window was convenient only for the Correctional Officers who had to execute head counts. This solid metal door was manufactured to make the most loud, God-awful clanks and noises when opened and closed. Studies had been done on this; millions spent, to craft an audible assault on inmates in an effort to make them uncomfortable, on edge, and contemplating the actions that had led them to their current place of residence.

The CO had awoken Grantes with a loud, mechanical unlatching, the grinding of metal as his cell door was sliding open at 5:30 AM.

"Grantes. You got 15 minutes to shit, shower 'n shave. Court. You'll get chow on the ride over."

"Yeah," he said between splashes of water on his face.

His grumbled reply indicated his malcontent, as this was to be a real shit day. It was to be a different kind of shit day, but a shit day all the same. All other days had the exact same schedule; filled with misery, meetings with so-called counselors, and a myriad of conversations with fellow inmates all of whom proclaim to be innocent or screwed by their lawyer. This day would be a shit day of a different color but a shade he knew quite well. Jacob Grantes had previously spent most of his adult life immersed in the muck and mire of the legal system, but on the other side of it. As an attorney, he knew exactly what this day would entail. The splashing of water on his face would make none of it go away.

"Jesus Christ, can you shut the fuck up? What time is it, bro?"

The shout came from a lump in the sheets, covering the body laying on the top bunk in his cell. Grantes's celly had a very low tolerance for anything beyond sleeping away his bid. This is known in prison as a bed-bid, and he is not the only one trying desperately to dream away the time.

"It's early. Sorry. I have court today. But it looks like you'll have the cell to yourself for the day."

"Goody." He said this without removing the covers which made him appear as though he was levitating five feet above a filthy concrete floor.

"You'll be able to shit in peace at least. I wish you'd spent a little time out of the cell so I could crap without an audience."

"You really gonna shower?"

"Yeah, I'm getting my shower bag ready now."

"That means that the door is gonna open and close a couple more times. Why you gonna shower anyways? Gonna be front and center with a jumpsuit and shackles anyway, clean ain't gonna matter."

"They'll let me change into a suit."

"Ha - you're funny. You're an idiot, but you're funny. Where are you gonna get a suit asshole?"

"I came here in a suit. My lawyer will have another one if they won't let me have that one out of property."

"You're gonna be in a holding tank, good luck getting one of the courthouse COs to let you change. Lazy assholes might have to do extra work," he said. "Whats today anyway?"

"February fif—"

"— the case moron. What part of the case is it?"

"Oh. Discovery and motions. It's when — "

" — I know what it is. Fifteen minutes tops bro. They're not lettin' you change into a fuckin' suit. Two bus rides and a day in the tank for fifteen minutes. Have fun."

"Shithouse lawyers."

It amazed him how much legal knowledge inmates had. Especially those with high recidivism. Grantes's cellmate had a very vast and intimate knowledge of the law from a certain prospective. He was, therefore, known throughout the prison as a good shithouse lawyer. His celly was of course aware that Jacob was a real lawyer, which only caused that many more passionate discussions.

"We'll see."

2

JACOB GRANTES AND HIS BEST FRIEND, Ryan Wells, had started a law practice together fifteen years prior. They had, over time, cornered the bustling criminal and legal market of nowhereville. The small southern New Hampshire town of Barstone, in Wayland County, was considered to be the other side of the tracks by the more affluent locals. Those elevated locals being the residents of the affluent town of Wayland, which was literally just across the tracks of the commuter rail into Boston, Massachusetts. The clichéd delineation was real. The constituents of Wayland Township made it quite clear to all of the inhabitants of Barstone, and really anywhere else for that matter but less vocally, that they were not welcome. The elected Sheriff of Wayland County, his office located in the town of Wayland by design, was well aware of what would happen if the petty crimes and riff-raff of Barstone were to bleed into the backyards of the wealthy community. And so the two towns within the same county coexisted; the town with the same name of the county reaped all the rewards, while the slums went about being the outcasts.

The law office of Grantes, Wells & Associates was strategically located in Barstone, on the border of the two towns. They needed the criminal element, and therefore the business from the Barstonians, and they wanted the much more civilized legal filings of Wayland. The two townships utilized the same courthouse as they were in the same county. Life was never boring for the two attorneys. Defending the proprietors of a Meth Lab one day; filing an uncontested, fourth divorce on behalf of the scorned trophy-wife on the next.

The *Associates* in the name of the firm was a mistruth. JG, as he was called, and Ryan were the only partners, the only lawyers, and there were no others seeking partnership. None would be sought out either as they were not seeking any new blood for such an arrangement. The associates consisted of their part-time private investigator, Warren Dennihan; and their full-time secretary in Ryan's wife, Angie. Warren had his own thriving business, with his own partner, and was subcontracted by the law firm whenever a top investigator was needed. He was rarely, if ever, in the office. Angie was in the office every business day, much to Ryan's chagrin, and she had almost no legal knowledge. What she lacked in legal prowess, she made up for in organization and efficiency. She was invaluable and JG had said in the past, in plain language to Ryan, that whatever problem he had with the arrangement, to get over it.

The arrangement had been Ryan's doing in the first place. He had hired Angie Grummond, as was her name at the time, without consulting JG on the spot at the first interview. Rather than ask the prospective employee out on a date upon their first meeting, which was ultimately what Ryan wanted to do, he decided to hire her instead. The would-be sexual harassment suit in waiting didn't last long, as they were officially an item by the time she was finished her training. JG didn't mind as much as he had initially let on, not even annoyed if truth be told. The headache of starting a firm was a larger migraine than that of an office romance. Besides, Ryan had been JG's best friend since law school, almost for as long as he could remember, and he had never seen his friend so happy.

The startup capital for the small firm came from the money bestowed to Jacob via his surrogate family. His in-laws had been more than good to him, they had filled a hole left in him by the passing of his natural parents. His wife, Anna, had come from money and while she had married for love, her parents could think of no reason for them to struggle financially. They had made the idle threats to rescind the money once they learned that Ryan was to be made full partner from the outset, but all concerned knew the threats were empty. Their apprehension came from genuine concern as they saw their son-in-law, Jacob, as the much more talented of the partnership. With Jacob viewed as having a much higher potential than his friend, especially since he had no money invested in the venture, they felt Ryan was there for the ride instead of the build.

Ryan was not a bad lawyer. He was no Shapiro either. He was talented but he was also a free-spirit. Wells would get caught up in the spirit of the law rather than the black letter. He took flyers. Rather than take on more legitimate claims, he often went to the hoop with little on evidence and heavy on the liberal sentiment. He would often take on the lost cause that was rejected by JG; acknowledging that he might win some, but he would lose more. Ryan was an idealist. He was interested in the law for the good it could do. He actually thought the lady with the scales was indeed blind. He still does to this day.

JG had depended on Ryan to bring in fees not necessarily wins. Winning of course would draw the big cases, but with a location in Barstone, New Hampshire, who was he kidding? JG had the wins, Ryan had the passion. But that was all in the past. What JG needed from his friend and partner now was a win. A big win. He needed him to win the case of his life. For Jacob's life.

3

"All RISE. PLEASE COME TO ORDER, court is now in session. The honorable Judge McCaglia presiding." The bailiff shouted with much too much in the way of volume. There were few people in the fourth session of the Wayland County Superior courtroom. It was entirely unnecessary to shout at that level, but Grantes decided that the loud volume coordinated nicely with the loud color of the neon, hazard-orange prison jumpsuit he was wearing.

He had asked the Correctional Officer, politely mind you, if he could change into a suit that his lawyer had brought for him to wear to court. He even bargained to leave on the shackles, but the request didn't warrant any response. He repeated the question in case the officer didn't hear him. The CO had heard the request because he gave the sternest of looks upon hearing it a second time, though he still gave no response. Ryan had then gotten involved when he arrived but the plea to the Deputy Sheriff was in vain. The officer didn't like the hippie lawyer in the linen suit, and never liked any inmate ever. He was appointed to rid the county of these unwanteds, and this nonconformist was working to free them. Chalk one up for the political right, getting one over on the liberal left.

"You may be seated," said the judge. She was the moderately attractive Judge Grace McCaglia. Wearing the usual black robe, matching black hair that may have been colored to do so, and mystic blue eyes that could virtually see through a person. She confidently presided with a no-nonsense efficiency.

In her late forties, she had accomplished more than most attorneys had in the course of their entire career, in a fraction of the time. In the *Live Free or Die* State of New Hampshire; there were rumors of political favoritism, affirmative action, and sleeping her way into a judgeship. Any explanation was more plausible than that she had earned her position. These whispers did not go unnoticed which is why she once prosecuted and now presided strictly but fairly. There would not be any second-guessing her rulings. She would not

394

allow anyone to be justified in criticizing her for not being the right person for the bench.

"Where are we in the matter of the State of New Hampshire v Grantes?"

"Where are Anna and Brady is the better question." JG whispered into Ryan's ear as they sat in their seats at the defendant's table. He looked around the room but with few people in it, it was quite clear that his wife and son were not present.

"No idea. Three messages without a response this morning. Maybe they are giving her a hard time about a four year old in the courtroom?"

Ryan finished whispering the response as he stood to address the judge.

"We would like to request a continuance, your honor."

"On what grounds? This has been ongoing for six months, time is ticking here sir."

"We are still in discovery, judge. Both theirs and ours."

"Theirs? A Grand Jury was convened and subsequent to Rule 8, they found probable cause to sustain an indictment. The 90-day threshold was met. Do you want to weigh in here counselor?"

She swiveled her chair to her right so she could face the prosecuting Assistant District Attorney. 'Weigh in' was a poor choice of words and she immediately realized it.

Pierce La Fontagne was an enormous man. Fat. He was an unhealthy glutton that could blame whatever or whomever he wanted to regarding his obesity, but it was a fact that he tipped the scales at over four hundred-fifty pounds. He was always disheveled and just as disorganized. How he had lasted as an ADA was a mystery, but his nickname was not so mysterious. They called him Jabba, after the enormous creature in *Star Wars*, behind his back. And he knew it. He spoke with as slow a purpose as his metabolism.

"We have. Ah. Given the defense and have enough to provide the state to move. Ah. Forward with the case, Judge. We. Ah. Don't need much, but we do need a little more time." The fat on his neck jiggled when he spoke. He never looked up to face the judge when he spoke to her, as he was still shuffling papers in the disorganized mess he had created at the prosecution table. Besides his disorganization, not making eye contact with her infuriated her. She felt it was a sign of disrespect.

"Does that mean you are ready or not? Kind of late in the game aren't we, counselor? You had enough to sustain the charges, do you have what you need to move forward or don't you?"

"Ah. We feel confident that the current evidence will prove our case beyond the threshold of reasonable doubt."

"I can tell." She had to pause to control her anger. She was a professional to her very core. She swiveled back toward the defendant.

"Mr. Wells. Have you received all of this said evidence? If so, then I'm confused. Speedy trial gentlemen. The defendant has the right to one, he is remanded and sitting in prison awaiting the disposition of this trial. So I would think his lawyer would be more adamant about moving this forward. He pleaded not guilty. ADA La Fontagne and the state requires a speedy trial, and frankly I demand it so I don't get backlogged. Six months gentlemen. This has been going long enough, wouldn't you both agree? We move ahead forthwith." Efficiency experts could learn a thing or two from Judge McCaglia.

"I agree that six months is a long time, your honor. Especially for my client, who was only remanded due to an imminent threat justification, which we will get to in a minute with the other motion you have before you."

Ryan had filed to have the issue of bail revisited. Jabba had used a justification that argued that Jacob Grantes was an immediate danger to society and should be remanded as to allay any danger to the community. She was already disgruntled with the prosecutor, he was hoping to use that to his and therefore his client's advantage.

"But with all due respect, judge, I do not agree with the a forthwith," Ryan continued. "In order to provide a proper defense against the charges, I need to ensure that the burden of proof and all pertaining evidence is met and provided to me by the prosecution. The ADA has just told you and I, after some equivocating I might add, that they now have all the evidence they plan to use when and if this goes to trial. I need time to assemble all the counter-evidence supporting our claim against the charges, and that proving that my client is innocent."

JG nodded his approval. His friend and partner was doing well. Unlike television and movies in Hollywood, the State cannot come out of nowhere in the last minute of the trial with a damning piece of evidence. It was now time for the prosecution to put up or shut up and Ryan had just spoken legalese saying so.

"OK. So we are moving forward to trial with this, correct gentlemen?"

The two opposing men nodded in agreement instead of stating it aloud for the court stenographer. The judge didn't make them, she continued instead.

"I don't see a green sheet with any deals on the table as of yet. So Mr. Wells, how long do you need?"

"We request ninety days your honor."

"Three months for discovery and prep for trial? You are joking right? Nice try. ADA La Fontagne, is there anything else you would like to state before I rule on this?"

"Ah. No your honor. I would just like to reiterate that — "

" - No need to reiterate anything, I heard you the first time. You've got thirty days." She turned toward the clerk to dictate. "Let's set a date for pretrial and jury selection at or about one month from today."

"Your Honor with that being settled, I would like to revisit the issue of bail. The motion should be before you," Ryan said.

He was hoping that since things had not exactly gone his way thus far, Judge McCaglia would throw him, and more importantly JG, a bone on the motion to revisit the issue of bail.

"That has already been denied. I denied it six months ago. Is there anything new to bring forth where I would reconsider?"

"He is a prominent attorney in the area, Judge. He has a family, is a husband, and father. He is the sole breadwinner. This has created an enormous hardship. His driver's license has been reinstated at this point, but we would surrender it again in lieu of incarceration if the State is still concerned that he is an imminent threat. But if we are now talking another thirty days before a trial is to even begin, I see no reason or threat to continue to remand him. He has been a model inmate, never been in trouble with the law prior to this case, and he has — "

"Save it Mr. Wells. You have nothing new here. A woman is dead. The allegation is that she is dead because of your client. Drinking and Driving is serious and a blight on our society. When a child is in the car on top of this, allegedly, it is reprehensible. I continue to believe that he may be an imminent threat. The fact that he is a prominent figure in this community; and that he is an attorney;

that has been before me and this court in the past; is not a reason for him to benefit. He cannot garner favor from a court that is supposed to judge his alleged crimes. Any defendant before me with these same allegations would get remanded, remain alcohol-free, surrender their license to drive a motor vehicle, and pending the outcome of the trial matriculate a Substance Abuse Program. I'm sorry Mr. Grantes, but you are to stay at the Wayland County House of Corrections pending trial. Stay in the Substance Abuse Program or there will be consequences, sir. As Mr. Wells just stated it is only thirty more days."

She paused only for a moment while she briefly looked over the rest of the documents regarding this case in front of her.

" So unless there are any other motions, we will resume these proceedings in thirty days. No more delays gentlemen, either one of you. Court is adjourned."

The gavel was only tapped onto the sound block but it sounded as though it was slammed through to the other side by a sledgehammer.

4

THE TRUTH WAS that the hardship the Grantes family was facing was not at all financial. It was Jacob who was suffering the most, but they were all unaccustomed to this torment. Not being able to see his wife and four year old child was all but killing him. Brady was not supposed to be without his father. He hadn't been in his life up to that point. Anna had been distant in recent months but they had dealt with serious difficulty in the past. They would get through it. Their college romance had started blissfully and had some serious downs despite their intense love for one another. Their eventual vows to take each other through good times and bad had taken significant meaning.

Norman and Olivia Craig had done whatever they could to encourage the college romance of their only daughter, Anna. Jacob, not Jake or JG as others called him (his natural parents had taken the time and effort to pick a name for him, and it was rude to bastardize that effort they had said repeatedly), was decidedly the perfect match for their Anna. Especially with the boys she had brought home in previous courtships. True, Jacob's family didn't come from wealth, nor had they built any. They had faith that this legacy would change with Jacob. He had work ethic, was smart, and pre-law. Yes, this is what they had in mind for their girl and they would do whatever they could, financially or otherwise, to support Jacob's goals. As long as Anna was included in the equation.

Jacob was always humbly appreciative, respectful in declining the offers of money or the "just because" expensive gifts, but would relent over time. Anna joined in on the pressure to accept these material tokens of affection for they were deemed as simple manifestations of parental approval. She viewed the entire subject as "only money". Of course it was only money to her, she had been privied to these same gestures and more over the course of her entire life. These were just an extension of her expectations from her wealthy parents.

"You should just get used to it honey, they won't let up. They love you and they just want to show you how much. Besides, you deserve to live a certain lifestyle even if you don't know it yet," she said in one of their more memorable spats on the subject. There had been more discussions regarding this very subject, all of which she won with some version of the same statement.

Jacob's fight for financial independence with her was a broken alliance, however. He would say things like, "I'm used to doing things for myself, babe. It's not that I am unappreciative of it, but there is something honorable in building a life for ourselves, by ourselves. I feel like I am forever indebted to them."

These declarations would fall on deaf ears and would either reluctantly fade or would be the impetus for a battle royale, depending on the value of the gesture and how much Jacob really wanted to press the issue. Eventually Jacob acquiesced, as he did every time. As the relationship developed, the lifestyle became de rigueur. He had lost every battle and the war as well. In truth, he had built up enormous debt and was very thankful for the financial help. Boston University was not cheap, Boston University School of Law even less so. The money, cars, apartments, the ability to go to Law School (only 11% of those applying to BU School of Law get accepted. The competition is stiff, but Mr. Craig was friends with someone on the Board of Trustees, or so he said).

"It's not bribery," Norman Craig had said. "I love Anna," he also said. It was to ensure that they had a strong foundation on which to build their life together. Of that, Jacob was sure.

Jacob's biological parents loved him with all of their hearts, albeit with fewer trinkets to show for it. Actually, there weren't any trinkets. Reginald and Elizabeth Grantes had to work and toil for every nickel of property or possession they owned, and even then the nickels didn't add up to anything of worth. They doled out hugs and kisses the way Norman Craig doled out money. Before the Craigs, Jacob had been a wealthy man. His parents attended or coached every athletic endeavor their only son struggled to perform. Neither parent had attended college but made it a priority for their son to get the education they did't have. They would not, could not, contribute financially. But they were motivating and supportive.

Young Grantes left upstate Vermont to attend Boston University and achieve his and his parent's goals for him. His parents remained there, driving south for visits or sending care packages of sweets to their starving student. They were pleased to learn that as of his sophomore year, their son would no longer struggle financially. The ends would more than meet. Unfortunately, in the end, they would never meet Anna.

✺✺✺✺✺

It was the start of Jacob's second semester, of his second year at BU that Reggie and Liz would drive down to Boston to visit their son for the last time. He had been home for Christmas break and every other sentence was, "Anna this" or "Anna that".

He had been a social mingler in high school, never the most popular kid but was a welcome addition to any clique. He was better than averagely attractive. He was polite, and was familiar with many a female as well, in large part because of his standing in a plethora of social circles. He had many dates, with a few sporadically retained as official girlfriends over the years. He certainly didn't have any that he had prattled on about for days on end.

His freshman year had been new and exciting, but also the most difficult endeavor he had undertaken in his life up to then. There were precious few stories regarding the fairer sex as he said there was no time. That was only half true. The other half was that going to University was not about settling down but about exploring, both academically and socially.   It was novel that this Anna would commandeer so much of a conversation, which made necessary the trip to Boston.

Interstate 89 is a long, windy, treacherous highway running north-south over and around the Green Mountains, crisscrossing Vermont and into New Hampshire.   This is one of two major highways in Vermont, and is the quickest way south to Boston, Massachusetts. The two lanes of patchy, frost-heaved road are tricky to negotiate any time of year; soft shoulders, ice, elevation changes, with notorious fog make it more so during bad weather.

January brings major snow storms almost every year, often dropping several feet of snow in a relatively few number of hours. This particular *Noreaster* should have postponed the trek south to Boston, the storm well-tracked and advised in advance. But in the

Northeast, weather personnel and meteorologists, were wrong as often as correct. Though every weather girl, on every channel, was forecasting the same snow advisory. But the days had been requested off, cashing in vacation and/or personal time, so the show must go on. And so on that January afternoon, Reg and Liz Grantes of Burlington, Vermont embarked on their journey south.

Jacob found it odd that his parents had not called him once they had arrived in Boston. They had a reservation with a late check-in scheduled at the Buckingham Hotel on Commonwealth Avenue, as was customary when they visited. When he had not heard from them, the thought of the big storm resonated in the back of his mind. He almost immediately disregarded it, however; his father had driven in the snow his entire life, had taught him how to drive in the stuff. He called the prepaid cellphone they used only when traveling, as cell phones were not the rage with the senior Granteses back then. He could not get through. Their voicemail was not set up, of course. It was not until he called the hotel and been informed that they had not checked in that he began to worry. More phone calls to their friends and to their places of work without a definitive answer to their whereabouts led to panic.

By 10:00 AM the following morning, panic became horrified shock. The Vermont State Police informed him by telephone that neither had survived a severe car crash. Neither had been alive when authorities had arrived at the scene.

"We hate to inform you over the phone," they said. "How very sorry we are," they also said. "Please come to Montpelier, Vermont to identify your parents."

They had not made it out of their own state. The reports showed that the snowy weather conditions inhibited sight; mixed with the unplowed snow on top of black ice, with an unfamiliar rental vehicle that was not equipped with all-wheel drive, were some of the elements contributing to the disastrous formula. The guard rail was ill-placed, meaning that there wasn't one in place. A guard rail would have at a minimum kept the vehicle on the road. The lack of this safety measure did the opposite and did not keep them on the road. The rental vehicle launched off the elevated highway into the icy ravine below. The final element in their premature demise.

The aftershock of the catastrophe had left Jacob scarred both emotionally and financially. Anna and her parents were there to reassemble the pieces as best they could. The financial piece was easy. Norman took care of the massive debt in one phone call. Anna was there for the emotional part. This was not as easy. But they dealt with it.

Reginald and Elizabeth Grantes, formerly of Burlington, Vermont, had loved life. They cared not for money but for the happiness it could provide from joyous memories. They loved each other and they loved their son, and in that they were rich. Realistically, they were not. They lived paycheck to paycheck and didn't manage those very well at all. There were always events deemed too important to pass up, spending money earmarked for bills; spending in lieu of life insurance, savings, or a 401k. They were upside down on their mortgage in part because of the market, but primarily because of the repeated refinancing and remortgaging.

Without life insurance, in their terrible financial condition, and most recently with the cost of their final expenses, they had left their only son with an enormous financial burden. He was already in debt because of his educational loans and the catastrophe would make him more so without a house or substantial property to sell. And so at the ages of 58 and 56, Reggie and Liz respectively, had left their son broken and broke. Had it not been for the Craigs, he would have been broke for the rest of his life.

5

JG WAS ANXIOUSLY AWAITING the arrival of his lawyer at the table in one of the courthouse conference rooms. He was immediately escorted there after his brief legal fray in the fourth session upstairs. Ryan had worked it out to conduct a meeting with his client before he was bussed back to prison, should he not make bail. Which to his misfortune is exactly what happened. Ryan seemed to be taking a long time doing whatever he was doing in the eyes of JG; leaving him alone in the dark, windowless conference room with a court officer standing watch in the corner. It was an awkward silence which made Ryan's absence seem even longer. He was not in any hurry to get back to his cell, nor his celly, but he was overwrought with how his case was progressing thus far. Or not progressing, which consumed his thoughts every minute of every day in prison.

The large wooden door opened with a start, ending the tension that had been building in the small room, adding a different sort of unease. Ryan moved quickly to a chair opposite his client, setting his leather briefcase down on the oversized table between them.

"I'd like to be alone with my client please," he said over his left shoulder to the officer.

"Sure thing. I'll be outside the door when you're finished."

Once the babysitter had left, the lawyer-client pretense was abandoned. "Well, that didn't go very well." The hearing had not gone well, they both knew it, and neither one would sugarcoat it to say that it had.

"Ya think?"

"Look pal, we have them on the ropes, right where we want them," Ryan said.

"Rope a dope, huh? Who's the dope? They're kicking our asses, Ry."

"Well I don't know what I could have done differently in retrospect. Thoughts? I mean what would the Great Jacob Grantes have done?"

JG's elbows were on the table, head in hands. He needed a lifeline. The sarcasm and mucking it up with his friend needed to cease. He was on the verge of breaking down.

"You did what you did, Ry. I mean you did what I would have done. That woman is a ball-buster."

"McCaglia has always been brutal, you knew that going in. You've been in front of her before. Hell, she was as an ADA, she is now on the bench. She has something to prove, always has, and she doesn't cut breaks unless she absolutely has to. And she doesn't have to here. We don't have anything going for us, and Jabba isn't chomping at the bit to cut a deal either."

"Exactly. So what do we have we going for us?"

"I was just speaking with tons-of-fun upstairs after our hearing. That's what took so long. I've got the 'one and only green sheet' right here. This is the only deal he is offering, or is ever going to offer, he says. It's not a good one, I'll warn you."

He reached into his briefcase on the table, removed the green court document the La Fontagne had given Ryan a few moments prior. It was conveniently on top and quickly slid directly in front of his jumpsuit-clad friend. A green sheet is a bargaining document with legalese and three vertical columns in the middle horizontal third. The form is on No Carbon Required (NCR) paper with three sheets; one for the ADA, one for the defense, and one for the judge. The first column is for the prosecutor, which offers a sentencing recommendation if the defense forgoes the expense of a trial. The middle column is the defense counter offer, which typically chips away at what the State wants. The final column on the right, is the deal formed between the two and goes to the judge. He or she reads the statutory minimums to ensure nobody is ponying up the courthouse, then usually rubber-stamps the deal. When all is said and done, all the judge wants is to clear their docket, keep justice moving just like everyone else. This is called a green sheet for the complicated reason in that the color of the document is a light green. Though it must be signed by all parties, it is only legally binding when and if a formal hearing takes place and agreed to on the record.

"He likes where he is," Ryan continued. "As you can see, the offer is Vehicular Manslaughter, OUI 1 with injury, leaving the scene. He drops the child endangerment, and puts a recommend of eight to ten on the VM, concurrent. Loss of licenses, two years after release on the drivers, law for life because we are talking felonies."

"Not much of a deal."

"You would get fifteen years on the VM alone at trial. Add in the OUI-with, leaving the scene, and indifference would get you another ten-plus separately. Add the child endangerment back into the charges if we go to the hoop, and you would not be able to see your kid without someone watching over your shoulder until he is legally an adult. Eight to ten, to run concurrent means with good time, two years off the minimum. You've been in for six months already, so you would be out in five and half. No child supervision, no probation. It's not good but it is the best we're gonna get I'm afraid."

The drivers license didn't make that much difference to JG. The loss of his ability to practice law could also be dealt with, he had money and he could always find something to occupy his days. Maybe he could teach. The five and a half years away from his family was intolerable. He could not lose his family for any longer than he already had. Supervised visits with Brady was unacceptable also but at least he would be able to see him other than through glass. These thoughts were going through his mind but he wasn't vocal about them, which caused a long pause. He continued to stare at the offer, lost in the ramifications if he agreed to what was written.

"What's going through your mind? Talk to me. There is nothing saying that you can't be behind the scenes at the firm, you just wouldn't be able to take cases when you get out."

"You think that is what's bothering me, Ry? How long have you known me? You really think that is what's hanging me up?"

"No, I don't. I'm just trying to help. But Jabba isn't going to budge. It's this or we go to the hoop. But you have given me nothing to work with on defense. We go to trial? I think unless we come up with something really damned compelling, you're going to go away for a long time."

"Have you been in touch with Anna yet? I'd like to discuss this with her."

"She isn't, nor was she, here today. No answer either. Voicemail is full. I'm really not sure where she is, but I'll keep trying." He pulled out some other documents from the briefcase, spreading out the pile on his side of the table. "What I would like to discuss is all of this circumstantial evidence and see if anything jogs your memory. Anything we can hammer away at. If we weaken anything he has, maybe the deal gets better."

"We've been through this, I don't remember anything about that night. Well, other than Sully's anyway."

"Yeah well we are going to go through it again. You admitted to quote, 'being hammered' when they picked you up at your house. You were passed out by the way. Again, Brady was upstairs asleep but unsupervised."

"I can't believe I drove in that condition, much less with Brady in the car. Then left him on his own like that in the house. I just can't believe it."

"Thats what they're going with. I have a statement from the bartender, Jenna, that you left Sully's between 8:00 and 8:15 PM. You also admitted to being at the bar in the back of the cruiser, which means you had to be really banged up. You, of all people, know better than to say anything to the police after you've been arrested. But anyway, you left and picked up Brady at the Destriers at 8:20 PM; the servant that was watching him told Chamille Destrier that she put him in his carseat in the back of the running car, that you never spoke or left the driver's seat. She said she found it odd behavior, but this is all third hand through Chamille because the servant doesn't speak English, apparently. The police never spoke to her directly to confirm or deny anything. Chamille was at the charity event next to your wife, so we strike the kid being in the car as hearsay. I think that is why the big-boy is dropping child endangerment, the kind soul."

"Yeah, what a sweetheart."

"Right. So you drove away and must have bounced off a tree, veering into the opposite lane where this poor woman happened to be coming right at you. She goes off the road and plays chicken with a big tree and an even bigger rock. She lost and you went home to sleep it off."

"It's not funny, Ry. Please don't make light of the fact that this woman was decapitated by a smoking-hot engine. I feel awful."

"Sorry, just trying to add some levity. Anyway, they have matching paint from the tree, black sapphire pearl, and the scrape on your Volvo has wood and bark all through it. Exact. No real credible argument there, I'm afraid. Furthermore the rubber zig-zagging on Wayland Country Club Road matches the Michelin 235/60R18s on your ride. Cops investigated your tires, they've got you dead to rights there too."

"Match? *Cops* are matching this all up? Can we get experts to refute them? Volvos are a dime a dozen in New England, hell I have two of them."

"Lab techs. This isn't *CSI,* they didn't stop everything they were doing and get top experts from all over the country to fly in on the state's dime, no. But you don't have to be an expert to see that all of this doesn't look good. Picking apart their lab technicians with our expensive ones is not going to win over a jury, if that's what you're thinking."

"That is exactly what I am thinking. The techs are overworked, underpaid, they make mistakes — "

" — this is New Hampshire, JG. They are neither overworked, nor are they underpaid. These aren't MIT grads by any stretch but they don't have a whole lot to investigate, trust me. Just between you and me, I looked at your car, the road, the tree. You killed this poor woman. If you were anybody else — "

" - So what are we doing here then?"

"You're my best friend. I'm trying to mitigate your responsibility here. I'm trying to help. I don't know, find a technicality. What we're doing here is trying to get the best deal we can."

"Great. Just great. You think five and half is the best I can do?"

"We haven't discussed the 911 call yet. Anonymous, but that is how they nailed you. How they knew to go to your house to grab you."

"What is there to discuss? You've already told me to take the deal, right?

Ryan paused. He shuffled the stack of papers containing all the condemning evidence. He really wasn't sure why he was against taking the deal but he was. He knew his friend, knew him better than any other male on the planet, and something was not right. Endangering the life of his only son, the one they had so much trouble conceiving, was not scanning. True, he had been drinking more in the months before the accident, but to get that blackout drunk was not something he would expect from his friend. He was mister safety. People disappointed. But not JG. Not Jacob Grantes. He had never disappointed. Not until now.

"Look, I'm not telling you to take the deal. At least not yet. We finally have all the evidence that fat-body has compiled; so we put Deni on it and see what he comes up with. I mean, the cops didn't pick you up at your house until 9:45 PM, which gives you a huge window to get shattered in the comfort of your own home. If everything comes back the way it looks here, which admittedly is really fucking bad, then we pick away at the bartender and the illegal lady."

"Please leave the vic alone. Arelia, right? Jenna too."

"Look. Jenna is a sweet girl, we go there and knock a few back and she is always good to us, but she over-served you. She claims not, but obviously she screwed up and is covering her ass. As far as the victim, she is dead. Which is unfortunate. But she shouldn't have been in this country to be dead. She was illegal. I feel for her just like you do, but when it comes to my friend or someone who may or may not even pay taxes? I might be a 'hippie' but I look out for my own. We've kinda got a role reversal here, huh? You're usually the cutthroat."

"Prison changes people I guess. Usually for the worse, not more sympathetic. But it is what it is."

"Maybe. But if shit goes south, all the cards lead to what we have before us, then we go after the ladies. The bartender has some responsibility here, and so does the vic. This *is* New Hampshire. We don't like drunk drivers but we don't like illegal aliens more."

"Not very Politically Correct of us, is it?"

"Unfortunately, like you said, it is what it is. Peace, love, and get a green card."

"Well lets hope it doesn't come to that. Just get Deni going because we don't have much time."

"I'm on it. I'm not going anywhere. You need anything?"

"Actually, yes."

"Name it."

"Find Anna."

6

RYAN WELLS WAS JG's longest and closest personal friend. They had both grown up poor but not impovered, had been instilled with a strong work ethic, and were the first in their respective families to go to college. They had met at BU during freshman orientation and were all but inseparable since. Grantes had been a loyal friend in pulling Wells into the fold of the partnership and Ryan had been loyal in many other ways, including during the death of Jacob's parents. They were each the brother to the other.

The two were so alike in so many ways that they could have been biological brothers. Ryan was good looking, tall and had what was once an athletic build. They would both be forty this year and had previously made plans for both families to go on vacation together to celebrate. Until the incarceration, all had looked forward to the time away. The only major difference between them was professionally. They were both strong advocates, but the hippie would live in the shadow of his more talented, leaning to the right, brother.

As Ryan left the courthouse, he pulled his iPhone out of his long winter overcoat to call Warren Dennihan, the firm investigator.

"Deni, how are you?" He immediately regretted not using his bluetooth ear device to make the call as he juggled his briefcase, the phone, and his car keys to open his parked car.

"Same shit, different pile. What's up?" Warren Dennihan was a *Southie*, or from the district of South Boston and had the severe accent to prove it. Bad. Or 'wicked bad, guy'. It was almost like he spoke a different language as *pahk tha cah in hah-vid yahd*, just doesn't quite describe how broken his English really was. He didn't pronounce *r's*, unless of course they were not in the word like *drawr* instead of draw. It was work to hold a conversation with him unless you were familiar with him or his kind.

"I just finished up with JG's hearing. It didn't go well."

"I figured. I got my partner workin' my other shit, so how much time do I gotta clear up?"

"Ah shit," Ryan said. He had dropped his phone while opening his car to get it started and warmed up. He had to retrieve it out of the snow but fortunately it still worked. With the new synthetic oils and the fact that he drove an Audi A6, he didn't need to get the car warmed up for performance reasons, but he couldn't get the winter-fighter to work on his cold body until the engine was pumping warm air at him.

"You ok?"

"Yeah, Yeah. I'm here. Just dropped something. So everything we talked about? That's what they've got. The whole shah-bang. We've gotta work on it."

"By we, ya mean me."

"It's been a tough morning, are you really gonna give me a hard time right now?"

"Always. Hey listen. I've been callin' WHOC, I know a few guys over there. Not much I can do to look after him in there. Its all political. He's a lawyer, so nobody trusts him, and he can't gang up. At least he knew not to PC, just take a beat'n like a man if thats what they wanna do."

"If it was going to happen, it would have happened by now."

"Not necessarily, but we can hope. How much longer?"

"That depends on you, Deni. Thirty days if this goes to the hoop. Trial will be probably about two weeks or so, after that depends on what we get. I was hoping we could get enough to kill a trial, maybe enough to get a deal. They are offering eight to ten, which means five and half when all is said and done."

"All depends on me? No pressure. Who's breakin' balls now?"

Ryan was still sitting in his car, which was starting to kick out the warm seventy-four degree air that was set on his in-dash computer. He still couldn't drive, however; the car had not yet picked up the signal for the phone and you cannot drive and talk on the phone in New Hampshire unless handsfree. "Hey where are you?"

"Around the corner from you, I'll be there in thirty secs or less."

"Good. This might be easier face to face. I have a ton of documents you should look at."

"Do you still drive the silver Audi?"

"Yes, of course. I love this — "

" — I'm behind ya."

"Holy crap. That was fast."

Deni parked his blacked-out Escalade and relocated to the passenger seat of Ryan's vehicle. This was the part that took the thirty-seconds. "Let's see it all," he said without explanation of how or why he was in the immediate area.

"So this is everything." He handed Warren the stack of evidential material from his briefcase, then continued. "I know we discussed it when this thing happened, and since, but something just isn't sitting right about this case. You think I'm nuts though don't you?"

"I don't think you're nuts, per se, but would you really go through all this bullsh for anybody but JG? I agree that somethin' isn't stirrin' the kool-aid, but you and I both know he did it. He was drinkin' like a fish for months before this all happened. I was thinkin' family trouble at the time, but who knows? That kid is his life, so I can't see him throwing that away. But we all fuck up, doesn't have to be on purpose for it to do damage."

"So does that mean that you are on board? I gotta know that you are on this."

"Loyal as lab, huh? Yeah, me too. I'm in, and you know it. I just need somethin' to work with here, guy."

"Look I never ask how you do what you do, because I'm not sure I want to know, but we are going to need all you've got on this. We need to dig into; Jenna, the bartender we know from Sully's Tavern, the Destrier servant or au pair or whatever she is, the 911 call is a bit wonky, and if all else fails — we make the vic the most despicable person who has ever illegally entered the borders of this country," Ryan said before pausing. "I was kind of hoping for a sliding scale on this one. I know you have to clear your calendar and this is going to take some time, but with me taking this case, I have all of his cases I have to work, and mine, and of course he isn't in the office taking cases so the firm is really financially tight right now and — "

" — hey relax, buddy. I can't dig up what ain't there, but I'm on it. As legit as possible anyway. As for the fee, don't worry about it. I owe tha kid. He's been good to me over the years."

"So what are you thinking?"

"I've got a couple of ideas. Mostly hunches, but I know people."

"I know you know people, that's why you are so good at what you do. Anyone I know?"

"Stop kissin' my ass Ry. I wanna check out the bar first. Jenna."

"Business or pleasure?"

"Both."

"I've got another project that's just as important."

"I'm listenin'."

"Find Anna and Brady. They didn't show up at court today and she is not answering phones. It's weirding me out, and JG is really freaking out."

"Huh. Lets go over to the house. You drive."

"Right now? Deni, I've got — "

" — you said it's important. Was that fact or bullsh?"

"Fact."

"Then start driving."

CRASH, and other novels in the Warren Dennihan series by Scott Wellinger can be purchased wherever books are sold.

www.ingramcontent.com/pod-product-compliance
Lightning Source LLC
Chambersburg PA
CBHW080820250626
47160CB00008B/2814